HEART'S DESIRE

The Story of a Contented Town, Certain Peculiar
Citizens, and Two Fortunate Lovers

A Novel by EMERSON HOUGH

1st WORLD
LIBRARY
Literary Society

Heart's Desire

Emerson Hough

© 1st World Library, 2007
PO Box 2211
Fairfield, IA 52556
www.1stworldlibrary.com
First Edition

LCCN: 2007927774

Softcover ISBN: 978-1-4218-4530-2
Hardcover ISBN: 978-1-4218-4446-6
eBook ISBN: 978-1-4218-4614-9

Purchase *"Heart's Desire"*
as a traditional bound book at:
www.1stWorldLibrary.com/purchase.asp?ISBN=978-1-4218-4530-2

1st World Library is a literary, educational organization
dedicated to:

- Creating a free internet library of downloadable ebooks

- Hosting writing competitions and offering book
  publishing scholarships.

1ˢᵗ World Library Literary Society

Giving Back to the World

"If you want to work on the core problem, it's early school literacy."

- James Barksdale, former CEO of Netscape

"No skill is more crucial to the future of a child, or to a democratic and prosperous society, than literacy."

- Los Angeles Times

"Literacy... means far more than learning how to read and write... The aim is to transmit... knowledge and promote social participation."

- UNESCO

"Literacy is not a luxury, it is a right and a responsibility. If our world is to meet the challenges of the twenty-first century we must harness the energy and creativity of all our citizens."

- President Bill Clinton

"Parents should be encouraged to read to their children, and teachers should be equipped with all available techniques for teaching literacy, so the varying needs and capacities of individual kids can be taken into account."

- Hugh Mackay

CONTENTS

CHAPTER I

THE LAND OF HEART'S DESIRE

This being in Part the Story of Curly, the Can of Oysters, and the Girl from Kansas

"It looks a long ways acrost from here to the States," said Curly, as we pulled up our horses at the top of the Capitan divide. We gazed out over a vast, rolling sea of red-brown earth which stretched far beyond and below the nearer foothills, black with their growth of stunted pines. This was a favorite pausing place of all travellers between the county-seat and Heart's Desire; partly because it was a summit reached only after a long climb from either side of the divide; partly, perhaps, because it was a notable view-point in a land full of noble views. Again, it may have been a customary tarrying point because of some vague feeling shared by most travellers who crossed this trail,— the same feeling which made Curly, hardened citizen as he was of the land west of the Pecos, turn a speculative eye eastward across the plains. We could not see even so far as the Pecos, though it seemed from our lofty situation that we looked quite to the ultimate, searching the utter ends of all the earth.

"Yours is up that-a-way;" Curly pointed to the northeast. "Mine was that-a-way." He shifted his leg in the saddle as he turned to the right and swept a comprehensive hand toward the east, meaning perhaps Texas, perhaps a series of wild frontiers west of the Lone Star state. I noticed the nice distinction in Curly's tenses. He knew the man more recently arrived west of the Pecos, possibly later to prove a backslider. As for himself, Curly knew that he would never return to his wild East; yet it may have been that he had just a touch of the home feeling which is so hard to lose, even in a homeless country, a man's country pure and simple, as was surely this which now stretched wide about us. Somewhere off to the east, miles and miles beyond the red sea of sand and *grama* grass, lay Home.

"And yet," said Curly, taking up in speech my unspoken thought, "you can't see even halfway to Vegas up there." No. It was a long two hundred miles to Las Vegas, long indeed in a freighting wagon, and long enough even in the saddle and upon as good a horse as each of us now bestrode. I nodded. "And it's some more'n two whoops and a holler to my ole place," said he. Curly remained indefinite; for, though presently he hummed something about the sun and its brightness in his old Kentucky home, he followed it soon thereafter with musical allusion to the Suwanee River. One might have guessed either Kentucky or Georgia in regard to Curly, even had one not suspected Texas from the look of his saddle cinches.

It was the day before Christmas. Yet there was little winter in this sweet, thin air up on the Capitan divide. Off to the left the Patos Mountains showed patches of snow, and the top of Carrizo was yet whiter, and even a portion of the highest peak of the Capitans carried a blanket of white; but all the lower levels were red-brown, calm, complete, unchanging, like the whole aspect of this far-away and finished country, whereto had come, long ago, many Spaniards in search of wealth and dreams; and more recently certain Anglo-Saxons, also dreaming, who sought in a stolen hiatus of the continental conquest nothing of more value than a deep and sweet oblivion.

It was a Christmas-tide different enough from that of the States toward which Curly pointed. We looked eastward, looked again, turned back for one last look before we tightened the cinches and started down the winding trail which led through the foothills along the flank of the Patos Mountains, and so at last into the town of Heart's Desire.

"Lord!" said Curly, reminiscently, and quite without connection with any thought which had been uttered. "Say, it was fine, wasn't it, Christmas? We allus had firecrackers then. And eat! Why, man!" This allusion to the firecrackers would have determined that Curly had come from the South, which alone has a midwinter Fourth of July, possibly because the populace is not content with only one annual smell of gunpowder. "We had trees where I came from," said I. "And eat! Yes, man!"

"Some different here now, ain't it?" said Curly, grinning; and I grinned in reply with what fortitude I could muster. Down in Heart's Desire there was a little, a very little cabin, with a bunk, a few blankets, a small table, and a box nailed against the wall for a cupboard. I knew what was in the box, and what was not in it, and I so advised my friend as we slipped down off the bald summit of the Capitans and came into the shelter of the short, black pinons. Curly rode on for a little while before he made answer.

"Why," said he, at length, "ain't you heard? You're in with our rodeo on Christmas dinner. McKinney, and Tom Osby, and Dan Anderson, the other lawyer, and me,— we're going to have Christmas dinner at Andersen's 'dobe in town to-morrer. You're in. You mayn't like it. Don't you mind. The directions says to take it, and you take it. It's goin' to be one of the largest events ever knowed in this here settlement. Of course, there's goin' to be some canned things, and some sardines, and some everidge liquids. You guess what besides that."

I told him I couldn't guess.

"Shore you couldn't," said Curly, dangling his bridle from the little finger of his left hand as he searched in his pocket for a match. He had rolled a cigarette with one hand, and now he called it a *cigarrillo*. These facts alone would have convicted him of coming from somewhere near the Rio Grande.

"Shore you couldn't," repeated Curly, after he had his bit of brown paper going. "I reckon not in a hundred years. Champagne! Whole quart! Yes, sir. Cost eighteen dollars. Mac, he got it. Billy Hudgens had just this one bottle in the shop, left over from the time the surveyors come over here and we thought there was goin' to be a railroad, which there wasn't. But Lord! that ain't all. It ain't the beginnin'. You guess again. No, I reckon you couldn't," said he, scornfully. "You couldn't in your whole life guess what next. We got a *cake*!"

"Go on, Curly," said I, scoffingly; for I knew that the possibilities of Heart's Desire did not in the least include anything resembling cake. Any of the boys could fry bacon or build a section of bread in a Dutch oven—they had to know how to do that or starve. But as to cake, there was none could compass it. And I knew there was not a woman in all Heart's Desire.

Curly enjoyed his advantage for a few moments as we wound on down the trail among the pinons. "Heap o' things happened since you went down to tend co'te," said he. "You likely didn't hear of the new family moved in last week. Come from Kansas."

"Then there's a girl," said I; for I was far Westerner enough to know that all the girls ever seen west of the Pecos came from Kansas, the same as all the baled hay and all the fresh butter. Potatoes came from Iowa; but butter, hay, and girls came from Kansas. I asked Curly if the head of the new family came from Leavenworth.

"'Course he did," said Curly. "And I'll bet a steer he'll be postmaster or somethin' in a few brief moments." This in reference to another well-known fact in natural history as observed west of the Pecos; for it was matter of common knowledge among all Western men that the town of Leavenworth furnished early office-holders for every new community from the Missouri to the Pacific.

Curly continued; "This feller'll do well here, I reckon, though just now he's broke a-plenty. But what was he goin' to do? His team breaks down and he can't get no further. Looks like he'd just have to stop and be post-master or somethin' for us here for a while. Can't be Justice of the Peace; another Kansas man's got that. As to them two girls—man! The camp's got on its best clothes right this instant, don't you neglect to think. Both good lookers. Youngest's a peach. I'm goin' to marry *her*." Curly turned aggressively in his saddle and looked me squarely in the eye, his hat pushed back from his tightly curling red hair.

"That's all right, Curly," said I, mildly. "You have my consent. Have you asked the girl about it yet?"

"Ain't had time yet," said he. "But you watch me."

"What's the name of the family?" I asked as we rode

along together.

"Blamed if I remember exactly," replied Curly, scratching his head, "but they're shore good folks. Old man's sort o' pious, I reckon. Anyhow, that's what Tom Osby says. He driv along from Hocradle canon with 'em on the road from Vegas. Said the old man helt services every mornin' before breakfast. More services'n breakfast sometimes. Tom, he says old Whiskers—that's our next postmaster— he sings a-plenty, lifts up his voice exceeding. Say," said Curly, turning on me again fiercely, "that's one reason I'd marry the girl if for nothing else. It takes more'n a bass voice and a copy of the Holy Scriptures to make a Merry Christmas. Why, man, say, when I think of what a time we all are going to have,—you, and me, and Mac, and Tom Osby, and Dan Anderson, with all them things of our'n, and all these here things on the side—champagne and all that,—it looks like this world ain't run on the square, don't it?"

I assured Curly that this had long been one of my own conclusions. Assuredly I had not the bad manners to thank him for his invitation to join him in this banquet at Heart's Desire, knowing as I did Curly's acquaintance with the fact that young attorneys had not always abundance during their first year in a quasi-mining camp that was two-thirds cow town; such being among the possibilities of that land. I returned to the cake.

"Where'd we git it?" said Curly. "Why, where'd you s'pose we got it? Do you think Dan Anderson has took to pastry along with the statoots made and pervided? As for Dan, he ain't been here so very long, but he's come to stay. We're goin' to send him to Congress if we ever get time to organize our town, or find out what county we're in. How'd our Delergate look spreadin' jelly cake? Nope, he didn't make it. And does it look any like Mac has studied bakery doin's out on the Carrizoso ranch? You know Tom Osby couldn't. As for me, if hard luck has ever driv me to cookin' in the past, I ain't referrin' to it now. I'm a straight-up cow puncher and nothin' else. That cake? Why, it come from the Kansas outfit.

"Don't know which one of 'em done it, but it's a honey," he went on. "Say, she's a foot high, with white stuff a inch high all over. She's soft around the aidge some, for I stuck my finger intoe it just a little. We just got it recent and we're night-herdin' it where it's cool. Cost a even ten dollars. The old lady said she'd make the price all right, but Mac and me, we sort of sized up things and allowed we'd drop about a ten in their recep*tic*le when we come to pay for that cake. This family, you see, moved intoe the cabin Hank Fogarty and Jim Bond left when they went away,—it's right acrost the 'royo from Dan Anderson's office, where we're goin' to eat to-morrer.

"Now, how that woman could make a cake like this here in one of them narrer, upside-down Mexican ovens—no stove at all—no nothing—say, that's some like adoptin' yourself to circumstances, ain't it? Why, man, I'd marry intoe that fam'ly if I didn't do nothing else long as I lived. They ain't no Mexican money wrong side of the river. No counterfeit there regardin' a happy home—cuttin' out the bass voice and givin' 'em a leetle better line of grass and water, eh? Well, I reckon not. Watch me fly *to* it."

The idiom of Curly's speech was at times a trifle obscure to the uneducated ear. I gathered that he believed these newcomers to be of proper social rank, and that he was also of the opinion that a certain mending in their material matters might add to the happiness of the family.

"But say," he began again shortly, "I ain't told you half about our dinner."

"That is to say—" said I.

"We're goin' to have oysters!" he replied.

"Oh, Curly!" objected I, petulantly, "what's the use lying? I'll agree that you may perhaps marry the girl—I don't care anything about that. But as to oysters, you know there never was an oyster in Heart's Desire, and never will be, world without end."

"Huh!" said Curly. "Huh!" And presently, "Is that *so*?"

"You know it's so," said I.

"Is that so?" reiterated he once more. "Nice way to act, ain't it, when you're ast out to dinner in the best society of the place? Tell a feller he's shy on facts, when all he's handin' out is just the plain, unfreckled truth, for onct at least. We got oysters, four cans of 'em, and done had 'em for a month. They're up there." He jerked a thumb toward the top of old Carrizo Mountain. I looked at the snow, and in a flash comprehended. There, indeed, was cold storage, the only cold storage possible in Heart's Desire!

"Tom Osby brought 'em down from Vegas the last time he come down," said Curly. "They're there, sir, four cans of 'em. You know where the Carrizo spring is? Well, there's a snowbank in that canon, about two hundred yards off to the left of the spring. The oysters is in there. Keep? They got to keep!

"Them's the only oysters ever was knowed between the Pecos and the Rio Grande," he continued pridefully. "Now I want to ask you, friend, if this ain't just a leetle the dashed blamedest, hottest Christmas dinner ever was pulled off?"

"Curly," said I, "you are a continuous surprise to me."

"The trouble with you is," said Curly, lighting another cigarette, "you look the wrong way from the top of the divide. Never mind about home and mother. Them is States institooshuns. The only feller any good here is the feller that comes to stay, and likes it. You like it?"

"Yes, Curly," I replied seriously, "I do like it, and I'm going to stay if I can."

"Well, you be mighty blamed careful if that's the way you feel about it," said Curly. "I got my own eye on that girl from Kansas, and I serve notice right here. No use for you or Mac or any of you to be a-tryin' to cut out any stock for me. I seen it first."

We dropped down and ever down as we rode on along the winding mountain trail. The dark sides of the Patos Mountains edged around to the back of us, and the scarred flanks of big Carrizo came farther and farther forward along our left cheeks as we rode on. Then the trail made a sharp bend to the left, zigzagged a bit to get through a series of broken ravines, and at last topped the low false divide which rose at the upper end of the valley of Heart's Desire.

It was a spot lovely, lovable. Nothing in all the West is more fit to linger in a man's memory than the imperious sun rising above the valley of Heart's Desire; nothing unless it were the royal purple of the sunset, trailed like a robe across the shoulders of the grave unsmiling hills, which guarded it round about. In Heart's Desire it was so calm, so complete, so past and beyond all fret and worry and caring. Perhaps the man who named it did so in grim jest, as was the manner of the early bitter ones who swept across the Western lands. Perhaps again he named it at sunset, and did so reverently. God knows he named it right.

There was no rush nor hurry, no bickering nor envying, no crowding nor thieving there. Heart's Desire! It was well named, indeed; fit capital for the malcontents who sought oblivion, dreaming, long as they might, that Life can be left aside when one grows weary of it; dreaming— ah! deep, foolish, golden dream—that somewhere there is on earth an Eden with no Eve and without a flaming sword!

The town all lay along one deliberate, crooked street, because the *arroyo* along which it straggled was crooked. Its buildings were mostly of adobe, with earthen roofs, so low that when one saw a rainstorm coming in the rainy season (when it rained invariably once a day), he went forth with a shovel and shingled his roof anew, standing on the ground as he did so. There were a few cabins built of logs, but very few. Only one or two stores had the high board front common in Western villages. Lumber was very scarce and carpenters still scarcer. How the family from Kansas had happened to drift into Heart's Desire— how a man of McKinney's intelligence had come to settle there—how Dan Anderson, a very good lawyer, happened to have tarried there—how indeed any of us happened to be there, are questions which may best be solved by those who have studied the West-bound, the dream-bound, the malcontents. At any rate, here we were, and it was Christmas-time. The very next morning would be that of Christmas Day.

CHAPTER II

THE DINNER AT HEART'S DESIRE

This continuing the Relation of Curly, the Can of Oysters, and the Girl from Kansas; and Introducing Others

There were no stockings hung up in Heart's Desire that Christmas Eve, for all the population was adult, male, and stern of habit. The great moon flooded the street with splendor. Afar there came voices of rioting. There were some adherents to the traditions of the South in regard to firecrackers at Yuletide, albeit the six-shooter furnished the only firecracker obtainable. Yet upon that night the very shots seemed cheerful, not ominous, as was usually the case upon that long and crooked street, which had seen duels, affairs, affrays,—even riots of mounted men in the days when the desperadoes of the range came riding into town now and again for love of danger, or for lack of *aguardiente*. It was so very white and solemn and content,—this street of Heart's Desire on Christmas Eve. Far across the *arroyo*, as Curly had said, there gleamed red the double windows of the cabin which had been preempted by the man from Leavenworth. To-night the man from Leavenworth sat with bowed head and beard upon his bosom.

Christmas Day dawned, brilliant, glorious. There was not

a Christmas tree in all Heart's Desire. There was not a child within two hundred miles who had ever seen a Christmas tree. There was not a woman in all Heart's Desire saving those three newcomers in the cabin across the *arroyo*. Yet these new-comers were acquainted with the etiquette of the land. There was occasion for public announcement in such matters.

At eleven o'clock in the morning the man from Leavenworth and the Littlest Girl from Kansas came out upon the street. They were ostensibly bound to get the mail, although there had been no mail stage for three days, and could be none for four days more, even had the man from Leavenworth entertained the slightest thought of getting any mail at this purely accidental residence into which the fate of a tired team had thrown him. Yet there must be the proper notification that he and his family had concluded to abide in Heart's Desire; that he was now a citizen; that he was now entitled by the length of his beard to be called "'Squire," and to be accepted into all the councils of the town. This walk along the street was notice to the pure democracy of that land that all might now leave cards at the cabin across the *arroyo*. One need hardly doubt that the populace of Heart's Desire was lined up along the street to say good morning and to receive befittingly this tacit pledge of its newest citizen. Moreover, as to the Littlest Girl, all Heart's Desire puffed out its chest. Once more, indeed, the camp was entitled to hold up its head. There were Women in the town! *Ergo* Home; *ergo* Civilization; *ergo* Society; and ergo all the rest. Heretofore Heart's Desire had wilfully been but an unorganized section of savagery; but your Anglo Saxon, craving ever savagery, has no sooner found it than he seeks to civilize it; there being for him in his aeon of the world no real content or peace.

"I reckon the old man is goin' to take a look at the

post-office to see how he likes the place," said Curly, reflectively, as he gazed after the gentleman whom he had frankly elected as his father-in-law. "He'll get it, all right. Never saw a man from Leavenworth who wasn't a good shot at a postoffice. But say, about that Littlest Girl— well, I wonder!"

Curly was very restless until dinner-time, which, for one reason or another, was postponed until about four of the afternoon. We met at Dan Anderson's law office, which was also his residence, a room about a dozen feet by twenty in size. The bunks were cleaned up, the blankets put out of the way, and the centre of the room given over to a table, small and home-made, but very full of good cheer for that time and place. At the fireplace, McKinney, flushed and red, was broiling some really good loin steaks. McKinney also allowed his imagination to soar to the height of biscuits. Coffee was there assuredly, as one might tell by the welcome odor now ascending. Upon the table there was something masked under an ancient copy of a newspaper. Outside the door of the adobe, in the deepest shade obtainable, sat two soap boxes full of snow, or at least partly full, for Tom Osby had done his best. In one of these boxes appeared the proof of Curly's truthfulness—three cans of oysters, delicacies hitherto unheard of in that land! In the other box was an object almost as unfamiliar as an oyster can,—an oblong, smooth, and now partially frost-covered object with tinfoil about its upper end. A certain tense excitement obtained.

"I wonder if she'll get *frappe* enough," said Dan Anderson. He was a Princeton man once upon a time.

"It don't make no difference about the frappy part," said Curly, "just so she gets *cold* enough. I reckon I savvy wine some. I never was up the trail, not none! No, I reckon not! Huh?"

We agreed on Curly's worldliness cheerfully; indeed, agreed cheerfully that all the world was a good place and all its inhabitants were everything that could be asked. Life was young and fresh and strong. The spell of Heart's Desire was upon us all that Christmas Day.

"Now," said Curly, dropping easily into the somewhat vague position of host, when McKinney had finally placed his platter of screeching hot steaks upon the table. "Now, then, grub pi-i-i-le!" He sang the summons loud and clear, as it has sounded on many a frosty morning or sultry noon in many a corner of the range. "Set up, fellers," said Curly. "It's bridles off now, and cinches down, and the trusties next to the mirror." (By this speech Curly probably meant that the time was one of ease and safety, wherein one might place his six-shooter back of the bar, in sign that he was in search of no man, and that none was in search of him. It was not good form to eat in a private family in Heart's Desire with one's gun at one's belt.)

We sat down and McKinney uncovered the cake which had been made by the wife of the man from Leavenworth. It appeared somewhat imposing. Curly wanted to cut into it at the first course, but Dan Anderson rebelled and coaxed him off upon the subject of oysters. There was abundance for all. The cake itself would have weighed perhaps five or six pounds. There was a part of a can of oysters for each man, any quantity of wholesome steaks and coffee, with condensed milk if one cared for it, and at least enough champagne for any one who cared for precisely that sort of champagne.

It was nightfall before we were willing to leave the little pine table. Meantime we had talked of many things; of the new strike on the Homestake, of the vein of coal lately found in the Patos, of Apache rumors below Tularosa, and other matters interesting to citizens of that land. We mentioned an impending visit of Eastern Capital bent upon investigating our mineral wealth. We spoke of the vague rumor that a railroad was heading north from El Paso, and might come close to Heart's Desire if all went well; and, generous in the enthusiasm of the hour, we builded upon that fancy, ending by a toast to Dan Anderson as our first delegate to Congress. Dan bowed gravely, not knowing the future any more than ourselves. Nor should it be denied that there was talk of the new inhabitants across the arroyo. The morning promenade of the man from Leavenworth had been productive of results; add to these the results of so noble a feast as this Christmas dinner of ours, and it was foregone that our hearts must expand to include in welcome all humanity west of the Pecos.

After all, no man is better than the prettiest woman in his environment. As to these girls from Kansas, it is to be said that there had never before been a real woman in Heart's Desire. You, who have always lived where there is law, and society, and women, and home,—you cannot know what it is to see all these things gradually or swiftly dawning upon your personal horizon. Yet this was the way of Heart's Desire, where women and law and property were not.

It was perhaps the moon, or perhaps youth, or perhaps this state of life to which I have referred. Assuredly the street was again flooded with a grand, white moonlight, bright almost as a Northern day, when we looked out of the little window.

Dan Anderson was the first to speak, after a silence which had fallen amidst the dense tobacco smoke. "It cost us less than fifteen dollars a plate," said he. "I've paid more for worse—yes, a lot worse. But by the way, Mac, where's that other can of oysters? I thought you said there were four."

"That's what I said," broke in Tom Osby. "I done told Mac I ought to bring 'em all down, but he said only three."

"Well," said McKinney, always a conservative and level-headed man, "I allowed that if they would keep a month, they would keep a little longer. Now you all know there's goin' to be a stage in next week, and likely it'll bring the president of the New Jersey Gold Mills, who's been due here a couple of weeks. Now here we are, hollerin' all the time for Eastern Capital. What's the right thing for us to do when we get any Eastern Capital into our town? This here man comes from Philadelphy, which I reckon is right near the place where oysters grows. What are you goin' to *do*? He's used to oysters; like enough he eats 'em every day in the year, because he's shore rich. First thing he hollers for when he gets here is *oysters*. Looks like you all didn't have no public spirit. Are we goin' to give this here Eastern man the things he's used to, kinder gentle him along like, you know, and so get all the closeter and easier to him, or are we goin' to throw him down cold, and leave him dissatisfied the first day he strikes our camp? It shore looks to me like there ain't but one way to answer that."

"And that there one answer," said Tom Osby, "is now a-reclinin' in the snowbank up on Carrizy."

"I reckon that's so, all right, Mac," assented Curly, reflectively. "I *could* have et one more oyster or so, but I can quit if it's for the good of the country."

"Well, I'm feeling just a little bit guilty as it is," said Dan Anderson, who was in fairly good post-prandial condition. "Here we are, eating like lords. Now who knows what that poor family from Kansas is having for Christmas dinner? Mac, I appoint you a committee of one to see how they are getting along. Pass the hat. Make it about ten for the cake. Come on, now, let's find out about these folks."

Curly was distinctly unhappy all the time McKinney was away. It was half an hour before the latter came back, but the look on his face betrayed him. Dan Anderson made him confess that he still had the ten dollars in his pocket, that he had been afraid to knock at the door, and that he had learned nothing whatever of the household from Kansas. McKinney admitted that his nerve had failed, and that he dared not knock, but he said that he had summoned courage enough to look in at the window. The family had either finished its dinner long ago, had not eaten, or did not intend to eat at all. "The table looked some shy," declared McKinney. Beyond this he was incoherent, distressed, and plainly nervous. Silence fell upon the entire group, and for some time each man in Dan Andersen's salon was wrapped in thought. Perhaps each one cast a furtive look from the tail of his eye at his neighbors. Of all present, Curly seemed the happiest. "Didn't see the Littlest Girl?" he asked. McKinney shook his head.

"Well, I guess I'll be gettin' up to see about my wagon before long," said Tom Osby, rising and knocking his pipe upon his boot-heel. "I've got a few cans of stuff up here in my load that I don't really need. In the mornin', you know—well, so long, boys."

"I heard that Jim Peterson killed a deer the other day," suggested Dan Anderson. "I believe I'll just step over and see if I can't get a quarter of venison for those folks."

"Shore," said McKinney, "I'll go along. No, I won't; I'll

take a *pasear* acrost the street and have a look at a little stuff I brung up from the ranch yesterday."

"No Christmas," said Curly, staring ahead of himself into the tobacco smoke, and indulging in a rare soliloquy. "No Christmas dinner—and this here is in Ameriky!"

It is difficult to tell just how it occurred; but presently, had any one of us turned to look about him, he must have found himself alone. The moonlight streamed brilliantly over the long street of Heart's Desire. . . . The scarred sides of old Carrizo looked so close that one might almost have touched them with one's hand. . . .

It was about three miles from the street, up over the foot-hills, along the fiat canon which debouched below the spring where lay the snowbank. There were different routes which one could take. . . .

I knew the place very well from Curly's description, and found it easy to follow up the trickle of water which came down the canon from the spring. Having found the spring, it was easy to locate the spot in the snowbank where the oysters had been cached. I was not conscious of tarrying upon the way, yet, even so, there had been feet more swift than mine. As I came up to the spring, I heard voices and saw two forms sitting at the edge of the snowbank.

"Here's another one!" called out Dan Anderson as I appeared; and forthwith they broke into peals of unrighteous laughter. "You're a little slow; you're number three; Mac was first."

"I thought I heard an elk as I came up," said I, as I sat down beside the others and tried to look unconcerned, although plainly out of breath.

Emerson Hough

"Elk!" snorted McKinney, as he arose and walked to the other edge of the snowbank. "Here's your elk tracks." McKinney, foreman on Carrizoso, was an old range-rider, and he was right. Here was the track, plunging through the snow, and here was a deep hole where an elk, or something, had digged hurriedly, deeply, and, as it proved, effectively.

"Elk!" said McKinney again, savagely. "Damn that cow puncher! He took to his horse, 'course he did, and not one of us thought of ridin'. Who'd ever think a man would ride up here at all, let alone at night? Come on, fellers, we might as well go home."

"Well, I'm pleased to have met you, gentlemen," said Anderson, lighting a philosophic pipe, "and I don't mind walking back with you. It's a trifle lonesome in the hills after dark. Why didn't you tell me you were coming up?" He grinned with what seemed to us bad taste.

When we got down across the foot-hills and into the broad white street of Heart's Desire, we espied a dark figure slowly approaching. It proved to be Tom Osby, who later declared that he had found himself unable to sleep. He had things in his pockets. By common consent we now turned our footsteps across the *arroyo*, toward the cabin where dwelt the family from Kansas.

The house of the man from Leavenworth was lighted as though for some function. There were no curtains at the windows, and even had there been, the shock of this spectacle which went on before our eyes would have been sufficient to set aside all laws and conventions. With hands in pockets we stood and gazed blankly in at the open window. There was a sound of revelry by night. The narrow Mexican fireplace again held abundance of snapping, sparkling, crooked pinon wood. The table was spread. At its head sat the next postmaster; near him a lately sorrowful but now smiling lady, his wife, the woman from Kansas. The elder daughter was busy at the fire. At the right of the man from Leavenworth sat none less than Curly, the same whose cow pony, with bridle thrown down over its head, now stood nodding in the bright flood of the moonlight of Heart's Desire. At the side of Curly was the Littlest Girl from Kansas, and she was looking into his eyes.

It was thus that the social compact was first set on in the valley of Heart's Desire.

A vast steaming fragrance arose from the bowl which stood at the head of the table. In the home of the girl from Kansas there was light, warmth, comfort, joy. It was Christmas, after all.

"By the great jumpin' Jehossophat!" said Tom Osby, "them's *our* oysters!"

"And to think," mused Dan Anderson, softly, as we turned away,—"we *fried* ours!"

CHAPTER III

TRANSGRESSION AT HEART'S DESIRE

Beginning the Cause Celebre which arose from Curly's killing the Pig of the Man from Kansas

A great many abdomens have been injured in the pastime known as the "double roll." Especially has this been the case with persons not native to the land of Heart's Desire or the equivalent thereof. Even those born to the manner, and possessed of the freedom of a vast landscape whose every particular was devoted to the behoof of any man seized with a purpose of attaining speed and efficiency with firearms, did not always reach that smoothness and precision in the execution of this personal manoeuvre which alone could render it safe to themselves or impressive to the beholder. The owner of this accomplishment was never apt to find himself much crowded with company, in the way either of participants or spectators. Yet the art was a simple and harmless one, pertaining more especially to youth, enthusiasm, and the fresh air of high altitudes, which did ever evoke saltpetreish manifestations.

The evolution of the "double roll" is executed by taking a six-shooter—let us hope not one of those pitiful toys of the East—upon each forefinger, each weapon so hanging balanced on the trigger-guard and the trigger itself that it shall be ready to turn about the finger as upon a pivot, and shall be ready for instant discharge, the thumb cocking the weapon as it turns; yet so that it shall none the less be discharged only when the muzzle of the weapon is pointed away from the operator's person and not toward it.

It is best for the ambitious to begin this little sport with an empty weapon. Thus one will readily observe that the click of the hammer is all too often heard before the whirl of the gun is fairly under way, and while the muzzle is pointed midway of the operator's person; the weight of the heavy gun being commonly sufficient to pull back the trigger and so discharge the piece. When the ambitious soul has learned to do this "roll" with one empty gun, he may try it with two empty guns. If he finds it possible thus to content himself, it will perhaps be all the better for him. To stand upright, with a gun in each hand, even an empty gun, and so revolve the same while its own cylinder is revolving, is not wholly easy, though when one has finally gotten both hemispheres of his brain into accord with his forefingers, he will ever thereafter be able to understand fully the double revolution of the earth upon its axis and around the sun; provided always that he is able to perform the "double roll" without hitch or break, pulling right and left forefinger alternately and rapidly until he has heard what in his tentative case must be a series of six double clicks.

This performance with an empty six-shooter is but a pale and spiritless form of the sport of high altitudes. Instead there should be twelve reports, so closely sequent as to sound as one string of explosion. Thus executed the game is a fine one, the finer for being risky. So to stand erect, with an eight-inch Colt in either hand, each arm at full length, one gun shooting joyously down the centre of the street of your chosen town, the other shooting as cheerfully up the same street—to do this actually, with bark of powder and attending puffs of dust cut—this is indeed delightsome when the heart is full of red blood, and the chest swells with charged wine o' life, and the eyes gleam and the muscles harden for very search of some endeavor immediate and difficult! It is the more delightsome when this moment of man-frenzy finds one in such a town as was this of Heart's Desire; where, indeed, a man could do precisely as he pleased; where it was not accounted wrong or ill-balanced to claim the whole street for a half moment or so of a cloudless morning, and so to ease one's self of the pressure of the joy of living. To own this little world, to live free of touch or taint of control or guidance, to be brother to the mountains, cousin of the free sky—to live in Heart's Desire and be a man—ah! would that were possible for all of us to-day! Were it so, then assuredly we should exult and take unto ourselves all the privileges of the domain, perhaps even to the extent of attempting the "double roll."

Curly's wooing of the Littlest Girl, sped apace by his unrighteous appropriation of our can of oysters, in which he had held no fee simple, but only an individual and indeterminate interest, had prospered beyond all just deserts of a red-headed cow puncher with a salary of forty-five dollars a month. He had already, less than two months after the installation of the new postmaster, announced to his friends his forthcoming nuptials, and ever since the setting of the happy date had comported himself with an air of ownership of the town and a mere tolerance of its inhabitants.

Perhaps, if we were each and every one of us a prospective bridegroom, as was Curly upon this morning in question, we should be all the more persuaded to execute the "double roll" in mid-street, as proof to the public that all was well. Perhaps, also, if there should thus appear to any of us, adown street upon either hand, an object moving slowly, pausing, resuming again across the line of gun-vision its slow advance—ah! tell me, if that slow-moving object crossing the bridegroom's joyous aim were a pig,—a grunting, fat, conceited pig,—arrogating to itself much of that street wherefrom one's fellow-citizens had for a moment of grave courtesy withdrawn—tell me, if you were a bridegroom, soon to be happy, and if you could do the "double roll" with loaded guns and no danger to your bowels, and if while so engaged you should see within easy range this black, sleek pig, with its tail curled tightly, egotistically, contemptuously, over its back, what, as a man, would you do? What, as a man, *could* you do in a case like that, in a land where there was no law, where never a court had sat, where never such a thing as a case at law had been known? Consider, what would be the abstract right and justice of this matter, repeating that you were a bridegroom and twenty-three, and that the air was molten wine and honey mingled, and that this pig—but then, the matter is absurd! There is but one answer. It was right—indeed, it was inevitable—that Curly should shoot the pig; because in the first place it had intruded upon his pastime, and because in the second place he felt like it.

And yet over this act, this simple, inevitable act of justice, arose the first law case ever known in Heart's Desire, a cause which shook that community to the centre of its being, and for a time threatened its very continuance. Ah, well! perhaps the time had come. Perhaps the sun was now to set over all the valleys of Heart's Desire. Perhaps this was the beginning of the end. The law, they say, must have its course. It had its course in Heart's Desire.

But not without protest, not without struggle. There were two factions from the start. Strange to say, that most bitterly opposed to Curly was headed by no less a person than his own intended father-in-law, the man from

Leavenworth. It was his pig. The rest of us had lived at Heart's Desire for a considerable time, but there had hitherto seemed no need for law. Order we already had in so far as order is really needed; though the importance of order, or indeed the importance of law, is a matter very much overrated. No man at Heart's Desire ever dreamed of locking his door. His horse might doze saddled in the street if he liked. No man spoke in rudeness or coarseness to his neighbor, as do men in the cities where they have law. No man did injustice to his neighbor, for fair play and an even chance were gods in the eyes of all, eikons above each pinon-burning hearth in all that valley of content. The speech of man was grave and gentle, the movements of man were easy and unhurried; neither did any man work by rule, or by clock, or by order. There was no such thing as want or hunger; for did temporary poverty encompass one, was there not always the house of Uncle Jim Brothers, and could not one there hang up his gun behind the door and so obtain credit for an indefinite length of time, entitling him to eat at table with his peers? Had there been such a thing as families in Heart's Desire, be sure such a thing as a woman or child engaged in any work had been utterly unknown. It was a land of men, big, grave, sufficient men, each with a gun upon his hip, and sometimes two, guaranty of peace and calm and content. And any man who has ever lived in a Land Before the Law knows that this is the only fit way of life. Alas! that this scheme, this great, happy simple, perfect scheme of society should be subverted. And, be it remembered, this was by reason of nothing more than a pig, an artless, lissom pig, it is true; an infrequent, somewhat prized, a little petted and perhaps spoiled pig, it is true; yet, after all, no fit cause of elemental strife.

But now came this man from Leavenworth, fresh from litigious soil, bearing with him in his faded blue army overcoat germs of civilization, seeds of discontent. He wailed aloud that the pride of the community, meaning this pig, which he had brought solitary in a box at the tail of the wagon when he moved in, was now departed; that there was naught left to distinguish this community from any other camp in the mountains; that the pig had been the light of his home, the apple of his eye, the pride of the community; that he had entertained large designs in connection with this pig the following fall; that its taking off was a shame, an outrage, a disgrace, an act utterly illegal, and one for which any man in Kansas would promptly have had the law of his neighbor.

Hitherto the "double roll," even in connection with a curly-tailed black pig, had not been considered actionable in Heart's Desire; but the outcry made by this man from Leavenworth, now the postmaster of the town and in some measure a leader in the meetings of the population, began to attract attention. It began to play upon the nicely attuned instrument of Public Spirit. What, indeed, asked the community gravely, was to separate Heart's Desire in the eye of Eastern Capital, from any other camp in the far Southwest? Once the town could claim a pig, which no other camp of that district could do. Now it could do so no more forever. This began to put a different look upon the face of things.

"It seems like the ole man took it some hard," said Curly, lighting a *cigarrillo*. "He don't seem to remember that I was due to be a member of the family right soon, same as the pig. I don't like to think I'm shy when it comes to comparison with a shoat. Gimme time, and I reckon I could take the place of the pig in my new dad's affections. But I say deliberate that pigs has got no call to be in a cow country, not none, unless salted. Say, can't we salt this one? Then, who's the worse *off* for it? What's all this furse about, anyway?"

"That's right, Curly," said Dan Anderson, who stood with hands in pockets and pipe in mouth, leaning against the door-jamb in front of his "law office." "You have enunciated a great principle of law in that statement. They have got to prove damages. Moreover, you have got a counter-claim. It's laceratin' to be compared to a shoat."

"And me just goin' to be married," said Curly.

"Sure, it ain't right."

"Andersen," said I, moving up to the group, "did you ever hear of such things as champerty and maintenance? The first thing you know, you'll get disbarred for stirring up litigation."

"Keep away from my client," said Dan Anderson, grinning. "You're jealous of my professional success, that's all. Neither of us has had a case yet, and now that it looks like I was going to get one, you're jealous. Do you want to pass up the first lawsuit ever held in the county? Come now, I'm bored to death. Let's have some fun."

Curly began to shift uneasily on his feet. His hat went still farther back on his red, kinky curls.

"Law!" said he. "Law! You don't mean—" For the first time in his life Curly grew pale. "Why, I'll clean out the hull bunch!" he said, the red surging back in his face and his hand instinctively going to his gun.

"No, you won't," said Dan Anderson. "Do you want to bust up your marriage with the girl from Kansas?"

"Sho'!" said Curly, and fell thoughtful. "This looks bad," said he; "mighty bad." He sat down and began to think. I do not doubt that Dan Anderson at that moment was a disgrace to his profession, though later he honored it. He winked at me.

"Don't you tamper with my client," said he; and then resumed to Curly; "What you need is a lawyer. You've got to have legal advice. It happens that the full bar of Heart's Desire is now present talking to you. Take your pick. I've got a mighty good idea which is the best lawyer of this bar, but I wouldn't tell you for the world that I'm the one. Take your pick. Here's the whole legal works of the town, us two. Try the Learned Counsel on my right."

"Law!" said Curly. "Why—law—lawyers! Then who— say, now, I'll *pay* for the pig. I didn't mean nothing, no way."

Then Dan Anderson rose to certain heights. "You can't settle it that way," said he. "That's too easy. Oh, you can pay for the *pig* easy enough; but how about the majesty of the law? Where is the peace and dignity of the common-wealth to come in? This is criminal. Nope, you choose. You need a lawyer."

"You—you-all got me *locoed*," said Curly, nervously. "Law! Why, I don't want no law. There ain't never been no co'te set here. Down to the county-seat, over to Lincoln, that's all right; but here—why, they don't *want* no law here. Besides, I can't choose between you two fellers. I like you both. You're both white men. Ef you could rope and shoot better, I could git either one of you a job cowpunchin' any day, and that's a heap better'n practisin' law. I couldn't make no choice between you fellers. Say, I'll have you *both*." This with a sudden illumination of countenance.

"That would be unconstitutional," said Dan Anderson, solemnly, "and against public policy as well. That would be cornering the whole legal supply of the community, Curly, and it wouldn't leave anybody for the prosecution."

"Sho'!" said Curly. Then suddenly he added: "There's the old man. Don't you never doubt he'd prosecute joyful. And there never was a man from Kansas didn't know some law. Why, onct, down on the Brazos—"

"He can't act as attorney-at-law," said Anderson. "He's never been admitted to the bar. Say, you flip a dollar."

The thought of chance-taking appealed to Curly. He flipped the dollar.

"Heads, me," said Dan Anderson; and so it fell. That young man smiled blithely. "We'll skin 'em, Curly," said he. "You'll be as free as air in less'n a week."

"Now," said Dan Anderson to me, "it's all right thus far. Next we have got to get a Justice of the Peace, and then we've got to get the prisoner arrested."

"'Rested!" said Curly. "Who? Me?"

"Of course," drawled his newly constituted attorney. "Didn't you kill the pig? You just hang around for a little, for when we need you, we don't want to have to hunt all over the country."

"All right," said Curly, dubiously.

"Where's Blackman?" said Dan Anderson, again addressing me. "We have got to have a judge, or we can't have any trial. Come on and let's hunt him up. Curly, don't you run away, mind. You trust to me, and I'll get you clear, and get you married, both."

"All right," said Curly again, "I'll just sornter down to the Lone Star, and when you-all want me I'll be in there, either takin' a drink or playin' a few kyards."

"Let's get Blackman now," said Curly's lawyer. Blackman was the duly constituted Justice of the Peace in and for Heart's Desire. Nobody knew precisely when or how he had been elected, and perhaps indeed he never was elected at all. There must be a beginning for all things. The one thing certain as to Blackman was that he had once been a Justice of the Peace back in Kansas, which fact he had not been slow to announce upon his arrival in Heart's Desire. Perhaps from this arose the local custom of calling him Judge, and perhaps from his wearing the latter title arose the supposition that he really was a judge. The records are quite silent as to the origin of his tenure of office. The office itself, as has been intimated, had hitherto been one purely without care. At every little shooting scrape or other playfulness of the male population Blackman, Justice of the Peace, became inflated with importance and looked monstrous grave. But nothing ever came of these little alarms, so that gradually the inflations grew less and less extensive. They might perhaps have ceased altogether had it not been for this malignant zeal of Dan Anderson, formerly of Princeton, and now come, hit or miss, to grow up with the country.

Blackman was ever ready enough for a lawsuit, forsooth pined for one. Yet what could he do? He could not go forth and with his own hands arrest chance persons and hale them before his own court for trial. The sheriff, when he was in town, simply laughed at him, and told his deputies not to mix up with anything except circuit-court matters, murders, and more especially horse stealings. Constable there was none; and policeman—it is to wonder just a trifle what would have happened to any such thing as a policeman or town marshal in the valley of Heart's

Desire! In short, there was neither judicial nor executive arm of the law in action. One may, therefore, realize the hindrances which Dan Anderson met in getting up his lawsuit. Yet he went forward in the attempt patiently, driven simply by ennui. He did not dream that he was doing something epochal.

Blackman, Justice of the Peace, was sitting in the office of the *Golden Age* when we found him, reading the exchanges and offering gratuitous advice to the editor. He was a shortish man, thick in body, with sparse hair and hay-colored, ragged mustache. His face was florid, his pale eyes protruded. He was a wise-looking man, excellently well suited in appearance for the office which he filled. We explained to him our errand. Gradually, as the sense of his own new importance dawned upon him, he began to swell, apparently until he assumed a bulk thrice that which he formerly possessed. His spine straightened rigidly; a solemn light came into his eye; a cough that fairly choked with wisdom echoed from his throat. It was a great day for Blackman, J. P.

"Do I know this man, this cow puncher?" said he. "Of course I know him, damn him, and I know what he done, too. Such a high-handed act never ought to be tolerated, sir! Destroyin' property—why, a-destroyin' of life *and* property, for he killed the pig—and this new family of citizens dependin' in part on the pig fer their sustenances this comin' season; to say nothin' of his nigh shootin' me up as I was crossin' the street from the post-office! Try him! Why, of *course* we ought to try him. What show have we got if we go on this lawless way? What injucement can we offer Eastern Capital to settle in our midst if, instead of bein' quiet and law-abidin', we go on a-rarin' and a-pitchin' and a-runnin' wide open, every man for hisself? What are we here for, you, and you, and me, if it ain't to set in trile over such britches of the peace?"

"You're in," said Dan Anderson, succinctly. "Get over to your 'dobe. We'll hold this trial right away. I reckon all the boys'll know about it by this time. I'll go over and get the prisoner. But, hold on! He ain't arrested yet. Who'll serve the warrant? Ben Stillson (the sheriff) is down on the Hondo, and his deputy, Poe, is out of town. There ain't a soul here to serve a paper. Looks like the court was some rusty, don't it?"

"Warrant!" said the Justice, "warrant! You don't need no warrant. Wasn't he seen a-doin' the act?"

"Oh, but it wasn't a real first-class felony," demurred Dan, with some shade of conscience left.

"Well, I'll arrest him myself," said the Justice. "He's got to be brought to trile."

"Well, now," I ventured to suggest, "that doesn't look exactly right, either, since you are to try the case, Judge. It's legal, but it isn't etiquette."

Blackman scratched his head. "Maybe that's so," said he. Then turning to me, "S'pose *you* arrest him."

"He can't," said Dan Anderson. "He's the prosecuting attorney—only other lawyer in town. It wouldn't look right for either the judge or prosecutor to make the arrest. Curly might not like it." This all seemed true enough, and we fell into a quandary.

"I'll tell you," said Dan Anderson at length. "I'd better arrest him myself. I'm going to defend him, so it would look more regular for me to bring him in. Looks like he wasn't afraid of the verdict. We ain't, either. I want you to remember, Judge, if you don't clear him—"

Here counsel for the Territory interrupted, feeling that the majesty of the law was not fully observed by threatening the trial judge in advance.

"Well, come along, then," said Anderson. "Let that part of it go. Come over and let's get out the warrant."

I was not with them when the warrant was issued, though that part of the proceeding might naturally have seemed rather the duty of the prosecution than of the defence. Dan Anderson afterward told me that Blackman could not find his law book (he had only one, a copy of the statutes of Kansas) for a long time, and then couldn't find the proper place in it. Legal blanks did not exist in Heart's Desire, and all legal forms had departed from Blackman's mind in this time of excitement. Dan Anderson himself drew the warrant. As it was read later by himself to Curly at the Lone Star, it did not lack a certain charm. It began with "Greeting," and ended with, "Now, therefore, in the name of God and the Continental Congress." Anderson did not crack a smile in reading it, and so far as that is concerned, the warrant worked as well as any and better than some. Curly, because he felt that he was in the hands of his friends, made no special demurrer to the terms of the "writ," and in a few moments the Lone Star was empty and Blackman's adobe was packed.

CHAPTER IV

THE LAW AT HEART'S DESIRE

Continuing the Story of the Pig from Kansas, and the Deep Damnation of his Taking Off

"Order! order! gentlemen!" called Blackman, Justice of the Peace, clearing his throat. "This honorable justice court is now in session. Gentlemen, what is your pleasure?"

He was a little confused, but he meant well. It seemed incumbent upon the prosecutor to make some sort of a statement, but the attorney for the defence interposed. He moved for the discharge of the prisoner on the ground that there was no Territorial law and no city ordinance violated; he pointed out that Heart's Desire was not a city, neither a town, but had never been organized, established, or begun, even to the extent of the filing of a town site plat; he therefore denied the existence of any municipal law, since there had never been any municipality; he intimated that the pig had perhaps been killed accidentally, or perhaps in self-defence; it was plain that the prisoner was wrongfully restrained of his liberty, etc.

The ire of Blackman, J. P., at all this was something to behold. He to be deprived of his opportunity thus lightly?

Emerson Hough

Hardly! He overruled the objections at once, and rapped loudly for order.

"The trile will go on," said he.

"Then, your Honor," cried Dan Andersen, springing to his feet, "then I shall resort to the ancient bulwark of our personal liberties. I shall sue out a writ of *habeas corpus*, and take this prisoner out of custody. I'll sue this court on its bond! I'll take a change of venue! We'll leave no stone unturned to set this innocent man free and restore him to the bosom of his family!"

This speech produced a great effect on the audience, as murmurs of approbation testified, but the doughty Justice of the Peace was not so easily to be reckoned with. He pointed out that there was no officer to serve a writ of *habeas corpus*; that the court had given no bond to anybody and did not propose to do so; that there was no other court to which to apply for a change of "vendew," as he termed it; and reiterated once more that the "trile must go on." The prosecution was, therefore, once more called upon to state the case. Again the attorney for the defence protested, a foreshadowing of his fighting blood reddening his face.

"I call for a jury," said he. "Does this court suppose we are going to leave the liberty of this prisoner in the hands of a judge openly and notoriously prejudiced as to the facts of this case? I demand a trial by a jury of the defendant's peers."

Blackman reddened, but was game. "Jury goes," said he. "Count out twelve fellers there, beginnin' next the door."

"Twelve!" said Dan Andersen, for the moment almost losing his gravity. "I thought this court might be content with six for a justice's jury; but realizing the importance of this court, we are willing to agree on twelve."

It was so agreed. The jury took in every man in the little room but three. "They'll do for a veniry," said Blackman, J. P., learnedly. Under the circumstances, one can perhaps forgive him for becoming at times a trifle mixed as to the legal proceedings.

At least, it was easy to agree as to the jury; for obviously the population of the place was fully acquainted with all the facts in the case, and each one had freely expressed his opinion upon the one side or the other. There seemed to be no reason for excusing any juror for cause; and upon the other hand, there are often very good reasons in a Land Before the Law for not bringing up personal matters of this kind. Indeed, the trial judge settled all that. He looked over the twelve good men and true thus segregated, and remarked briefly: "They're his peers, all right. The trile will now proceed."

Whereupon he swore them solemnly and made a record in his fee book, to the later consternation of his jurors. "Ain't this court a notary, too?" said Blackman later. "And ain't a notary entitled to so much fee for administerin' a oath? And didn't I administer twelve oaths?" There was small answer to this, after all. The laborer is worthy of his hire; and Blackman really labored in this case as in all likelihood few justices have before or since.

The prosecuting attorney, who, it may be seen, held his office much as did the justice of the peace, by the doctrine of *nemine contradicente*, now arose and made the opening statement. There, was some doubt as to whether this was a civil or criminal trial, but there was no doubt whatever of the existence of a trial of some kind; neither did there exist any doubt as to the importance of this, the first case the prosecuting attorney had ever tried, outside of moot courts. It was the first speech he had ever made in public, barring college "orations," carefully memorized, and an occasional Fourth of July speech, which might have been better for more memorizing. The attorney for the prosecution, however, arose to the occasion—at least to a certain extent. He spoke in low and feeling tones of the struggling little community of hardy souls thus set down apart in the far-off mountain country of the West; of its trials, its hopes, its ambitions, of its expectations of becoming a mountain emporium which should be the pride of the entire Territory; he went on to mention the necessity for law and order, pointing out the danger to the public interests of the community which must lie in a general reputation for ruffianism and lawlessness, showing how Eastern Capital must ever be timid in visiting a town of such reputation, apart from investing any money therein; then, changing to the personal phases of the case, he spoke of the absolute disregard of law shown in the act charged, mentioned the red-handed deed of this lawless and dangerous person who had thus slain a pig, no less the pride of the community than the idol of the family now bereft.

At this point the jury began to look much perturbed and solemn, and the prisoner very red and uneasy. Prosecution closed by offering to prove all charges by competent testimony. This latter was a dangerous proposition to advance. We could not well ask the jurymen to testify, and of the "veniry," more than half had now slipped out for a hurried and excited visit to the Lone Star, there to advise any possible new arrivals of what was going on at Blackman's adobe.

Counsel for the defence arose calmly to make his opening statement. The man was a natural trial lawyer. It was simply destiny which had driven him into this comedy, as destiny had driven him to Heart's Desire. It was not comedy now, when Dan Anderson faced judge and jury here in Blackman's adobe. There came a swift, sudden chill, a gripping as of iron, a darkening, a shrinking of the heart of each man in that little room. It was the coming of the Law! Ah! Dan Anderson, you ruined our little paradise; and now its walls are down forever, even the walls of our city of content.

Dan Anderson stood, young, tall and grave, one hand in the bosom of his shirt, for hardly one present wore a coat. He had his audience with him before he spoke. When he began he caught them tighter to his cause, using not merely flowing rhetoric of speech, but the close-knit, advancing, upbuilding argument of a man able to "think on his feet,"—that higher sort of oratory which is most convincing with an American audience or an American jury.

The statement of the prosecution, said Dan Anderson, was on the whole a fair one, and no discredit to the learned brother making it. None would more readily than himself yield acquiescence to the statement that law and order must prevail. Without law there could be nothing but anarchy. Under anarchy progress was at an end. The individual must give up something of his rights to the state and the community. He gave up a certain amount of liberty, but received therefor an equivalent in protection. The law was, therefore, no oppressor, no monster, no usurer, no austere being, reaping where it had not sown. The law was nothing to be dreaded, nothing to be feared; and, upon the other hand, it was nothing to be scorned.

There must be a beginning, continued Dan Anderson. There must be something established. The pound measure was one pound, the same all over the country; a yard measure was a yard, and there was no guesswork about it.

It was the same. It was a unit. So with the law. It must be the same, a unit, soulless, unfeeling, just, unchangeable. There was nothing indeterminate in it. The attitude of the law was thus or so, and not otherwise. It was not for the individual to pass upon any of these questions. It was for the courts to do so, the approved machinery set aside, under the social compact, for reducing the friction of the wheels of society, for securing the permanency of things beneficial to that society, and for removing things injurious thereto. The Law itself was immutable. The courts must administer that Law without malice, without feeling, impersonally, justly.

In so far as there had hitherto been no Law in Heart's Desire, went on the speaker, thus far had our citizens dwelt in barbarism, had indeed been unfit, under the very definition of things, to bear the proud title of citizens of America, the justest, the most order-loving, as well as the bravest and the most aggressive nation of the world. The time had now come for the establishment in this community of the Law, that beneficent agency of progress, that indispensable factor, that inseparable attendant upon civilization. Upon the sky should blaze no more the red riot of anarchy and barbarism. Upon the summit of the noble mountain overtopping this happy valley there should sit no more the grinning figure of malevolent and unrestrained vice, but the pure form of the blind Goddess of Justice, holding ever aloft over this happy land the unfaltering sword and the unwavering scales, so that all might look thereon, the rightdoers in smiling security, the wrong-doing in terror of their deeds. This was the Law!

"And now, gentlemen of this jury," said Dan Anderson, "I stand here before you to make no excuses for this Law, to palliate nothing in the way of its workings, to set no tentative or temporizing date for the time of the arrival at this place of the image of the Law. I say to you here to-day, at this hour, that image now sits there enthroned above us. The Law is not to come—it has come, it is here!"

The old days were, therefore, done, he went on. Henceforth we must observe the Law. We were here now with the intention of observing that Law. Should we therefore fear it? Should we dread the decision of this distinguished servant of the Law? By no means. To show that the Law was no dragon, no demon, he would now, in the very face of that Law, proceed to clear this innocent man of that cloud of doubt and suspicion which for a brief moment the social body had cast upon him. He would show to the gentlemen of this jury and to this honorable court that there had been no violation of the Law through any act of this honest, open-faced, intelligent young gentleman, long known among them as an upright and fair-dealing man. The Law, just and exact, would now protect this prisoner. The Law was no matter of haphazard. The prosecution must show that some specific article of the Law had been violated.

"Now," continued Dan Anderson, casting an eye about him as calmly as could have done any old trial lawyer examining the condition of his jury, "what are the charges made by the Territory? The prosecution specifies no section or paragraph of the statutes of this Territory holding it unlawful to shoot any dangerous wild beast at large in this community. But we do not admit that this prisoner shot anything, or shot at anything whatever. We shall prove that at the time mentioned he was engaged in a simple, harmless, and useful pastime, a pastime laudable of itself, since it tends to make the participant therein a better and more useful citizen. There is no Territorial law forbidding any act which he is here charged with committing. Neither has the body social in this thriving community placed upon its records any local law, any indication that a man may not, without let or hindrance, do any act such as those charged vaguely against this good young man, who has only availed himself of his right under the Constitution to bear arms, to assemble in public, and to engage in the pursuit of happiness."

The prosecution, he said, had introduced reference to a certain pig, alleging that it was slain by the act of the prisoner. He would not admit that there had been any pig, since no *corpus delicti* was shown; but in any event this was no civil suit now in progress. We were not here to assess value upon a supposititious pig, injured in a supposititious manner, and not represented here of counsel. No law had been violated. Why, then, his client had been thus ruthlessly dragged into court, to his great personal chagrin, his loss of time, his mental suffering, the attorney for defence could not say. It was injustice of a monstrous sort! Prosecution might well feel relieved if no retaliatory action were later taken against them for false imprisonment. This innocent young man must at once be discharged from custody.

When Dan Anderson sat down there was not a man in the jury who was not bathed in perspiration. Abstruse thought was hard at work. Blackman, J. P., perspiring no less than any member of the jury, drew himself up, but he was troubled.

"Evidence fr the State," the Judge finally managed to stammer, turning to the attorney for the prosecution.

But it never came so far along as that. There was a sound of many footsteps; voices came murmuring, growing louder. The door was pushed open from without, and in came much of the remaining population of Heart's Desire, so far as it could gain room. The man from Leavenworth was there, his whiskers wagging unintelligibly. McKinney was there, and Doc Tomlinson and Tom Osby, and everybody else; and, pushing through the crowd, there came the Littlest Girl from Kansas, her apron awry, her hair blown, her face flushed, her eyes moist with tears.

"Curly!" cried she as at last her eyes caught sight of him. "Come right on out of here, this minute! Come along!"

What would you have? The Law is the Law; but there are such things as supreme courts. It was useless for Blackman, J. P., to rap and call for order. It had probably been useless for any man to undertake to stop the prisoner at the bar, thus adjured. At any rate he arose and said politely to the jurors, "Fellers, I got to go"—and so went, no man raising hand to restrain him.

As to Dan Anderson, he himself admitted his wish that the case had gone on. "I wanted to cross-examine," said he.

That night, over by the *arroyo*, we met Curly and the Littlest Girl walking in the moonlight. Curly was quiet. The Littlest Girl was tremulous, content. Curly, pausing as we approached, mumbled some shamefaced thanks.

"Curly," said Dan Anderson, his voice queer, "I didn't do it for pay. I did it—I don't know why—"

A new mood was upon him. A lassitude as of remorse appeared to relax him, body and mind. An hour later he and I sat in the glorious flood of the light of the moon of Heart's Desire, and we fell silent, as was the way of men in that place. At length Dan Anderson turned his face to the top of old Carrizo, the restful, the impassive. He gazed long without speaking, as though he plainly saw something there at the mountain top.

Emerson Hough

"Listen," he whispered to me, a moment later, and his eyes did not quite keep back the tears. "She's there—the Goddess. The Law has come to Heart's Desire. May God forgive me! Why could we not have stayed content?"

But little did Dan Anderson foresee that day how swiftly was to come further ruin for the kingdom of oblivion which we thought that we had found.

"There'll be *women* next!" I said to him bitterly; though this was a vague threat of a thing impossible.

His reply was a look more than half frightened.

"Don't!" he said.

CHAPTER V

EDEN AT HEART'S DESIRE

This being the Story of a Paradise; also showing the Exceeding Loneliness of Adam

Two months had passed since the wedding of Curly and the Littlest Girl, and nothing further had happened in the way of change. The man from Philadelphia had not come, and, to the majority of the population of Heart's Desire at least, the railroad to the camp remained a thing as far distant as ever in the future. Life went on, spent in the open for the most part, and in silent thoughtfulness by choice. Blackman, J. P., now languished in desuetude among the fallen remnants of an erstwhile promising structure of the law; and there being no further occupation for the members of the bar, the latter customarily spent much of the day sitting in the sun.

"You might look several times at me," said Dan Andersen one day, without preface or provocation, "and yet not read all my past in these fair lineaments."

This seemed unworthy of notice. A man's past was a subject tabooed in Heart's Desire. Besides, the morning was already so warm that we were glad to seek the shade of an adobe wall. Conversation languished. Dan Anderson absent-mindedly rolled a *cigarrillo* with one hand, his gaze the while fixed on the horizon, on which we could see the faint loom of the Bonitos, toothed upon the blue sky, fifty miles away. His mind might also have been fifty miles away, as he gazed vaguely. There was nothing to do. There was only the sun, and as against it the shade. That made up life at Heart's Desire. It was a million miles away to any other sort of world; and that world, in so far as it had reference to a past, was a subject not mentioned among the men of Heart's Desire. Yet this morning there seemed to be something upon Dan Andersen's mind, as he edged a little farther along into the shade, and felt in his pocket for a match.

"No, you wouldn't think; just to look at me, my friend," said he, "you wouldn't think, without runnin' side lines, and takin' elevations for dips, spurs, and angles, that I had ever been anything but a barrister; now, would you? Attorney and Counsellor-at-law, all hours of the day and night: that bill of specifications is engraved on my brow, ain't it? You like enough couldn't believe that I was ever anything else—several things else, could you?"

His speech still failed of interest, except as it afforded additional proof of the manner in which Yale, Harvard, Princeton, and the like disappeared from the speech of all men at Heart's Desire. Dan Anderson sat down in the shade, his long legs stretched out in front of him. "My boy," said he, "you can gaze at me if you ain't too tired. As a matter of fact, in this pernicious age of specialization I stand out as the one glitterin' example of success in more than one line. Why, once I was a success as a journalist—for a few moments."

There was now a certain softness and innocence in his voice, which had portent, although I did not at that time suspect that he really had anything of consequence upon his soul. Without more encouragement he went on.

"My brother," said he, "when I first came out of Princeton I was burnin' up with zeal. There was the world, the whole wide world, plunged into an abyss of error and wrongdoin'. I was the sole and remainin' hope. Like all great men, I naturally wanted to begin the savin' as early as possible; and like everybody else who comes out of Princeton, I thought the best medium for immediate salvation was journalism. I wasn't a newspaper man. I never said that at all. I was a journalist.

"Well, dad got me a place on a paper in New York, and I worked on the dog-fight department for a time, it havin' been discovered that I was noted along certain lines of research in Princeton. I knew the pedigree and fightin' weight of every white, black, or brindle pup in four States. Now, a whole lot of fellows come out of college who don't know that much; or if they do, they don't know how to apply their knowledge. Now dogs, that's plumb useful.

"I was still doin' dogs when the presidential campaign came along, or rather, that feature of our national customs which precedes the selection of the People's Choice. First thing, of course, the People's Choice had to take a run over the country—which was a good thing, too, because he didn't know much about it—and let the people in general know that he was their choice. I went along to tell the other people how he broke it to them."

I confess I sat up at this, for there was now so supreme an innocence in Dan Anderson's eye that one might have been morally certain that something was coming. "From dogs to politics—wasn't that a little singular?" I asked.

"Yes," said he; "but you have to be versatile in

Emerson Hough

journalism. The regular man who was to have gone on that special presidential car got slugged at an art gatherin'. I didn't ask for the place. I just went and told the managin' editor I was ready if he would give me an order for expense money. It wouldn't have been good form for him to look up and pay any attention to me, so I got the job. I needed to see the country just as much as the People's Choice did.

"Three other fellows went along,—newspaper men. I was the only real journalist. We did the presidential tour for ten towns a day. I watched what the other fellows did, and in about two hours it was easy. Everything's easy if you think so. Folks made a lot of fuss about gettin' along in the world. That's all a mistake.

"People's Choice tore it off in fine shape. Comin' into Basswood Junction he turns to his Honorable Secretary, and says he, 'Jimmy, what's this?' Jimmy turns to his card cabinet, and says he: 'Prexie, this is Basswood Junction. Three railroads come in here—and get away as soon as they can. Four overall factories and a reaper plant. Population six thousand, and increasin' satisfactory. Hon. Charles D. Bastrop, M.C., from this district, on the straight Republican ticket for the last three hundred years; world without end.'"

"Then the train would pull into this station to the sad sweet notes of the oompah horn, and the delegation of leadin' citizens would file in behind the car, and the first leadin' citizen would get red in the face with his Welcome talk, while we four slaves of the people were hustling the President's speech to the depot telegraph wire before he said it. People's Choice, he stands on the back platform with one hand in his bosom, and says he: 'Fellow-citizens of Basswood Junction, I am proud to see before me this large and distinguished gatherin' of our noble North

American fauna. My visit to your pleasant valley is wholly without political significance. These noble et cetera; these smilin' et cetera; these beautiful et cetera, fill me with the proudest emotions of et cetera. This, our great and glorious et cetera; Basswood Junction has four magnificent factories, and is the centre of three great trunk lines of railroad which radiate et cetera; it is destined to be a great commercial et cetera. And what could be more confirmatory of the sober, practical judgment of the citizens of this flourishing community than the fact that they have produced and given to the world that distinguished statesman and gentleman, the Hon. Charles D. Bastrop, who is your representative in the Congress of the United States and who has always et cetera, et cetera? 'Fellow-citizens, the issue before this country to-day—' and that was where he would hit his gait.

"He had three of these, and on the schedule laid out by the chairman of the Central Committee he couldn't spring any two alike closer together than a hundred miles. The whole business would take about five minutes to a station. We would put number Two, or number Three, or whichever it was, on the wire, while the People's Choice was talkin', provided we could catch the station agent, who on such occasions was bigger than the President. Then, toot! toot! and we were off for the next Basswood Junction, to show 'em who was their spontaneous choice.

"Well, that was all right, and it was easy work to report. The only thing was not to get number One speech mixed up with number Two or number Three at any given point. The Honorable Secretary had to attend to that. So all the time we were bored for something to do. What we was hopin' and longin' for all the time was that some one in the opposition at some station would haul off and throw a brick at the car. Then we would have had some News."

"Oh," said I, "you got to wanting news! You had a narrow escape."

"Maybe," said Dan Anderson. "I admit I got to likin' the game. I think, too, I did get to understandin' what news was. So one day, when I was mighty tired of the four-factory, railroad-centre, leadin'-citizen business, I mixed up the speeches on the Honorable Secretary between stations." Dan Anderson blew a faint wreath of blue smoke up toward the blue sky and remained silent for a time.

"The next particular Basswood Junction happened to be a Democratic minin' town, instead of a Republican agricultural community. It didn't have any overall factories at all. They didn't relish bein' told that they had voted the straight Republican ticket ever since Alexander Hamilton, and that they had given to the public that distinguished citizen, James K. Blinkensop, when the man they had really given to the public was Dan G. Healy. Oh, the whole thing got all mixed up! Now, that was News! And they fired me by wire that night! The People's Choice was awful hostile. And me raised tender, too!"

"Well, then, what did you do?" asked I, getting interested in spite of myself.

"I was far, far from home. But not thus easily could I be shaken out of my chosen profession. In thirty-eight minutes I was at work as managin' editor of a mornin' paper. That particular Basswood Junction was just startin' a daily, the kind the real-estate men and the local congressman have to support or go out of the business. Their editor had been raised on a weekly, and had been used to goin' to sleep at eight o'clock in the evening. The rumor spread that a metropolitan journalist had fallen out of a balloon into their midst. That morning's paper was two days late. So I just went in and went to work. I sent every one else home to bed, and sat down to write the paper.

"Of course, I began with dogs, for on account of my early trainin' I knew more about that. Two columns of dogs as a Local Industry. Then I took up Mineral Resources, about half a column. Might have played that up a little stronger, but I was shy on facts. Then I did the Literary and Dramatic. I shuddered when I struck that, because when a man on a paper gets put on Literary and Dramatic, it usually isn't far to his finish. He don't have to send out after trouble—it comes to him spontaneous. Next, I had to do Society. Didn't know anybody there, so that was a little hard. Had to content myself with the Beautiful-and-Accomplished-Who-Shall-be-Nameless,—that sort of thing. Why," said Dan Anderson, plaintively, "it's awful hard to write society and local news in a town when you've only been there fifteen minutes. But a real metropolitan journalist ought to be able to, and I did.

"By this time the office force was standin' around some awed. I sent the foreman of the pressroom out for a bottle of fizz. Sarsaparilla was the nearest he could come to it, but it went. Then I turned my hot young blood loose on the editorial page. 'This,' said I, 'is my opportunity to save the country, and I'm goin' to save it, right here.' It was then eleven hours, forty-five minutes, and eight seconds by the grandpa clock which adorned the newly furnished sanctum." Dan Anderson again sat silent a few moments, the stub of his *cigarrillo* between his fingers.

"Oh, well," said he, "it might, perhaps, have been worse, although I admit that was unlikely. I couldn't prove an alibi, but there were extenuatin' circumstances. The fact was, I got the politics of the place mixed up almost as bad as the People's Choice. That community woke up as one man at six-thirty the next morning, and turned out to see the evidence of their progress. I never did see so many Democrats in my life. Or was it Republicans? I forget. I had given 'em a good, hot, mixed Princeton paper,—dog, international law, society, industrial progress, footlight favorites, and the whole business; had Sermons from Many Lands, and a Conundrum Department, as well as a Household Corner—How to get Beautiful for the ladies, How to get Rich for the men, How to get Strong for the advertisers—why, if I do say it, I don't believe any one fellow was ever much more cosmopolitan in all his life, inside the space of one night's writin'. But they didn't like me. I was too good for them. Ah, well!"

Dan Anderson sighed softly. The lazy sun crawled on. Nobody came into the street. There was nothing to happen. It might have been an hour before Dan Anderson leaned over, picked up a splinter to whittle, and went on with his story, back of which I was long before this well convinced there remained some topic concealed, albeit beneath inconsequent and picturesque details.

"At that state of my *entwickelung*, as the French say, I still wore my trousers with a strong crimp at the bottom and cut pear-shaped at the hips. That pair was. The next one wasn't. It was a long, long way to that next pair. I forgot how many years.

"You see, by that time—although I did still say 'rully,' account of having roomed with a man who had been in Harvard for a while—I was really beginning to wake up just a little bit. My dad still supposed I was doing dog on the dramatic page in New York, whereas the facts were I had been fired twice. But that did me good. I sort of woke up about then, and realized there were such things in the world as folks. I wasn't the People's Choice,—not yet,— but I was learnin' a heap more about the Basswood

Junctions of this world. And I want to say to you that after all's said and done, Princeton hasn't got Basswood Junction skinned no ways permanent. There's several kinds of things in life, when you come to find it out. It ain't all in the gay metropolis.

"At half-past four one afternoon I turned the roll down out of my trousers and took account of the world. Says I to myself: 'Journalism is not a science. It ain't exact enough.' Then I thought of studyin' medicine. Bah! That's not a science. It's a survival. I clerked for a while, but I couldn't stand it. What I was lookin' for was a science. At last I concluded to take up law, because I thought it was more of a science than any of these other things. I wanted some place where I could sort of reason things out, and have them fit and hang together. Well, the law—well, you know the law isn't just exactly that way. But it's a beautiful thing if you just hang to the principles, and don't believe too much of the practice. The law is disgraced— but at bottom what the law meant to do was to give humanity some sort of a square deal; which, of course, it doesn't. It ain't a science; but I love it, because it might have been."

He fell silent once again for a time, after his fashion, but now his gaze was softened, although he went on with his light speech. "I rather thought I would take up the science of the law as the most possible line of activity for a man of my attainments. I began to read a little on the side. Then I didn't know whether to have contempt for us fools who live and endure the eternal folly, or whether I ought to pity Basswood Junction and Princeton, because life is all so awfully hard and hopeless. Meantime, Old Mr. World went right on—didn't stop to ask me anything.

"You can understand these things took a little time. Meantime, my dad had sized me up as one more young man ruined by college life. The old man had a heap of sense in him, and he did the right thing. He told me to go to the devil."

"So you came West?"

"So I came West. Same pants."

"But you haven't told me about the girl," said I, quietly.

Ah, that was it, then! I could see his eyelids twitch. A moisture broke out on his lower lip, in that country where perspiration was so little known. "And you!" he said. "But then, it didn't take much brains to guess that. It was the same way with you. We all of us came here to Heart's Desire because some time, some where, there was a Girl."

So now we both were silent. Indeed, all the world was silent. The calm valley lay unwinking in the sun. The grave mountains stood about unperturbed, unagitated, calm. The blue sky swept above, peaceful, unflecked by any moving cloud. There was not a leaf in all that land to give a rustle, nor any water which might afford a ripple. It was a world silent, finished, past and beyond life and its frettings, with nothing to trouble, and with nothing which bade one think of any world gone by. Here was no place for memories or dreams. The rush of another world might go on. Folk might live and love, grieve and joy, and sorrow and die, and it mattered nothing. These things came not to Heart's Desire.

Presently Dan Anderson was guilty of a thing revolutionary, horrible! He sat silent as long as he could, but at length there broke from him a groan that was half a sob. He rose and flung out an arm at the great blue heaven. "Girl!" he cried. "Girl!" Then he sank down, burying his face in his hands. One might have heard falling, faint and far off, the shattered crystals of the walls that had long hedged sacredly about the valley of Heart's Desire. One might have heard, sweeping the soft and silken curtains of its oblivion, the rough rush of a disturbing wind!

Dan Anderson's back was in shame turned to me as he gazed down the valley. "Friend," said he, "I swore never to think of her once more. Of course, the old ways had to end. Her people wouldn't have it. She told me she could not be happy with a dreamer; that it was no time for dreamers; that the world was run by workers. She told me—well, I came West, and after a while a little farther West.

"I hadn't begun, I know that. It was fair enough to suppose I never would begin. But at least I didn't holler. I sat down to read law. Ah, don't let's talk of it. Her face was on the pages. I would brush it off, and read over a page a dozen times. I had to force it into my mind. I worked so hard— but maybe it was all the better for me. I not only learned my law, but I remember to this minute every misplaced comma and every broken type on every page I read; and I know how type looks, irregularly set around a roll of brown hair and a pair of gray eyes that look straight at you. My boy, when the principles of law are back and under that kind of a page illustration, they are hard to get, and you don't forget them when they're yours. It wasn't hard to learn things in Princeton. It's the things out of college that are hard to learn.

"Well, you know how that is. A fellow lives because this physical machine of ours is wound up for threescore years and ten, and unless the powers of evil get their fingers in the works, it runs. Well, one time, after I was admitted to the bar back there, I was sitting one night reading Chitty on Pleading. That was the worst of all the books. Contracts, notes and bills, torts, replevin, and ejectment—all those things were easy. But when I got to Chitty, the girl's face would always get on the page and stick there. So one night, seeing that I was gone, I took Chitty on Pleading, girl's face and all, and screwed it shut, tight and fast in the letter-press. I allowed she couldn't get out of there! Then I pulled my freight. I punched a burro into Heart's Desire, two hundred miles, just as you did. I have lived here, just as you have. No life, no trouble, no woman—why, you know, this is Heart's Desire!"

"It was," said I; "God bless it."

"And amen! We'd all have been in the Army, or burglary, or outlawry, if it hadn't been for Heart's Desire. God bless it."

"But she got out," said I. "Some one unscrewed the press?"

"Yes," said Dan Anderson. "She's out. They're out. I tell you, they're out, all over the world!

"We were three hundred men here, and it was Heaven. One vast commune, and yet no commune. Everything there was if you asked for it, and nothing you could take if you didn't ask. Not a church, because there wasn't a woman. Not a courthouse, because there wasn't any crime, and that because there wasn't a woman. Not a society—not a home—and I thank God for it. I knew what it was back there—every man suspicious, every man scared, every man afraid of his own shadow—not a clean, true note in all the world; and incidentally a woman behind every tree, in every corner, whichever way you turned. Life in the States was being a *peon* with a halter around your neck. But it was never that way here. There never was any crime in Heart's Desire. It's no crime to shoot a man when he's tired of living and wants you to kill him. Why, this was Heart's Desire until—"

"Until the press got loose?"

"It's loose all over the world!" cried Dan Anderson. "They've got out. You can't keep them in. How did Charlie Allen get killed over at Sumner? Woman in it. When the boys arrested this fellow Garcia over at the Nogales, what was it all about? A woman. What set the desperado Arragon on the warpath so the boys had to kill him? That was a woman, too. What made Bill Hilliard kill Pete Anderson? Woman moved in within fifty miles of them on the Nogales. Here's Curly; good man in his profession. Night-wrangler, day-herder, bog-rider, buster, top-waddy—why, he'd be the old man on the range for his company if that Kansas family hadn't moved down in here and married him. It's Paradise Lost, that's what it is. Arizona next, and it's full of copper mines and railroads. Where shall we go?" The sweat stood full on his lip now, and a deep line ran across his forehead. "Where shall we go?" he repeated insistently. "Come!"

In my own bitterness at all this I grew sarcastic with him. "Sit down," said I. "Why all this foolishness about a college girl with a shirtwaist and a straw hat?"

"Oh, now," and his forehead puckered up, "don't you be deceived for one minute, my friend. This wasn't ordinary. No plain woman; no common or crimping variety. Just a specimen of the great 'North American Girl!" He took off his hat. "And may God bless her, goin' or comin'!" said he.

This was the most untoward situation ever yet known in the valley of Heart's Desire. Dan Andersen was proving recreant to our creed. And yet, what could be done?

Dan Anderson presently made the situation more specific. "May old Jack Wilson just be damned!" said he. "If he hadn't found that gold prospect up on the Homestake, we might have lived here forever. Besides, there's the coal fields yonder on the Patos, no one knows how big."

Coal! That meant Eastern Capital. I could have guessed the rest before he told it.

"Oh, of course, we've got to sell our coal mines, and get a lot of States men in here monkeyin' around. And, of course, it couldn't have been anybody else but the particular daddy of this particular girl who had to come pokin' in here to look at the country! He's got money literally sinful."

"But, man," I cried, "you don't mean to say that the girl's coming, too?"

He nodded mutely. "They're out," said he, at last. "You can't get away from 'em. They're all over the world."

Here, indeed, was trouble, and no opportunity for speech offered for a long time, as we sat moodily in the sun. At about this time, Tom Osby drove his freight wagon down the street and outspanned at the corral of Whiteman the Jew, just across the street. Tom tore open a bale of hay, and threw down a handful of precious oats to each of his hump-backed grays, and then sat down on the wagon-tongue, where, as he filled a pipe, he began to sing his favorite song.

"I never *loved* a fond gazel-l-l-e,"

he drawled out. Dan Andersen drew his revolver and fired a swift shot through the top of Tom Osby's wagon. Tom came up, rifle in hand, like a jack-in-the-box, and bent on bloodshed.

"Shut up," said Dan Anderson.

"Well, I ain't so sure," said Tom, judicially rubbing his chin. "It's a new wagon-bow for you fellers; and next time just you don't get quite so funny, by a leetle shade."

I interfered at this point, for trouble had begun in Heart's Desire over smaller things than this. "Don't you know it's Sunday?" I asked Tom Osby.

"I hadn't noticed it," said he.

"Well, it is," said Dan Anderson. "You come here, and tell me what time the stage gets in from Socorro."

"I ain't no alminack," said Tom Osby, "and I ain't no astrollyger."

"He's *loco*, Tom," said I.

"Well, I reckon *so*. When a man begins to worry about what time the Stage'll come in, he's gettin' too blamed particular for this country."

"This," said I, "is a case of Eastern Capital—Eastern Capital, Eve and the Serpent, all on one stage. The only comfort is that no Eastern Capital has ever been able to stay here more than one day. She'll go back, shirtwaist and all, and you can begin over again." But the dumb supplication in Dan Anderson's eye caused me swift regret.

There was no telegraph at Heart's Desire. It was ninety miles to the nearest wire. The stage came in but occasionally from the distant railroad. Yet—and this was one of the strange things of that strange country, which we accepted without curiosity and without argument—there was, in that far-away region, a mysterious fashion by which news got about over great distances. Perhaps it was a rider in by the short trail over Lone Mountain who brought the word that he had seen, thirty miles away by the longer road up the canon, the white smoke of the desert dust that said the stage was coming. This news brought little but a present terror to Dan Anderson, as I looked at him in query.

"Man," said he, as he gripped my arm, "you see, up there on Carrizo, the big canon where we hunt bear. You know, up there at the end, there's a big pine tree. Well, now, if you or any of the citizens of this commercial emporium should require the legal services of the late Daniel Anderson, you go up the canon and look up the tree. I'll be there. I'm scared."

By this I knew that he would, in all likelihood, meet the stage and help Eve to alight at Heart's Desire. Moreover, I reproached him as having been deliberately a party to this invasion. "You've been writing back home to the girl," I said. "That is not playing the game. That's violation of the creed. You're renegade. Then go back home. You don't belong here!"

"I'm not! I won't! I didn't!" he retorted. "I didn't write—at least only a few times. I tried not to—but I couldn't help it. Man, I tell you I couldn't *help* it."

CHAPTER VI

EVE AT HEART'S DESIRE

How the Said Eve arrived on the Same Stage with Eastern Capital, to the Interest of All, and the Embarrassment of Some.

The sun drew on across the enchanted valley and began to sink toward the rim of the distant Baxter Peak. The tremendous velvet robes of the purple evening shadows dropped slowly down upon the majestic shoulders of Carrizo, guardian of the valley. A delicious kindness came into the air, sweet, although no flower was in all that land, and soft, though this was far from any sea, unless it were the waters immeasurably deep beneath this sun-dried soil. There was no cloud even at the falling of the sun, but the gun had no harshness in his glow. There was a blue and purple mystery over all the world, and calm and sweetness and strength came down as it were a mantle. Ah, never in all the world was a place like this Eden, this man's Eden of Heart's Desire!

A gentle wind sighed up the valley from the narrow canon mouth, as it did every day. There was no variableness. Surprises did not come thither. The world ran always in one pleasant and unchanging groove. But the breeze this evening brought no smile of content to Dan Anderson's face as he sat waiting for the coming of the new and fateful visitor to our ancient Eden.

"They'll be about at the Carrizoso Springs now," said Dan Anderson, "twelve miles away down the trail. Can't you smell the cold cream?"

This was beyond ken, but he became more explicit. "Cold cream to the eyes and ears," said he. "To the untutored face, the sun of this heathen district is something sinful; and like enough she never heard of collodion for cracked lips in an alkali country. And a veil—oh, sacred spirits! that veil and its contents is now hatin' Carrizoso flats and all the inarticulate earth till fare-ye-well! Wrapped up to the topmast in a white veil,—or one of was-white,—gray travelling gown, common-sense boots. Gloves—ah, yes. And hate—hate—why, can't you feel the simmerin', boilin' hatred of that States girl just raisin' the temperature of this land of Canaan? Hate us? Why, she'll be poisonous. Ninety miles in the sun, at ninety in the shade. Water once at the Mal Pais, and it alkali."

I reminded Dan Anderson that in view of his promise to absent himself at the time of the arrival of the Socorro stage, he was not conducting himself with the proper regard either to decorum or historical accuracy.

"I want to go," said Dan Anderson, "and I ought to go. I ought to go climb that tree and leave a pink and lavender card of regrets for the lady and her dad. I reckon I will go, too, if I can ever get this faintness out of my legs. But somehow I can't get started. I'd look well, tryin' to climb a tree with my legs this way, wouldn't I? Man, haven't you any sympathy?"

So we sat on a log out in front of Uncle Jim Brothers's hotel, and waited for the worst to happen.

"Don't you go away," said Dan Anderson. "I want you for my second. You can go for the doctor. I ain't feelin' very well."

Now, there was no doctor in Heart's Desire, nor had there ever been, as Dan Anderson knew. Neither did he look in need of any help whatsoever. He made no foolish masculine attempt at personal adornment, but his long figure, with good bony shoulders and a visible waist line, looked well enough in the man's garb of blue shirt and belted trousers. A rope of hair straggled from under his wide hat; for in Heart's Desire wide hats were worn of right and not in affectation. He was a manly man enough, in a place where weak men were rare. The one most vitally concerned in all the population of Heart's Desire, he was now the one least visibly affected. All the rest of the settlement, suddenly smitten by the news that the stage was coming with Eastern Capital and a live Woman, had hastened under cover in search of coats and neckties. Dan Anderson sat out on the street just as he had been, and watched the purple mysteries dropping on the mountains, and waited grimly for that which was to come to him. True, there was the slight moisture on his brow and on his under lip, but otherwise his agitation displayed itself only in an occasional exuberance of metaphor.

For my own part, I remained unreconciled to these impending events. "What will you do?" I asked Dan Anderson bitterly, "now that you've been ass enough to allow this girl to come on down in here? You'll have some one killed in this town before long. Besides, where can a white girl live in this place? There's not a bedspread or a linen sheet in the whole town."

"You talk like a chambermaid," said Dan Anderson, scornfully. "Do you suppose a Wellesley girl, accustomed steady to high thinkin', can't get along with a little plain livin' once in a while? As for women folks, why can't Curly's girl take care of her? Does a chance lady caller in this city need a *thousand* women to entertain her? And blankets—why, you know well enough, that blankets are better after sundown here than much fine linen. Heart's Desire'll be here calm and confident after this brief pageantry has passed from our midst."

As he spoke, he half turned and started, with a broken exclamation. I followed his gaze. The street was vacant, barren of the accustomed throng that usually awaited near the post-office the arrival of the infrequent stagecoach. But there, at the mouth of the canon, almost under the edge of the deepening shadow from the purple-topped mountain, appeared the dusty top of the creeping vehicle that bore with it the fate of Heart's Desire. Dan Anderson was pale now, and he put his hand to his shirt collar, as though it were too tight; but he sat gazing down the valley.

"That old fool, Bill Godfrey, is showin' them our sign," said he, in exasperation. "That's a nice thing, ain't it, for Eastern Capital, or a woman, to see the first thing?"

It was Charlie Lee, a landscape artist of Heart's Desire, who subsequently turned his studio into a shop for sign-painting, who had prepared the grim blazonry on the canon wall to which Dan Anderson had made reference. "Prepare to meet thy God!" was the sign that Charlie Lee had painted there. It was the last thing he did on his way out of town. That was the day after certain outlaws had killed a leading citizen. Charlie's emotions, of necessity, turned to paint for expression; and there had never been any other funeral sermon. The inhabitants had always left the sign standing there. But at this time it seemed not wholly suitable, in the opinion of Dan Anderson.

"They ain't goin' to understand that," said he. "They can't think the way we do. Oh, why didn't that old fool Godfrey call their attention the other way? Oh, that'll set fine, won't it, with a man comin' to buy a coal mine, and a girl with a pot of white vaseline on her face and a consumin' vision of tarantulas in her soul! This'll be another case of New Jersey Gold Mill. Old Mr. Eastern Capital, why, he'll run out at the same door wherein he went; that's what he'll do. And, oh, doctors and saints, look at that, now!" Bill Godfrey was leaning out of the coach-box and pointing with his whip. "He's showin' them the town now," said Dan Anderson. "Why—I hadn't thought before but what this place was all right."

I looked anxiously about, sharing his consternation. It had been our world for these years, a world set apart, distant and unknown; but it had been satisfactory until now. Never before that moment had the scattering little one-story cabins of log and adobe seemed so small and insignificant, so unfit for human occupancy. We were suddenly ashamed.

Dan Anderson, awaiting his fate, did not fly, but sat gravely on the log in front of Uncle Jim's hotel, and waited for the creaking, stage, white with far-gathered dust, to climb the last pitch of the road up from the arroyo and come on with the shambling trot of a pair of tired mules for the final nourish at the end of the long, dry trail.

He waited, and as the stagecoach, stopped, arose and walked steadily forward. Another man might have smiled and stammered and nervously have offered assistance to the newcomers; but Dan Anderson was master of his faculties.

The curtains still concealed the tenant of the farther side of the rear seat, when there appeared the passenger nearest to our side of the coach,—a citizen of the eminently respectable sort, forty inches in girth, and of gray chin whiskers and mustache. He was well shod and well clad; so much could be seen as he climbed down between the wheels and stood stamping his feet to shake the travel cramp out of his legs. He looked thirsty and unhappy and bored. A flush of recognition crossed his face when he saw the tall figure approaching him.

"Well, Andersen," Mr. Ellsworth said, extending a hand, "how are you? Got here at last—awful drive. Where do we stop? You know my daughter, of course."

What treachery to Heart's Desire was here! Dan Anderson, a man who had come to stay, shaking hands on terms of old acquaintanceship, apparently, with Eastern Capital itself; and not content with that, advancing easily and courteously, hat in hand, to greet the daughter of Eastern Capital as though it were but yesterday that last they met. Moreover, and bitterest of all for a loyal man of Heart's Desire, was there not a glance, a word between them? Did Dan Anderson whisper a word and did she flush faint and rosy? or was it a touch of the light? Certain it was he reached up his hand to take hers, shaking it not too long nor too fervently.

"I do remember Miss Ellsworth very well, of course, Mr. Ellsworth," said he. "We are all very glad to see you."

"And we're very glad to *see* you!" echoed the girl. "Oh! the dust, the dust!" She spoke in a full, sweet voice, excellent even for outlanders to hear. If there were agitation in her tones, agitation in Dan Andersen's heart, none might know it. This meeting, five years and two thousand miles from a parting, seemed the most natural and ordinary thing in all the world. Mr. Ellsworth was of the belief that he himself had planned it so far as himself and Dan Anderson were concerned.

"My daughter was on her way out to California, you see," Ellsworth began again; "down at El Paso she took a sudden freak for coming up here to see about the climate—lots of folks go West nowadays, you know, even in the spring. I'll warrant she's sick of the trip by now. A good climate has to have dust to season it. One of the mules went lame—thought we would never get here. And now tell me, where'll she stop?" The personification of Eastern Capital looked about him dubiously at the only hotel of Heart's Desire, before which the coach had pulled up as a matter of course. "Any women folks in town, anywhere?" he inquired, bringing his roving eye to rest upon Dan Andersen's impassive face.

"I was upon the point of saying, Mr. Ellsworth," replied Dan Anderson—and vaguely one felt that his diction was once more that of Princeton—"that my friend here, a prominent member of the bar, will go with Miss Ellsworth to the house of a nice little woman, wife of—er—a cow gentleman of our acquaintance. That will be best for her. I'll try to take care of you myself, sir, if you like, while the Learned Counsel goes with Miss Ellsworth."

There were introductions and further small talk, and presently Learned Counsel found himself climbing up to the seat beside Eve; beside the Temptress who, he made no manner of doubt, had come to put an end to Paradise.

But ah! she was Eve enough for any Eden—a tall girl, rounded, firm formed, with a mass of good brown hair, and a frank gray eye, and a regular and smooth forehead. Her garb was a cool, gray serge, and, a miracle here in this desert, it was touched here and there with immaculate white, how, after that cruel ninety miles, none but a woman might tell. A cool, gray veil was rolled about her hatbrim. Her hands, shapely and good, were gloved in gray. Her foot, trim and well shaped,—for even a desolate pariah might note so much,—was shod in no ultra fashion, but in good feminine gear with high and girlish heels, all unsuited to gravel and slide-rock, yet exceeding good, as it seemed at that time. The girl raised her eyes, smiling frankly. There was no cold cream traceable. The first thought of Learned Counsel was that her complexion would brown nicely under sunburn; his second thought was that he had on overalls,—a fact which had escaped him for more than four years.

If Eve, new come within Heart's Desire, felt any surprise, or if she even experienced any pique at the calm deportment of Dan Anderson, she masked it all and put all at ease with a few words spoken in that manner of voice which is an excellent thing in woman. In a sort of dream the coach trundled on up the street, to pause for half an instant in front of the commercial emporium of Whiteman the Jew. Whiteman came out with his hat above his head, and said, "Velgome."

The girl looked backward down the street as they turned to cross the *arroyo* beyond which stood the house of the Kansas family, where Curly lived. The off mule limped. "Poor little fellow," she said; "I wanted them to stop. They have no pity—"

"No," said Learned Counsel to her, "there is no such thing as pity in all the world." She fell silent at this, and looked back once more, unconsciously, down the street, as one who would gladly pity, or be pitied. But soon the coach was at Curly's house, and there came out to meet it, already forewarned of her guest, the Littlest Girl, wiping her hands on her apron, which means Welcome on the frontier.

The Littlest Girl, uncertain and overawed by her visitor, came forward and took a first look. Then she suddenly held out her arms; and Constance Ellsworth, from the East, lonely, perhaps grieved, walked straight into the outstretched arms and straight into the heart of the Littlest Girl from Kansas.

Emerson Hough

CHAPTER VII

TEMPTATION AT HEART'S DESIRE

Showing how Paradise was lost through the Strange Performance of a Craven Adam

The hotel of Uncle Jim Brothers, to which Dan Anderson led Mr. Ellsworth, was a long, low adobe, earthen roofed. The window-panes were very small, where any still remained. The interior of the hotel consisted of a long dining room, a kitchen, a room where Uncle Jim slept, and a very few other rooms, guest chambers where any man might rest if very weary from one cause or another. The front door was always open. The hotel of Uncle Jim Brothers, not being civilized but utterly barbaric, was anchorage for the Dead Broke, in a way both hotel and bank.

There was in Heart's Desire, at least before this coming of Eastern Capital, only three hundred dollars in the total and combined circulating medium. That was all the money there was. No one could be richer than three hundred dollars, for that was the limit of all wealth, as was very well known. To many this may seem a restricting and narrowing feature; but, as a matter of fact, three hundred dollars is not only plenty of money for one man to have, but it is plenty for a whole town to have, as any man of

Heart's Desire could have told you.

A stranger dropping into that hostelry, and taking a glance behind the front door, might have thought that he was in an armory or some place devoted to the sale of firearms. There were many nails driven into the wooden window-facings, the door-jambs, and elsewhere, and all these nails held specimens of weapons. Excellent weapons they were, too, as good and smooth-running six-shooters as ever came out of Colt's factory; and Winchesters which, if they showed fore-ends bruised by saddle-tree and stocks dented by rough use among the hills, none the less were very clean about the barrels and the locks. At times there were dozens of these guns and rifles to be seen on the wall at Uncle Jim's hotel. The visible supply fluctuated somewhat. Any observer of industrial economics might have discovered it to move up or down in unison with the current amount visible of the circulating medium.

Uncle Jim never asked cash or security of any man. If a man paid, very well. If he did not pay, it would have been unkind to ask him, for assuredly he would have paid if he could, as Uncle Jim very well knew. And if he could not pay, none the less he needed to eat, as Uncle Jim also knew very well. There were no printed rules or regulations in Uncle Jim's hotel. There was no hotel register. There were no questions ever asked. Uncle Jim felt that his mission, his duty, was to feed men. For the rest, he often had to do his own cooking, for Mexicans are very undependable; and if a man is busy in the kitchen, how can he attend to the desk? Indeed, there was no desk. The front door was always open, the tables were always spread.

That any man should take advantage of this state of affairs was something never dreamed in Heart's Desire. Yet one day a sensitive young man, fresh from the States, who had blundered, God knows how, down into Heart's Desire, and who was at that time reduced to a blue shirt, a pair of overalls, one law book, one six-shooter, and one dime, slipped into the hotel of Uncle Jim Brothers, since by that time he was very hungry. He sat on the edge of the bench and dared not ask for food; yet his eyes spoke clearly enough for Uncle Jim. The latter said naught, but presently returned with a large beefsteak which actually sputtered and frizzled with butter, a thing undreamed! "Get 'round this," said Uncle Jim, "and you'll feel better." The young man "got 'round" the beefsteak. Perhaps it was the feeling about the butter, which of itself was a thing unusual. At any rate, as he went out, he quietly hung up his six-shooter behind the door. This act meant, of course, that for the time he was legally dead; he no longer existed. The six-shooter hung there for nearly four months, and Uncle Jim said nothing of pay, and the meals were regular and good. The intention of every man in that little valley to do "about what was right" was silently and fully evidenced. That a man would give up his gun was proof enough of that. So this became the custom of the place, the unwritten law. When by any chance a man got hold of enough of the three hundred dollars to settle his bill with Uncle Jim, he walked in, handed over the cash, and without comment of his own or of any one else, took down his gun from behind the door, and then walked off down the street with his head and his chest much higher in the air. It is astonishing how much business, how much safe and valid business, can be done in a community with three hundred dollars and a good general supply of six-shooters.

On this particular day in question, thanks to certain pernicious activity of Johnny Hudgens, junior partner at the Lone Star, on the night previous, nearly all the six-shooters of Heart's Desire were hanging behind the door of Uncle Jim Brothers, pending the arrival of better days.

The financial situation stood thus: Johnny Hudgens had all the three hundred dollars, and Uncle Jim Brothers had all the guns. Temporarily, male Heart's Desire did not exist.

Certainly, there could have been no time more unhappy than this to display the charms of the community to the critical eyes of the man who—as the rapid word spread to all—had come to look into the gold-mines on Baxter side of the valley, and the new coal-fields up Patos way; and who, moreover, so said swift rumor, was the real head and front of the railroad heading northward from El Paso! Humiliated, Heart's Desire stepped aside and let its chosen representative, Dan Anderson, do the talking.

"I didn't know you had a militia company here, Mr. Anderson," said Ellsworth, as they entered Uncle Jim's hotel. "Lately organized?" He swept an inquiring hand toward the array behind the door.

"That? Oh, that's not the arsenal," replied Dan Anderson; "that's the clearing-house. If a man's broke, he just hangs up his gun, you know. I don't know that I can just explain everything in this country to you right at once, sir. You see, it's different. Now, out here, a six-shooter is part of a man's clothes. That's why the fellows stay out. They're ashamed—don't feel properly dressed, you know."

"Not much law and order, eh?"

"Not much law, but plenty of order, and not the least pretence about it."

"The courts—"

"No courts at all, or at least within sixty miles. Why, we haven't even a town organization—not a town officer.

There was never even a town-site plat filed."

Mr. Ellsworth turned on him suddenly. "Where's your titles?" he asked.

"We haven't needed any, so far. Now that you've come, with talk of a railroad and all that—"

"Oh, well, you know, that's just talk. I'm not responsible for that."

"I hope you like canned tomatoes," said Dan Anderson, "or, if you don't, that you're very fond of beefsteak. There won't be much else till Tom Osby gets back from Las Vegas with a load of freight. Tom Osby's our common carrier. I hope the new railroad will do as well."

Mr. Ellsworth was a gentleman, and a very hungry one, so there was no quarrel over the tomatoes, which were Special XXX, nor over the beefsteak, which might have been worse. An hour later he went out on the street with his host, whose conduct thus far, he was forced to admit, had been irreproachable. They strolled up the rambling street, past many straggling buildings, and at length paused before the little building, made of sun-dried brick, and plastered with mud, where Dan Anderson had his residence and his law office.

"You'll excuse me, Mr. Ellsworth," said that young gentleman, "for bringing you here, but the truth is I thought you might be thirsty and might get poisoned. You have to do these things gradually, till you get immune. Now, under my bed, I've got a bottle which never has been opened and which ought to be safe. I don't bother corks a great deal, only when we are welcoming distinguished guests."

"It's just a little soon after dinner," demurred Ellsworth, "but, ahem! That dust—yes, I believe I will."

There was a dignity about Dan Anderson now which left Ellsworth distinctly uncomfortable. The latter felt himself in some fashion at a disadvantage before this penniless adventurer, this young man whom once he had not cared to have as a regular visitor at his own home back in the far-off East.

"You don't mean to tell me, young man," he spoke after a long period of silence, "that this is the way you live?"

"Certainly," said Dan Anderson. "I know I'm extravagant. I don't need a place as good as this, but I always was sort of sensuous, you know." Ellsworth looked at him without any comprehension, from him to the bed with blankets, and the bare table. "Come in," said Dan Anderson, "and sit down. Better sit on the chair, I reckon. One leg of the bed is sort of dicky."

"So this is the way you live?" repeated Ellsworth to Dan Anderson, who was now on his hands and knees and searching under the bed. "Now, about my daughter—is there any hotel—are there any women?"

"Three, from Kansas," said Dan Anderson. "That is, three real ones. All the female earth, Mr. Ellsworth, comes from Kansas, same as all the baled hay. Oh, yes, here she is!"

He had been speaking with his voice somewhat muffled under the bed, but now emerged, bearing a dusty bottle in his hand.

Mr. Ellsworth looked at him a bit keenly; for, after all, he was not a bad judge of men. "How long has that bottle been there?" asked he, abruptly.

"Oh, a couple of years, maybe."

"And you've never opened it?"

"No, why should I? You hadn't come yet. Of course, I knew you'd be along some day. I kept it to drink to your very good health, Mr. Ellsworth—the health of the man who told me not to come around his house—told me I was an unsettled ne'er-do-well, and not suitable company for his—why, I don't think I have any corkscrew at all." His voice was slow, but harder now in quality.

Ellsworth sat on the chair, the bottle in his hand hanging between his knees. He looked at Dan Anderson steadily. "You've got me guessing in a good many ways," he said; "I don't know why you came here—"

"No?"

"Nor how you live, nor what encouragement or prospects you find here. For instance, about how much did you make last year in your business?"

"My law practice? Oh, you mean down at the county-seat? There is no law court here. How much did the boys pay me?"

"Yes."

"Two hundred and sixty-eight dollars and seventy-five cents."

"What?"

"Oh, I know it's a heap of money; but I made it."

"Enough for tobacco money!"

"Sir," said Dan Anderson, "more. I ate frequent. Why, sir, did you ever stop to think that our total circulating medium here is only three hundred dollars? I had almost all of it one time or another. Now, not doubting your intentions in the least, did you ever come that near to corralling the whole visible supply of cash in your own town? Moreover, I am attorney for the men who own the coal-mines. I'm the lawyer for both the gold mills. We've got one or two mines here, and I'm in. Besides, I've just got the law business from Pitzer Chisum, down on the Seven Rivers, He's got maybe a hundred thousand head of cattle. Now, I'm going to rob Pitzer, because he needs it. He's got money scandalous."

Mr. Ellsworth put the bottle down on the floor, and sat up on the chair with his hands in his pockets, wondering. "But why?" he demanded sternly, "why? What are you doing out here? Why have you thrown away your life? Come—you're a bright young man, and you—"

"Friend," said Dan Anderson, with a sudden cold quality in his voice, "I think that'll about do. I am no brighter than I was a few years ago."

"But this is no place to live."

"Why isn't it? It takes a man to live here. Do you reckon you could qualify?" The older man raised his head with a snort, but Dan Anderson stood looking at him calmly. "Now let me tell you one thing," said he. "If you heard of our coal-mines here through me, at least I didn't ask you to come out here, and I didn't ask you to bring anybody along with you. I've played fair with you. You don't come here to do me any favor, do you?"

"Oh, well,"—began the other.

"Then you think there might be something here, after all?"

"What is there here?"

"A very great deal. There's just as much here as there is anywhere else in the world."

Mr. Ellsworth arose and stepped to the door. For a moment he stood looking out at the twilight. He turned suddenly to the young man. "I'll tell you," said he. "There's something to you—I don't know what. Drop all this. Come on back. I'll think it over—I'll give you a place in my office."

"You'd give me *what*? Did you ever stop to think that you can't give me *anything*?"

Surprise sat on his visitor's face. "*Nada!*" cried Dan Anderson. "Me go back there and work on a salary for you? Me check my immortal soul on your hat-rack? Me live scared of my life, like all the rest of the slaves in that infernal system of living, that hell? If I should do that, I'd be giving you some license for the opinion of me you once expressed, before you really knew me."

"But what have you got out here?" repeated the other, stupidly.

Dan Anderson made no answer, except a sweep of his hand to the mountains, and an unconscious swell of the broad chest beneath his blue shirt.

"What made you come?" insisted Mr. Ellsworth, feeling around for the neck of the bottle, which had been forgotten.

"You know almighty well why I came. But let that go. Let's say I came for the express purpose of handling your local interests when you buy our coal-mines and try to get a railroad somewhere near our valley if you have luck later. I'm going to be your kind and loving partner in that deal, and I'll soak you the limit in everything I do for you. You watch me. I'm going to stay here, and I'm going to work all I want to. When I don't want to, there isn't any living mortal soul that's going to crack a whip over me and tell me I've got to."

"Things seem rather strange," began Mr. Ellsworth. "You talk as though I were obliged to put money into these mines."

"Of course you will. You can't help it. You never saw a better opportunity for investment in all your life. But now let me tell you another thing, which I oughtn't to tell you if I served you right. You go slow while you're here. There is plenty of gold in this valley. There isn't a fellow in this settlement who hasn't got a quart glass fruit-jar full of gold nuggets and dust under his bed, and who isn't just waiting and pining to show it to some stranger like yourself. You're Glad Tidings in this town. You couldn't walk to-morrow if you took all the free samples of solid gold the boys would offer you. You'd get dizzy looking down prospect holes. You wouldn't know where you were; and when you came to; you'd own about fifty gold-mines, with all the dips, spurs, and angles, and all the variations of the magnetic needle to wit and aforesaid. Now, I oughtn't to take care of you. I don't owe you a thing on earth. But because you brought—well, because—anyhow, I'm *going* to take care of you, while you're here, and see that you get a square deal."

"By the way, my daughter—" said Mr. Ellsworth, sitting up uneasily.

"Never mind," said Dan Anderson, gently. "Miss Constance is all right. They'll take care of her just as well as I'll take care of you. Everybody will be more sociable by about noon to-morrow. The whole town's scared yet."

"I don't see anything very terrible about me," said Mr. Ellsworth.

"Oh, it isn't *you*," said Dan Anderson, calmly. "Nobody's afraid of *you*. It's your daughter—it's the woman. Don't you reckon Adam was about the scaredest thing in the wide, wide world about the time old Ma Eve set up her bakeshop under the spreading fig tree? I don't know that I make myself right plain—you see, it's sort of funny here. We aren't used to women any more."

"Oh, well, now, my dear sir, you see, my daughter—"

"I know all about her," said Dan Anderson, sharply.

"I don't doubt she thought I was a mere trifler. She couldn't understand that it isn't right for a man to stick to anything until he's found the right thing to stick to. I don't blame her the least bit in the world. She could only see what I *wasn't* doing. I knew what I was *going* to do, and I know it now." There was a gravity and certainty about Dan Anderson now that went through the self-consciousness of the man before him. Ellsworth looked at him intently. "We'll be here for a day or so," said he, "and meantime, it will seem a little strange for my daughter, I suppose—"

"You don't need to tell me about anything," said Dan Anderson. "Of course, her coming is a little inopportune. You see, Mr. Ellsworth, the morning stars are inopportune, and the sunrise every day, and the dew of heaven."

Ellsworth looked at him half in terror, and in his discomfort murmured something about going to look up his daughter.

"Now, that's mighty kind of you," said Dan Anderson. "But I know the way over there alone, and after I have taken you back to Uncle Jim's, I am going over there—alone. Wait till I get my coat. I don't wear it very often, but we'll just show you that we can dress up for the evening here, the same as they do in the States."

As Dan Anderson, his head bent down and his hands in his pockets, crossed the *arroyo* alone, he met Curly coming the other way. Curly's brow was wrinkled, though he expressed a certain consciousness of the importance of his position in society at the time.

"Say, man," said he, jerking his thumb toward the house, "that new girl is the absolute limit. She dropped in just like we'd been expectin' her. I was some scared; but *she's* just *folks*!"

Dan Anderson hardly heard him. He passed on into the house, where he had long ago made himself easily at home with the women of the place. It was a half hour later that he spoke directly to the girl. "I was just thinking," said he, "that after all the dust and heat and everything you might like to walk, for just a minute or so, over to our city park. Foliage, you know; avenues, flowers; sweetness and light."

She looked at the man quietly, as if she failed to understand the half-cynical bitterness, the half-wistfulness in his voice, yet she rose and joined him. All human beings in Heart's Desire that evening fell in with the plans of Dan Anderson without cavil and without possible resistance.

Emerson Hough

A short distance up the *arroyo*, toward the old abandoned stamp mill, there was a two-inch pipe of water which came down from the Patos spring, far up on the mountain side. At the end of this pipe, where the water was now going to waste, the Littlest Girl from Kansas had taken in charge the precious flow, and proposed a tiny garden of her own. Here there were divers shrubs, among these a single rose bush, now blossomless. Dan Anderson broke off a leafy twig or so, and handed them to Constance, who pinned them on her breast.

"This is our park," said he, very gravely; "I hope you have enjoyed your stroll along the boulevard. I hope, also, that the entertainment of the cow gentleman was not displeasing."

"Not a word!" she answered, her cheek flushing; "you shall not rail at them. These people are genuine."

"I'm not apologizing," he said quickly; "there are just a few things a fellow learns out here. One is not to apologize; and another is not to beg. Sit down." There were two white boulders beside which the trickle of water rippled. Obeying him, she seated herself. Presently Dan Anderson settled himself upon the other, and for a time they sat in silence. The purple shadows had long ago deepened into half darkness, and as they looked up above the long, slow curve of old Carrizo, there rose the burnished silver of the wondrous moon of Heart's Desire. The bare and barren valley was softened and glorified into a strange, half-ghostly beauty. The earth has few scenes more beautiful than Heart's Desire at moonlight. These two sat and gazed for a time.

"And so this is your world!" the girl spoke at length, more to herself than to him.

"Yes," he replied almost savagely, sweeping his hand toward the mountain-rimmed horizon. "Yes, it's mine."

"It is very beautiful," she murmured softly.

"Yes," said Dan Anderson, "it's beautiful. Some time there'll be a man who'll learn something in such a place as this. I don't know but I've learned a little bit myself in the last few years."

"The years!" she whispered to herself.

"It seems forever," said he. "The time when a fellow's taking his medicine always seems long, I reckon, I have almost forgotten my life of five years ago—almost, except a part of it. It's been another world here. Nothing matters much, does it?"

Whether there was now bitterness or softness in his speech she could not tell, but she found no reproach for herself in word or tone.

"Look," said she at length, pointing down at the valley of Heart's Desire, now bathed in the full flood of the unveiled moonlight. "Look! It is unspeakable."

He looked at her face instead. "I've seen you right here," he said, "right at this very place, a thousand times. It's Eden. It's the Garden. It's the Beginning."

"It is the world," she whispered vaguely.

"Yes, yes—" Words burst from his lips beyond his power to control. "It is Eden, it is Paradise, but a vacant Eden, a Paradise incomplete. Constance—"

The girl felt herself shiver at this sound of a voice which

all too often these past five years had come to her unbidden when she found moments of self-communion in her own restless and dissatisfied life. Walls had not shut it out, music had not drowned it, gayety had not served to banish it. She had heard it in her subjective soul ofttimes when the shadows fell and the firelight flickered. Now, beneath a limitless sky, under a strange radiance, in a wild primeval world—in this Eden which they two alone occupied—she heard him, the man whom in her heart she loved, speaking to her once more in very person, and speaking that very thought which was in her own heart that hour. Her bosom rose tumultuously, her throat fluttered. Instinctively she would have fled, but a hand on her shoulder pressed her back as she would have arisen, and she obeyed—as she had always obeyed him—as she always would.

"Paradise unfinished—" he whispered, his face close to hers. "You know what it is that's missing."

Ah! could not a woman also know the longing, the vacancy, the solitude of an Eden incomplete! She turned to him trembling, her lips half open, as though to welcome a long-hoped-for draught of happiness.

Alas! it was not happiness, but misery that came; for Constance Ellsworth now got taste of those bitter waters of life which are withheld from none. There was a sound of a distant shout—the chance call of some drunken reveller—far down the street, a tawdry, unimportant incident, but enough to break a spell, to destroy an illusion, to awaken a conscience for a man, if that phrase be just. Dan Anderson turned to look down the long street of Heart's Desire. It was as though the physical act restored him to another realm, another mental world. He started, and half shivered as his hand dropped to his side. His face showed haggard even in the moonlight.

"My God! what am I saying?" he murmured to himself.

Then presently he drew himself up, smiling bitterly. "Some prominent citizens of the place enjoying themselves," he said and nodded toward the street. "Don't you think you'd like Heart's Desire?"

The moment of Eve—the woman's moment—the instant for her happiness was past and gone! The light of the moon lay ghostly over all the world, but there was no radiance, no joy nor comfort in it now.

The girl herself was silent. She sat looking out over the street below, instinctively following Dan Anderson's gaze. Voices came to them, clamorous, strident, coarse. There lay revealed all that was crude, all that was savage, all that was unlovable and impossible of Heart's Desire. It had been a dream, but it was a man's dream in which he had lived. For a woman—for her—for this sweet girl of a gentler world, that dream could be nothing else than hideous. "Be just! Be fair!" Dan Anderson's soul demanded of him; and as best he saw justice and fairness to the woman he loved he answered for himself.

"Come," said the girl, gently, rousing herself from the lassitude which suddenly assailed her, "we must go in."

His face was averted as he walked beside her. There was no word that he could say. Accord being gone from all the universe, he could not know that in her heart, humbled and shamed as it was, she understood and in some part forgave.

"It has been very beautiful to-night," she said, as he turned back at length from the door of Curly's house.

Choking, he left her. As he stumbled blindly back, over

the *arroyo*, there crossed on the heavens the long red line of a shooting star. Dully he watched it, and for him it was the flaming sword barring the gates of Eden.

Hours later—for sleep was not for him—Dan Anderson stood waiting for the sun to rise over old Carrizo. Far off, along the pathway of the morn, lay his former home, the States, the East, the fight, the combat, and the grovelling. "No, not for me; not there!" he said, conviction coming to him once more.

He turned then and glanced down the single street of Heart's Desire, a street as straggling and purposeless as his own misdirected life—a wavering lane through the poor habitations of a Land of Oblivion. Longer he looked, and stronger the conviction grew. "No, no," he said, clenching his hand; "not here for her—not here!"

CHAPTER VIII

THE CORPORATION AT HEART'S DESIRE

This being the Story of a Parrot, Certain Twins, and a Pair of Candy Legs

Time wore on at Heart's Desire, uncalendared and unclocked. The sun rose, passed through a sky impenetrably blue, and sank behind Baxter Peak at evening. These were the main events of the day. All men had apparently long ago forgotten the departure of the stagecoach that had borne away at one voyaging both Eve and Eastern Capital. Eve had gone forever, as she supposed, although Capital secretly knew full well that it, at least, was coming back again.

The population shifted and changed, coming and going, as was the wont of the land, but none questioned the man booted and spurred who rode out of town or who came into town. Of late, however, certain booted and bearded men wandered afoot over the mountain sides, doing strange things with strange instruments. A railroad was about to cross the country somewhere. Grave and moody, Heart's Desire sat in the sun, and for two months did not mention the subject which weighed upon its mind. Curly broke the silence one morning at a plebiscite of four men who gathered to bask near Whiteman's corral.

"I hit the trail of them surveyors," said he, "other side of Lone Mountain, day before yestiday. They've got a line of pegs drove in the ground. Looks like they was afraid their old railroad was goin' to git lost from 'em, unless they picketed it out right strong."

Reproachful eyes were turned on Curly, but he went on.

"It's goin' to run right between Carrizoso ranch and the mouth of our canon," said he. "You'll have to cross it every time you come to town, McKinney. When she gits to runnin' right free and general, there'll be a double row of cow corpses from here to Santa Rosa. What this here new railroad is a-goin' to do to your English stockholders, Mac, is a deep and abidin' plenty."

McKinney made no reply, but looked stolidly out across the valley.

"Them fellers come up into town for tobacco, Doc." Curly threw out the suggestion cheerfully.

"Tobacco ain't *drugs*," said Doc Tomlinson, annoyed. He was sensitive about allusions to his stock of drugs, which had been imported some years before, and under a misapprehension as to Heart's Desire's future.

"We might shoot up the surveyors," said Curly, tentatively. But Dan Anderson shook his head.

"That's the worst of it," he answered, "We might shoot any one of us here, and the world wouldn't care. But if we shot even a leg off one of the least of these, them States folks would never rest content. For me, I'm goin' in with the railroad. Looks like I'd have to be corporation counsel."

"Well, I reckon we won't have to drive our cows quite so far to market," apologized McKinney, striving to see the silver lining.

"Oh, drop it," snapped Doc Tomlinson. "I might as well say I could get in my drugs easier. Cows can walk; and as for importin' things, everybody knows that Tom Osby can haul in everything that's needed in this valley."

The members of the plebiscite fell silent for a time, willing to wait for Tom Osby's arrival, whenever that might be.

"Now, we ain't downtrod none in this country," finally began Doc Tomlinson, who had made political speeches in Kansas.

"Is *any*body?" asked Curly, who had never lived anywhere but on the free range.

"We've had three squares a day," said McKinney. "This country's just as good as the States."

"States!" cried Dan Anderson. "We've got a state of our own, or did have, right here, the Free State of Heart's Desire. But it ain't good enough for us. We want to hitch our little wagon to the star of progress. I reckon we oughtn't to holler if the star travels some fast. It was ours, the Free State of Heart's Desire! And we—well—"

"Well," said Curly, ruminatingly, "I don't see as ole Carrizo is frettin' any about these here things." He glanced up at the big mountain whose shadow lay athwart the valley. Dan Anderson gazed thither as well. McKinney sat looking quietly up the street.

"No use frettin' about it, anyhow," said he, in his

matter-of-fact way. "And as to Tom Osby, fellers, I'll bet a plug of tobacco that's him pullin' in at the head of town right now."

"Just like I said," exclaimed Doc Tomlinson. "He's good enough railroad for any one, and he's safe! I wonder what did he bring this time."

What Tom Osby brought this time, besides sundry merchandise for Whiteman the Jew, was a parrot and a pair of twins. Neither of these specialties had ever before been seen in Heart's Desire.

"Twins!" exclaimed Dan Anderson, when the facts were divulged, "and a parrot!"

Tom Osby, after making known the full nature of his cargo, discharged divers boxes, bales, and other packages at the store of Whiteman the Jew. The parrot was not disposed to wait for the close of these formalities. From under the white cover of the wagon there came sounds of profane speech. Tom Osby paused and filled his pipe. "Him?" said he, jerking his head toward the cover, as he scratched a match on the side of the wagon seat. "He's a shore peach. Talked to me all the way from Vegas down."

"Quork!" said the parrot. "Look out! Look out! Brrrrrrr—awk—awk! Quork!"

"I told you so," said Tom.

"Oh, dang it, I'm tired!" continued the bird.

"This," remarked Dan Anderson, "seems to be a cultivated gentleman. But how about the twins? Where are they? And might we—er—ask whose are they?"

"Them?" said Tom. "Why, they're for Curly. They're asleep down under the seat here. Now, between the parrot and them twins, my trip down ain't been any lonesome to speak of."

All eyes were turned on Curly, the newly wedded cow puncher, who blushed a bright brick red to the roots of his hair. "Wh—where did they come from?" stammered he.

"I presume, Curly," said Dan Anderson, gravely, "like enough they came from somewhere over on the Brazos, your earlier home. Why didn't you tell us you were a married man?"

"I ain't—I never was!" cried Curly, hotly. "I never did have no twins nowhere. Where'd you git 'em, Tom?"

The freighter threw his leg across the seat. "Oh, they're yours all right, I reckon, Curly," said he. "Mother's dead. No relations. They come from Kansas, where all the twins comes from. I found 'em waitin' up there in Vegas, billed through to you. Both dead broke, both plumb happy, and airy one of 'em worth its weight in gold. Its name is Susabella and Aryann, or somethin' like that. Shall I wake it up? It's both alike."

"Now, why, my woman's folks," began Curly, "up there in Kansas—I reckon maybe *that's* how it happened! She had a sister done married a Baptis' preacher, onct. Say, now, I bet a horse that's right how this here happened. Say, they was so pore they didn't have enough to eat."

"Letter come with 'em," said Tom, taking out a handful of tobacco from his pocket with the missive. "I reckon, that explains it, I wouldn't take a thousand dollars for 'em if they was mine. Here, you kids, get out of there and come and see the nice gentlemen. Here they are, fellers."

He haled forth from beneath the wagon cover two solemn-eyed and sleepy little girls, perhaps five years of age, and of so close a personal resemblance to each other as impressed all as uncanny. The four men stepped to the wagon side, and in silence gazed at the curly-headed pair, who looked back, equally silent, upon the strange group confronting them. At length the twins buried their faces in Tom Osby's overalls.

"Look here, friend," said Tom Osby to Curly, with asperity, "if you don't want these here twins, why, I'll take 'em off your hands mighty damn quick. They're corral broke and right well gentled now, half good stock anyway, and is due to be right free steppers. If you don't want 'em, they're mine for the board bill."

But Curly stepped up and laid an awkward hand on the head of each of the twins. "Fellers," said he, "I ain't got a whole lot of experience in this here twin game, but this goes. These here twins is mine. This is some sudden, but I expect it'll tickle the little woman about half to death. I reckon I can get enough for 'em all to eat, somehow."

McKinney looked at him with anger in his gaze. "I told you, Curly," he reminded the cow puncher with undue emphasis, "that you was drawin' ten extry from day before yestiday. I reckon the stockholders can stand that."

"That'll make it about break even," Curly answered simply.

"Now," said Doc Tomlinson, "if either of them twins should need any drugs—"

"Drugs!" snorted Dan Anderson. "What would they want with drugs? After they've run around in here for two weeks, you couldn't kill 'em with an axe. If the coyotes don't catch 'em, there's nothing else can happen to 'em."

"I'll give you about eight dollars for the green canary, Tom," said Doc Tomlinson. "I want to hang him in my store."

"But I want to hang him in my wagon," objected Tom Osby. "He's company. You fellers plumb rob me every time I come to town." His voice was plaintive.

"The court rules," observed Dan Anderson, judicially, "that the parrot goes with the twins." And it was finally so decided by the referendum. Whereupon Tom Osby, grumbling and bewailing his hard lot as common carrier, drove off with Curly across the *arroyo* in search of a new mother for the twins.

The Littlest Girl, Curly's wife, read the letter which Tom offered. Tears sprang to her eyes; and then, as might have been expected of the Littlest Girl, she reached up her arms to the homeless waifs, who stood at the wagon front, each clasping a stubby forefinger of Tom Osby's hand.

"Babies!" cried she. "You poor little babies! Oh!" And so she gathered them to her breast and bore them away, even though a curly head over each shoulder gazed back longingly at the gnarled freighter on his wagon seat. Tom Osby picked up his reins and drove back across the *arroyo*. Thus, without unbecoming ostentation, Heart's Desire became possessed of certain features never before known in its history.

Within a few weeks the parrot and the twins had so firmly established themselves in the social system of the place as to become matters of regular conversation. Curly never appeared at the forum of Whiteman's corral without finding himself the recipient of many queries.

"Why, them twins," he replied one day, "they're in full charge of the *rodeo*. They've got me and the woman hobbled, hitched, and side-lined for keeps. Dead heat between them and Bill, the parrot. They're in on all the plays together. Wherever they go, he's right after 'em, and he night-and-day-herds 'em closer'n a Mexican shepherd dog does a bunch of sheep. Now, I blew in last night, intoe their room, and there was old Bill, settin' on the foot of the bed, watchin' of 'em, them fast asleep. 'Too late now,' says he to me. 'Too late. All over now!' I didn't know what he meant till I looked under the bedclothes; and there was a pan full of ginger cakes the woman had made for the fam'ly. You needn't tell me a parrot can't think."

"It would seem," said Dan Anderson, meditatively, "that we may report progress in civilization."

"But say, fellers," remarked Curly, taking off his hat and scratching his head perplexedly, "sometimes I wish Bill was a chicken hawk instead of a talker. There is rats, or mice, or something, got into this valley at last."

"Do you want any drugs?" asked Doc Tomlinson, suddenly.

"No, not yet," Curly shook his head. "Never did see airy rat or mouse round here, but still, things is happenin' that looks right strange.

"It's this-a-way, fellers," he continued, "—set down here and let me tell you." So they all sat down and leaned back against the fence of Whiteman's corral.

"Last Christmas," Curly began at the beginning, "why, you see, my girl, she got a Christmas present from some of her folks back in Kansas, in the States. It was a pair of candy legs."

"What's that, Curly?" said Dan Anderson, half sitting up.

"Legs," said Curly, "made out of candy, about so long, or maybe a little longer. Red, and white, and blue—all made out of candy, you know. Shoes on the feet, buckles on the shoes, and heels. Sort of frill around on top. The feller that made them things could shore do candy a-plenty. They was too pretty to eat up, so the little woman, she done put 'em in the parlor,—on the table like, in the middle of the floor; tied 'em together with a blue ribbon and left 'em there. Now, you all know right well that's the only pair of candy legs in Heart's Desire."

"That's legitimate distinction, Curly," Dan Anderson decided. "It entitles your family to social prominence."

"Oh, we wasn't stuck up none over that," laughed Curly, modestly, "but we always felt kind of comfortable, thinkin' them there legs was right there on the parlor table in the other room. You can't help feelin' good to have some little ornyment like that around the place, you know, special if there's women around. But now, fellers, what I was goin' to say is, there's mice, or rats, got in on this range some how, and they—"

"Why didn't you put 'em in a box?" asked McKinney, severely. "You ain't got sense enough to know the difference between a hair rope and a can of California apricots."

"Put 'em in a box?" cried Curly. "Why? Them was *ornyments*! Now you ain't got a ornyment on your whole place, except a horned toad and four tarantulas in a teacup. Now a real ornyment is somethin' you put on the parlor table, man, and show it free and open. It's sort of

Emerson Hough

sacred like."

"Not for rats," said McKinney.

"You'd better keep your eye on that parrot," warned Doc Tomlinson. "About to-morrow, you tell us what you find out."

But on the morrow the mystery remained unsolved. "One heel's plumb gone," said Curly, sighing. "And they've begun on the toe of the other foot."

Bill, the parrot, remained under increasing suspicion. "He's got a wall eye," said McKinney, "and I never seen a wall eye in a man, woman, or mustang, that it didn't mean bad. This here bird ain't no Hereford, nor yet a short-horn. He's a dogy that ain't bred right, and he ain't due to act right." All Curly could do was to shake his head, unpersuaded.

Meantime, there went on in the little cabin across the *arroyo*, a reproduction of an old, old drama. Should we, after all, criticise these two descendants of the first sweet human woman of the world? Consider; to their young and inexperienced eyes appealed all the fascinations of this august but tempting object, new, strange, appealing. For a time their hearts were strong, upon their souls rested the ancient mandate of denial. They gazed, short breathed, in awe, upon this radiantly bestriped, unspeakably fascinating, wholly and resplendently pulchritudinous creation. They must have known that it was a part of the family pride, a part of the parlor—a part, indeed, of the intermingled fabric of the civilization of Heart's Desire! And yet—alas!

One morning the twins foregathered in the parlor. The hour of temptation, as is always the case, found all things well ordered for the success of evil.

"Everybody's gone," whispered Suzanne. "There ain't nobody here at all."

"Only Bill," said Arabella, looking at the parrot, which regarded them with a badly bored aspect. "I wonder if he'd tell?"

"Oh, dang it all!" remarked Bill; "I'm tired!"

"He's awful," remarked Arabella. "He swears. Folks that swears goes to the bad place. Besides, Bill wouldn't tell, would you, Bill?"

"He'll go to sleep," said Suzanne. "Besides, we ain't goin' to bite off only just a little *bit* of a *bite*! Nobody'll never notice it."

Twofold Eve edged up to the centre table. "You first," said Arabella.

"No, you."

"You first," insisted Arabella. "I'm afraid. Bill, he's lookin'."

"I ain't afraid," Suzanne asserted boldly, and stretched out her hand.

That was the time when the first heel disappeared. Even as Suzanne's white teeth closed upon it, the parrot gave a vast screech of disapproval. "Quork!" cried he. "Look out! Look out!" At which warning both the twins fled precipitately underneath the bed; whence presently their heads peered out, with wide and frightened eyes.

"I didn't have my bite," whimpered Arabella.

"It's only Bill!" Suzanne was disgusted with herself for running. "Come on. Who's afraid?" Arabella chose the toe of the other foot.

Thus it was that temptation, at first insidious, at length irresistible, had its way. The lustre paled and dimmed on one gaudily bepainted leg. The remaining heel disappeared. A slight nick became visible on the cap of the right knee.

"Well, I'll be darned!" said Curly, scratching his head, as he observed these developments.

"So'll I," remarked Bill, in frank friendship. "Ha! Ha!"

Curly looked at him pugnaciously for a moment. "For one cent, Bill," said he, "I'd wring your cussed green neck for you. I'll bet a hundred you're the feller that's been a-doin' all this devilment. Here you,—Susy—Airey,—have you seen Bill a-eatin' the ornyment?" Both the young ladies solemnly and truthfully declared that they had never noticed any such thing; and pointed out that parrots, in their belief, did not eat candy.

The next day amputation and subtraction had proceeded yet further. Only Bill was present when Arabella broke out into tears.

"What's the matter?" asked stout-hearted Suzanne.

"Why, we—we—we—can't eat it but *once*," mourned Arabella. "Now—now—now it's most *gone*! OO—oo—oo!"

"It's good," said Suzanne.

"Will we go to the bad place?" asked Arabella.

Suzanne evaded this question. "How can we *help* it, when it looks so pretty, and tastes so good? They ought to put 'em in a *box*. I c-c-can't help it!" And now tears broke from her eyes also. They leaned their heads upon each other's shoulders and wept. But even as they did so, the hand of either, upon the side nearest to the table, reached out toward the disfigured remnant. A week later the last bite was taken. The parlor table was bare and vacant. Heart's Desire, in all its length and breadth, contained no parlor ornament!

That was the last day when Curly reported to the group at the side of Whiteman's corral. "They're gone, up to both knees now," said he, gloomily. "The finish ain't far off. You all come on over across the *arroyo* with me, and if you can find a sign showin' how this thing happened, I'll make you a present of the whole shootin' match."

It was thus that Curly, Dan Anderson, Doc Tomlinson, McKinney, and Learned Counsel rose and adjourned across the *arroyo*. They found Suzanne and Arabella industriously carrying in aprons full of pinon chips for the kitchen stove.

The clean-swept room at which the visitors entered was the neatest one in Heart's Desire. The tall, narrow fire-place of clay in the corner of the other room was swept clean, spick and span. A chair stood exactly against the wall. The parlor table—ah, appalling spectacle! the parlor table, bare and empty, held upon its surface no object of any sort whatever!

"They're gone!" cried Curly, "plumb gone!" His hand instinctively reached toward his hip, and he cast a swift glance upon Bill, the parrot, who sat blinking at the edge of the table.

"All over now!" remarked Bill. "All over! Too late! Quork!"

"Rope him and throw him," urged Doc Tomlinson, "Search his person. We got to look in his teeth."

"Not necessary," said Dan Anderson. "He hasn't got any teeth." The entire party looked with enmity at Bill, but the latter turned upon them so brave and unflinching a front that none dared question his honor.

Dan Anderson, his hands in his pockets, turned and strolled alone into the other room, and thence out of the door into the sunlight, where the twins were still continuing their unwonted industry at the chip pile. He stood and looked at them, saying no word, but with a certain smile on his face. A corner of each apron fell down, spilling the chips upon the ground. The other hand of each twin was raised as though to wipe a furtive tear. Dan Andersen put out his arms to them.

"Come here, little women," he said softly, and took them in his arms. One chubby face rested against each side of his own. His long arms tightened around them protectingly. Tears now began to wet his cheeks, falling from the eyes of the twins.

"You—you won't tell?" whispered Suzanne, in his right ear, and Arabella begged as much upon the left.

"No," said Dan Anderson, hugging them the tighter, "I won't tell."

"It's gone!" said Suzanne, vaguely.

"Yes," said Dan Anderson, "it's gone." He turned at the sound of voices. Curly appeared at the door, carrying in his hand a limp, bedraggled figure.

"That," said Dan Anderson, "I take to be the remains of our late friend Bill, the parrot. What made you, Curly?"

"Well," said Curly, defensively, as he held the body of Bill suspended by the head between two fingers, "I was lookin' for his teeth, to see if he had any candy in 'em, and he bit my finger nigh about off. So I just wrung his neck. Do you reckon he'd be good fried?"

"He'd like enough be tolerable tough," said McKinney. "Them parrots gets shore old."

"You ought to have some drugs to tan his hide," Doc Tomlinson volunteered hopefully. "It'd be right stylish on a hat."

Dan Anderson gazed at Curly with reproach in his eyes. "Now, I just wrung his neck," repeated the latter, protesting.

"Yes," said Dan Anderson, "and you've wrung the wrong neck. Bill was innocent."

"Then who done et the legs?"

"That," said Dan Anderson, "brings me again to the position which I enunciated this morning. In these modern days of engineers, mining companies, parrots, and twins, the structure of our civilization is so complex as to require the services of a highly intelligent corporation counsel. You ask who ate the candy ornament, representation, or image formerly existent on your premises. I reply that in all likelihood it was done by a corporation; but these matters must appear in court at a later time."

"Well," said McKinney, "it looks like the joke was on us."

Dan Anderson smiled gravely. "In the opinion of myself and the consolidation which I represent," said he, and he hugged the twins, who looked down frightened from his arms, "the joke is on Bill, the prisoner at the bar."

The group would have separated, had it not been for a sudden exclamation from Curly. "Ouch!" cried that worthy, and cast from him the body of Bill. supposedly defunct. "He bit me again, blame him!" said Curly, sucking his thumb.

"If he bit you for true," said McKinney, who was of a practical turn of mind, "like enough he ain't been dead at all."

Corroboration was not lacking. The prisoner at the bar, thrown violently upon the ground, now sat up, half leaning against a pinon log, and contemplated those present with a cynical and unfriendly gray eye.

"Now," said Doc Tomlinson, regarding him, "you get him a few drugs, and he'll be just as good as new, right soon."

"All I got to say," grumbled Curly, "is, for a thing that ain't got no teeth, and that's dead, both, he can bite a leetle the hardest of anything I ever did see."

"Yet it is strange," remarked Dan Anderson, "that the innocent bystander should sit up and take notice, after all. How are you feeling, friend?"

This to Bill, who was now faintly fanning a wing and ruffling up his yellow crest.

"I'm mighty tired," said Bill.

"I don't blame you," remarked Dan Anderson, cheerfully, turning to put down Suzanne and Arabella safe within the door, "but as corporation counsel I am bound to protect the interests of my clients. Run, you kids!

"As to you, Curly," he continued, "you represent, in your ignorance, ourselves and all Heart's Desire. We have intrusted to us a candy palladium of liberty, which, being interpreted, means a man's chance to be a grown man, with whiskers, in a free state of Heart's Desire. What do we do then? Ask in a railroad corporation, and shut our eyes!"

"And a corporation," said Curly, meditatively, "can be a shore cheerful performer."

CHAPTER IX

CIVILIZATION AT HEART'S DESIRE

How the Men of Heart's Desire surrendered to the Softening Seductions of Croquet and other Pastimes

"Go on, Curly, it's your next shot. Hurry up," said McKinney, who was nervous.

"Now you just hold on, Mac," replied the former. "This here croquet is a new style of shootin', and with two dollars on the game I ain't goin' to be hurried none."

"It ain't a half-decent outfit, either," complained Doc Tomlinson. "Hay wire ain't any good for croquet arches; and as for these here balls and mallets you bought sight-unseen by mail, they're a disgrace to civilization."

"*Pronto! Pronto!* Hurry up!" called Dan Anderson from his perch on the fence of Whiteman's corral, from which he was observing what was probably the first game of croquet ever played between the Pecos and Rio Grande rivers. There were certain features of the contest in question which were perhaps not usual. Indeed, I do not recall ever to have seen any other game of croquet in which two of the high contracting parties wore "chaps" and spurs and the other two overalls and blue shirts. But in spite of all admonition Curly stood perplexed, with his hat pushed back on his forehead and his mallet held gingerly between the fingers of one hand, while a cigarette graced those of the other.

"The court rules," resumed Dan Anderson, "that this game can't wait for arguments of counsel. Curly, you are a disgrace. You and McKinney ought to skin Doc and the Learned Counsel easy if you had a bit of savvy. Can't you hit that stake?"

"I could if you'd let me take a six-shooter or a rope," said Curly. "I ain't fixed for this here tenderfoot game you-all have sprung on me. If it wasn't for that there spur, I'd have sent Doc's ball plumb over Carrizy Mountain that last carrom. You watch me when onct I get the hang of this thing."

"You can't get the hang of nothing," said McKinney. "A cow puncher ain't got no sense except to ride mean horses and eat canned tomatoes."

"Maybe you don't like your pardner," said Curly. "Now you change around next game, and I'll bet me and the lawyer can skin Doc and you to a finish. Bet you three *pesos*. Of course, I can't play this thing first jump like a borned tenderfoot. I wonder what my mammy'd say to me if she caught me foolin' around here with this here little wooden tack hammer."

"It all comes of Mac's believin' everything he saw in an advertisement," said Dan Anderson.

"Well, you put me up to it," retorted McKinney, flushing.

"Now, there you go!" exclaimed Dan Anderson. "I didn't figure on what it might do to our mortality tables. You fellows can't play the game wearin' spurs, and I'm afraid to see you try any further with your guns on. Here, all of you, come over here. The umpire decides that you've got to check your guns during the game. I don't mind bein' umpire in the ancient and honorable game of croquet, but I ain't goin' to assume no unpaid obligations as coroner."

With some protests all those engaged handed their belts to Dan Anderson, who casually flung them over a projecting cedar limb of the fence. "For shame! Curly," said he. "Talk about tenderfeet! Here you are, wearin' a pearl handle on your gun, just like a cheap Nebraska sheep-herder with social ambitions. I thought you was a real cowman. The court fines you—"

"It ain't my fault," said Curly, blushing. "The girl—the little woman—that's my wife—she done that last Christmas. She allowed it was fine—and it goes."

"Yes, and put enough money into this handle to buy a whole new croquet set for the family. Ain't that awful! All this comes of takin' a daily newspaper once a month and readin' the advertisin' columns. We're going to be plumb effete, if we ain't mighty careful, down in here."

"That's so," said McKinney, scratching his head. "Times is changin'. That reminds me, I ordered a new suit of clothes by mail from Philadelphy, and they ought to be just about due when Tom Osby comes down; and that ought to be to-day."

"That's so," assented Doc Tomlinson. "He's got a little bill of goods for me, too."

"Oh, why, oh, why this profligacy, Doc?" said Dan Anderson. "Didn't you order two pounds of alum the last trip Tom made? What do you want of so many drugs, anyhow?"

"Hush, fellers," said Curly. "Listen a minute!"

Curly's ears had detected the rattle of distant wagon wheels. "That's Tom comin' now," said he. "He's a heap more regular than the Socorro stage. That's him, because I can hear him singin'."

"Tom, he's stuck on music," said McKinney.

Afar, but approaching steadily, might be heard the jolting vehicle coming down the canon; and presently there was borne to our ears the sound of Tom Osby's voice in his favorite melody:—

"I never *lo-o-oved* a fo-o-o-o-nd ga-a-a-z-elle!"

He proclaimed this loudly.

We knew that Tom would drive up to Whiteman's store, hence we waited for him near the corral fence. As he approached and observed our occupation he arrested his salutations and gazed for a moment in silent meditation.

"Prithee, sweet sirs," said he, at length, "what in blazes you doin'?"

"These gentlemen," said Dan Anderson from the fence, "are engaged in showin' the endurin' quality of the Anglo-Saxon temperament. Wherever the Saxon goes he sets up his own peculiar institutions. What! Shall New Mexico be behind New York, or New England? This croquet set cost eighteen dollars to get here from Chicago. Get down, Tom, you're in on the game."

But Tom picked up his reins and clucked to his team.

"Excuse *me*, fellers," said he. "That there looks too frisky for me. I got to think of my business reputation." He passed on up the street.

"What's the matter with Tom?" asked Curly. "Seems like he wasn't feelin' right cheerful, some way." Dan Anderson gazed after the teamster pensively.

"Methinks you are concealing something from us, Tom," said he. "Let's go find out what it is, fellows." He disengaged the respective six-shooters from their place on the fence, and thus again properly clad, we wandered over toward Whiteman's commercial emporium, where Tom Osby was now proceeding to discharge the cargo of his freight wagon. This done, he did not pause for a pipe and a parley, but, climbing up to the high front seat, picked up the reins and drove off; not, as was his wont, to the corral, or to Uncle Jim Brothers's restaurant, but to his own adobe down the *arroyo*. We looked at each other in silence.

"Something on his mind," said Dan Anderson.

"He didn't bring my clothes," said McKinney.

"Nor my drugs," said Doc Tomlinson.

"And yet," said Curly, who was observant, "he kep' one box in the wagon. Couldn't see the brand, but she's there all right."

"Curly," said Dan Anderson, "you are appointed a committee of one to follow the accused down to his house and find out what all this means."

Curly deployed as a skirmisher, and finally arrived in front of Tom Osby's adobe. The tired horses stood in the sun still hitched to the wagon, and Curly, out of pity, made it his first business to hunt under the wagon seat for the picket ropes and halters. He then began to search for the oats bag, but while so engaged his attention was attracted by something whose nature we, at a distance, could not determine. With a swift glance into the back of the wagon, and another at the door of the cabin, Curly dropped his Good Samaritan work for Tom Osby's team and came up the street at as fast a gait as any cow puncher can command on foot. When he reached us his freckled brow was wrinkled in a frown.

"Fellers," said he. "I didn't think it of him! This here ain't right. Tom Osby's got a baby in there, and he's squeezin' the life out of it. Listen! Come on now. Do you hear that? How's that? Why, I tell you—why, dang *me* if it ain't *singin'*!"

There came to our ears, as we approached, a certain wailing melody, thin, quavering, distant, weird. As it rose upon the hot afternoon air it seemed absolutely strange, unimaginable, impossible. The spine of each man crawled.

Dan Anderson, of the entire party, seemed to be the only one who maintained his self-possession. He smiled gently. "Now," said he, "we certainly are fixed; Heart's Desire ain't benighted any after this."

"What's the matter with you?" Curly questioned.

"Poor cow puncher," replied Dan Anderson, "I have to do the thinkin' for you, and I ain't paid for it. Who, if not the Learned Counsel on my right and myself, organized the social and legal system of this community? Who paved these broad boulevards of our beauteous city? Who put up the electric lightin' and heatin' plant, and installed the forty-eight miles of continuous trolley track all under one transfer system? Who built the courthouse and the red brick schoolhouse, with nine school-teachers fresh from Connecticut? Who planned the new depot? Who got a new leather lounge for the managin' editor of our daily newspaper? Who built the three new smelters? Who filled our busy streets each evenin' with throngs of happy-faced laborers pacin' home at night after four hours' pleasant work each day in our elegantly upholstered quartz mines? Was it you, Curly, who made these different and several *pasears* in progress? Was it you, Doc, you benighted stray from the short-grass Kansas plains, where they can't raise Kafir corn? Was it you, McKinney, you sour-dispositioned consumer of canned peas? Nay, nay. It was myself and my learned brother. You ought to send us both to Congress."

We gazed up the long, silent street of Heart's Desire, asleep in the all-satisfying sun, and it almost seemed to us that we could indeed see all these things that he had named. The spell was broken by a renewal of the thin, high voice of this mysterious Thing in Tom Osby's house.

"And now," resumed Dan Anderson, "as I remarked, havin' turned our hands to the stable things of life, and havin' builded well the structure of an endurin', permanent society, there remained for us no need save for the softenin' and refinin' touch of a higher culture. We lacked nothing but Art. Now, here she is!

"What you're listenin' to, my countrymen, is music. It ain't a baby, Curly. Music, heavenly maid, is young in Heart's Desire, but it ain't any baby that you're listenin' to. I told Tom Osby myself to look into the phonograph business some time if he got a chance. Gentlemen, I now bid you follow me, to greet Art upon its arrival in our midst. I must confess that Tom Osby is actin' like a blamed swine over this thing, tryin' to keep it all to himself."

The phonograph inside the adobe switched from one tune to another. "Don't that sound like the Plaza Major in old Chihuahua by moonlight?" cried McKinney, as a swinging band march came squealing out through the door. "That's a piece by a Mexican band. Can't you hear the choo-choo, and the wee-wee, and the bum-bum? They're all there, sure's you're born!"

"If she plays 'La Paloma,' or that 'Golondrina' thing, I'm goin' to shoot," threatened Curly. "I've done danced to them things at more'n a thousand *bailes* here and in Texas, and if this is Art, she's got to do different."

"Gentlemen," Dan Anderson suggested, "let us go in and watch Tom Osby gettin' his savage breast soothed."

Tom Osby started as he saw shadows on the floor; but it was too late. He was discovered sitting on the bed, in rapt attention to the machine industriously grinding away upon the table. Dan Anderson, with great gravity, took up a collection of four pins from each of the newcomers and handed them to Tom. "No bent ones," said he. "It's a good show; but, tell us, what are you doin'? This is worse than croquet. And we asked you in on our game, too. Ain't you playin' it just a little bit lonesome this way?"

Tom frowned in perturbation. "Well, I was goin' to spring her on you about to-night, up at the Lone Star," said he; "but I couldn't wait. Ain't she a yaller flower? Say, I played her every night from Vegas down for five nights— Pecos Crossin', Salt Wells, Maxwell's, Hocradle Canon, Jack's Peak—all the way. After I'd get my horses hobbled out and get my bed made down, I'd set her up on the front seat and turn her loose. Coyotes—you'd ought to heard 'em! When you wind her up plumb tight and turn the horn the right direction, you can hear her about a mile."

"That," said Dan Anderson, "must have been a gladsome journey."

"For sure," said Tom Osby. "Look at the reecords—whole box of 'em. Some of the stylishest singers in the business are in here. Some of 'em's Dago, I reckon. Here's one, 'Ah, no Ginger.'"

"That, probably," said Dan Anderson, "is 'Ah, non Giunge.' Yes, it's Dago, but not bad for a lady with a four-story voice."

"Here's another," said Tom; "'Down Mobile.'"

"I know that one," said Curly.

"Let me see it," said the impresario in charge. "Ah, as I thought; it's 'La Donna e Mobile.' This, bein' translated, means that any lady can change her mind occasionally, whether she comes from Mobile or not."

"That's no dream," said Curly. "Onct on the Brazos—"

"Never mind, Curly. Just feed that 'Donna' into the machine, Tom, and let's hear how it sounds once more."

And so Tom Osby, proud in his new possession, played for his audience, there in the adobe by the *arroyo*; played all his records, or nearly all; played them over and over again. It was nearly night when we left the place.

"Excuse me," said Dan Anderson to me, with a motion as though adjusting a cravat upon my neck, "but your white tie is slipping around under your ear again." And as we walked, I was sure that I saw an opera hat under his arm, though sober reason convinced me that we both were wearing overalls, and not evening clothes.

"But did you notice," said Curly, after a while, "Tom, he's holdin' out on us. That there music, it's all tangled up in my hair." He removed his hat and ran a questioning hand through the matted tangle on his curly front. "But," he resumed, "there was one piece he didn't play. I seen him slip it under the blankets on the bed."

"How could he!" said Dan Anderson. But memories sufficient came trooping upon him to cause him to forget. He fell to whistling "La Donna e Mobile" dreamily.

CHAPTER X

ART AT HEART'S DESIRE

How Tom Osby, Common Carrier, caused Trouble with a Portable Annie Laurie

The shadows of night had fallen when at length Tom Osby crept stealthily to his door and looked around. The street seemed deserted and silent, as usual. Tom Osby stepped to the side of the bed and withdrew from under the blankets the bit of gutta-percha which Curly had noticed him conceal. He adjusted the record in the machine and sprung the catch. Then he sat and listened, intent, absorbed, hearkening to the wonderful voice of one of the world's great contraltos. It was an old, old melody she sang,—the song of "Annie Laurie."

Tom Osby played it over again. He sat and listened, as he had, night after night, in the moonlight on the long trail from Las Vegas down. The face of a strong and self-repressed man is difficult to read. It does not change lightly under any passing emotion. Tom Osby's face perhaps looked even harder than usual, as he sat there listening, his unlit pipe clenched hard between his hands. Truant to his trusts, forgetful of the box of candy which regularly he brought down from Vegas to the Littlest Girl, Curly's wife; forgetful of many messages, commercial and social,—forgetful even of us, his sworn cronies,—Tom Osby sat and listened to a voice which sang of a Face that was the Fairest, and of a Dark blue Eye.

The voice sang and sang again, until finally four conspirators once more approached Tom Osby's cabin. He had forgotten his supper. Dinner was done, in Heart's Desire, soon after noon. Dan Anderson stood thoughtful for a time.

"Let him alone, fellows," said he. "I savvy. That fellow's in love! He's in love with a Voice! Ain't it awful?"

Silence met this remark. Dan Anderson seated himself on a stone, and we others followed his example, going into a committee of the whole, there in the night-time, on the bank of the *arroyo*.

"Did you notice, Curly," asked Dan Anderson—"did you get a chance to see the name on the record of the singer who—who perpetrated this?"

"No," said Curly. "I couldn't get a clean look at the brand, owin' to Tom's cuttin' out the thing so sudden from the bunch. It was somethin' like Doughnuts—"

"Exactly—Madame Donatelli! I thought I rather recognized that voice my own self."

"Dago!" said McKinney with scorn.

"By trainin', though not by birth," admitted Dan Anderson. "Georgia girl originally, they tell me, and Dagoized proper, subsequent. All Yankee girls have to be Dagoized before they can learn to sing right good and strong, you know. They frequent learn a heap of things besides 'Annie Laurie'—and besides singin'. Oh, I can see the Yankee Dago lady right now. Fancy works installed in the roof of her mouth, adjacent and adjoinin' to her tongue, teeth, and other vocal outfit.

"Now, this here Georgia girl, accordin' to all stories, has sung herself into about a quarter of a million dollars and four or five different husbands with that voice of hers; and that same 'Annie Laurie' song was largely responsible. Now, why, *why*, couldn't she have taken a fellow of her size, and not gone and made trouble for Tom Osby? It wasn't fair play.

"Now, Tom, he sits humped over in there, a-lookin' in that horn. What does he see? Madame Donatelli? Does he see her show her teeth and bat her eyes when she's fetchin' one of them hand-curled trills of hers? Nay, nay. What he sees is a girl just like the one he used to know—"

"Whoa! Hold on there; that'll about do," said McKinney. "This country's just as good as—"

"No, let him go on," said Curly to McKinney. "Onct over on the Brazos—"

"Sometimes I think you fellows are inclined to be provincial," said Dan Anderson, calmly. "Now, I'm not goin' to talk if you don't leave me alone. Listen. What does Tom Osby see in that horn that he's lookin' into? I'll tell you. He sees a plumb angel in white clothes and a blue sash. She's got gray eyes and brown hair, and she's just a little bit shorter than will go right under my arm here when I stretch it out level."

"That's about right!" said McKinney.

"She's got on white," resumed Dan Anderson, casting a glance about him in the dusk of the evening. "The girl's got to have on white. There ain't no man can hold out when they come in white and have on a blue sash—it's no use tryin' then.

"Now, there she is, a-settin' at the piano in there in the front parlor; daddy's gone out into the country after a load of wood, like enough; old lady's gone to bed, after a hard day's labor. Honeysuckles bloomin' all around, because in New Jersey—"

"It wasn't in New Jersey," said Learned Counsel, hastily, before he thought.

"No, it was in New York," said McKinney, boldly.

"You're all liars," said Curly, calmly; "it was onct on the Brazos."

"Gentlemen," said Dan Anderson, "you are right. It was once on the Brazos, and in Iowa, and in New York, and in New Jersey, and in Georgia. Thank God, it was there, once upon a time, in all those places. . . . And, as I was sayin', the birds was just twitterin' in the evergreen trees along the front walk, some sleepy, because it was just gettin' right dark. Vines, you know, hangin' over the edge of the front porch, like. Few chairs settin' around on the porch. Just a little band of moonlight layin' there on the front steps, leadin' up like a heavenly walk, like a white path to Paradise—which was there in the front parlor, with the best angel there at home.

"The high angel of this here Heaven, like I told you, she's a settin' there in white," he went on; "and with a blue sash—it was blue, now, wasn't it, fellows? And she's lettin' her fingers, God bless 'em, just tra-la-loo-loo, loo-loo-la-la, up and down the keys of the piano her dad gave her when she graduated. And now she's sort of singin' to herself—half whisperin', soft and deep—I hate a thin-voiced woman, or a bad-tempered one, same as you do—she's just singin' about as loud as you can hear easy down as far as the front gate. And—why, she's a singin' that same tune there, of 'Annie Laurie'! . . . And in your heart you know it's true, every word of it, all the time, and at any station!" said Dan Anderson.

"At any station!" said Curly.

"At any station!" said McKinney,

"At any station!" said Learned Counsel.

There were no hats on at that moment. To be sure, the evening air was a trifle warm.

"And now," said Dan Anderson, after a while, "it's got Tom. Now, why couldn't it have been a man-Dago to sing that air into the tuneful horn of the mechanical heavenly maid yonder? No reason, only it's got to be a woman to sing that man's song of 'Annie Laurie.' A man couldn't any more sing 'Annie Laurie' than you could make cocktails without bitters. The only way we can get either one of them here is in bulk, which we have done. It's canned Art, that's all. Owin' to our present transportation facilities, everything has to come here in cans."

Dan Anderson arose and stretched out his arm. "Gentle-men," said he, "I present to you Art!" He raised before him an imaginary glass, which we all saw plainly. "I present to you the cool, pink, and well-flavored combi-nation of life and longing with a cherry at the bottom of it. Thanks to Tom Osby, we have Art! We are not quite provincial. Listen at Madame Donatelli tearin' it off in there! . . . Shoot him up, boys!" he cried suddenly. "I'm damned if I'm going to look all my days on the picture of a girl in a blue sash! The chief end of man is to witness an ecru coyote and a few absolute human failures like you and me. Down with the heavenly maid! Shoot him up! He's a destroyer of the peace!"

So we shot up Tom's adobe for a time, joyously peppering the thick walls, until at length that worthy came out annoyed, a phonograph record in one hand and a gun in the other.

"Don't, fellers," said he. "You might break something."

"Come out," said Dan Anderson. "Not even grand opera lasts all night. Besides, the price of the box seats is exorbitant. Come on. Get ready to play croquet to-morrow. It's safer."

And so Tom Osby's entertainment came to an end for that evening. Our little party straggled on up the long, deserted street of Heart's Desire. Dan Anderson turned in at the post-office to see if the daily paper from El Paso had come in that month.

It was something that Dan Anderson saw in the daily paper that caused him on the following day to lead Tom Osby aside. "Did you know, Tom," said he, "that that opera singer you've got in your box, the 'Annie Laurie' artist, is goin' to be down in this part of the world before long?"

"I never *loved* a fo-o-o-nd ga-aze-ll-lle!" began Tom Osby, defensively.

"Well, it's true."

"What are you tellin' me?" said Tom, scornfully. "Comin' down here? Why, don't it say that them things is all sung by *artists*?"

"So they are."

"Well, now, a artist," said Tom Osby argumentatively, "ain't never comin' within a thousand miles of this here country. Besides, a *artist* is somebody that's *dead*."

"There's something in that," admitted Dan Anderson. "You've got to be dead to make a really well-preserved, highly embalmed success in art, of course. It's true that in a hundred years from now that song will be just what it is to-day. That's Art. But I'm tellin' you the truth, Tom. The woman who sang into that machine is alive to-day. She belongs to a grand opera troupe under the management of a gent by the name of Blauring, who is in hot water with these stars all his life, but makes so much money out of them that he can't bear to be anything but boiled continuous.

"Now, these people are bound for California, for an early season. They are goin' six hundred miles at a jump, and they stop at El Paso for a moment, to catch a little of their financial breath. The Southern Pacific raineth on the just and the unjust in the matter of railroad fares. Now, as they are still goin' to be too early for the season on the coast, Monsieur Blauring has conceived in his fertile brain the idea that it will be an interestin' and inexpensive thing for him to sidetrack his whole *rodeo* for a few weeks up in the Sacramentos, at the Sky Top hotel,—that new railroad health resort some Yankees have just built, for lungers and other folks that have money and no pleasure in livin'.'"

"How do you know *she'll* be there?" asked Tom.

"Well, this El Paso daily has got about four pages about it. They think it's news, and Blauring thinks it's advertising so they're both happy. And this very lady who sang into your tin horn, yonder, will be down there at Sky Top just about ten days from now."

Tom Osby was silent. The Sacramentos, as all men knew, lay but a hundred miles or so distant by wagon trail. "It ain't so," said Tom, at length. "A singin' artist would choke to death in El Paso. The dust's a fright."

"Oh, I reckon it's so," said Dan Anderson. "Now, the bull-ring over at Juarez would be a fine place for grand opera—especially for 'Carmen'—which, I may inform you, Tom, is all about a bull-fight, anyway. Yes," he went on softly, "I hope they'll sing 'Carmen' over there. I hope, also, they won't see the name on the Guggenheim smelters and undertake to give Wagner under a misapprehension. If Blauring has any judgment at all, he'll stick to 'Carmen' at El Paso. He'd have to hire a freight train to get away with the money.

"But now," resumed he, "after they get done at El Paso, whatever they sing, the grub wagon will be located in the Sacramentos, while old Blauring, he goes on in advance and rides a little sign out near 'Frisco and other places, where Art is patronized copious. Yes, friend, 'Annie Laurie,' she'll be up in Sacramentos; and from all I can figure, there'll be trouble in that particular health resort."

"Sometimes I think you're *loco*," said Tom Osby, slowly; "then again I think you ain't, quite. The man who allows he's any better than this country don't belong here; but I didn't think you ever did."

"No!" cried Dan Anderson. "Don't ever say that of me."

"Of course, I know folks is different," went on Tom Osby, presently. "They come from different places, and have lived different ways. Me, I come from Georgy. I never did have much chanct for edication, along of the war breakin' out. My folks was in the fightin' some; and so I drifted here,"

"You came from Georgia?" asked Dan Anderson. "I was born farther north. I had a little schooling, but the only schooling I ever had in all my life that was worth while, I got right here in Heart's Desire. The only real friends I ever had are here.

"Now," he went on, "it's because I feel that way, and because you're going to punch your freight team more than a hundred miles south next week to see if you can get a look at that 'Annie Laurie' woman—it's because of those things that I want to help you if I can. And that's the truth—or something resemblin' it, maybe.

"Now listen, Tom. Madame Donatelli is no Dago, and she's not dead. She was a Georgia girl herself—Alice Strowbridge was her name, and she had naturally a wonderful voice. She went to Paris and Italy to study long before I came out West. She first sang in Milan, and her appearance was a big success. She's made thousands and thousands of dollars."

"About how old is she?" asked Tom Osby.

"I should think about thirty-five," said Dan Anderson. "That is, countin' years, and not experience."

"I'm just about forty-five," said Tom, "countin' both."

"Well, she came from Georgia—"

"And so did I," observed Tom Osby, casually.

Dan Anderson was troubled. His horizon was wider than Tom Osby's.

"It's far, Tom," said he; "it's very far."

"I everidge about twenty mile a day," said Tom, not wholly understanding. "I can make it in less'n a week."

"Tom," cried Dan Anderson, "don't!"

But Tom Osby only trod half a pace closer, in that vague, never formulated, never admitted friendship of one man for another in a country which held real men.

"Do you know, Dan," said he, "if I could just onct in my life hear that there song right out—herself singin', words and all—fiddles, like enough; maybe a pianny, too—if I could just hear that! If I *could* just hear—*that*!"

"Tom!"

They wandered on a way silently before the freighter spoke. "There is some folks," said he, "that has to do things for keeps, for the rest of the folks that can't do things for keeps. Some fellers has to just drive teams, or run a ore bucket, or play the cards, or something else common and useful—world's sort of fixed up that way, I reckon. But folks that can do things for *keeps*—I reckon they're right proud, like."

"Not if they really do the things that keep. That sort ain't proud," said Dan Anderson.

"Now, I can just see her a-settin' there," went on the freighter. "It sounded like there was fiddles, and horns, and piannys all around."

"She was maybe standin' up."

"She was a-settin' there," said Tom Osby, frowning; "right there at the pianny herself. Can't you see her? Don't you ever sort of imagine things yourself, man?"

"God forbid!" said Dan Anderson. "No, I can't imagine things. That's fatal—I try to forget things."

"Well," said Tom Osby, "I reckon I've been imaginin' things. Now, there she's settin', right at the pianny, and sort of lettin' her fingers run up and down—"

"Tra-la-loo-loo, loo-loo-la-la?" said Dan Anderson.

"Sure. That's just it. Tra-la-la-loo, loo-la-la-la, up and down the whole shootin' match. And she sings! Now what does she sing? That song about Gingerbread? That Mobile song? No, not none. It's 'Annie Laurie' she sings, man, it's 'Annie Laurie'! Now, I freighted to El Paso before the railroad, and I know them boys. They'll tear up the house."

"She'll be wearin' black lace and diamonds," said Dan Anderson, irrelevantly; "and when she breathes she'll swell up like a toy balloon. She'll bat her eyes. They got to do those things."

"Man," said Tom Osby, "there's times when I don't like you."

"Well, then, cut out the lace. I'll even leave off the diamonds."

"She's settin' right there," said Tom Osby, wagging his forefinger, "and she's dressed in white—"

"With a blue sash—"

"Sure! And she sings! And it's 'Annie Laurie'! And because I want my own share of things that's for keeps, though I ain't one of the sort that can do things for keeps, why, I want—why, you see—"

"Yes, Tom," said Dan Anderson, gently, "I see. Now, as you said, it's only a few days' drive, after all. I'm goin' along with you. There's watermelons near there—"

"You *are loco*!"

"Not yet," said his friend. "I only meant to point out that the best melons these embalmed Greasers raise in their little tablecloth farmin' operations is right down there in the valley at the foot of the Sacramentos. Now, you may have noticed that sometimes a fellow ought to cover up his tracks. What's to hinder you and me just takin' a little *pasear* down in toward the Sacramentos, on the southeast side, after a load of melons? They're better than cactus for the boys here. That's straight merchandisin', and, besides, it's Art. And—well, I think that's the best way.

"We don't all of us always get our share, Tom," resumed Dan Anderson; "we don't always get our share of the things that are for keeps; but it's the right of every man to try. Every once in a while, by just tryin' and pluggin' along on the dead square, a fellow gets something which turns out in the clean-up to be the sort that was for keeps, after all, even if it wasn't just what he thought he wanted."

"Then you'll go along?"

"*Si, amigo*! Yes, I'll go along."

They parted, Dan Anderson to seek his own lonely adobe.

There he closed the door, as though he feared intrusion. The old restlessness coming over him, he paced up and down the narrow, cagelike room. Presently he approached a tiny mirror that hung upon the wall, and stood looking into it intently. "Fool!" he muttered. "Liar, and fool, and coward—you, you! You'll take care of Tom, will you? But who'll take care of *you*?"

He seated himself on the blanketed bed, and picked up the newspaper which he had brought home with him. He gazed long and steadily at it before he tore it across and flung it on the floor. It held more news than he had given to Tom Osby. In brief, there was a paragraph which announced the arrival in town of Mr. John Ellsworth, President of the new A. P. and S. E. Railway, his legal counsel, Mr. Porter Barkley, also of New York, and Miss Constance Ellsworth. This party was bound for Sky Top, where business of importance would in all likelihood be transacted, as Mr. Ellsworth expected to meet there the engineers on the location of the road.

"I ought not to go," said Dan Anderson to himself, over and over again. "I *must* not go . . . But I'm going!"

CHAPTER XI

OPERA AT HEART'S DESIRE

Telling how Two Innocent Travellers by mere Chance collided with a Side-tracked Star

Many miles of sand and silence lay between Heart's Desire and Sky Top, by the winding trail over the high plateau and in among the foot-hills of the Sacramentos. The silence was unbroken by any music from the "heavenly maid," which lay disused beneath the wagon seat; nor did the two occupants of Tom Osby's freight wagon often emerge from the reticence habitual in a land where spaces were vast, men infrequent, and mountains ever looking down. The team of gnarled gray horses kept on their steady walk, hour after hour, and day after day; and bivouac after bivouac lay behind them, marked by the rude heap of brush piled up at night as an excuse for shelter against the wind or by the tiny circle of ashes where had been a small but sufficient fire. At last the line of the bivouacs ended, far up toward the crest of the heavily timbered Sacramentos, after a weary climb through miles of mountain canons.

"We'll stop at the lowest spring," said Tom Osby, who knew the country of old. "That'll leave us a half mile or so from where they've built their fool log hotel. It beats the dickens how these States folks, that lives in cities, is always tryin' to imertate some other way of livin'. Why didn't they build it out of boards? They've got a saw-mill, blame 'em, and they're cuttin' off all the timber in these mountings; but they got to have logs to build their house with. Folks that builds real log houses, and not toys, does it because they ain't got no boards. But these States folks always was singerler."

By this time Tom Osby was unhitching and feeding his team, and throwing out the blanket rolls upon the ground. "Go easy on the 'Annie Laurie' machine there," called out Dan Anderson, hearing a suspicious rattling of brass against the wagon box. But his companion heeded him little, casting the phonograph at the foot of a tree, where the great horn swung wide, disconsolately.

"A imertation," said Tom, "is like I was just sayin'. It ain't the real thing.

"Now look here, friend," he went on a moment later, "you've got to do like you said you would. Of course, I know melons don't grow up here in the pine mountains, even if they was ripe yet; but you said you was comin' along to see fair play, and you got to do it."

Dan Anderson looked at him queerly. "Wait," said he; "it'll be night before long. Then you go on up to the house, and prospect around a little. If you get scared, come back, and I'll—I'll take care of you. I'll be around here somewhere, so you needn't be afraid to go right on in alone, you know. Tell her you know her preserved songs, and liked them so much you just had to come down here. Tell her about the watermelons. Tell her—"

"You're actin' a *leetle* nervous your own self, man," said Tom Osby, keenly. "But you watch Papa. I been married four times, or maybe five, so what's a woman here or there to me? What is there to any woman to scare a feller, anyway?"

"I'm damned if I know!" replied Dan Andersen;—"there isn't—of course there isn't, of course not. You're perfectly safe. Why, just go right on up. Have your sand along!"

"Sure," said Tom Osby. "All right; I'll just mosey along up the trail after a while."

And after a while he did depart, alone, leaving Dan Anderson sitting on the wagon tongue. "You come up after a while, Dan," he called back. "If you don't hear nothing from me, you'd better stroll along up and view the remains."

Madame Alicia Donatelli paced up and down the long room in the somewhat dismal hotel building which constituted the main edifice of Sky Top. She was in effect a prisoner. El Paso seemed like a dream, San Francisco a figment of the brain, and New York a wholly imaginary spot upon some undiscovered planet, lost in the nebulous universe of space. She trod the uneven floor as some creature caged, on her face that which boded no good to the next comer, whoever he might be.

The next comer was Signer Peruchini, the tenor. Unhappy Peruchini! He started back from the ominous swish of the Donatelli gown, the deep cadence of the Donatelli voice, the restless Donatelli walk, now resumed.

"How dare you!" cried the *diva*. "How dare you intrude on me?"

"The saints!" cried Signer Peruchini. "What service is zere here? I knock, but you do not hear. Madame, what horror is zis place!"

"Ah, that Blauring!" cried Madame Donatelli, in her rage. "The beast! How dare he bring me here—*me*!" (she smote her bosom)—"who have sung in the grand in the best houses of the Continent—in Italy, Paris, London, St. Petersburg! I shall not survive this!"

"*Perfide*!" cried Peruchini, in assent. "*Perfide*! R-r-rascal! *Cochon*! Pig unspikkab'!"

"But, madame," he resumed, with gestures and intonations suitable for the scene. "Behole! It is I who have lofe you so long. To lofe—ah, it is so divine! How can you riffuse?"

Madame Donatelli withdrew with proper operatic dignity. "Never!" she cried. "You have sufficiently persecuted me ere this. I bid you go. Begone!"

"Vooman, you mad meh!" cried Peruchini, rushing forward, his hands first extended with palms upward, then clenched, his hair properly tumbled, his eyes correctly rolling. "I vill not be teniet! Your puty, it is too much! Vooman, vooman, ah, have you no harret? Py Heaven, I—"

With a swift motion he grasped her wrists. Color rose to the Donatelli cheek. Her eyes flashed. She was about to sing. She checked herself in time. "Unhand me, sir!" she cried.

The two wrestled back and forth, their hands intertwined. And now the log fire, seeing the lack of better footlights, blazed up loyally to light for them this unusual stage. They did not hear the door open behind them, did not hear the click of high bootheels on the floor, as there came toward them an unbidden spectator, who had by some slack servant been directed thither.

The door did open. In it stood Tom Osby, unannounced. He was dressed in his best, which was not quite so picturesque as his worst, but which did not disguise him nor the region which was his home. His boots were new, sharp at toe and heel. His hat, now removed, was new, but wide and white. His coat was loose, and under it there was no waistcoat, neither did white collar confine his neck.

A quick glance took in the scene before him. A little dark man was contending with a superb female of the most regally imperious beauty that he had ever seen or dreamed. Tom Osby stepped a swift pace into the room. There had come to his ear the note of a rich, deep voice that brought an instant conviction. This—this was the Voice that he had worshipped! This was that divine being whom he had heard and seen in so many sweet imaginings in the hot days and sweet, silent nights afar in the desert lands. She was assailed. She was beset. There swept over him the swift instinct for action which was a part of life in that comer of the world. In a flash his weapon leaped from its scabbard, and an unwavering, shining silver point covered the figure of this little, dark man, now obviously guilty of sacrilege unspeakable.

"Git back, you feller'" cried Tom Osby. "Leggo! What are you doin' there? Break, now, and git out. This ain't right."

And that was all he ever knew of Signer Peruchini, for the latter sprang back and away into an immediate oblivion. Tom Osby from that instant was himself swept on by the glory of this woman's presence. Confronting her, he stood half trembling, at once almost longing for warlike action rather than that now grown needful.

Madame Donatelli, for the first time in years jarred from the standards of her artificial life, and so, suddenly, become woman rather than actress, fell into a seat, turning toward the newcomer a gaze of wide-eyed astonishment. She had read in certain journals wild stories of doings of wild men. Was that sort of thing actually true?

"Sir," she said, "how dare you!" At this, Tom Osby stood upon one leg.

"I beg your pardon, ma'am," said he, at length. "I didn't know anybody was in here. I just come in lookin' for somebody."

She did not answer him, but turned upon him the full glance of a deep, dark eye, studying him curiously.

"I don't live here, ma'am," resumed Tom. "I'm camped down the hill by the spring. I left my *compadre* there. I—I belong to Heart's Desire, up north of here. I—I come along in here this mornin'. They said there wasn't any one in the parlor—they said there might be some one in the parlor, though, maybe. And I was—I was—ma'am, I was lookin'—I reckon I was lookin' for you!"

He laid his hat and gun upon the table, and stood with one hand against its edge. "Yes, I come down from Heart's Desire," he began again.

"From where?" broke in a low, sweet voice. "From Heart's Desire? What an exquisite name! Where is it? What is it? That sounds like heaven," she said.

"It might be, ma'am," said Tom Osby, simply, "but it ain't. The water supply ain't reg'lar enough. It's just a little place up in the mountains. Heaven, ma'am, I reckon is just now located something like a hundred miles south of Heart's

Desire!" And he laughed so sudden and hearty a man's laugh at this that it jostled Alicia Donatelli out of all her artificiality, and set the two at once upon a footing. It seemed to her that, after all, men were pretty much alike, no matter where one found them.

"Sit down," she said, ceasing to bite at her fingertips, as was her habit when perturbed. "Tell me about Heart's Desire."

"Well, Heart's Desire, ma'am," said Tom Osby, "why, it ain't much. It's mostly men."

"But how do you live? What do you do?"

"Well, now, I hadn't ever thought of that. But now you mention it, I can't say I really know. The fellers all seem to get along, somehow."

"But yourself?"

"Me? I drive a freight wagon between Las Vegas and Heart's Desire. There is stores, you know, at Heart's Desire, and a saloon. We held a co'te there, onct. You see, along of cattle wars and killings, for a good many years back, folks has been kind of shy of that part of the country. Most of the men easy scared, they went back home to the States. Some stayed. And it's—why, I can't rightly explain it to you, ma'am—but it's—it's Heart's Desire."

The face of the woman before him softened. "It's a beautiful name," said she. "Heart's Desire!" She said it over and over again, wistfully. The cadence of her tone was the measure of an irrevocable loss. "Heart's Desire!" she whispered—"I wonder—

"Tell me," she cried at length, arising and pacing restlessly, "what do you do at Heart's Desire?"

"Nothing," said Tom Osby. "I just told you, I reckon."

"Do you have any amusements? Are there ever any entertainments?"

"Why, law! no, ma'am!"

She threw back her head and laughed. There rose before her the picture of a primitive world, whose swift appeal clutched at her heart, saturated and sated with unreal things grown banal.

"Besides," went on Tom Osby, "if we had an op'ry house, it wouldn't do no good. Why—I don't want to be imperlite, but I've heard that op'ry singers cost as high as ten dollars a night, or maybe more. We couldn't afford it. Onct we had a singin'-school teacher. Fellow by the name of Dawes come in there from Kansas, and he taught music. He used to sing a song called the 'Sword of Bunker Hill.' Used to have a daughter, and she sung, too. Her favoright song was 'Rosalie, the Prairie Flower.' They made quite a lot of money holdin' singin'-school. The gal, she got married and moved to Tularosa, and that broke up the singin'-school. There ain't been any kind of show at Heart's Desire for five years. But say, ma'am," he interrupted, "about that feller that had hold of you when I come in. Did he hurt you any?"

"That's our leading tenor, Signer Peruchini! He's a great artist." She laughed, a ripple of soft, delicious laughter. "No, don't bother him. We'll need him out on the Coast. Don't you know, we are just here in the mountains for a little while."

"Don't you like these mountings, ma'am?" asked Tom Osby, sinking back into his seat. "I always did. They always remind me of the Smokies, in Car'lina, back South."

"You came from the South?"

"Georgy, ma'am."

"Georgia! So did I! We should be friends," she said, and, smiling, held out her hand. Tom Osby took it.

"Ma'am," said he, gravely, "I'm right glad to see you. I've not been back home for a good many years. I've been all over."

"Nor have I been home," said she, sadly. "I've been all over, too. But now, what brought you here? Tell me, did you want to see me?"

"Yes!" Tom Osby answered simply. "I said that's why I come!"

"You want me to come up to Heart's Desire to sing? Ah, I wish that were not impossible."

"No, there's no one sent me," said Tom Osby. "Though, of course, the boys would do anything for you they could. What we want in Heart's Desire—why, sometimes I think it's nothing, and then, again, everything. Maybe we didn't want any music; and then, again, maybe we was just sick and pinin' for it, and didn't know it."

She looked at him intently as he bent his head, his face troubled. "Listen," said he, at length, "I'll tell you all about it. Up at Vegas I heard a funny sort of singin' machine. It had voices in it. Ma'am, it had a Voice in it.

It—it sung—" he choked now.

"And some of the songs?"

Strangely enough, he understood the question of her eyes. She flushed like a girl as he nodded gravely. "'Annie Laurie,'" he said.

"I am very glad," said she, with a long breath. "It reconciles me to selling my art in that way. No, I'm very glad, quite outside of that."

Tom Osby did not quite follow all her thoughts, but he went on.

"It was 'Annie Laurie,'" said he. "I knew you sung it. Ma'am, I played her all the way from Vegas down."

"But why did you come?" She was cruel; but a woman must have her toll. The renewed answer cost courage of Tom Osby.

"Ma'am," said he, "I won't lie to you. I just come to see you, or to hear you, I can't rightly tell which. It must have been both." Now he arose and flung out a hand, rudely but eloquently. "Ma'am," he went on, "I knowed you come from Georgy onct, the same as me. And I knowed that a Georgy girl, someway, somewhere, somehow, would have a soft spot in her heart. I come to hear you sing. There's things that us fellers want, sometimes."

The woman before him drew a deep, long breath.

"I reckon you'll have to sing again," the man went on. "You'll have to sing that there song, 'Annie Laurie,' like I heard it more than onct, before I went away from home."

The soft Georgia speech came back to his tongue, and she followed it herself, unconsciously.

"My friend," said she, "you're right. I reckon I'll have to sing."

"When?" said Tom Osby.

"Now," said Alice Strowbridge. She rose and stepped toward the piano open near the fire.

The color was full on her cheek now; the jewels glanced now above a deep bosom laboring in no counterfeit emotion. A splendid creature, bedecked, bejewelled, sex all over, magnificent, terrible, none the less, although the eyes of Alice Strowbridge shone sombrely, her hands twined together in embarrassment, as they did the first time she sang in public as a child. The very shoulders under the heavy laces caught a plaintive droop, learned in no role of Marguerite in any land. The red rose at her hair—the rose got from some mysterious source—half trembled. Fear, a great fear—the first stage fright known in years—swept over Alice Strowbridge, late artist, and now woman. There sat upon her soul a sense of unpreparedness for this new Public, this lone man from a mysterious land called Heart's Desire—a place where men, actual men, earnest men, were living, vaguely yearning for that which was not theirs. She felt them gazing into her soul, asking how she had guarded the talents, how she had prized the jewels given her, what she had done for the heart of humanity. Halfway across the floor she stopped, her hand at her throat.

"I know this here is right funny," said Tom Osby, misunderstanding, "for me to do this-a-way. It's right embarrassin' for a lady like you to try to oblige a feller like me. But, ma'am, all I can say is, all the boys'll be

Emerson Hough

mightily obliged to you."

She flashed upon him a smile which had tears in it. Tom Osby grew more confident, more bold.

"Ma'am," said he, clearing his throat, "I want you to forgive me; but I reckon how, when you great people sing different things, you-all sort of dress up, different like, at different times, accordin' to the things you are singin' right then. Ain't that so?"

"We have many costumes," said she, simply. "We play many parts. Sometimes we hardly know we are ourselves."

"And when you sung that 'Annie Laurie' song, did you have any coschume to go along with that?"

"You mean—"

"Well, now, ma'am, when us fellers was talkin' it over, it always seemed to us, somehow, like the Annie Laurie coschume was right *white*." He blushed and hastened to apologize. "Not sayin' anything against that dress you've got on," he said. "I never saw one as fine as that in all my life. I never saw any woman, never in all my life, like you. I—I—ma'am"—he flushed, but went on with a Titanic simplicity—"I *worship* you, right where you stand, in that there dress; but—could you—"

"You are an artist yourself!" cried she. "Yes! Wait!"

In an instant she was gone from the room, leaving Tom Osby staring at the flickering fire, now brighter in the advancing shades of evening. In perhaps half an hour Alice Strowbridge reappeared. The rich black laces, and the ripe red rose, and the blazing jewels, all were gone.

She was clad in simple white—and yes! a blue sash was there. The piled masses of her hair were replaced by two long, glossy braids. By the grace of the immortal gods all misdeeds were lifted from her that night. For once in many years she was sincere. Now she was a girl again, and back at the old home. Those were the southern mountains half hidden in the twilight; and yonder was the moon of the old days, swinging up again. There was the gallery at the window of the old Georgia home, and the gate, and the stairs, and the hedgerow, and the trailing vines, and the voices of little birds; and Youth—Youth, the unspeakable glory of Youth—it all was hers once more! The souls of a thousand Georgia mocking-birds— the soul of that heritage which came to her out of her environment—lay in her throat that hour.

And so, not to an audience, but to an auditor—nay, perhaps, after all, to the audience of Heart's Desire, an audience of unsated souls—she sang, although of visible audience there was but one man, who sat crumpled up, shaken, undone.

She could not, being a woman, oblige any man by direct compliance; she could not deprive herself of her own little triumph. Or perhaps, deliberately, she sought to give this solitary listener that which it would have cost thousands of dollars for a wider public to hear. She sang first the leading *arias* of her more prominent operatic roles. She sang the Page's song, which had been hers in her first appearance on a critical stage. "*Nobil signors*," she sang, her voice lingering. And then presently there fell from her lips the sparkling measures of Coquette, indescribably light, indescribably brilliant in her rendition. Melody after melody, score after score, product of the greatest composers of the world, she gave to a listener who never definitely realized what privilege had been his. She slipped on and on, forgetting herself, revelling, dreaming;

and it was proof at least of the Alice Strowbridge which might have been, that there came to her fingers and her throat that night no sound of cheap sensuous melody, no florid triviality from any land. With a voice which had mastered the world, she sang the best of the masters of the world. So music, with all its wooing, its invitation, its challenge, its best appeal, for a time filled and thrilled this strange auditorium, until forsooth later comers might, as was the story, indeed have found jewels caught there in the chinks of the rude-hewn walls.

All at once the voice of the artist, the subsidiary voice of the piano broke, dropped, and paused. And then, with no more interlude, that great instrument, a perfect human voice, in the throat of a perfect human woman, swept gently into the melody of the old song of "Annie Laurie." At the beginning of it there was a schoolgirl of Georgia, and a freighter of the Plains, and at the end of it there was a woman with bowed head, and a man silent, whose head also was bowed.

Neither of the two in the great room heard the footfalls of one who approached in the dusk across the puncheon floor of the wide gallery. Dan Andersen, for reasons of his own, had also come on up the trail to the hotel. Perhaps he intended to make certain inquiries; but he never got even so far as the door. The voice of Donatelli caught and held him as it had her other auditor. He stopped midway of the gallery, listened to the very last note, then turned and quietly stole away, returning to the lonely bivouac beneath the pines. He started even at the whisperings of the trees, as he threw down his blankets beside the little fire. He could not sleep. A face looked at him out of the dark, eyes gazed down at him, instead of stars, out of the heavens. The night, and the stars, and the pines, and the desert wind reproached him for his faithlessness to themselves as comforters; but abjectly he admitted he could make no plea, save that he had heard once more of a Face that was the Fairest.

He heard the sound of slow footsteps after a time. It was Tom Osby, who came and sat down by the fire, poking tobacco into his pipe with a crooked finger, and smoking on with no glance at the recumbent figure on the camper's bed. Yet the outdoor sense of Tom Osby told him that his companion was not asleep.

"I was just thinking" said Tom Osby, at length, scarce turning his head as he accosted Dan Anderson, "that since watermelons don't grow very much up here in the mountings, we might take a load of passengers back home with us."

"Passengers?" A voice came from the blankets.

"Yes. Whole bunch of them railroad folks comin' up on the mornin' train from El Paso. Old man and the girl both, and a lawyer fellow, Barkley, I believe his name is. I reckon he's attoreney for the road."

Deep silence greeted this. Tom reached forward and picked up a brand to light his pipe more thoroughly.

"I just want to thank you," said he, "for comin' along down here to take care of me."

CHAPTER XII

THE PRICE OF HEART'S DESIRE

Concerning Goods, their Value, and the Delivery of the Same

In the morning the travellers arose with the sun, and after breakfast Tom Osby began methodically to break camp as though preparing for the return up-country. Neither made reference to any event occurring since their arrival, or which might possibly occur in the near future. Dan Anderson silently watched his partner as he busied himself gearing up his horses. All was nearly ready for the start on their journey down the east side of the Sacramentos, when they heard afar a faint and wheezy squeak, the whistle of a railway train climbing up the opposite slope.

"There's the choo-choo cars," said Tom, "comin' a-rarin' and a-pitchin'. The ingine has to side-step and back-track about eight times to get up the grade. Didn't notice my old grays a-doin' that none, when we come up, did you? I'm the railroad for our town, and I've got that one beat to a frazzle. Now listen to that thing, Dan; that's the States comin' to find us out." Dan Anderson made no reply.

"Well, let her come," Tom resumed cheerfully; "I come

from Georgy, and in that country, it ain't considered perlite to worry if you've got one square meal ahead. Which, by the way, reminds me that that's about all we've got ahead now. You just set here with the team a while, while I take a *pasear* down the canon to see if I can get a deer for supper to-night. I hope the old railroad ain't scared 'em all away. Besides, we might as well stay here for a hour or so anyway, now, and see what the news is, since the cars has got in."

He tapped the muzzle of his old rifle against the wagon wheel to shake out the dust, and then took a squint into the barrel. "I can see through her," he said, "or any ways, halfway through, and I reckon she'll go off." Next he poked the magazine full of cartridges, and so tramped off down the mountain side.

Dan Anderson sat down on a bundle of bedding, and fell into a half dream in the warm morning sun. There was time even yet for him to escape, he reflected. He had but to step into the wagon, and drive on down the canon. Constance Ellsworth—if indeed it were true that she had come again so near to him—need never know that he had been there. How could he learn if she had indeed come? How could he ever face her now? Surely she could never understand. She could only despise him. Dan Anderson sat, irresolute, staring at the breakfast dishes piled near the mess-box ready for packing.

Meantime, in the dining room at Sky Top hotel, there was a certain flutter of excitement as there entered, just from the train, the party of Mr. Ellsworth, president of the new railway company now building northward. Ellsworth beckoned Porter Barkley to him for talk of business nature, so that Constance sat well-nigh alone when Madame Alicia Donatelli came sweeping in, tall, comely, sombre, and, it must be confessed, hungry. Donatelli hesitated politely, and Constance made room for her with a smile and gesture, which disarmed the Donatelli hostility for all well-garbed and well-poised young women of class other than her own.

"And you're going up the country still farther?" asked Donatelli, catching a remark made by one of the men. "I wish I could go as well. You go by buckboard?"

Constance nodded. "I like it," said she. "I am sure we shall enjoy the ride up to Heart's Desire."

"Heart's Desire?" repeated the diva, with an odd smile.

Constance saw the smile and challenged it. "Yes," she replied briefly, "I was there once before."

"What is it like?" asked Donatelli.

"Like nothing in the world—yet it's just a little valley shut in by the mountains."

"A man was here from Heart's Desire last night," began Donatelli. "You know, I am a singer. He had heard in some way. My faith! He came more than a hundred miles, and he said from Heart's Desire. I've wondered what the place was like."

The Donatelli face flushed hotly in spite of herself. A queer expression suddenly crossed that of Constance Ellsworth as well. She wondered who this man could be!

"It was just a couple of campers who travelled down by wagon," explained the diva. "Only one of them came up to the house. Their camp is by the springs, a half mile or so down the east side. He told me they had no music at Heart's Desire."

In the heart of Constance Ellsworth there went on jealous questionings. Who was this man from Heart's Desire, who had come a hundred miles to hear a bit of music? What other could it be than one? And as to this opera singer, surely she was beautiful, she had charm. So then—

Constance excused herself and returned to her room. She did not even descend to say farewell to Donatelli and her bedraggled company, who steamed away from Sky Top slopes in the little train whose whistlings came back triumphantly. She admitted herself guilty of ignoble joy that this woman—a singer, an artist, a beautiful and dangerous woman as she felt sure—was now gone out of her presence, as indeed she was gone out of her life. But as to this man from Heart's Desire, how came it that he was not here at the hotel, near to his operatic divinity? Why did he not appear to say farewell?

Ellsworth and Barkley betook themselves to the gallery after breakfast, and paced up and down, each with his cigar. "I ordered our head engineer, Grayson, to meet us," said Ellsworth, "and he ought to be camped not far away. I told him not to crowd the location so that those Heart's Desire folks would get wind of our plans. For that matter, we don't want to take those men for granted, either. Somehow, Barkley, I believe we've got trouble ahead."

"Nonsense!" said Barkley. "The whole thing's so easy I'm almost ashamed of it."

"That last isn't usually the case with the Hon. Porter Barkley," Ellsworth observed grimly.

Barkley laughed a strong, unctuous laugh. He was a sturdy, thick-set man, florid, confident, masterful, with projecting eyebrows and a chin now beginning its first threat of doubling. Well known in Eastern corporation life as a good handler of difficult situations, Ellsworth valued his aid; nor could he disabuse himself of the belief that there would be need of it.

"If I don't put it through, Ellsworth," reiterated Barkley, biting a new cigar, "I'll eat the whole town without sugar. If I failed, I'd be losing more than you know about." He turned a half glance in Ellsworth's way, to see whether his covert thought was caught by the suspicion of the other. The older man turned upon him in challenge, and Barkley retreated from this tentative position.

"Maybe you can do it," said Ellsworth, presently, "but I want to say, if I'm any judge, you've got to be mighty careful. Besides, you've never been out here before. We'll have to go slow."

"Why'll we have to? I tell you, we can go in and take what we want of their blasted valley, and they can't help themselves a step in the road."

"I don't know," demurred Ellsworth. "They're there, and in possession."

"Nonsense!" snorted Barkley. "How much title have they got? You say yourself they've never filed a town-site plat. We can go in there and take the town away from under their feet, and they can't help themselves. More than that, I'll bet there's not one mining claim out of fifty that we can't 'adverse' in the courts and take away from its dinky locater. These fellows don't work assessments. They never complete legal title to a claim. There never was a mine in the Rocky Mountains that was located and proved up on without a fight, if it was worth fighting for. Bah! we just walk in and see what we want, and take it, that's all."

"Well," said Ellsworth, "it's the best-looking deal I've

seen for a long while, that's sure, and I don't see how it's been covered up so long. And yet if you come to talk of law-suits, I've noticed it a dozen times that when Eastern men have gone against these Western propositions, they've got the worst of it. They're a funny lot, these natives. They'll live in a shirt and overalls, without a *sou marque* to bless 'emselves with. They'll holler for Eastern Capital, and promise Eastern Capital the time of its life, if it'll only come; and when Eastern Capital does come—why, then they *give* it the time of its life!"

"Nonsense," rejoined Barkley, walking up and down with his hands under the tails of his coat. "We'll eat 'em up. I'm not afraid of this thing for a minute. What I want to do now is to get in touch with that Grayson fellow, the head engineer."

"I'm not so sure about that," commented Ellsworth, seating himself in the sun at the edge of the gallery. "If you want to see the real head engineer of this whole Heart's Desire situation, the man you want isn't Grayson, but a young fellow by the name of Anderson, a lawyer up there."

"Lawyer?"

"Yes, and I shouldn't wonder if he was a pretty goodish one, too. Oh, don't think these people are all easy, Barkley, I tell you. This isn't my own first trip out here."

"What about this lawyer of yours?"

"Well, he's a young man that I knew something about before he went West. He knows every foot of the ground up there, and every man that lives there, and I want to tell you, he's got the whole situation by the ear. That gang will do pretty hear what he tells them to do. He's got

Emerson Hough

nerve, too. He's the most influential man in that town."

"Oh, ho! Well, that's different. I'm always right after the man who's got the goods in his pocket. We'll trade with Mr. Anderson mighty quick, if he can deliver the goods. What does he hold out for? What does he want?"

"Well, I don't know. He talked to me rather stiff, up there, and we didn't hitch very well. He sort of drifted off, and I didn't see him at all the day I left, when I'd laid out to talk to him. He's the fellow that put me on to this deal, too. It was through him I got word there was coal in that valley."

"How would it do to charter him for our local counsel? Is he strong enough man for that?"

"Strong enough! I'm only afraid he's *too* strong."

"Well, now, let's not take everything for granted, you know. Let's go at this thing a little at a time. There's got to be a system of courts established in here, and we've got to know our judiciary, as a matter of course. Then we've got to know our own lawyers, as another matter of course. Did you say you knew him before, that is, to get a line on him, before he came out here?"

Ellsworth colored just a trifle. "Well, yes," he admitted. "He's a Princeton man. He comes of good family—maybe a little wild and headstrong—wouldn't settle down, you know. Why, I offered him a place in my office once, and he—well, he refused it. He started out West some five years ago. Of course—well, you know, in a good many cases of this sort, there's a girl at the bottom of the Western emigration."

"What girl?" asked Porter Barkley, sharply.

"One back East somewhere," said Ellsworth, evasively.

Porter Barkley came and seated himself beside the older man, leaning forward, his elbows resting on his knees, meditatively crumbling a bit of bark in his hands.

"I was just going to say, Mr. Ellsworth," said he, "that a girl in a case like this—always provided that this man is as influential as you think—may be a mighty useful thing. Maybe you couldn't buy the man for himself, but you could buy him for the girl. Do you see?"

Ellsworth did not answer.

"He wants to make good, we'll say," went on Barkley. "He wants to go back East with a little roll. Now, we give him a chance to make good. We give him more money than he ever saw before in his life, and set him up as leading citizen, all that sort of thing. For the sake of going back and making a front before that girl, he'll be willing to do a heap of things for us. You've seen it a thousand times yourself. A woman can do more than cash, in a real hard bit of work. Now, Ellsworth, you furnish the girl, and leave the rest to me. I'll deliver Heart's Desire in a hand-bag to you, if the man's half as able as you seem to think he is."

Porter Barkley never quite understood why Mr. Ellsworth arose suddenly and walked to the far end of the gallery, leaving him alone, crumbling his bits of bark in the sunshine.

CHAPTER XIII

BUSINESS AT HEART'S DESIRE

This Describing Porter Barkley's Method with a Man, and Tom Osby's Way with a Maid

Dan Anderson sat for a long time on his blanket roll, looking at the dribbling smoke from the ends of the charred pinon sticks. So deep was his preoccupation that he did not at first hear the shuffle of feet approaching over the carpet of pine needles; and when the sound came to his consciousness, he wondered merely how Tom Osby had gotten around the camp and come in on that side of the mountain. Then he looked up. It was to see the face that had dwelt in his dreams by night, his reveries by day, the face that he had seen but now—the "face that was the fairest"! He sat stupid, staring, conscious that Fate had chided him once more for his unreadiness. Then he sprang up and stared the harder—stared at Constance Ellsworth coming down the slope between her father and a well-groomed stranger.

The girl looked up, their eyes met; and in that moment Porter Barkley discovered that Constance Ellsworth could gaze with brightening eye and heightened color upon another man.

When Ellsworth and Barkley had started from the hotel in search of the engineer's camp, Constance had joined them ostensibly for the sake of a walk in the morning's sun. If it had been in her mind to discover the mystery of this man from Heart's Desire, she had kept it to herself. But now as they approached the dying fire, she gained the secret of this stranger who had travelled a week by wagon to listen to a bedizened diva of the stage! The consciousness flashed upon her sharply. Despite her traitorous coloring, she greeted him but coolly.

Porter Barkley, noticing some things and suspecting others, drew a breath of sudden conviction. With swift jealousy he guessed that this could be none other than the man to whom Ellsworth had referred,—Anderson, the lawyer of Heart's Desire. Why had not Ellsworth told him that Constance also knew him? Porter Barkley ran his eye over the tall strong figure, the clean brown jaw, the level eyes, sizing up his man with professional keenness. He instantly rated him as an enemy dangerous in more ways than one.

After the first jumbled speeches of surprise, Ellsworth introduced the two. Maugre his coatless costume, Dan Anderson was Princeton man upon the moment, and Barkley promptly hated him for it, feeling that in the nature of things the stranger should have been awkward and constrained. Yet this man must, for business reasons, be handled carefully. He must be the business friend, if the personal enemy, of Hon. Porter Barkley, general counsel for the A. P. and S. E. Railway.

The States had come to Sky Top, as Tom Osby had said, and this group, gathered around a mountain fireside, became suddenly as conventional as though they had met in a drawing-room. "Who could have suspected that you were here, of all places, Mr. Anderson?" Constance remarked with polite surprise.

"Why, now, Dolly," blundered Mr. Ellsworth, "didn't the hotel fellow tell you that some one had come down from Heart's Desire to hear the latest from grand opera— private session—chartered the hall, eh? You might have guessed it would be Mr. Anderson, for I'll warrant he's the only man in Heart's Desire that ever heard an opera singer before, or who would ride a hundred miles—that is— anyhow, Mr. Anderson, you are precisely the man we want to see." He finished his sentence lamely, for he understood in some mysterious fashion that he had not said quite the right thing.

"I am very glad to hear that," replied Dan Anderson, gravely, "I was just sitting here waiting for you to come along."

"Now, Mr. Anderson," resumed Ellsworth, "Mr. Barkley, here, is our general counsel for the railroad. He's going up to Heart's Desire with us in a day or so to look into several matters. We want to take up the question of running our line into the town, if proper arrangements can be made."

"Take chairs, gentlemen," said Dan Andersen, motioning to a log that lay near by. He had already seated Constance upon the corded blanket roll from which he himself had arisen. "I will get you some breakfast," he added.

"No, no," Mr. Ellsworth declined courteously. "We just came from breakfast. We were moving around trying to find our engineer's camp; Grayson, our chief of location, was to have been here before this. By the way, how did you happen to come down here, after all, Anderson?"

Dan Anderson was conscious that this question drew upon

him the gaze of a pair of searching eyes, yet none the less he met the issue. He glanced at the battered phonograph which leaned dejectedly against a tree.

"As near as I can figure," said he, "I made this pilgrimage to hear a woman's voice." Saying which he leaned over and deliberately kicked the phonograph down the side of the hill.

"I hope you enjoyed it," commented Constance, viciously, her cheeks reddening.

"Very much," replied Dan Anderson, calmly, and he looked squarely at her.

Porter Barkley, quiet and alert, once more saw the glance which passed between these two. Into his mind, ever bent upon the business phase of any problem, there flashed a swift conviction. This was the girl! Here, miraculously at hand, was the girl whom Dan Anderson had known back in the East, the girl who had sent him West, perhaps the same girl to whom her father had referred! If so, there was certainly a solution for the riddle of Heart's Desire. Piqued as he was, his heart exulted. For the time his own jealousy must be suppressed. His accounting with Dan Anderson on this phase of the matter would come later; meanwhile he must handle the situation carefully—literally for what it is worth.

"As I was saying," continued Dan Anderson, "what's a breakfast or two among friends?"

"If it is among friends," replied Ellsworth, "and if you'll remember that, we'll eat with you."

In answer Dan Anderson began to kick together the embers of the fire and to busy himself with dishes. He was resolved to humiliate himself before this girl, to show her how absolutely unfit was the life of this land for such as herself.

Suddenly he stopped and listened, as there came to his ear the distant thin report of a rifle. Ellsworth looked inquiringly at his host.

"That's my friend, Tom Osby," explained Dan Anderson, "He went out after a deer. Tom and I came down together from the town."

"I presume you do have some sort of friends in here," began Barkley, patronizingly.

"I have never found any in the world worth having except here," replied Dan Anderson, quietly.

"Oh, now, don't say that. Mr. Ellsworth tells me that he has known you for a long time, and has the greatest admiration for you as a lawyer."

"Yes, Mr. Ellsworth is very fond of me. He's one of the most passionate admirers I ever had in my life," said Dan Anderson.

Barkley looked at him again keenly, realizing that he had to do with a quantity not yet wholly known and gauged.

Socially the situation was strained, and he sought to ease it after his own fashion. "You see," he resumed, "Mr. Ellsworth seems to think that he can put you in a way of doing something for yourself up at Heart's Desire."

It was an ugly thing for him to do under the circumstances, but if he had intended to humiliate the other, he met his just rebuke.

"I don't often talk business at breakfast in my own house," said Dan Anderson. "Do you use tabasco with your *frijoles*?"

"Oh, we'll get together, we'll get together," Barkley laughed, with an assumed cordiality which did not quite ring true.

"Thank you," Dan Anderson remarked curtly; "you bring me joy this morning."

He did not relish this sort of talk in the presence of Constance Ellsworth. Disgusted with himself and with all things, be arose and made a pretence of searching in the wagon. Rummaging about, his hand struck one of the round, gutta-percha plates which had accompanied the phonograph. With silent vigor he cast it far above the tree tops below him on the mountain side.

"That," he explained to Constance as he turned, "is the 'Annie Laurie' record of the Heart's Desire grand opera. The season is now over." The girl did not understand, but he lost the hurt look in her eyes. Irritated, he did not hear her soul call out to him.

"It's the luckiest thing in the world that you happen to be here." Mr. Ellsworth took up again the idea that was foremost in his mind. "You fit in like the wheels in a clock. We're going to run our railroad up into your town—I don't mind saying that right here—and we're going to give you plenty of law business, Mr. Anderson; that is to say, if you want it, and will take it."

"Thank you," said Dan Anderson, quietly. But now in spite of himself he felt his heart leap suddenly in hope. Suppose, after all, there should be for him, stranded in this out-of-the-way corner of the world, a chance for some sort of business success? Suppose that there should be, after all, some work for him to do? Suppose that, after all, he should succeed—that, after all, life might yet unfold before him as he had dreamed and planned! Unconsciously he stole a glance at the gray-clad figure on the blanket roll.

Constance sat cool, sweet, delicate but vital, refreshing to look upon, her gray skirt folded across her knees, the patent-leather tips of her little shoes buried in the carpet spread by the forest conifers. He could just catch the curve of her cheek and chin, the droop of the long lashes which he knew so well. Ah, if he could only go to her and tell her the absolute truth—if only it could be right for him, all his life, to tell her the truth, to tell her of his reverence, his loyalty, his love, through all these years! If, indeed, this opportunity should come to him, might not all of this one day be possible? He set his mind to his work, even as the girl held her heart to its waiting.

There came the sound of a distant whistle approaching up the trail, and ere long Tom Osby appeared, stumbling along in his pigeon-toed way, his rifle in the crook of his arm. Tom saluted the strangers briefly, and leaned his rifle against the wagon wheel. Dan Anderson made known the names of the visitors, and Tom immediately put in action his own notions of hospitality. Stepping to the wagon side he fished out a kerosene can, stoppered with a potato stuck on the spout. He removed the potato, picked up a tin cup, and proceeded calmly to pour out a generous portion.

"I always carry my liquor this way, gentlemen," said he, "because it's convenient to pour in the dark, and ain't so apt to get spilled. This here liquor sometimes makes folks forget their geogerphy. 'Missin' me one place, search another,' as Walt Whitman says. If a fellow gets a drink of this, he may take to the tall trees, or he may run straight on out of the country. You never can tell. Drink hearty."

Ellsworth and Barkley, for the sake of complacency, complied with such show of pleasure as they could muster.

"Now," said Tom, "I'll cook you a real breakfast. My *compadre*, here, can't drink and he can't cook."

"Three breakfasts before ten o'clock?" protested Constance.

But Tom was inexorable. "Eat when you get a chanct," he insisted. "That's a good rule."

Barkley drew Ellsworth to one side. "I can't figure these people out," he complained.

Ellsworth chuckled. "I told you you'd need help, Barkley," he said. "They've got ways of their own. You can't come in here and take that whole town without reckoning with the people that live there. Now suppose we get Anderson to himself and talk things over with him a little? We may not have another chance so good."

Ellsworth beckoned to Dan Anderson, and he readily joined them. The three walked a little way apart; which left Constance to the tender mercy of Tom Osby.

"That's all right, ma'am," said he, when she objected to his cleaning the knives by sticking them into the sand. "I don't reckon you do that way back home, but it's the only way you can get a knife plumb clean."

"So this is the way men live out here?" mused Constance, half to herself.

"Mostly. You ought to see him"—he nodded toward Dan Anderson—"cook flap-jacks. The woman who marries him will shore have a happy home. We're goin' to send him to Congress some day, maybe."

Constance missed the irrelevance of this. "I wonder," said she, gently, "how he happened to come out here—how any one happened to come out here?"

"In his case," replied Tom, "it was probably because he wanted to get as far away from Washington as he could— his mileage will amount to more. This is one of the best places in America, ma'am, for a man to go to Congress from." Constance smiled, though the answer did not satisfy her.

"There are folks, ma'am," Tom Osby continued, "that says that every feller come out here because of a girl somewheres. They allow that a woman sent most of us out here. For me, it was my fifth wife, or my fourth, I don't remember which. She never did treat me right, and her eyes didn't track. Yes, I'll bet, ma'am, without knowing anything about it, there was a girl back some- where in Dan Anderson's early ree-cords, though whether it was his third or fourth wife, I don't know. We don't ask no questions about such things out here."

He went on rubbing sand around in the bottom of the frying-pan, but none the less caught, with side-long glance, the flush upon the brown cheek visible beneath its veil.

"I'm mighty glad to see you this mornin', ma'am," he went on; "I am, for a fact. It more'n pays me—it more'n pays him—" and he nodded again toward Dan Anderson, "for our trip down here. We wasn't expectin' to meet you."

"How did you happen to come?" asked Constance, feeling as she did so that she was guilty of treachery.

Tom Osby again looked her straight in the face. "Just because we was naturally so blamed lonesome," said he. "That is to say, I was. I allowed I wanted to hear a woman sing. It wasn't him, it was me. He come along to take care of me, like, because he's used to that sort of thing, and I ain't. He's my chaperoon. He didn't know, you know—didn't either of us know—but what I might be took advantage of, and stole by some gipsy queen."

"But—but the phonograph—"

Tom looked around. "Where is it?" he asked.

"Mr. Anderson kicked it down the hill."

"Did he? Good for him! I was goin' to do it my own self. You see, ma'am, I come down here to hear a song about Annie Laurie. I done so. Ma'am, I heard about a 'face that was the fairest.' Him? Was he surprised to see you-all this morning? Was, eh? Well, he didn't seem so almighty surprised, to my way of thinkin', last night when I told him you was comin' up here from El Paso. I don't know how he knowed it, and I ain't sayin' a word."

A strange lightening came to Constance Ellsworth's heart. The droop at the corners of her mouth faded away. She slid down off the blanket roll and edged along across the ground until she sat at his side. She reached out her hand for the skillet.

"That spider isn't clean in the least," said she.

"Oh, well," apologized Tom Osby, leaning back against the wagon wheel and beginning to fill a pipe. "I suppose there might be just a leetle sand left in it, but that don't hurt. Do you want a dish towel? Here's one that I've used for two years, freightin' from Vegas to Heart's Desire. Me and it's old friends."

"Let your dishes dry in the sun if you can't do better than that," reproved Constance. "Ah, you men!"

"You're right hard to get along with, ma'am. Us gettin' you two breakfasts, too!"

They looked into each other's faces and Constance laughed. "The air is delightful—isn't it a beautiful world?" she exclaimed joyously.

"It shore is, ma'am," rejoined Tom Osby, "if you think so. It's all in the way you look at things."

"I came out here for my health, you know," said she, carefully explanatory.

"Yes, I know. You ain't any healthier than a three-year-old deer on good pasture. Ma'am, I'm sorry for you, but I wouldn't really have picked you out for a lunger. You know, I don't believe Dan Andersen's health is very good, either. He's needin' a little Sky Top air, too,"

She froze at this. "I don't care to intrude into Mr. Andersen's affairs," she replied, "nor to have him intrude into my own."

"Who done the intrudin'?" asked Tom Osby, calmly. "Here's me and him have flew down here as a bird to our mountings. We was wantin' to hear about a 'face that was the fairest.' We was a-settin' here, calm and peaceful, eating *frijoles*, who intruded? Was it us? Or, what made us intrude?" He looked at her keenly, his eyes narrowed in the sunlight.

Constance abandoned the skillet and returned to the blanket roll.

"Now," went on Tom Osby, "things happens fast out here. If I come and set in your parlor in New York, it takes me eight years to learn the name of your pet dog. Lady comes out and sets in my parlor for eight minutes, and I ain't such a fool but what I can learn a heap of things in that time. That don't mean necessary that I'm goin' to tell any *other* fellow what I may think. It *does* mean that I'm goin' to see fair play."

The girl could make no protest at this enigmatic speech, and the even voice went on.

"How I know things is easy," he continued. "If you think he"—once more nodding his head toward the group beyond—"come down here to hear a op'ry singer sing, I want to tell you he didn't. That was me. He come to give me fair play in regards to a 'face that was the fairest.' I'm here to see that he gets fair play in them same circumstances—"

"I just came down with my father," Constance interrupted hotly, suddenly thrown upon the defensive, she knew not why. "He's been ill a great deal. I've been alarmed about him. I *always* go with him."

"Of course. I noticed that. Your dad's goin' to run the railroad into Heart's Desire, and we'll all live happy ever after. You come along just to see that your dad didn't get sun stroke, or Saint Vitus dance, or cerebrus meningittus, or something else. I understood all that perfectly, ma'am. And I understand too, perfectly, ma'am," he continued, tapping his pipe on a wagon wheel, "that back yonder in the States, somewhere, Dan Anderson knowed a 'face that was the fairest'; I reckon he allowed it was 'the fairest that e'er the sun shone on.' Now, I'm old and ugly, and I don't even know whether I'm a widower any or not; so I know, ma'am, you won't take no offence if I tell you it's a straight case of reasonin'; for *yore* own face, ma'am,—and I ain't sayin' this with any sort of disrespect to any of my wives,—is about the fairest that Dan Anderson ever did or could see—or me either. I don't reckon, ma'am, that he's lookin' for one that's any fairer."

Constance Ellsworth turned squarely and gazed hard into the eyes of the man before her. She drew a breath in sharply between her lips, but it was a sigh of content. She felt herself safe in this man's hands. Again she broke into laughter and flung herself upon the convenient frying-pan, which she proceeded to scrub with sudden vigor. Tom Osby's eyes twinkled.

"Whenever you think that skillet's clean enough, us two will set up and cook ourselves some breakfast right comfterble. As for them fellers over there, they don't deserve none."

So presently they two did cook and eat yet again. A strange sense of peace and content came to Constance, albeit mingled with remorse. She had suspected Dan Anderson of worshipping at the shrine of an operatic star, whereas he had made the long journey from Hcart's Desire to see herself! She knew it now.

"I'm goin' to take you up to the hotel, ma'am," said Tom Osby, after Constance had finished her third breakfast, "and then, after that, I'm goin' to take Dan Anderson back home to Heart's Desire. We'll see you up there after a while.

"One thing I want to tell you, ma'am, is this. We've got along without a railroad, all right, and we ain't tearin' our clothes to have one now. If that railroad does get into our town, it's more'n half likely that it'll be because the boys has took a notion to you. I never did see you before this mornin'; but the folks has told me about you—Curly's wife, you know, and the rest. We'd like to have you live there, if only we thought the town was good enough for you. It's been mostly for men, so far."

CHAPTER XIV

THE GROUND FLOOR AT HEART'S DESIRE

Proposing Certain Wonders of Modern Progress, as wrought by Eastern Capital and Able Corporation Counsel

Tom Osby and Constance walked up the trail toward the hotel, and Dan Anderson from a distance saw them pass. He watched the gray gown move through sun and shadow, until it was lost beyond the thickening boles of mountain pines. She turned once and looked back, but he dared not appropriate the glance to himself, although it seemed to him that he must rise and follow, that he must call out to her. She had been there, close to him. He had felt the very warmth of her hand near to his own. There flamed up in his soul the fierce male jealousy. He turned to this newcomer, this man of the States, successful, strong, fortunate. In his soul was ready the ancient challenge.

But—the earth being as it is to-day, a compromise, and love being dependent upon property, and chastity upon chattels, and the stars of the Universe upon farthing dips—though aching to rise and follow the gray gown, to snatch its wearer afar and away into a sweet wild forest all their own, Dan Anderson must sit silent, and plan material ways to bring the gray gown back again to his eyes according to the mandates of our society. Because the gray gown was made in the States, he must forget the lesson of Curly and the Littlest Girl. Because the wearer of the gown lived in the States, he must pull down in ruins the temple of Heart's Desire. Such is the sweet logic of these days of modern progress, that independence, friendship, faith, all must yield if need be; even though, and after all, man but demands that himself and the woman whom he has sought out from all the world may one day be savage and sweet, ancient and primitive, even as have been all others who have loved indeed, in city or in forest, from the beginning of the world.

"As Mr. Ellsworth has told me," went on Porter Barkley, "you are an able man, Mr. Anderson,—far too able to be buried down here in a mountain mining town."

"Thank you," said Dan Anderson, sweetly; "that's very nice of you."

"Now, I don't know what induced you to hide yourself out here—" went on Barkley, affably.

"No," replied Dan Anderson, "you don't. As for myself personally, it's no one's damned business. I may say in a general way, however, that the prevailing high prices of sealskins and breakfast food in the Eastern States have had a great deal to do with our Western civilization. The edge of the West is mostly inhabited by fools and philosophers, all mostly broke."

"I think I follow you," assented Barkley; "but I'd rather classify you as a philosopher."

"Perhaps. At least I am not fool enough to talk about my own affairs. You say you are here to talk business. It is your belief that I understand some of the chemical constituents of the population of Heart's Desire. Now, in what way can we be useful to each other?"

Ellsworth broke in, "It's as Barkley says; I've been watching you, Mr. Anderson, and I've had an interest in you for quite a while."

"Indeed?"

"Yes, I have. I want to see you win out. Now, if you won't go to the mountain, the mountain will have to come to you. If you won't go back and live in the States, we will have to bring the States to you; and they'll follow mighty quick when the railroad comes, as you know very well."

"My friend Tom Osby used those very words this morning, when he heard the whistle of your esteemed railroad train."

"Precisely," Ellsworth went on. "We'll give you a town to live in. We'll give you professional work to do."

"So you'll build me a town, in order to get me work? That's very nice of you, indeed."

"Now, there you go with your infernal priggishness," protested Ellsworth, testily. "Have we asked you to do anything but straight business?"

"Exactly," said Barkley.

They were playing now with Dan Anderson's heartstrings, but his face did not show it. They were putting him in the balance against Heart's Desire, but his speech offered no evidence of it. They were making Constance Ellsworth the price of Heart's Desire, but Dan Anderson did not divulge it, as he sat and looked at them.

"Gentlemen," said he, at length, "I am a lawyer, the best one in Heart's Desire. The law here is complex in practice. The titles are very much involved. Between Chitty on Pleading and the land grants the Spanish crown, the law may be a very slow and deliberate matter in this country. Now, I understand the practice. I speak the language—I don't need an interpreter—so that I am probably as good as any lawyer you can secure at this time. In straight matters of business I am open for employment."

"Now you are beginning to talk," said Barkley. "And just to get right *down* to business, and show you we're not all talk, I want to give you a little retainer fee. I'm sorry it isn't larger, but it'll grow, I hope." He drew a goodly wallet from his breast pocket, and counted out ten one-hundred-dollar bills, which he threw down carelessly on the pine needles in front of Dan Anderson. "Is that satisfactory?" he asked.

"Yes," said the latter; but he did not take up the money.

"Oh, there'll be more," suggested Mr. Ellsworth. "This business ought to net you between five and ten thousand dollars this year. It might mean more than that if we got into town without a fight."

"That would be about the only way you would get in at all," and Dan Anderson smiled incomprehensibly.

"Exactly! And now, since you are our counsel—" Barkley spoke with an increased firmness—"we want to know your idea on the right-of-way question. What's the nature of the titles in that town, anyhow?"

"As near as I can tell," replied Dan Anderson, "since you retain me and ask my legal opinion, the fundamental title to the valley of Heart's Desire lies in the ability of every fellow there to hit a tin can at forty yards with a six-shooter. There's hardly a tin can in the street that you could cook a meal in," he added plaintively.

"I see," said Barkley, his laughter a little forced. "But now, I heard there never was a town site filed on."

"There was a story," replied Dan Anderson, ruminatingly, "that Jack Wilson laid out a town there soon after he made the Homestake strike. He had McDonald, the deputy surveyor, plat it out on a piece of brown paper,—which was the only sort they had,—and Jack started over with the plat to file at the county seat. He got caught in a rain and used the paper to start a fire with. After that he forgot about it, and after that again, he died; so there never was any town site. The boys just built their houses where they felt like it; and since then they have been so busy about other things—croquet, music, embroidery, antelope hunting, and the like—that they haven't had time to think about town lots or town sites, or anything of that sort."

Barkley's eyes gleamed. "That will simplify matters very much," said he.

"You really do need local counsel," Dan Anderson observed. "On the contrary of that, it will complicate matters very much."

"Well, we'll see about that," rejoined Barkley, grimly. "We'll see if a little mining camp can hold up a railroad corporation the size of this! But why don't you put your money in your pocket? It's yours, man."

Dan Anderson slowly picked up the bills, folded them,

and tucked them into a pocket. "This," said he, "is a great deal more than the entire circulating medium of Heart's Desire. I'm likely to become a disturbing factor up there."

"That's what we want you to become," said Barkley. "We know there're a lot of good mining claims in there, especially the coal lands on the east side of the valley. It isn't the freight and passenger traffic that we're after—we want to get hold of those mines. Why, the inside gang of the Southern Pacific—you'll keep this a professional secret, of course—has told us that they'll take coal from us for their whole system west of Houston. In a couple of years there'll be a town there of eight or ten thousand people. Why, man, it's the chance of your life. And here's Mr. Ellsworth putting you in on the ground floor."

Dan Anderson looked at him queerly.

"By the way," began Ellsworth, taking from his pocket an engineer's blue-print map, "one of the first things we want to settle is the question of our depot site. The only place we can lay out our side tracks is just at the head of the canon, and at the lower end of the valley. Do you know anything about this house here? It's the first one as you go into town from the lower end of the valley."

Dan Anderson bent over the map. "Yes, I know it perfectly," said he. "That's the adobe of our friend Tom Osby here, the man who came down with me from Heart's Desire. He just went up the trail with your daughter, sir."

"The yards'll wipe him out," said Barkley.

"The valley is so narrow," went on Ellsworth, "according to what our engineers say, that we've got to clean out the whole lower part of the town, in order to lay out the station grounds."

Dan Anderson started. The money in his pocket suddenly burned him.

"The trouble with your whole gang," resumed Barkley, striking a match on a log, "has been that you've been trying to stop the world. You can't do that."

Dan Anderson, silent, grim, listened to what he had not heard for many months, the crack of the whip of modern progress. Yet, before his eyes he still saw passing the vision of a tall, round figure, sweet in the beauty of young womanhood, even as he was strong in the strength of his young manhood.

"I'll help you all I can honorably, gentlemen," said he, at length, rising; "we'll talk it over up at the town itself. I don't know just what we can do in the way of recognizing existing rights, but in my opinion force isn't the way to go about it."

"Well, we'll use force if need be; you can depend on that!" said Barkley, harshly. "I've got to get back home before long, and it will be up to you after that."

He and Ellsworth also arose and brushed from their clothing the clinging dust and pine needles. The three turned towards the trail and walked slowly up to the edge of the open space in which stood the Sky Top edifice.

"Quite a house, isn't it?" said Ellsworth, admiringly.

Dan Anderson did not look at the building. Constance was sitting alone at the edge of the gallery. Wishing nothing so much in the world as to go forward, Dan Anderson turned back at the edge of the grounds.

Some jangling mountain jays flitted from tree to tree

about him. They seemed to call out to him to pause, to return. The whispering of the pines called over and over to him, "Constance! Constance!"

Once more he turned, and retraced his steps, the trees still whispering. At the edge of the opening he paused unseen. He saw the girl, with one hand each on the arm of her father and of Barkley, laughing gayly and walking across the gallery. Each had offered her an arm to assist her in arising, and her act was, in fact, the most natural one in the world. Yet to Dan Anderson, remote, morose, solitary, his soul out of all perspective, this sight seemed the very end of all the world.

CHAPTER XV

SCIENCE AT HEART'S DESIRE

This being the Story of a Cow Puncher, an Osteopath, and a Cross-eyed Horse

"That old railroad'll shore bust me up a heap if it ever does git in here," remarked Tom Osby one morning in the forum of Whiteman's corral, where the accustomed group was sitting in the sun, waiting for some one to volunteer as Homer for the day.

There was little to do but listen to story telling, for Tom Osby dwelt in the tents of Kedar, delaying departure on his accustomed trip to Vegas.

"A feller down there to Sky Top," he went on, arousing only the most indolent interest, "one of them spy-glass ingineers—tenderfoot, with his six-shooter belt buckled so tight he couldn't get his feet to the ground—he says to me I might as well trade my old grays for a nice new checkerboard, or a deck of author cards, for I won't have nothing to do but just amuse myself when the railroad cars gets here."

No one spoke. All present were trying to imagine how Heart's Desire would seem with a railroad train each day.

"Things'll be some different in them days, mebbe so." Tom recrossed his legs with well-considered deliberation.

"There's a heap of things different already from what they used to be when I first hit the cow range," said Curly. "The whole country's changed, and it ain't changed for the better, either. Grass is longer, and horns is shorter, and men is triflin'er. Since the Yankees has got west of the Missouri River a ranch foreman ain't allowed to run his own brandin' iron any more, and that takes more'n half the poetry out of the cow business, don't it, Mac?" This to McKinney, who was nearly asleep.

"Everything else is changing too," Curly continued, gathering fluency as memories began to crowd upon him. "Look at the lawyers and doctors there is in the Territory now—and this country used to be respectable. Why, when I first come here there wasn't a doctor within a thousand miles, and no need for one. If one of the boys got shot up much, we always found some way to laundry him and sew him together again without no need of a diplomy. No one ever got sick; and, of course, no one ever did die of his own accord, the way they do back in the States."

"What's it all about, Curly?" drawled Dan Anderson. "You can't tell a story worth a cent." Curly paid no attention to him.

"The first doctor that ever come out here for to alleviate us fellers," he went on, "why, he settled over on the Sweetwater. He was a allopath from Bitter Creek. What medicine that feller did give! He gradual drifted into the vet'inary line.

"Then there come a homeopath—that was after a good many women folks had settled in along the railroad over west. Still, there wasn't much sickness, and I don't reckon the homeopath ever did winter through. I was livin' with the Bar T outfit on the Oscura range, at that time.

"Next doctor that come along was a ostypath." Curly took a chew of tobacco, and paused a moment reflectively.

"I said the first feller drifted into vet'inary lines, didn't I?" he resumed. "Well, the ostypath did, too. Didn't you never hear about that? Why, he ostypathed a horse!"

"Did *what?*" asked Tom Osby sitting up; for hitherto there had seemed no need to listen attentively.

"Yes, sir," he went on, "he ostypathed a horse for us. The boys they gambled about two thousand dollars on that horse over at Socorro. It was a cross-eyed horse, too."

"What's that?" Doc Tomlinson objected. "There never was such a thing as a cross-eyed horse."

"Oh, there wasn't, wasn't there?" said Curly. "Well, now, my friend, when you talk that-a-way, you simply show me how much you don't know about horses. This here Bar T horse was as cross-eyed as a saw-horse, until we got him ostypathed. But, of course, if you don't believe what I say, there's no use tellin' you this story at all."

"Oh, go on, go on," McKinney spoke up, "don't pay no attention to Doc."

"Well," Curly resumed, "that there horse was knowed constant on this range for over three years. He was a outlaw, with cream mane and tail, and a *pinto* map of Europe, Asia, and Africa wrote all over his ribs. Run? Why, that horse could run down a coyote as a moral pastime. We used him to catch jack rabbits with between meals. It wasn't no trouble for him to *run*. The trouble was to tell when he was goin' to *stop* runnin'. Sometimes it was a good while before the feller ridin' him could get him around to where he begun to run. He run in curves natural, and he handed out a right curve or a left one, just as he happened to feel, same as the feller dealin' faro, and just as easy.

"Tom Redmond, on the Bar T, he got this horse from a feller by the name of Hasenberg, that brought in a bunch of has-beens and outlaws, and allowed to distribute 'em in this country. Hasenberg was a foreign gent that looked a good deal like Whiteman, our distinguished feller-citizen here. He was cross-eyed hisself, body and soul. There wasn't a straight thing about him. We allowed that maybe this Pinto *caballo* got cross-eyed from associatin' with old Hasenberg, who was strictly on the bias, any way you figured."

"You ain't so bad, after all, Curly," said Dan Andersen, sitting up. "You're beginning now to hit the human interest part. You ought to be a reg'lar contributor."

"Shut up!" said Curly. "Now Tom Redmond, he took to this here Pinto horse from havin' seen him jump the corral fence several times, and start floatin' off across the country for a eight or ten mile sasshay without no special encouragement. He hired three Castilian busters to operate on Pinto, and he got so he could be rode occasional, but every one allowed they never did see any horse just like him. He was the most aggravatinest thing we ever did have on this range. He had a sort of odd-lookin' white eye, but a heap of them *pintos* has got glass eyes, and so no one thought to examine his lookers very close, though it was noticed early in the game that Pinto might be lookin' one way and goin' the other, at the same time. He'd be goin' on a keen lope, and then something or other might get on his mind, and he'd stop and untangle hisself from all kinds of ridin'. Sometimes he'd jump and snort like he was seein' ghosts. A feller on that horse could have roped antelopes as easy as yearlin' calves, if he could just have told which way Mr. Pinto was goin'; but he was a shore hard one to estermate.

"At last Tom, why, he suspected somethin' wasn't right with Pinto's lamps. If you stuck out a bunch of hay at him, he couldn't bite it by about five feet. When you led him down to water, you had to go sideways; and if you wanted to get him in through the corral gate, you had to push him in backward. We discovered right soon that he was born with his parallax or something out of gear. His graduated scale of seein' things was different from our'n. I don't reckon anybody ever will know what all Pinto saw with them glass lamps of his, but all the time we knowed that if we could ever onct get his lookin' outfit tuned up proper, we had the whole country skinned in a horse race; for he could shore run copious.

"That was why he had the whole Bar T outfit guessin' all the time. We all wanted to bet on him, and we was all scared to. Sometimes we'd make up a purse among us, and we'd go over to some social getherin' or other, and win a thousand dollars. Old Pinto could run all day; he can yet, for that matter. Didn't make no difference to him how often we raced him; and natural, after we'd won one hatful of money with him, we'd want to win another. That was where our judgment was weak.

"You never could tell whether Pinto was goin' to finish under the wire, or out in the landscape. His eyes seemed to be sort of moverble, but like enough they'd get sot when he went to runnin'. Then he'd run whichever way he was lookin' at the time, or happened to think he was lookin'; and dependin' additional on what he thought he saw. And law! A whole board of supervisors and school commissioners couldn't have looked that horse in the face, and guessed on their sacred honor whether he was goin' to jump the fence to the left, or take to the high sage on the outside of the track.

"Onct in a while we'd git Pinto's left eye set at a angle, and he'd come around the track and under the wire before she wobbled out of place. On them occasions we made money a heap easier than I ever did a-gettin' it from home. But, owin' to the looseness of them eyes, I don't reckon there never was no horse racin' as uncertain as this here; and like enough you may have observed it's uncertain enough even when things is fixed in the most comf'terble way possible."

A deep sigh greeted this, which showed that Curly's audience was in full sympathy.

"You always felt like puttin' the saddle on to Pinto hind end to, he was so cross-eyed," he resumed ruminatingly, "but still you couldn't help feelin' sorry for him, neither. Now, he had a right pained and grieved look in his face all the time. I reckon he thought this was a hard sort of a world to get along in. It is. A cross-eyed man has a hard enough time, but a cross-eyed *horse*—well, you don't know how much trouble he can be for hisself, and every one else around him.

"Now, here we was, fixed up like I told you. Mr. Allopath is over on Sweetwater creek, Mr. Homeopath is maybe in the last stages of starvation. Old Pinto looks plumb hopeless, and all us fellers is mostly hopeless too, owin' to his uncertain habits in a horse race, yet knowin' that it ain't perfessional for us not to back a Bar T horse that can run as fast as this one can.

"About then along comes Mr. Ostypath. This was just

about thirty days before the county fair at Socorro, and there was money hung up for horse races over there that made us feel sick to think of. We knew we could go out of the cow-punchin' business for good if we could just only onct get Pinto over there, and get him to run the right way for a few brief moments.

"Was he game? I don't know. There never was no horse ever got clost enough to him in a horse race to tell whether he was game or not. He might not get back home in time for supper, but he would shore run industrious. Say, I talked in a telyphome onct. The book hung on the box said the telyphome was instantaneous. It ain't. But now this Pinto, he was a heap more instantaneous than a telyphome.

"As I was sayin', it was long about now Mr. Ostypath comes in. He talks with the boss about locatin' around in here. Boss studies him over a while, and as there ain't been anybody sick for over ten years he tries to break it to Mr. Ostypath gentle that the Bar T ain't a good place for a doctor. They have some conversation along in there, that-a-way, and Mr. Ostypath before long gets the boss interested deep and plenty. He says there ain't no such a thing as gettin' sick. We all knew that before; but he certainly floors the lot when he allows that the reason a feller don't feel good, so as he can eat tenpenny nails, and make a million dollars a year, is always because there is something wrong with his osshus structure.

"He says the only thing that makes a feller have rheumatism, or dyspepsia, or headache, or nosebleed, or red hair, or any other sickness, is that something is wrong with his nervous system. Now, it's this-a-way. He allows them nerves is like a bunch of garden hose. If you put your foot on the hose, the water can't run right free. If you take it off, everything's lovely. 'Now,' says Mr. Ostypath, 'if, owin' to some luxation, some leeshun, some temporary mechanical disarrangement of your osshus structure, due to a oversight of a All-wise Providence, or maybe a fall off'n a buckin' horse, one of them bones of yours gets to pressin' on a nerve, why, it ain't natural you ought to feel good. Now, is it?' says he.

"He goes on and shows how all up and down a feller's backbone there is plenty of soft spots, and he shows likewise that there is scattered around in different parts of a feller's territory something like two hundred and four and a half bones, any one of which is likely any minute to jar loose and go to pressin' on a soft spot; 'In which case,' says he, 'there is need of a ostypath immediate.'"

"For instance,' he says to me, 'I could make quite a man out of you in a couple of years if I had the chanct.' I ast him what his price would be for that, and he said he was willin' to tackle it for about fifty dollars a month. That bein' just five dollars a month more than the boss was allowing me at the time, and me seein' I'd have to go about two years without anything to wear or eat—let alone anything to drink—I had to let this chanct go by. I been strugglin' along, as you know, ever since, just like this, some shopworn, but so's to set up. There was one while, I admit, when the Doc made me some nervous, when I thought of all them soft spots in my spine, and all them bones liable to get loose any minute and go to pressin' on them. But I had to take my chances, like any other cow puncher at forty-five a month."

"You ought to raise his wages, Mac," said Doc Tomlinson to McKinney, the ranch foreman, but the latter only grunted.

"Mr. Ostypath, he stayed around the Bar T quite a while," began Curly again, "and we got to talkin' to him a heap

Emerson Hough

about modern science. Says he, one evenin', this-a-way to us fellers, says he, 'Why, a great many things goes wrong because the nervous system is interfered with, along of your osshus structure. You think your stomach is out of whack,' says he. 'It ain't. All it needs is more nerve supply. I git that by loosenin' up the bones in your back. Why, I've cured a heap of rheumatism, and paralysis, and cross eyes, and—'

"'What's that?' says Tom Redmond, right sudden.

"'You heard me, sir,' says the Doc, severe.

"Tom, he couldn't hardly wait, he was so bad struck with the idea he had. 'Come here, Doc,' says he. And then him and Doc walked off a little ways and begun to talk. When they come up toward us again, we heard the Doc sayin': 'Of course I could cure him. Straybismus is dead easy. I never did operate on no horse, but I've got to eat, and if this here is the only patient in this whole blamed country, why I'll have to go you, if it's only for the sake of science,' says he. Then we all bunched in together and drifted off toward the corral, where old Pinto was standin', lookin' hopeless and thoughtful. 'Is this the patient?' says the Doc, sort of sighin'.

"'It are,' says Tom Redmond.

"Doc he walks up to old Pinto, and has a look at him, frontways, sideways, and all around. Pinto raises his head up, snorts, and looks Doc full in the face; leastwise, if he'd 'a' been any other horse, he'd 'a' been lookin' him full in the face. Doc he stands thoughtful for quite a while, and then he goes and kind of runs his hand up and down along Pinto's spine. He growed plumb enthusiastic then, 'Beautiful subject,' says he. 'Be-yoo-tiful ostypathic subject! Whole osshus structure exposed!' And Pinto shore was a dream if bones was needful in the game."

Curly paused for another chew of tobacco, then went on again.

"Well, it's like this, you see; the backbone of a man or a horse is full of little humps—you can see that easy in the springtime. Now old Pinto's back, it looked like a topygraphical survey of the whole Rocky Mountain range.

"Doc he runs his hand up and down along this high divide, and says he, 'Just like I thought,' says he. 'The patient has suffered a distinct leeshun in the immediate vicinity of his vaseline motor centres.'"

"You mean the vaso-motor centres," suggested Dan Anderson.

"That's what I said," said Curly, aggressively.

"Now, when we all heard Doc say them words we knowed he was shore scientific, and we come up clost while the examination was progressin'.

"'Most extraordinary,' says Doc, feelin' some more. 'Now, here is a distant luxation in the lumber regions.' He talked like Pinto had a wooden leg.

"'I should diagnose great cerebral excitation, along with pernounced ocular hesitation,' says Doc at last.

"'Now look here, Doc,' says Tom Redmond to him then. 'You go careful. We all know there's something strange about this here horse; but now, if he's got any bone pressin' on him anywhere that makes him *run* the way he does, why, you be blamed careful not to monkey with that there particular bone. Don't you touch his *runnin'* bone, because *that's* all right the way it is.'"

"'Don't you worry any,' says the Doc. 'All I should do would only be to increase his nerve supply. In time I could remedy his ocular defecks, too,' says he. He allows that if we will give him time, he can make Pinto's eyes straighten out so's he'll look like a new rockin' horse Christmas mornin' at a church festerval. Incidentally he suggests that we get a tall leather blinder and run it down Pinto's nose, right between his eyes.

"This last was what caught us most of all. 'This here blinder idea,' says Tom Redmond, 'is plumb scientific. The trouble with us cow punchers is we ain't got no brains—or we wouldn't be cow punchers! Now look here, Pinto's right eye looks off to the left, and his left eye looks off to the right. Like enough he sees all sorts of things on both sides of him, and gets 'em mixed. Now, you put this here harness leather between his eyes, and his right eye looks plumb into it on one side, and his left eye looks into it on the other. Result is, he can't see nothing at *all*! Now, if he'll only run when he's *blind*, why, we can skin them Socorro people till it seems like a shame.'"

"Well, right then we all felt money in our pockets. We seemed most too good to be out ridin' sign, or pullin' old cows out of mudholes. 'You leave all that to me,' says Doc. 'By the time I've worked on this patient's nerve centres for a while, I'll make a new horse out of him. You watch me,' says he. That made us all feel cheerful. We thought this wasn't such a bad world, after all.

"We passed the hat in the interest of modern science, and we fenced off a place in the corral and set up a school of ostypathy in our midst. Doc, he done some things that seemed to us right strange at first. He gets Pinto up in one corner and takes him by the ear, and tries to break his neck, with his foot in the middle of his back. Then he goes around on the other side and does the same thing. He hammers him up one side and down the other, and works him and wiggles him till us cow punchers thought he was goin' to scatter him around worse than Cassybianca on the burnin' deck after the exploshun. My experience, though, is that it's right hard to shake a horse to pieces. Pinto, he stood it all right. And say, he got so gentle, with that tall blinder between his eyes, that he'd 'a' followed off a sheepherder.

"All this time we was throwin' oats a-plenty into Pinto, rubbin' his legs down, and gettin' him used to a saddle a little bit lighter than a regular cow saddle. Doc, he allows he can see his eyes straightenin' out every day. 'I ought to have a year on this job,' says he; 'but these here is urgent times.'"

"I should say they was urgent. The time for the county fair at Socorro was comin' right clost.

"At last we takes the old Hasenberg Pinto over to Socorro to the fair, and there we enters him in everything from the front to the back of the racin' book. My friends, you would 'a' shed tears of pity to see them folks fall down over theirselves tryin' to hand us their money against old Pinto. There was horses there from Montanny to Arizony, all kinds of fancy riders, and money—oh, law! Us Bar T fellers, we took everything offered—put up everything we had, down to our spurs. Then we'd go off by ourselves and look at each other solemn. We was gettin' rich so quick we felt almost scared.

"There come nigh to bein' a little shootin' just before the horses was gettin' ready for the first race, which was for a mile and a half. We led old Pinto out, and some feller standin' by, he says, sarcastic like, 'What's that I see

Emerson Hough

comin'; a snow-plough?' Him alludin' to the single blinder on Pinto's nose.

"'I reckon you'll think it's been snowin' when we get through,' says Tom Redmond to him, scornful. 'The best thing you can do is to shut up, unless you've got a little money you want to contribute to the Bar T festerval.' But about then they hollered for the horses to go to the post, and there wasn't no more talk.

"Pinto he acted meek and humble, just like a glass-eyed angel, and the starter didn't have no trouble with him at all. At last he got them all off, so clost together one saddle blanket would have done for the whole bunch. Say, man, that was a fine start.

"Along with oats and ostypathy, old Pinto he'd come out on the track that day just standin' on the edges of his feet, he was feelin' that fine. We put Jose Santa Maria Trujillo, one of our lightest boys, up on Pinto for to ride him. Now a Greaser ain't got no sense. It was that fool boy Jose that busted up modern science on the Bar T.

"I was tellin' you that there horse was ostypathed, so to speak, plumb to a razor edge, and I was sayin' that he went off on a even start. Then what did he do? Run? No, he didn't *run*. He just sort of passed *away* from the place where he started at. Our Greaser, he sees the race is all over, and like any fool cow puncher, he must get frisky. Comin' down the homestretch, only needin' about one more jump—for it ain't above a quarter of a mile—Jose, he stands up in his stirrups and pulls off his hat, and just whangs old Pinto over the head with it, friendly like, to show him there ain't no coldness.

"We never did rightly know what happened at that time. The Greaser admits he may have busted off the fastenin' of that single blinder down Pinto's nose. Anyhow, Pinto runs a few short jumps, and then stops, lookin' troubled. The next minute he hides his face on the Greaser and there is a glimpse of bright, glad sunlight on the bottom of Jose's moccasins. Next minute after that Pinto is up in the grandstand among the ladies, and there he sits down in the lap of the Governor's wife, which was among them present.

"There was time, even then, to lead him down and over the line, but before we could think of that he falls to buckin' sincere and conscientious, up there among the benches, and if he didn't jar his osshus structure a heap *then*, it wasn't no fault of his'n. We all run up in front of the grandstand, and stood lookin' up at Pinto, and him the maddest, scaredest, cross-eyedest horse I ever did see in all my life. His single blinder was swingin' loose under his neck. His eyes was right mean and white, and the Mexican saints only knows which way he *was* a-lookin'.

"So there we was," went on Curly, with another sigh, "all Socorro sayin' bright and cheerful things to the Bar T, and us plumb broke, and far, far from home.

"We roped Pinto, and led him home behind the wagon, forty miles over the sand, by the soft, silver light of the moon. There wasn't a horse or saddle left in our *rodeo*, and we had to ride on the grub wagon, which you know is a disgrace to any gentleman that wears spurs. Pinto, he was the gayest one in the lot. I reckon he allowed he'd been Queen of the May. Every time he saw a jack rabbit or a bunch of sage brush, he'd snort and take a *pasear* sideways as far as the rope would let him go.

"'The patient seems to be still laborin' under great cerebral excitation,' says the Doc, which was likewise on the wagon. 'I ought to have had a year on him,' says he, despondent like.

"'Shut up,' says Tom Redmond to the Doc. 'I'd shoot up your own osshus structure plenty,' says he, 'if I hadn't bet my gun on that horse race.'"

"Well, we got home, the wagon-load of us, in the mornin' sometime, every one of us ashamed to look the cook in the face, and hopin' the boss was away from home. But he wasn't. He looks at us, and says he;—

"'Is this a sheep outfit I see before me, or is it the remnants of the former cow camp on the Bar T?' He was right sarcastic. 'Doc,' says he, 'explain this here to me.' But the Doc, he couldn't. Says the boss to him at last, 'The *right* time to do the explainin' is before the hoss race is over, and not after,' says he. 'That's the only kind of science that goes hereafter on the Bar T,' says he.

"I reckon the boss was feelin' a little riled, because he had two hundred on Pinto hisself. A cross-eyed horse shore can make a sight of trouble," Curly sighed in conclusion; "yet I bought Pinto for four dollars, and—sometimes, anyway—he's the best horse in my string down at Carrizosy, ain't he, Mac?"

In the thoughtful silence following this tale, Tom Osby knocked his pipe reflectively against a cedar log. "That's the way with the railroad," he said. "It's goin' to come in herewith one eye on the gold mines and the other on the town—and there won't be no blind-bridle up in front of old Mr. Ingine, neither. If we got as much sense as the Bar T feller, we'll do our explainin' before, and not after the hoss race is over. Before I leave for Vegas, I want to see one of you ostypothetic lawyers about that there railroad outfit."

CHAPTER XVI

THE PARTITION OF HEARTS DESIRE

Concerning Real Estate, Love, Friendship, and Other Good and Valuable Considerations

"You see, it's just this-a-way," began Tom Osby, the morning after Curly's osteopathic horse saga; "I've got to go on up to Vegas after a load of stuff, and I'll be gone a couple of weeks. Now, you know, from what we heard down at Sky Top about this railroad, a heap of things can happen in two weeks. Them fellers ain't showin' their hands any, but for all we know their ingineers may come in any day, and start in to doin' things."

"They've got to make arrangements first," replied Dan Anderson.

"That's all right; and so ought we to make arrangements. We seen this place first. Now, Dan—" and he extended a gnarled and hairy hand—"you've always done like you said you would. You took care of me down there to Sky Top. I want you to keep on a-takin' care of me, whether I'm here or not. Now, there's my house and yard, right at the head of the canon, where they've got to come if they get in. That little old place, and my little old team, is about all I've got in the world. If old Mr. Railroad comes up this *arroyo*, what happens to me? You tell 'em to go somewheres else, because I seen this place first, and I like it. Ain't that the law in this country? Ain't it *always* been the law?"

Dan Anderson nodded. He held out his hand to Tom Osby and looked him straight in the eye. "I'll take care of you, Tom," he promised.

"Then that'll be about all," said Tom; "giddup, boys!"

In some way news of the early advent of the railroad had gotten about in Heart's Desire, and Dan Anderson found talk of it on every tongue, talk very similar to that of Tom Osby. Uncle Jim Brothers, owner of the one-story hotel and restaurant, the father and the feeder of all Heart's Desire when the latter was in financial stress, was the next to come to him; and Uncle Jim was grave of face.

"See here, man," said he, "how about this here new railroad? Do we want it, or *do* we? Seems to me like we always got along here pretty well the way things was."

Dan Anderson nodded again. Uncle Jim shifted from one large foot to the other, and thrust a great hand into the pocket of one trouser leg.

"All I was going to say to you, Dan," he went on, "is, if it comes to takin' any sides, we all know which side you're on. You're with *us*. Now, there's my place down there, where you've et many a time with the rest of the boys. You've helped me build the tables in the dining room— done a lot of things which makes me feel obliged to you." (Ah! lovable liar, Uncle Jim, who could feed a man broke and hungry, and still let him feel that the operation was a favor to the feeder!) "Now, I just wanted to say, Dan, I was sure, in case any railroad ever did come cavortin' around here, you'd sort of look after the old place. Will you do that?"

"Of course he will," broke in Doc Tomlinson, who had strolled down the street and overheard the conversation. "Dan Anderson, he's our lawyer. We've got him retained permanent, ain't we, Dan? Now, there's my old drug store—ain't much in it, but it's where I settled when I first driv into the valley, and I like the place. Ain't no railroad going to boost me out without a scrap."

Dan Anderson turned away, sick at heart. For three days he kept to his cabin on the far side of the *arroyo*.

But if hesitation sat on the soul of any man of the community, if doubt or questionings harassed the minds of any, there was no uncertainty on the part of the management of the railroad, whose coming was causing this uneasiness. One day Dan Anderson was startled to hear a knock at his door, and to see the dusty figure of Porter Barkley, general counsel of the A. P. and S. E., just from a long buckboard ride from the head of the rails. With him came Grayson, chief engineer. Dan Anderson invited them in.

"Well, Mr. Anderson," said Barkley, "here we are, close after you. We're following up the right-of-way matters sharp and hard now. We can't hold back our graders, and before the line gets abreast of this canon, we've got to know what we can do here. Now, what can you tell us by this time?"

"I can tell you, as I said, the status of every town lot and every mining claim in this valley," replied Dan Anderson. "It's all simple so far as that is concerned."

"How about that town site? Grayson, here, is ready to go

ahead with the new plat. If you never had any town site filed, how were real-estate transfers made?"

"There never were any transfers made. There has not been a town lot sold in ten years."

"Real estate just a little dull?" laughed Barkley, sarcastically.

"We hadn't noticed it," said Dan Anderson, simply.

"But how about your courts? Next thing you'll be telling me there wasn't any court."

"There never was, except when we acquitted a man for shooting a pig. I was his counsel, by the way."

"Nor any town election?"

"Why should there be?"

"No government—no nothing? for five years?"

"Over twelve years altogether, to be exact. I'm rather a newcomer myself."

"No organization—no government—" Barkley summed it up. "Good God! what kind of a place is this?"

"It's Heart's Desire," said Dan Anderson. No man of that valley was ever able to say more, or indeed thought it needful to say more.

Porter Barkley gave a contemptuous whistle, as he turned on his heel, hands in pockets, his bulky form filling the doorway as he looked out. "So you were a lawyer here," he said. "You must have had rather more leisure than law practice, I should think."

"It left me all the more time for my reading," said Dan Anderson, gravely. "You've no idea how much a law practice interferes with one's legal studies." Barkley looked at him, but could discover no sign of levity.

"Well, there is one thing mighty sure," said he, shutting his heavy jaws tight; "this valley is, or was, open to settlement under the United States land laws."

"Certainly," assented Dan Anderson. "The first men in here were mining men from every corner of the Rockies, and they knew their business. All these mountains were platted, and 'adversed,' and litigated. Then, before the second discoveries, and before any coal veins were located on the other side of the valley, the gold veins pinched out. Everybody got broke, and nearly everybody got up and walked away. Meantime, the courts had only been sitting over at Lincoln once in a while—when Billy the Kid allowed it. I'll have to admit that things were a trifle tangled as to title."

"Well, I should say so!" Barkley was irritable, Grayson, the engineer, silent and smiling.

"There was so much room after the mining boom broke, that nobody cared for a town lot. Every fellow just picked out the place he liked, built where he liked, and went in as his own butler, chambermaid, and cook.

"You are seeing this country now, gentlemen," he went on, "pretty much as God made it, and as Coronado saw it three hundred years ago. I deprecate any undue haste on your part. We've been three hundred years in getting this far along. We've done very well without either a town site or a city council."

Barkley was utterly unable to comprehend either Dan Anderson or Heart's Desire. "This is the absolute limit!" he rapped out. "At least we'll end this now. Come on, Grayson, we three'll go out and have a look at the place, and see what is the best way to lay out the streets. I suppose, Anderson, you can tell us how we can get title under government patent—mineral lands—coal lands—desert lands—homestead—whatever we can dig out the quickest?"

"Oh, yes," said Dan Anderson, "but don't dig too deep, or you may run against a land grant from Ferdinand and Isabella to some well-beloved *hidalgo* whose descendants may now be herding sheep on the Pecos, or owning the earth along the Rio Grande. Cabeza de Vaca may own this valley, for all I know. Maybe Coronado owns it. *Quien sabe?* We only borrowed the place. We thought that probably Charles IV, or Philip II, or whoever it was, wouldn't mind very much, seeing that he's dead anyhow, in case we returned the valley in good condition, reasonable wear and tear excepted, after we were dead ourselves. Of course, this railroad coming in complicates matters a good deal. Do I make all this clear to you, gentlemen? I never did see a place just like this, myself."

"No?" snapped Barkley.

"So we called it Heart's Desire."

"We'll call it Coalville now," retorted Barkley.

They passed out into the bright sunlit street of Heart's Desire. Stern-browed Carrizo, guardian through centuries of calm and secrecy, gazed down on them unwinking. Dan Anderson looked up at the grim sentinel of the valley, and mockery left his speech. He looked about at the wide and vacant spaces of the little settlement, lying content, secure, and set apart, and a horror came upon his soul. He was about to be a traitor, a traitor to Heart's Desire! Law—title—security—what more of these could these men bring to Heart's Desire than it had long had already? What wrong here had ever been left unrighted? Truth, and justice, and fairness, and sincerity, those priceless things—why, he had known them here for years. Were they now to be made more obvious, or more strong? He had believed his friends, had had friends to believe; would these walking at his side be better friends? These men of Heart's Desire, these simple children who had left the smother of civilization to seek out for themselves a place of strength and simplicity, these strong and fearless giants, these friends of his—had he not promised them that they would be safe in his hands? Hitherto there had never been a traitor among all the men of Heart's Desire. Was he, their accepted friend, to be the first? Dan Anderson passed his hand over a forehead suddenly grown moist. He dared not look up at the chiding front of old Carrizo.

"I was saying," said Porter Barkley, turning from the taciturn engineer as they walked along the hillside, "that this place seems to have been laid off with a circular saw. I can't see any idea of streets at all."

"There is a sort of a street along the *arroyo*," said Dan Anderson, dully. "There never were any cross streets. The boys just built where they felt like it."

"And great builders they were! I didn't know men ever lived in such places. What's that joint there?" He pointed out a ruined *jacal* of upright mud-chinked logs, now leaning slantwise far to one side. "Was that a house, too? It hasn't even a chimney,"

"That was the residence and law office of a former

supreme judge of the State of Kansas," replied Dan Anderson. "He didn't need any chimney. You've no idea how useless a chimney really is. He never stopped to cut any wood, but just fed a log in through the front door into the fire, and let the smoke go out the window. He had a pet wildcat that shared his legal studies—oh, I admit that some of our ways may seem strange to you, just fresh from New York."

"But didn't you live in New York once yourself?"

"Yes, once."

"What made you come away?"

"Objected to, as irrelevant, immaterial, and incompetent; and objection sustained," replied Dan Anderson. "The first thing I learned in this country was not to inquire about any man's past. That's a useful thing for *you* to learn, too."

Porter Barkley, accustomed to dominating those around him, flushed red, but managed to suppress his rising choler for the time. "And by the way, what's that old shell over there, across the ditch?" he asked.

"I regret your irreverence," said Dan Anderson. "That's the New Jersey Gold Mills. Eighty thousand of Eastern Capital went in there at one time. They didn't understand the ways of the country."

"Humph! Well, it's a more practical layout you've got in here this time. You can gamble that Ellsworth and our gang are not going to sink their roll here, by a long ways, unless they get something for it."

"You'll get a run for your money, in all likelihood,"

remarked Dan Anderson.

"As I said, now, Grayson, don't pay any attention to this gully here," went on Barkley. "We'll fill this ditch and put in drains at the crossings, and run the main street north and south. We'll take the ramshorn crooks out of this town in about two days, when we get started."

"I see no reason why we could not run the cross streets at right angles," said Grayson, the constructive. "Of course, we'll catch a good many of these buildings—" he hesitated, pointing at the time to Doc Tomlinson's drug store.

"The corner of this fence would be inside the line of the main street," he went on, sighting along his lead pencil to the angle of Whiteman's corral. It was the very spot where Dan Anderson had sat in council with his cronies many a time. He bit his lip now as he followed the gaze of the engineer.

"How about the stone house down the *arroyo*?" asked he of Grayson. This was Uncle Jim Brothers's hotel, sanctuary for the homeless of Heart's Desire, a temple of refuge, a place where the word "Friendship," unspoken, never written, was known and understood among men gathered from all corners of this unfriendly world.

"That would have to go," replied Grayson.

"As to that shanty down below, at the head of the canon," growled Barkley, pointing to Tom Osby's adobe, "that's going to be the first thing we'll tear down, street or no street. We need that place for our depot yard, and we're going to take it. Besides, there was something about that Osby fellow I didn't like when we met him over at Sky Top. He's too damned independent to suit me."

Dan Anderson straightened up as though smitten, his face a dull red. The dancing heat mist blurred before his eyes. He said nothing. They turned presently and strolled down toward the foot of the *arroyo*. Barkley pushed his hat back on his furrowed forehead.

"There is a lot in this thing for me, Andersen," said he, "and there'll be a lot in it for you. Have you got any claims of your own in here? Mineral, I mean?"

"Of course," Dan Anderson replied. "We all have claims. This is the only valley in the West, so far as I know, where there is good coal on one side, and paying gold quartz on the other. But that's the case here. We haven't overlooked it."

Barkley whistled. "I wouldn't ask a better show than you'll have here," said he, contemplatively. "The only wonder to me is that some one hasn't broken into this long ago."

"There might be some few difficulties," suggested Dan Anderson.

"Difficulties! What do you care about that? We'll wear 'em out, pound 'em out, break 'em up, I tell you. We're the first ones to find this country—"

"Except maybe Coronado, De Vaca and Company."

"Who were they?"

"The same as you and me," replied Dan Anderson, enigmatically. "Ask the mountains."

"Oh, rot!" said Barkley. "I'll tell you, once for all, I'm not interested in dreams or foolishness. Now, if you want to go in with us, that's one thing. If you don't, we want to find it out mighty quick."

"You might do worse," said Dan Anderson. "The other lawyer is worse than myself. At times I suspect him of being lazy."

"Well, well, let's get together," urged Barkley, impatiently. "Now, Grayson thinks it will take about three hundred and fifty acres for the first plat, without additions; we'll supersede the old Jack Wilson patent. He's dead, you say? Never left a will, or any heirs? Never did get his town site platted and filed? Well, he never will, now. You go with Grayson to-morrow and run out these lines quietly, and help him get an idea of the best mining claims on both sides of the valley, too. There'll be plenty for you to do."

Dan Anderson nodded, but made no comment. Many things were revolving in his mind.

"Meantime," concluded Barkley, "I've got to get back down the line to meet Mr. Ellsworth. We'll come up again. You can readily see that we've got to have a town meeting before very long. Get things in line for it. Will you attend to this?"

"Yes," replied Dan Anderson, slowly and musingly; "yes, I'll attend to it."

Barkley looked once more upon the impassive face of his local counsel, and departed more than ever puzzled and exasperated. He liked Dan Anderson as little as he understood him. "I'll handle him, though," he muttered to himself. "There's a way to handle every man, and I rather think that this one'll come to his feed before we get done with him."

CHAPTER XVII

TREASON AT HEART'S DESIRE

Showing the Dilemma of Dan Anderson, the Doubt of Leading Citizens, and the Artless Performance of a Pastoral Prevaricator

"Learned Counsel," said Dan Anderson on the morning following the preliminary survey of Heart's Desire, "I want you to take my case."

"What's up?" asked Learned Counsel. Dan Anderson pointed down the street, where a group stood talking among themselves, casting occasional side-long glances in his direction. "They're milling like a bunch of scared longhorns," he said. "Something's wrong, and I know it mighty well. I want you to take my case. Come along."

Contrary to the ancient custom of the forum at Whiteman's corral, the group did not move apart to admit them to the circle. "The gentleman from Kansas was addressing the meeting," said Dan Anderson. Doc Tomlinson continued speaking, but still the circle made no move.

"Say it!" burst out Dan Anderson. "Tell it out! What's on your minds, you fellows?"

"We don't like to believe it," McKinney began, facing toward him. "We hope it ain't true."

"What's not true?" he demanded, looking from one averted face to another. At length Doc Tomlinson resumed his office as spokesman. "They say you've sold us out. They say you're bought by the railroad to clean us out; that the scheme is to steal the town, and you're in the steal. Is that so?"

"Is it true?" asked McKinney.

"We want to *know* if it's true," insisted Doc Tomlinson. "You was all over town with them fellers. Now they've let it out they're goin' to grab the town site and make a re-survey."

"We know there wasn't ever any town site here," added Uncle Jim Brothers, "but what need was there? Wasn't there plenty of room for everybody?"

"You can't try any hurrah game on us fellers here," said McKinney, facing Dan Anderson squarely.

"Nor you with me," retorted Dan Anderson. "Don't any of you undertake that."

"Hold on there," called Learned Counsel, lifting his hand for attention. "This man is my client! You're not hearing both sides."

"Tell the other side, Dan," said Uncle Jim Brothers. Dan Anderson shook his head.

"Why can't you?" asked Uncle Jim.

"I can't!" broke from Dan Andersen's dry lips. "If you

knew, you wouldn't ask me to."

"That's no argument," exclaimed Doc Tomlinson. "What we do know is that you were figurin' to run the street right past here, maybe through my store and Uncle Jim's place, maybe takin' Tom's place for depot yards. That outfit's been all over the hills lookin' for claims to jump. It's a case of gobble and steal. They say you're hired to help it on, and are gettin' a share of the steal. Now, if that's so, what would you do if you was in our place?"

"I'd run the fellow out of town," said Dan Anderson. "If there was that sort of a traitor here, by God! I'd kill him."

"We never did have no man go back on us here," Uncle Jim Brothers remarked.

"Don't say that to me!" Dan Andersen's voice was shaken. "You've fed me, Uncle Jim. Don't say that to me."

"Then what *shall* we say, man?" replied Uncle Jim. "We want to be fair with you. But let me tell you, *you* don't own this valley. *We* own it. There's other places in the world besides the States, and don't you forget that. We didn't think you'd ever try to bring States ways in here."

"To hell with the States!" said McKinney, tersely.

"And States ways with them!" added Doc Tomlinson. "I'd like to see any railroad, or any States, or any United States government, try to run this place." Unconsciously he slapped his hand upon the worn scabbard at his hip, and without thought others in the group eased their pistol belts. It was the Free State of Heart's Desire.

"Well, by God!" said Uncle Jim Brothers, snapping and throwing away the pinon twig which he had been fumbling, "if we don't want no railroad, we don't *have* it, and that goes!"

"Of course," broke in Learned Counsel. "We all know that. That's a small thing. The big question is whether or not we've been fair to my client. I've not had time yet to go fully into his case. We'll have to continue this trial. We've got to have fair play."

"That's right enough," assented McKinney, and the others nodded.

"Then wait a while. You can't settle this thing until my client has had time to talk with me. I'll find out what he ought to tell."

"All right for that, too," agreed Uncle Jim Brothers. "But about that railroad, we'll hold court right here. We'll send out a summons to them folks, and have a meetin' here, and we'll see which is which and what is what in this town."

"That's fair enough," assented Learned Counsel. "We'll try the railroad, and we'll try my client at the same time."

"Write out the summons," said Doc Tomlinson. "Send word down to them railroad folks to come up here and be tried. It's time we knew who was boss, them or us. Go ahead, you're a lawyer; fix it up."

They ignored Dan Anderson, their long-time leader in all matters of public interest! Eventually it was Doc Tomlinson himself who drafted the document, one of the most interesting of the Territorial records—a summons whereby civilization was called before the bar of primitive man. These presents being signed and sealed, a messenger was sought for their delivery. None better offered than a half-witted sheepherder commonly known as Willie, who chanced to be in town by buckboard from the lower country. This much accomplished, the meeting at Whiteman's corral broke up.

Learned Counsel took his client by the arm and led him away. "You need not say much to your lawyer," he remarked; "but while I don't ask you to incriminate yourself even with your counsel, I only want to say that a Girl is, in a great many decisions of the upper courts, held to be an extenuating circumstance." He watched the twitch of Dan Anderson's face, but the latter would not speak.

"I don't know just where the girl exists now in this case," went on Learned Counsel, "or how; but she's somewhere. It is not wholly necessary that you should specify."

"My God!" broke out Dan Anderson. "I wanted—I hoped so much? It was my opportunity, my first—"

"That's enough," said Learned Counsel. "You needn't say any more. Every fellow has something of that sort in his life. What brought McKinney here, and Doc Tomlinson, and all the rest?"

"Ribbons!" said Dan Anderson. "Tintypes!"

"Precisely. And who shall cast the first stone? If the boys knew—"

"But they don't know, they can't know. Do you think I'd uncover her name, even among my friends—make her affairs public? No."

"Then your only defence cannot be brought into court."

"No. So what do you advise?"

"What do you advise your counsel to advise you?" asked Learned Counsel, bitterly.

"Nothing. I'm done for, either way it goes."

Dan Anderson turned a drawn face. "What shall I do?" he asked at length again.

For once Learned Counsel was wise. "In this sort of crisis," said he, "one does not consult a lawyer. He decides for himself, and he lives or dies, succeeds or fails, wins or loses forever, for himself and by himself, without aid of counsel or benefit of clergy." He stood and watched the iron go home into the soul of a game man. Dan Anderson was white, but his reply came sharp and stern.

"You're right! Leave me alone. I'll take the case now myself."

They shook hands and separated, not to meet again for days; for Dan Anderson shut himself up in his cabin and denied himself to all. Gloom and uncertainty reigned among his friends. That a crisis of some sort was imminent now became generally understood. At length the crisis came.

There arrived in town, obedient to the summons of Heart's Desire, the dusty buckboard driven by Willie the sheep-herder. Upon the front seat with him was Mr. Ellsworth; on the back seat sat Porter Barkley and Constance. The chief actors in the impending drama were now upon the stage, and all Heart's Desire knew that action of some sort must presently follow.

With due decorum, however, all Heart's Desire stood

apart, while the three travellers, dusty and weary, buried themselves in the privacy of Uncle Jim Brothers's best spare rooms. Then Heart's Desire sought out Willie the sheepherder.

"Now, Willie," said Doc Tomlinson, "look here—you tell us the truth for once. There's a heap of trouble goin' on here, and we want to get at the bottom of it. Maybe you heard something. Now, say, is this here railroad figurin' on comin' in here, or not?"

"Shore it'll come," said Willie, sagely. "Them folks has got money to do just what they want. Railroad'll be here in a few days if they feel like it."

"Maybe *we* don't feel like it," said Doc Tomlinson, grimly. "We'll see about that to-night."

"The girl, she's the one," said Willie, vaguely.

"What's that you mean?" commanded Doc Tomlinson.

"The funniest thing," said Willie, "is how things is mixed. Lord John, he rides on the front seat; and Lord Peter Berkeley,—that's the lawyer for the railroad,—he rides on the back seat with her, and he sues for her hand, he does, all the way up from the Sacramentos. Says he to Lord John, says he, 'Gimme the hand of this fair daughter of thine, and the treasure shall be yours,' says he."

"Ah, ha!" said Doc Tomlinson. "I shore thought that girl was mixed up in this somehow. But I didn't understand. Wonder if Dan Anderson told us everything he knew?"

"They set on the back seat," continued Willie, glancing importantly at the listeners to his romance, "a-lookin' into each other's eyes. And says the bold juke, to her, says he,

'Constance!' like that. 'Constance,' says he, 'I've loved you these many years agone.'"

"What did she say then?"

"I didn't ketch what she said. But by'm by the proud earl—"

"You said the bold juke."

"It's the same thing. The proud earl laughs, scornful of restraint, like earls always is, and says he agin, 'Lord John, the treasure shall be thine, but the proudest treasure of me life is this fair daughter of thine that sets here by me side, Lord John,' says he. From that I thought maybe the Lady Constance had said something I didn't ketch. Of course, I was busy drivin' the coach."

The men of Heart's Desire looked from one to the other. "Well, I'll be damned!" said Doc Tomlinson.

Curly chewed tobacco vigorously. "To me," he said, "it looks like Dan was throwed down. That girl was over to my house, too; and I didn't think that of her."

"Throwed down hard," affirmed Uncle Jim Brothers; "but now, hold on till we get all this straight. Maybe Dan wouldn't work for this outfit if he knew all that's goin' on. Seems to me like, one way or another, the girl's kind of up at auction. If she's part of the railroad's comin' into Heart's Desire, why, then, we want to know about it. I wish 't Dan Anderson was here,"

But Dan Anderson was not there, neither was he to be found at his *casita* across the *arroyo*. As fate would have it, he had caught Willie in his wanderings and had done some questioning on his own account. Willie escaped

Emerson Hough

alive, and presently left town. Whereafter Dan Anderson, half dazed, walked out into the foot-hills, seeking the court of old Carrizo, to try there his own case, as he had promised; and that of the woman as well.

At first his fairness, his fatal fairness, had its way with him. Resolutely he slurred over in his own mind the consequences to himself, and set himself to the old, old task of renunciation. Then, in his loneliness and bitterness, there came to him thoughts unworthy of him, conclusions unsupported by fair evidence.

Far up on the flank of Carrizo he sat and looked down upon the little straggling town in the valley below. These hills, he thought, with all their treasures, were to be sold and purchased for a price, for a treasure greater than all their worth,—the hand of the woman whom he loved. She had consented to the bargain. She had been true to the States, and not to Heart's Desire. She had been true to her class, and not to him, who had left her class. She had been true to her sex, and not to him, her unready lover. Ah, he had not deserved her remembrance; but still she ought to have remembered him! He had not been worthy of her, but still she ought to have loved him! He had offered her nothing, he had evaded her, shunned her, slighted her— but in spite of that she ought to have waited for him, and to have loved him through all, and believed in him in spite of all!

He sat, befooled and befuddled, arguing, accusing, denying, doubting, until he knew not where treachery began or faith had ended. It was late when he descended the mountain and walked dully down the street.

All this time Constance, in ignorance of everything except the absolute truth, sat in the meagre room of the little stone hotel. She wondered if there would ever be any change in her manner of life, if there would ever be anything but this continuous following of her father from one commercial battle into another. She wondered why Dan Anderson did not come. Surely he was here. Surely his business was with his employers; and more surely than all, and in spite of all, his place was here with her; because her heart cried out for him. In spite of all, he was her heart's desire. Why did he not come?

She arose, her hands clenched; she hated him, as much as she had longed for him.

CHAPTER XVIII

THE MEETING AT HEART'S DESIRE

How Benevolent Assimilation was checked by Unexpected Events

There are two problems in life, and only two: food and love. Civilization offers us no more, nor indeed does barbarism; for civilization and barbarism are not far apart. The great metropolis which sent its emissaries out to the little mountain hamlet never held within its teeming confines any greater or graver questions than those which were now to come before the town meeting of Heart's Desire.

Down at the stone hotel of Uncle Jim Brothers the tables had been cleared away to make room for this event, the first of its kind ever known in that valley. Heretofore there had been no covenant among these men, no law save that which lay in leather on each man's thigh. It was a land of the individual; and a sweeter land than that for a man was never known in all the world. Now these men were coming together to debate what we call a great question, but what is really a small question—that of an organization under the laws of what is denominated civilization; that compact which the world devised long ago, when first man's flocks and herds became of value, and against which the world has since then rebelled, and ever will rebel, until there is no longer any world remaining, nor any worth the name of man.

The long room, low and bare, was filled with silent, bearded men. Two or three smoky little lamps but served to emphasize the gloom. At the farther end, on chairs raised a few inches above the level of the floor, sat John Ellsworth and Porter Barkley. The latter was the first to address the meeting, and he made what might have been called an able effort.

Ignoring the fact that civilization had been summoned to the bar of Heart's Desire for trial, and assuming that barbarism was put upon its defensive, he pointed out to the men of Heart's Desire that they had long been living in a state of semi-savagery. To be sure, they had not yet had among them men of executive and organizing minds, but the fulness of years had now brought this latter privilege.

He paused, waiting a space for applause, but no applause came. He felt upon him scores of straight-forward eyes, unwavering, steady.

The town, in its new shape, he hurried on to explain, ought, of course, to wipe out and forget its past. Even the name, "Heart's Desire," was an absurd one, awkward, silly, meaning nothing. They had tremendous coal-fields directly at their doors. He suggested the name of Coalville as an eminently practical one for the reconstructed community. His suggestion brought out a stir, a shuffle, a sigh; but no more.

Mr. Barkley declared that there must be a fundamental revolution as to the old ideas of Heart's Desire. There had been no courts. There had been no government, no society. It was time that the old days of the mining camp and cow town were done, time that miner's law and no law at all should give way to the laws of the Territory, to the laws of the United States government, and to the greater law of industrial progress.

He additionally, and with a hardening of his voice, pointed out that, under the provisions of the laws of society and civilization, property belonged only to the man who held the legal title to it. The gentlemen representing this new railroad were the first to assume legal title to this town site; they had taken all necessary steps, and intended to hold this town site in the courts as their own. Their expenses would be very large, and they proposed to be repaid. They felt that their holdings in the valley would warrant them in going ahead rapidly with their plans of development. They had bought some few claims in the coal-fields, had filed on others for themselves, and had taken over other and abandoned claims on both sides of the valley. Their disposition was not to be hostile. They hoped, after the preliminary organization of the town government should have been completed, to have the unanimous ratification of all their actions. They felt most friendly, most friendly indeed, toward the hardy citizens of this remote community. They proposed to help them all they could. He felt it a distinguished privilege for himself to be the man to take the first steps for the organization of the new commercial metropolis of Coalville.

But it was distinctly to be understood by all that the gentlemen whom he represented did not propose to entertain, and would not tolerate, any interference with their plans. He begged, in conclusion, to present to them, with the request for a respectful and intelligent hearing, that able, that distinguished, that benevolent gentleman, well known in financial circles of the East, Mr. John Ellsworth of New York, who would now address them.

Barkley sat down, and, with customary gesture of the orator, passed his handkerchief across his brow. Then he gazed up, surprised. The applause was long in coming. He straightened in his chair. The applause did not come at all. The men of Heart's Desire sat hard and grim, each silent, each looking straight ahead, nor asking any counsel.

Ellsworth felt the chill which lay upon the audience, and understood its meaning. He stood before them, a rather portly figure, clean, ruddy, well clad, fully self-possessed, and now, by intent, conciliatory. With hands behind his back, he told a certain funny little story with which he had been wont to conquer, at least in social gatherings. No ripple came in response. The eyes of the men of Heart's Desire looked as intolerably keen and straight at him as they had at his predecessor. He could feel them plainly in the gloom beyond.

Unconsciously on the defensive now, he explained in detail the undeniable advantages which would accrue to Heart's Desire on the advent of this railroad and the carrying out of the plans that had been outlined. He did not deny that he considered the opinion of his counsel valid; that the valley was in effect open to settlement; that they had taken steps to put the first legal possession in their own names. Yet, he stated, although they had taken over a number of claims to which there seemed to be no legal title, they did not propose to interfere, if it could be avoided, with the holdings of any man then living in Heart's Desire. The re-survey of the town would naturally make some changes, but these should sit as lightly as possible upon those affected. Of course, the railroad company could condemn and confiscate, but it did not wish to confiscate. It desired to take the attitude of justice and fairness. The gentlemen should bear in mind that all these improvements ran into very considerable sums of money. A hundred miles of the railroad below them must pass over a barren plain, a cattle country and not an agricultural region, and hence offering relatively small support to a railroad enterprise. As yet, artesian water was unknown in that country, and might remain always a problem. No natural streams crossed that great dry table land which lay to the west, or the similar plateau to the east. All their hopes lay in this one valley and its resources, and while without doubt those resources were great, while the coal-fields upon the one side of the valley and the gold claims upon the other had been proved beyond a peradventure to be of value, the gentlemen should nevertheless remember that all this road building and mine developing cost money, a great deal of money. Of course, no capital could be invested except under the protection of a stable and adequate system of the law.

These gentlemen before him, Ellsworth said in conclusion, had chosen for their habitation one of the most delightful localities he had ever seen in all his travels. He congratulated them. He looked forward to seeing a prosperous city built up in this happy valley. The country was changing, and it must change, the line of the frontier passing steadily from the east to the west across the continent. They could not forever escape civilization. Indeed, it had now come to them. He hoped that they would receive it, and that they would receive him as their friend.

As he closed, Ellsworth found himself not dictating, but almost pleading. The stern gravity of his audience removed the edge of any arrogance he might have felt. He sat down and in turn passed his hand across his forehead, as perplexed as had been Barkley before him. Both grew uneasy. There was a shifting in the seats out in the half-lighted interior before them, but there came no sound of applause or comment. Ellsworth leaned over and whispered to his associate.

"There's something up," said he. "We haven't got them going. What's on their minds? Where's Anderson? He ought to be here. Get him, and let's nominate him for mayor, or something. This thing's going to split!"

"I'll go out and find him," whispered Barkley, and so slipped out of the room.

He did find him, aloof, alone, pacing slowly up and down the street, the one man needed by both divergent interests, and the one man absent. "Good God! Anderson," protested Barkley. "What are you doing out here by yourself? We need you in there. They're like bumps on a log. We can't get them started at all."

"That's funny," said Dan Anderson.

"Funny! I don't *think* it's very funny. You are the one supposed to understand these men, and we want you now to deliver the goods."

"If you will pardon me, sir," said Dan Anderson, facing him with his hands in his pockets, "I don't exactly like that expression."

"Like it or not," retorted Barkley, hotly. "You belong in there, and not out here in the moonlight studying over your maiden speech. What are you afraid of?"

"Of nothing," said Dan Anderson, simply. "Or, of nothing but myself."

"But we need another strong talk to stir them up."

"Go make it, then."

"What's that!" cried Barkley, sharply; "you'll not

come in."

"No, I'm done with it."

"Why, damn your soul! man, you don't mean to tell me that you've flunked—that you've gone back on us?"

Dan Anderson bit his lip, but continued silent.

"You've taken our money!" exclaimed Barkley. "We've hired you, bought you! We won't stand for any foolishness, and we won't put up with any treachery, I want you to understand that. Your place is in there, at the meeting —and here you are standing around as though you were mooning over some girl."

"I hadn't noticed the moonlight," said Dan Anderson. "As to the rest of it, the street of this town has usually been free for a man to think as he pleased."

"You're a traitor and a squealer!" cried Barkley.

"You're a damned cad!" retorted Dan Anderson, calmly. He stepped close to the other now, although his hands remained in his pockets. "I dislike to make these remarks to an oiled and curled Assyrian ass," he went on, smiling, "but under the circumstances, I do; and it goes."

Porter Barkley, dominant, arrogant, aggressive, for years accustomed to having his own way with men, felt a queer sensation now—a replica, fourfold intensified, of that he had experienced before the silent audience he had left within. He was afraid. Dan Anderson stepped still closer to him, his face lowered, his lips smiling, his eyes looking straight into his own.

"It's just what I said," began Barkley, desperately, "I

told Constance—"

The wonder was that Barkley lived, for the resort to weapons was the only remedy known in that land, and Dan Anderson knew the creed, as Barkley should have known it. His weapon leaped out in his hand as he drew back, his lean body bent in the curve of the fanged rattler about to strike. He did strike, but not with the point of flame. The heavy revolver came to a level, but the hooked finger did not press the trigger. Instead, the cylinder smote Porter Barkley full upon the temple, and he fell like a log. Dan Anderson checked himself, seeing the utter unconsciousness of the fallen man. For a moment he looked down upon him, then walked a few steps aside, standing as does the wild stag by its prostrate rival. The fierce heats of that land, still primitive, now flamed in his soul, gone swiftly and utterly savage. It was some moments before he thrust the heavy weapon back into its scabbard, and, turning, strode toward the door.

As he entered the crowded room he was recognized, and heard his name called again and again. The audience had wakened, was alive! Ellsworth, sitting, alone and anxious, looked up hopefully and beckoned Dan Anderson to his side. The latter seemed scarce to know him, as he walked to the end of the hall and, without preliminary, began to speak.

"Gentlemen," said he,—"boys—I am glad to answer you. I have twice been invited to speak at this meeting. Rather I should say that I am now invited by you. A moment ago I was commanded, ordered to speak, by a man who seemed to think he was my owner.

"He thought himself my owner by reason of this!" He drew from his pocket the roll of bills which had been untouched since he had received them at Sky Top. "Here's

Emerson Hough

my first fee as a lawyer. It's a thousand dollars. I wanted the money. My business is that of the law. I am open to employment. You ought not to blame me—you shall not blame me." He held the money in his hand above his head.

The silent audience looked at him gravely, with eyes level and straight, as it had regarded the speakers preceding him.

"But—" and here he stiffened—"I did not know I was asked to help steal this town, to help rob my friends. These men have proposed to take what was not theirs. They have wanted no methods but their own. They have not asked, but ordered. If this is their way, they'll have to get some other man."

The men of Heart's Desire still looked at him gravely, silently.

"Now," said Dan Anderson, "I've had my chance to choose, and I've chosen. The choice has cost me much, but that has been my personal cost, with which you have nothing to do. I am throwing away my chance, my future, but I do throw them away!"

As he spoke he flung at Mr. Ellsworth's feet the roll of bills. "Sir," said he, "it is the sense of this meeting that the railroad shall not come into Heart's Desire. Is it so?" he asked of the eyes and the darkness; and a deep murmur said that it was so.

Dan Anderson stepped down from the little platform out into the room. Hands were thrust out to him, but he seemed not to see them. He pushed on out, haggard; and presently the assemblage followed, breaking apart awkwardly, and leaving Ellsworth standing alone at the rear of the room.

Ellsworth was now wondering what had become of Barkley, and in his discomfiture was turning around in search, when he heard a voice behind him, and passing back encountered Barkley, staggering and bloody, as he entered through a side door of the building.

"Great God! man, what's the matter?" exclaimed Ellsworth. "What's happened to you?"

"That fellow struck me with a gun. Let me in! Let me get fixed for him! By God! I'll kill him."

"Kill whom? Who did it? Wait! Wait, now!" expostulated Ellsworth, following him toward his room; but Barkley still fumed and threatened. "That fellow Anderson—" Ellsworth caught.

The sound of their voices reached other ears. Constance came running from her own room, questioning.

"Barkley's been hurt," explained her father, motioning her away. "Some mistake. He and Anderson have had trouble over this railroad business, some way."

"By God! I'll kill him!" shrieked Barkley again, in spite of her presence, perhaps because of it. "Where can I get a gun?"

"You forget—my daughter—" began Ellsworth. But Constance avenged the discourtesy for herself.

"Never mind, papa," she said coldly. "Mr. Barkley, you look ridiculous. Go wash your face; and then, if you want a gun, go get one in the front room. The wall's full of them." A glint of scorn was in her eyes, which carried no mercy for the vanquished, nor any concern for the victor. She drew her father with her into her own room.

"By the Lord! girl," exclaimed he, "things have come out different from what we expected. I never thought—"

"No," said Constance, "you never thought. You didn't know." She spoke bitterly.

Ellsworth sank down in a chair, his hands in his pockets. "Well, we're whipped," said he. "The game's up. That fellow Anderson did us up, after all,—and look here, here's the money he threw back, almost in my face. They went with him like so many lambs. Confound it all, I don't more'n half believe I ever understood that fellow."

"No, you never did," said Constance, slowly. She was sitting upon the edge of the bed, gazing at her father quietly. "And so he threw away his chance?"

"Just what he did. Said it meant a lot for him to throw away his future, but he was going to do it."

"Did he say that?" asked the girl.

"Sure he said it! There's not going to be any railroad at Heart's Desire; and incidentally Mr. Daniel Anderson isn't going to be mayor, or division counsel with a salary of ten thousand dollars a year. Oh, well, to-morrow we'll pull out of here."

Constance was deliberate with her reply. "One thing, dad, is sure," said she; "when we go, you and I go together. Let Porter Barkley take the stage to-morrow if he likes. You and I'll go back by way of Sky Top; and we'll go alone."

Ellsworth pursed his lips into a whistle, many things

perplexing him. "He's lucky to get away at all," he remarked at length. "From what he said, it looks like there'd be more trouble."

"Trouble!" She flung out her hand in contempt. "There'll be no trouble if it waits for him to make it. If I know Porter Barkley, he'll know enough to stay right there in his room. If he does not—"

"By Jinks! Dolly," exclaimed her father, "you remind me all the time of your mother. I never could fool that woman; and no one ever could scare her!"

She looked at him without reply, and though he stroked her hair softly, he departed in discontent, his own head bowed in reflection.

Meanwhile, out in the long street of Heart's Desire, little groups of men gathered; but they held to the sides of the street, within the shelter of angles and doorways. In the centre of the street there paced slowly up and down, his hands behind his back and not fumbling his weapon, a tall figure, with head bent slightly forward as in thought, although with eyes keenly watching the door of the hotel. Uncle Jim Brothers himself had brought out word of Barkley's threatenings, and according to the only known creed there was but one issue possible. That issue was now awaited decently and in order. The street was free and fair. Let those concerned settle it for themselves. Incidentally, Heart's Desire was willing that its question should be settled at the same time. Here was its champion, waiting.

The watchers in the street grew restless, but nothing happened to interrupt their waiting. Upon the side of the house nearest them, lights shone from three windows. Presently one of these, that in the room of Constance

Ellsworth, was extinguished. A second window black-ened; Mr. Ellsworth had retired. The third light disapp-eared. Porter Barkley, not yet exactly of the proper drunkenness to find courage for his recently declared purpose, had concluded to go to sleep instead.

In the street Heart's Desire waited patiently, gazing at the darkened house, at the shaded door. Half an hour passed, an hour. Dan Anderson, without speech to any one, walked slowly up the street and across the *arroyo*. The light in his own casita flickered briefly and then vanished.

"I told you all along he was game!" said Curly, emerging from the corner of Whiteman's store and offering everybody a chew from his plug of tobacco. "They ain't runnin' him any, I reckon. Huh?"

"Shucks!" remarked Uncle Jim, disgustedly. "From the way that feller Barkley roared around, I shore thought he was a-goin' to tear up the earth. He's so yellow that in the mornin' I'm goin' to tell him to move on out of town. I've always kep' a respectable house before now, and I never did harbor a man who wouldn't shoot *some*!"

"In the mornin'," added Doc Tomlinson, as the group broke up, "I'm goin' to take Dan Anderson that saddle of mine that's layin' around in my store. Why, what does a man want of a *saddle* in a drug store? I just want to *give* the boy something."

CHAPTER XIX

COMMERCE AT HEART'S DESIRE

Showing Wonders of the Thirst of McGinnis, and the Faith of Whiteman the Jew

There was a barber at Heart's Desire, a patient though forgotten man, who had waited some years in the belief that eventually a patron would come into his shop in search of professional services. No one did come, but still the barber hoped. He was one of those who had clamored most loudly for Eastern Capital. After the town meeting the courage of the barber failed him. He declared himself as at length ready to abandon his faith in Heart's Desire, and to depart in search of a community offering conditions more encouraging. In this determination he was joined by Billy Hudgens of the Lone Star, a man also patient through long years of adversity, who now admitted that he might be obliged to close up and move to Arizona.

The news of these impending blows fell upon a community already gloomy and despondent. Some vague, intangible change had come over Heart's Desire. The illusion of the past was destroyed. Men rubbed their eyes, realizing that they had been asleep, that they had been dreaming. There dawned upon them the conviction that perhaps, after all, the old scheme of life had not been sufficient. The lotus plant was robbed of its potency.

It was at this time that McGinnis came to town. His advent was the most fortunate thing that could have happened. Certainly, it was hailed with joy and accepted as an omen; for, as was known of all men over a thousand miles of mining country in the Rockies, McGinnis was the image and emblem of good luck.

Not that this meant prosperity for McGinnis himself, for that gentleman continued in a very even condition as to worldly goods, being steadily and consistently broke,—a sad state of affairs for one who had brought so much happiness to others. History proved to the point of proverb that whenever McGinnis visited a camp,—and he had followed scores of strikes and stampedes in all the corners of the metalliferous world,—that camp was destined to witness a boom at no distant day.

McGinnis was not actually a newcomer at Heart's Desire, but upon the contrary one of the autochthones of that now decadent community. He was a friend and former bunk-mate of old Jack Wilson, discoverer of the Homestake mine. Five years ago, however, at the breaking of the Heart's Desire boom, he had silently stolen away, whether for Alaska or the Andes no one knew nor asked. Returning now as though from temporary absence, he punched an ancient and subdued burro into town, and unrolled his blankets behind Whiteman's corral, treating his return, as did every one else, entirely as a matter of course. Seeing these things, a renewed cheerfulness came to the lately despondent. Whiteman the Jew, ever a Greatheart, openly exulted, and voiced again his perennial confession of commercial faith in Heart's Desire.

"Keep your eye on Viteman," said he. "Der railroat may

go, der barber may go, der saloon may go, but not Viteman. My chudgment is like it vas eight years ago. Dis stock of goots is right vere I put it. If no one don't buy it, I keeps it. I know my pizness. Should I put in twenty thousand dollars' vort of goots, and make a mistake of der blace vere a town should be? I guess not! Viteman stays. By and by der railroat comes to Viteman. You vatch. Keep your eye on Viteman."

He stood in the door of his long log store building, squat, stocky, bristling, blue shirted like the rest, and cast his eye down counters and shelves piled with clothing and hats, boots and gloves, pick-axes, long-handled shovels, saddles, spurs, wagon bows, flour, bacon, and all manner of things which come in tin cans. Dust was over all; but above the dust was expectancy and not despair. The Goddess of Progress had her choicest temple in the frontier store.

"I toll you poys years ago," Whiteman went on, "you should blat der town. Ve blat it oursellufs now. Ve don't act like childrens no more. Ve meet again. Ve holt a election. Ve make Viteman gounty dreasurer. Dan Anderson should be mayor, and McGinney glerk. Ve make a town gouncil, and ve go to vork like ve should ought to did. Ve move Nogales City over here and make dis der gounty seat. Ve bedition for a new gounty—ve don't vant to belong to dot Becos River gow outfit. Ve make a town for oursellufs. Viteman didn't put in dis stock of goots for noddings. You vatch Viteman."

This speech turned the tide, coming as it did with the arrival of McGinnis. Billy Hudgens decided to wait for a few more days, although for the time he was out of business for lack of liquids. It was fortunate that McGinnis did not know this latter fact.

The capital of McGinnis, aside from his freckles and his thirst, was somewhat limited. His blankets were thin and ragged, his pistol minus the most important portion of a revolver—to wit, the cylinder—and withal so rusted that even had it boasted all the component parts of a six-shooter, it could not have been fired by any human agency. He had a shovel, a skillet, and a quart tin cup. He had likewise a steel-headed and long-handled hammer, in good condition; this being, indeed, the only item of his outfit which seemed normal and in perfect repair. McGinnis was a skilled mechanic and a millwright and could use a hammer as could but few other men.

On the morning after his arrival McGinnis rolled early out of his blankets, ate his breakfast of flapjacks and water, and put his hammer in his hip pocket, where some men put a gun who do not know how to carry a gun. McGinnis spoke to no one in particular, but headed up into the mouth of the curving valley where stood the silent works of the New Jersey Gold Mills Company. He was not cast down because he found no one whom he could ask for work. He whistled as he walked through the open and barn-like building, looking about him with the eye of a man who had seen gold mills before that time.

"They've got their plates fixed at a lovely angle!" said he; "and there's about enough mercury on 'em to make calomel for a sick cat. There's been *talent* in this mill, me boy!"

He crawled up the ore chute into the bin, and cast a critical gaze upon the rock heaped up close to the crusher. Then he examined the battery of stamps with silent awe. "This," said McGinnis, softly to himself, "is the end of the whole and intire earth! Is it a confectionery shop they've got, I wonder? They do well to mash sugar with them lemon squeezers, to say nothing of the Homestake refractories."

He passed on about the mill in his tour of inspection, still whistling and still critical, until he came to the patent labor-saving ore crusher, which some inventor had sold to the former manager of the New Jersey Gold Mills Company, along with other things. McGinnis drifted to this instinctively, as does the born mechanician, to the gist of any problem in mechanics.

"Take shame to ye fer this, me man, whoivver ye were," said McGinnis, and the blood shot up under his freckles in indignation. "This is so bad it's not only unmechanical and unprofissional—it's absolutely unsportsmanlike!"

His ardor overcame him, and, hammer in hand, he swung down into the ore bin underneath the crusher. "Here's where it is," said he to himself. "With the jaw screwed that tight, how cud ye hope to handle this stuff— especially since the intilligent and discriminatin' mine-boss was sendin' down quartz that's more'n half porphyry! Yer little donkey injin, and yer little sugar mashers, and yer little lemon squeezer of a crusher—yah! It's a grocery store ye've got, and not a stamp mill. Loose off yer nut on the lower jaw, man; loose her off!"

McGinnis was a man of action. In a moment he was tapping at the clenched bolt with the head of his bright steel hammer. Slowly at first, and sullenly, for it had long been used to treatment that McGinnis called "unsports-manlike"; then gently and kindly as it felt the hand of the master, the head of the bolt began to turn, until at length the workman was satisfied. Then he turned also the corresponding nut on the opposite face of the jaw, swung the great steel jaw back to the place where he fancied it, and made all fast again. "She's but a rat-trap," said he to himself, "but it's only fair to give the rat-trap its show."

McGinnis went out and sat down upon a pile of ore. It was a bright and cloudless morning, such as may be seen nowhere in the world but in Heart's Desire. The Patos Mountains, across the valley, seemed so close that one might lay his hand upon them. The sun was bright and unwinking, and all the air so golden sweet that McGinnis pushed back his hat and gloried simply that he was alive. He did not even note the cottontail that came out from behind a bush to peer at him, nor mark the sweeping shadow of a passing eagle that swung high above the little valley. His eye now and again fell upon the abandoned mill, gaunt, idle and silent; yet he regarded it lazily, the spell of the spot and the languor of the air filling all his soul.

But at last the sun grew more ardent, and McGinnis, knowing the secret of the dry Southwest, sought shade in order that he might be cool. He rose and strolled again into the mill, looking about him as before, idly and critically. "Av ye was all me own, it's quite a coffee mill I cud make of ye, me dear," said he, familiarly. And at this moment a thought seemed to strike him.

"It has always been me dream to be a captain of industhry," soliloquized McGinnis. "I've always longed to hear the busy hum of me own wheels, and to feel that I was the employer and not merely the employeed." He mused for a few moments, too lazy to think far at one flight.

"It wud be nice," he resumed later, "to see the smoke of your own facthory ascendin' to the sky, and to feel that yerself 'uz the whole affair, cook and captain bold, ore shoveller, head ingineer, amalgamator and main squeeze."

"All capital," continued McGinnis, "is too much depindent upon labor. The only real solution—" he paused to feel his pockets for a match—"the only real solution is to be *both* capital and labor. Then, av ye've anny kick, take it to yourself, and settle it fair fer both!" He paused again, and again the light of his idea showed upon his countenance. "This," said McGinnis, "is Accajyun!"

He wandered over to the little boiler which drove the engine, and took inventory of the pile of crooked pinon wood that lay heaped up near by. He sounded the tank on top of the engine house, and found that it was half full. Then, calmly and methodically, he took off his coat, folded it, and laid it across a bench. He picked up a piece of board, whittled a little pile of shavings, thrust them into the ashy grate, and piled some wood above them. Then he scraped a match, and turning a cock or so to satisfy himself that the boiler would not go out through the roof in case he did get up steam, sat down to await developments. "She'll steam for sure," he ruminated. "She'll steam as much as wud do for a peanut wagon, av ye give her time."

Before the morning was gone the little boiler began to thump and churn and threaten. McGinnis ran the belt on to the stamp shaft. He went up and connected the crusher and shovelled a few barrows of ore into the hopper. Not long afterwards there was a dull and creaking rumble. The shaft of the stamps turned half around, slipped and stopped with a rusty squeak. Then came further creaks, groans, and rumbles. McGinnis walked calmly from place to place, tightening, loosening, shaking, testing, shovelling, and watching.

"It's wonderful," said he to himself, softly. "It's just wonderful what human bein's can do! If I, hadn't ever seen this mill, I wuddn't have believed it! But I'll say at this point meself, that I'm not looking a gift mill in the mouth. Moreover, this runnin' of your own mill, not bein' beholden to any sordid capitalist, nor yet depindent on anny inefficient labor, is what I may call a truly ijeel situation in life. I'll stay here till the wood runs out. Not that I'll cut wood for annybody. Capital must draw the line somewhere!"

No one noticed the smoke from the abandoned gold mill. McGinnis ran it by himself and undisturbed until his woodpile waned. Then he disconnected, blew off, and set to work to scrape his plates, whereon to his experienced eye there now appeared a gratifying roughness in the coating. He got off a lump of amalgam as big as his fist, and was content. "It's ojus there's no retort here," said he, "but like enough I'll find some way to vollituize this mercury."

He crossed the *arroyo*, and went to the cabin which had once been the office of the assayer. The latter was now an *emigre*, but he had left his crucibles and his furnace behind him; because it is not convenient to carry such things when one is afoot. McGinnis found a retort, adjusted it, set it going, volatilized the mercury from his amalgam, and in time had his button of dirty but quite valid gold. It lay heavy in his hand and rested heavy in his pocket. "As a captain of industhry," said he, "I must see what I can do for poor sufferin' humanity." He chuckled, and passed out into the street.

"As capital," said McGinnis to himself, walking on in the moonlight, "I am entitled to the first drink meself, and after that to one or two as a laborer. Then, if there's anny left, after treatin' all round, I'll buy the town a public liberry, pervidin' the town'll make it sufficiently and generally understood that I'm a leadin' and public-minded citizen that has reached success by the grace of God and a extraordinary brain."

But McGinnis in his philanthropic intentions met difficulty. He wandered into the Lone Star, and placing his crude bullion upon the counter, swept about him a comprehensive hand. To his wonder there was no response. A few of the assembled populace shifted uneasily in their seats, but none arose. "Do you take this for a low-down placer camp?" asked Billy Hudgens, with a dull show of pride, when McGinnis demanded the gold scales.

"No," said McGinnis, "it's a quartz camp right enough, and all it needs is developin'. At this speakin', I'm capital and labor both, and crew of the *Nancy Brig*. What's the matter?"

A sigh escaped from the audience, as Billy Hudgens made reply. "Not a drop," said he; "all gone. Nothing till Tom Osby gets back from Vegas, and maybe not then. I owe Gross & Blackwell over two hundred now."

McGinnis's voice dropped into a low, intent whisper. "Do you mean to tell me that?" he said. "Me, with my thirst?" He laid a hand on Billy's shoulder. "Friend," said he, "I've walked two hundred miles. I've developed your place. I'm in a position to give this town a public liberry worth maybe forty dollars. Now, do you mean to say to me—do you mean—" He gulped, unable to proceed. Hudgens nodded. McGinnis let fall his hand from the counter, turned and silently left the place.

He moved up the street to the adobe where the barber had his shop. The barber was gloomily sitting inside, waiting. McGinnis entered, and looked about him with the ease of one revisiting familiar scenes.

In a case upon the wall were rows of shaving mugs, now

dusty and abandoned, mute witnesses of a former era of glory. Indeed, they remained an historical record of earlier life in Heart's Desire.

Once there had been rivalry between McGinnis and Tom Redmond for the affections of a widow who kept a boarding-house in Heart's Desire, the same long since departed. There came by express one day, addressed to Tom Redmond, a shaving mug of great beauty and considerable size, whereon the name of Tom Redmond, handsomely emblazoned, led all the rest. The fame of this work of art so spread abroad that Tom Redmond, as befitted one who had attained social distinction, became the recipient of increased smiles from the widow aforesaid. McGinnis bided his time. Thirty days later, there arrived by stage for him a shaving mug of such stature and such exceeding art as cast that of Tom Redmond completely in the shade! Thenceforth the widow smiled upon McGinnis. Tom Redmond, unable to endure this humiliation, and in the limitation of things wholly unable to raise the McGinnis ante in shaving mugs, was obliged to leave the town. McGinnis hung upon the handle of the Redmond mug a goodly card bearing the legend, "Gone, but not forgotten." Shortly after that McGinnis himself left town. Alas! at the instance of the widow the barber hung upon the McGinnis mug a similar card; it having appeared that McGinnis had emigrated without paying either his board bill or his barber's bill.

This evidence of his early delinquency now confronted McGinnis as he stepped into the shop for the first time in these years. He regarded it with displeasure. "Take it off," said he to the barber, sternly. "I paid the widdy in Butte, two years ago. As for yourself, I have come six hundred miles to pay my bill to you. Take it out of that." He presented his heavy button of gold.

The barber protested that he could not make change on this basis, but cheerfully extended the credit. He was glad to see McGinnis back again, for he was most promisingly hairy.

"I am back, but I'll not be stayin' long," said McGinnis. "Have ye annything to drink?"

The barber mournfully shook his head, even as had Billy Hudgens. McGinnis, refusing to believe such heavy news, walked up to the mantle, picked up a tall bottle labelled "Hair tonic," smelled of it, and without asking leave, raised it to his lips and drained it to the bottom.

"For industhrial purposes, friend," said he. In twenty minutes he was lying in a deep and dreamless sleep.

"In some ways this fellow has talent," said Billy Hudgens, as he looked in on McGinnis later; "but like enough he's come to a show-down now."

Until noon the next day McGinnis slept soundly. Then he sat up on the floor. "How're you feelin' now, man?" asked Billy Hudgens.

"Friend," said McGinnis, "I'm feelin' some dark and hairy inwardly; but I'm a livin' example of how a man can thriumph over circumstances." Wherewith he smiled gently, sank back, and slept again till dark.

"It wud have been too bad," said McGinnis to the barber when he awoke, "if you had left this town before I came. What ye've all been needin' is some one to give ye a lesson in not gettin' discouraged.

"As for combinin' hair tonic and strong drink into one ingradyint, if anny one tells you it's a good thing, you may say for me the report lacks confirmashun. But we'll not despair. Aside from the proverb about the will and the way, 'tis well known that no disgrace can come to a real captain of industhry through a timporary change in the industhrial conditions. I'm sayin' to you, get in a new chair, and get ready for the boom."

CHAPTER XX

MEDICINE AT HEART'S DESIRE

How the Girl from the States kept the Set of Twins from being broken

Even as the stouter-hearted captains of Heart's Desire began to voice their confidence, a sudden sense of helplessness, of personal inadequacy, came upon Porter Barkley, erstwhile leader of the forces of the A. P. and S. E. Railway Company. With emotions of chagrin and humiliation he found himself obliged wholly to readjust his estimate of himself and his powers. He had come hither full of confidence, accustomed to success, animated by a genial condescension toward these benighted men; and now, how quickly had the situation been reversed! Nay, worse than reversed. He, Porter Barkley, a man who had bought a legislature in his time, was ignored, forgotten by these strangers, as though he did not exist! More than that, Ellsworth was reticent with him; and worst of all, when he met Constance at the table she gave him no more than a curt nod and a polite forgetfulness of his presence.

Porter Barkley wished nothing so much as speedily to get away from the scene of his twofold defeat, although he knew that farewell meant dismissal. He knew also that he could restore himself to the respect of Heart's Desire in only one way; but he did not go out on the street in search of that way, although the Socorro stage was a full day late in its departure, and he was obliged to remain a prisoner indoors.

Indeed, Constance and her father were little better than prisoners as well, for no possible means of locomotion offered whereby they could get out of town; and all Heart's Desire remained aloof from them, not even the Littlest Girl coming across the *arroyo* to call on Constance at the hotel.

"I'd like to have her come over to see the twins," said Curly to his spouse, "but I reckon like enough she's sore."

"I'd be mighty glad to have a good square talk with some woman from the States," rejoined the Littlest Girl, hesitatingly. "I'd sort of like to know what folks is wearin' back there now. Besides that—"

"Besides what?"

"I don't more'n half believe her and Dan Anderson is gettin' along very well, someway."

"That so? Well, I don't see how they can, the way he throwed the spurs into her pa the other night."

"He just worships the ground that girl walks on."

"You oughtn't to talk so much. That ain't our business— but how do you know?"

"Well, because I *do* know," responded the Littlest Girl, warmly. "Don't you suppose I can see? I've talked with Dan every time he come up here to buy a pie—talked about that girl. He buys more pies now than he used to. I reckon I *know*."

"That may all be. Question is, how's she a-feelin' toward *him* these days?"

"Curly," after a little silence, "I'm going to put on my bonnet and go over there and see that girl. She's all alone. I'll take her a pie. I always did think she was nice."

"Well, all right. There's Bill Godfrey drivin' the stage out of his barn now. I'll go over to the post-office and help the old man with the mail. May ride out as far as the ranch with Bill and see if Mac has anything special to do. There was talk of that Nogal sheep outfit gettin' in on the lower end of our range. If they do, something'll pop for sure. You go on over to the hotel if you want to. Ma'll take care of the twins."

The departure of the stage for Socorro occurred once a week or so, if all went well, and the event was always one of importance. Even Mr. Ellsworth and Constance found themselves joining the groups which wandered now toward the post-office, next door to Whiteman's store, in front of which Bill Godfrey regularly made his first stop preparatory to leaving town. As they two passed up the street from the hotel, they missed the Littlest Girl, who crossed the *arroyo* above them by a quarter of a mile; Heart's Desire being, in view of its population, a city of magnificent distances.

The man from Leavenworth, postmaster, had nearly finished the solemn performance of locking up the emaciated mail-bag for Socorro, and Bill Godfrey was looking intently at his watch—which had not gone for six months—when all at once the assemblage in and around the post-office was startled by shrieks, screams, and calls of the most alarming nature. These rapidly approached from the direction of the *arroyo*, beyond which lay the residence portion of Heart's Desire. Presently there was to be distinguished the voice of a woman, raised in terrified lamentations, accompanied with the broken screams of a child in evident distress. There appeared, hastening toward the group in front of the store, Curly's mother-in-law, wife of the postmaster of Heart's Desire, and guardian as well of the twins of Heart's Desire. It was one of these twins, Arabella, whom she now hurried along with her, at such speed that the child's feet scarce touched the ground. When this latter did happen, Arabella seemed synchronously to catch her breath, becoming thus able to emit one more spasmodic wail. There was pain and fright in the cries, and the whole attitude of the woman from Kansas was such that all knew some tragedy had occurred or was impending.

"Good Lord!" cried Curly, "I'll bet a thousand dollars the kid's got my strychnine bottle this time! I left it in the window. There was enough to poison a thousand coyotes!"

He sprang forward to catch the other arm of the sobbing child. The man from Kansas, postmaster of Heart's Desire, hastened to join his wife in the street, wagging his gray beard in wild queries. In half a moment all the population was massed in front of Whiteman's store, incoherent, frightened, utterly helpless.

"She's dyin'!" cried the woman from Kansas. "Poison! Oh, Willyam, what shall we do?" But the postmaster was unable to offer any aid or counsel.

"I just left it there in the window," explained Curly, excitedly; "I was goin' to put out some baits around a water hole, about to-morrow."

"Oh, it's awful!" sobbed the woman from Kansas. "What shall we do? What shall we do?"

"Doc," said Curly to Doc Tomlinson, "you run the drug store—ain't you got no anecdote for this?" Doc Tomlinson could only shake his head mournfully. A ring of bearded, beweaponed men gathered about the little sufferer, hopeless, at their wits' end.

Constance and her father, hurrying to learn the cause of the commotion, received but incoherent answers to their questions. "Good Lord! girl, that child's hurt!" cried Ellsworth, helpless as the others. "What'll we do?"

Constance did not even reply to him. Without his assistance, indeed without looking to right or left, she made straight through the circle of men, who gave way to admit her.

"What's the trouble here? What's wrong?" she demanded sharply, catching the weeping woman by the arm, even as she reached out a hand toward the suffering Arabella.

"Poison!" wailed the woman from Kansas again. "She's goin' to die! There ain't no way to help it."

"What poison—what has the child taken?" asked Constance.

"It was strychnine, ma'am, like enough," ventured Curly. "There was some—"

"Nonsense! It's not strychnine," cried the girl. In an instant her eye had caught what every other individual present had overlooked, although it was certainly the most obvious object in all the landscape,—the half-empty can which still remained tightly clutched in Arabella's free hand.

"Why, here it is!" she exclaimed. "The child has eaten concentrated lye. Quick! Get her in somewhere. What are you standing around here for—get out of the way, you men!"

They scattered, and Constance glanced about her. "Where's some grease—some lard? Quick!" she called out to Whiteman, who was looking on.

"In here, lady—dis vay," he answered eagerly; but she outfooted him to the rear of the store, carrying Arabella in her arms. Spying a lard tin, she thrust off the cover, and plunged in a hand. Immediately the sobs of Arabella changed to sputterings, for the physician in charge had covered her face, lips, and a goodly portion of the interior of her mouth and throat with the ameliorating unguent! At this act of first aid, the wails of the woman from Kansas ceased also, and a vast sigh of relief arose from the confederated helplessness of Heart's Desire.

"Is she going to die?" gasped the woman from Kansas.

"No," said Constance, scornfully. "I've seen much worse burns. The lye has perhaps lost a little of its strength, too. The burns are all well in the front of the mouth and tongue, and I don't think she swallowed any of it. Lard is as good as anything to stop the burn. Why didn't you think of it?"

"I don't know, ma'am," confessed the woman from Kansas.

A sudden loquacity now seized upon all those recently perturbed and silent.

"Now," said Curly, "it's this-a-way; the women they must have left that can of lye settin' around. It's mighty careless of 'em. I *needed* my strychnine, but there ain't no *sense* in leavin' lye settin' around. Them twins was due to eat it, shore. Why, they was *broke* to eat anything that comes in tin cans!"

Constance gathered Arabella in her arms. The tailored gown was ruined now. One hand remained gloved, but both were grease-laden to the wrists. She was unconscious of all this. Her gaze, frowning, solicitous, maternal, bent itself upon the face of her patient. The men of Heart's Desire looked on, silent, relieved, adoring. A few began to edge toward the open air.

"You ain't no kind of a drug-store man," said the postmaster, scornfully, to Tomlinson.

"Why ain't I?" retorted the latter, hotly. "What *chance* does a merchant get in this town? What do I get for carrying a full line of drugs here for years? Now, *lard* ain't drugs. It ain't in the pharmacopy."

"I don't know but it's a good thing for that kid," said Curly. "She ought to be plumb soft-spoken all her life, after all that lard in her frontispiece. But it won't do 'em no good,—they'll eat my strychnine next. This here stage-coach—with her along," jerking his thumb towards the physician in charge, "won't be any more'n out of sight before that twin corporation will be fryin' dynamite on the kitchen stove. I shore thought that set of twins was busted this time for keeps. Unless there's two of 'em, twins ain't no good!"

"Ma'am, your dress is just ruined," said the woman from Kansas; "you are lard clean from head to foot!"

"I know it," cried Constance, gayly, the color coming to her cheeks; "but never mind, the baby's all right now."

"Well, you've got to come over to our house and get fixed up. Was you goin' out on the stage? You stay here for a day or so and watch that child; we'd like it mighty well if you would."

It was a flag of truce from Heart's Desire. Nevertheless, Constance seemed to hesitate. Ah! wily Constance. A great many things might happen which had not yet happened, but which ought to happen. And in all that group Dan Anderson was nowhere to be seen. Perhaps after a time he might come!

Constance hesitated just long enough. The dignity of Bill Godfrey had to be sustained. His stagecoach had not started on the appointed and stipulated time any day these many months; yet for that stage, ready equipped for its journey, to stand waiting idly upon the convenience of any mortal after the "mails" had been brought out from the post-office and placed safely in the boot, was mortal affront to any stage-driver's reputation. Bill Godfrey again looked solemnly at his watch and gathered up the reins. "All aboard!" he cried. "Git up!" and so swung a wide circle and headed down the street to the hotel. Presently he departed. He carried a solitary passenger. Constance and her father were still prisoners, or guests, in Heart's Desire for an indefinite time! And in an indefinite time many things may occur.

In his house across the *arroyo* Dan Anderson endured the silence and loneliness as long as he could, turning over and over again in his mind the old questions to which he had found no answer. Most of all, one question was insistent. Had he been just to her, to Constance, in allowing himself to accept her alleged conduct as a motive for his own actual conduct? He had taken for granted much—all—and upon what manner of testimony? The babblings of a half-witted herder! He had asked the men of Heart's Desire to hear both sides of his own case. The men of Heart's Desire had heard both sides of the railroad's case. But he had condemned without trial the woman whom he loved—her—Constance! It was impossible, unbelievable of any man.

When the horror of this thought broke upon him fully, Dan Anderson sprang up, caught his hat, and started fast as he might for the hotel. He crossed the *arroyo* below the post-office, and so did not know, at the time, of the peril and rescue of Arabella. Nor did he know that all of Heart's Desire was penitent regarding her and her father; nor that both were to remain for yet a little time.

Dan Anderson approached the stone hotel in time to watch the stage depart, himself unobserved. Then he stepped farther toward the hotel door. He met the Littlest Girl just emerging from the building, whither she had gone upon the same errand as his own.

"She ain't here, Mr. Anderson," explained the Littlest Girl; "her and her pa has just went to the post-office."

He looked at her silently. "Oh, I know who you come to see," asserted the Littlest Girl, "and I don't blame you. It's *time* you did, too."

Without a word he turned and walked with her up the street, there to miss Constance by three moments, which, potentially, might have been a life-time.

CHAPTER XXI

JUSTICE AT HEART'S DESIRE

The Story of a Sheriff and Some Bad Men; showing also a Day's Work, and a Man's Medicine

"Dad, you've been drinking!" burst out Constance as her father met her at the door of Curly's house. She had heard footsteps, and hastened to meet the visitor. Perhaps it was disappointment, perhaps indignation with herself that she had listened, that she had waited, which caused her to greet her parent with such asperity.

"You wrong me, daughter!" protested Mr. Ellsworth, solemnly; "only took one or two little ones, to celebrate the saving of the twin. You've made a great hit with those people over there. They'd all celebrate, if there was anything to drink. I had to stock the Lone Star myself out of my valise. They won't have anything in till Tom Osby comes.

"I say," he resumed, taking his daughter's arm with genial gallantry as they stepped out into the sunlight together, "these people are not so bad. They're warming up right along now. If you and I could stay here awhile, we'd get along with 'em all right—better understanding all around."

Her face brightened. "Then you don't give up the railroad?"

"No; by no means. I never give up a thing I want. Besides, I wouldn't mind coming here to live for a while. The climate's glorious."

"You live here? You'd look well in a wide hat and a blue shirt, wouldn't you, dad?"

"More irreverence! Of course I'd look well. And it's worth something to eat the way I do here. I'm getting better every day. Why, they tell me no one has died out here in a hundred years. A man can eat anything from cactus to sole leather, and keep hearty. I saw a lot of fellows over there just now, sitting flat on the ground in the sun out in the middle of the street, eating dried beef and canned tomatoes, and they looked so happy that I sat down and took a bite with them. They are just travelling through,— sheriff's party from somewhere, going somewhere after somebody."

"What's that, Mr. Ellsworth?" the woman from Kansas came out and inquired; for she knew better than he what that meant. "Sheriff? Was he a tall, slim man, longish mustache, sorter thin?"

Ellsworth nodded; the woman wiped her hands on her blue-checked apron. Constance glanced at her serious face, and wondered.

"Then it's Ben Stillson," the woman from Kansas said, "the sheriff of Blanco. He's after somebody. Did he summons any of our men along?"

"I don't know, madam," answered Ellsworth. The woman said no more; she only watched and listened.

It was this posse, headed by the sheriff of Blanco, that Dan Anderson and the Littlest Girl saw when they reached a point midway between Uncle Jim Brothers's hotel and the post-office. The little group of riders, dusty and travel-stained, had come at a steady trot down the street. Stillson, tall, grim-featured, and bronzed, looked neither to the right nor to the left. He stopped, and ordered his men to dismount and eat. They swung out of their saddles without a word, loosening the cinches to breathe their horses. The men of Heart's Desire began to gather around them.

"What's up, Ben?" asked McKinney, the one most apt to be concerned; for cow men had borne the brunt of outlawry in that land for more than a generation. "Has Chacon come across from Arizona, or has the Kid broke out again?"

The sheriff looked at him gravely. "The Kid's out," said he. "We had him and two others at Seven Rivers, but he broke out four days ago. He killed the jailer and a couple of Mexicans farther up the river. There's four in his bunch now, and we've trailed them this far. They're likely headed for Sumner. We dropped in here, across the Patos, to get a couple of men or so. How are you fixed here?"

"Wait till I get a Winchester," said McKinney, briefly, and started down the street.

"Whiteman," Doc Tomlinson volunteered, "you 'tend to my drug store while I'm away, and if anybody wants any drugs, you go get 'em."

"You all hold on a minute," said Curly, hurrying forward, "while I run over home and git saddled up." He did not see the Littlest Girl approaching, but the sheriff did.

"Never mind, Curly," said the sheriff, quietly, pointing to her. "I want one more man, a single man."

"You, Curly!" interrupted his spouse, "you stay right where you are. You get some one else, Mr. Stillson. He's got a family, and besides, he's *such* a fool."

Curly flushed. "Was it *my* fault I got married?" he began hotly. "And them twins, was they mine, real? Now look here—" But the sheriff shook his head. He looked at Dan Anderson inquiringly.

"Certainly I'll go," said he. "Wait till I get fixed."

"That's as many as I'll need," said Stillson. "Hurry up, all of you."

Dan Anderson hastened across the *arroyo* to his house, first asking Curly to get him a horse. Curly departed to his own home with the Littlest Girl; so that Constance presently got fuller news of the arrival of the sheriff's party, and learned also that Dan Anderson was to join them.

"But, Curly," cried Constance, "isn't it dangerous? Won't some one get hurt?" She winced. The steady flame of her own brave heart flickered at this new terror.

"*Kin savvy?*" grinned Curly. "The Kid's gang shore'll fight. A good many fellers has got hurt goin' after him. But what you goin' to do? Let 'em steal all the cows they want, and kill everybody they feel like?"

"That's work for the officers," insisted Constance.

"There ain't no police out here," Curly replied, "and not sherfs enough to go around; so a feller sorter has to go when he's asked. They won't let me, because I got twins—though they ain't mine. But, now, I've got to take this here horse over to Dan Anderson." He mounted and rode away.

It was Dan Anderson himself who presently came at a gallop across the *arroyo*. A heavy revolver swung at his hip, a rifle rested in the scabbard under his leg, and a coat was rolled behind his saddle, plainsman fashion. Constance noted these details, but passed them in her eagerness and pleasure that he should come at least to say good-by. Something of the joy faded from her eyes as he approached. She had seen his face wear this same expression before,—fierce, eager, forgetful of all but a purpose.

He did not smile. He stooped from his saddle and grasped her hand. He looked squarely into her eyes, but said no word of salutation or farewell. He did not look back, as upon the instant, he whirled and galloped away! For her there were to be yet more days of waiting; for him the relief of action and of danger.

That afternoon Tom Osby drove into town from the northern trail. Mr. Ellsworth welcomed him and his rude vehicle as the first feasible means of getting back to Sky Top. By noon of the following day they were well upon their way, leaving behind them problems enough unsolved, and breaking touch with pending events which might cut short all problems for at least one loyal heart. It was a sad and silent Constance who looked back and said good-by to the rambling street of Heart's Desire, lying in the sun empty, empty!

As for the sheriff of Blanco and his men, they trotted on steadily toward the northeast, hour after hour. They crossed the Patos divide, and a few miles beyond took up the trail of their quarry, at the point where Stillson had earlier left it. This they followed rapidly, crossing wide plains of sage brush and cactus throughout the day. They slept in their saddle-blankets that night, and were up and off again by dawn for the second day of steady travel. There were seven men in the posse, three besides Stillson from the Seven Rivers country, employees of the cow men on the Pecos,—slim, brown, thin-featured fellows, who talked little either in the saddle or at the bivouac fire by night.

The second night out they spent by a water hole in the desert; and on the morning of the third day they ran into their game, earlier than they had expected. The sheriff, riding in advance, suddenly pulled up at the crest of a low ridge which they were ascending, and came back motioning to his men to remain under cover.

"That's the Pinos Altos ranch house just ahead," he explained, "and there's smoke coming out of it. Old Frazee's friendly enough with the Kid, and more'n likely the bunch has stopped in there to get something to eat. Hold on a little till I have a look." He took a pair of field-glasses from his saddle, and crawling to the top of the ridge lay examining the situation.

"It's them, all right," he said when he returned. "I know some of the horses. It's the Kid and about three others. They are all saddled up—probably stopped in to cook a meal. We'll get 'em sure. Now, all of you hitch back here, and crawl around to the *arroyo* below, there. That'll put us within a hundred yards or so of the house."

Each man, dismounting, hitched his horse, then quietly ran over the cylinder of his revolver, blew the dust out of the rear sight of his Winchester, tested the magazine, and cleared the breech action. This done, each crept to the place assigned to him. Dan Anderson found himself moving mechanically, dully, with a strange absence of excitement. He almost felt himself looker-on at what other men were doing.

For some time Stillson lay behind a little bush at the edge of the gully, peering critically at the house, from which came nothing to indicate that their approach had been discovered. At length, without a word, he slowly raised his short-barrelled rifle and fired. One of the horses hitched to the beam above the door stumbled forward and sank across the opening, blocking it. The bullet had caught it at the butt of the ear, and it fell stone dead, its neck bent up by the shortened rein.

In response, without a word of parley, a thin cloud of smoke gushed out of the only window facing the attack. Puffs of sand arose along the front of the *arroyo*, searching out each little bush top which might possibly offer cover. Stillson heard a smothered spat and a short sound, and turned his head quickly. He saw Jim Harbin, one of the boys from the lower range, turn over with a sigh, and lie with arms spread out. He had been shot straight through the neck. Dan Anderson, the man nearest to him, drew him back. He would have raised the head of the wounded man, but the choking warned him. Harbin lay out on his back, looking up, his breath gurgling in his throat. "No use," he whispered thickly. "Leave me alone. I've got to take my medicine." In ten minutes he was dead.

The day's work went on. The sheriff fired three or four more deliberate shots, but finally turned around. At each shot, the other horse tied to the beam sprang back.

"Can't you hit it?" grinned McKinney.

"I don't want to kill the horse," said Stillson; "I know that horse, and it's a good one. I want to turn it loose. Here you, Anderson, can you see that rope from where you are? Shoot it off, if you can, close up to the beam."

Dan Anderson, in spite of Stillson's hasty warning to keep down, rose at full height at the edge of the cover, and took a deliberate off-hand shot. They saw him whirl half around, and look down at his left arm; but as he dropped lower, he rested his rifle on a bit of sage brush, and fired once more. With a snort the horse, which had been pulling back wildly on its lariat, now broke free and went off, saddled as it was.

"Good shot!" commented the sheriff. "That'll about put 'em on foot. What, did they get you?"

Dan Anderson drew back from the crest and rolled up his shirt-sleeve above an arm now wet with blood. A bullet had cut through the upper arm above the elbow.

"Serves you mighty near right," called McKinney to him, "standing up, like a blamed fool! You suppose them fellers can't shoot, same as us?"

Doc Tomlinson crawled over to him and examined the hurt. "It's all right," said he. "Bone ain't touched. Let me tie her up."

A half hour passed without further firing. Stillson edged around to the point nearest the house. "Here you, Kid," he called out. "Come on out. We've got you on foot, and you might as well give up."

A dirty rag was thrust out of a window at the end of a rifle-barrel. "That you, Ben?" called a muffled voice from the adobe.

"You know it is, Kid. Drop it, and come on out. We've got

you sure."

The day's work was over. Dan Anderson remembered afterward how matter of fact and methodical it all had seemed. A few moments later a short, dirty young man appeared at the door, crawling over the prostrate horse. He held up his hands, grinning. He was followed by two others, both chewing tobacco calmly. The sheriff ordered down his men to meet them. McKinney unbuckled the belts. The captives seated themselves a few feet apart on the ground.

"This all the men you've got?" asked the Kid.

The sheriff nodded. "You've killed Jim Harbin," he added, jerking a thumb toward the *arroyo*.

"Why didn't he stay home, then?" said the Kid, peevishly. No one seemed disposed again to mention an unpleasant subject.

"Where you goin' to take us?" the Kid inquired.

"Vegas. It's a United States warrant, and you go dead or alive, either way you want."

"Oh, that's all right, Ben. We'll take the chance of stayin' alive a while."

Stillson now appeared to experience his first concern in regard to his casualties. "Doc," said he, "you take the ranch wagon here and carry Jim back to the settlements. You go along, Anderson. Doc, you drive."

"You busted up our breakfast," said the Kid, in an aggrieved tone. "Don't we eat?" He spoke complainingly. The day's work was thus concluded.

It was a long ride back for Dan Anderson, lying part of the time himself prone at the bottom of the wagon, too faint to sit with comfort on the narrow, jolting seat. The long, muffled body of the dead man, wrapped tightly in its blankets, at times rolled against him as the wagon tilted, and he pushed it back gently. The day's work had been savage, stern, and simple. The lesson of the landscape, the lesson of life, came to him as he had never felt it before. He saw now how little a thing is life, how easy to lay down—gayly, bitterly, lightly, or quietly perhaps; but not cheaply. He remembered the last words of the boy who now lay there, shrouded and silent,—"I've got to take my medicine."

"It's not a question of being happy," thought Dan Anderson, "but of doing your work, and taking your medicine."

Emerson Hough

CHAPTER XXII

ADVENTURE AT HEART'S DESIRE

The Strange Story of the King of Gee-Whiz, and his Unusual Experience in Foreign Parts

In the absence of McKinney with the sheriff's posse, Curly became, by virtue of seniority, acting foreman on the Carrizoso ranch. Grieving over the edict which held him home from sheriffing, and disconsolate now that Ellsworth and Constance had departed, he sought an outlet for his feelings. "I'll show folks what a real cow foreman is like," he asserted, and forthwith began plans which, in his opinion, had been too long deferred by the more conservative McKinney.

The wagons of the Carrizoso cow outfit came into town one morning, with a requisition for all the loose .44-caliber ammunition that could be bought, begged, or commandeered under the plea of urgent necessity. Whiteman burrowed through his stock from top to bottom, but still the new foreman growled at the insufficiency.

"There's more'n five thousand sheep in that bunch that has just crossed the Nogales," said he, "and we've got to kill 'em, every one. Do you suppose my men is goin' to take to clubs, like Digger Injuns?"

Whiteman could only shrug. There had always been ammunition in Heart's Desire sufficient for all benevolent and social purposes. No one had suspected sheep. The Carrizoso plateau had been sacred ground, and it was unsupposable that it could ever be desecrated by the trampling hoofs and scissor noses of these woolly abominations. Grumbling, Curly rode away with his wagons, surrounded by a group of be-Winchestered cow punchers, not unlike that which had accompanied Stillson out at the other end of the town.

It was two days before they returned. When they did so, two of the men were not in their saddles, but at the bottom of a wagon. Beside them, bucked up and bound, lay a strange and long-haired figure, at which the new foreman occasionally looked back with a gaze of mingled curiosity and respect.

It appeared that Carrizoso cow honor had been maintained. The five thousand sheep had been rounded up in a box canon, and scrupulously killed to the last item, while two herders went flying westward in fright such as might have warranted euchre upon their stiffly extended coat-tails.

Willie, the half-wit, one of the sheep outfit, had readily taken the oath of allegiance; beyond that, however, there had been a hitch in the proceedings. The man causing this hitch—the long-haired figure at the bottom of the wagon—had been presumptuous enough to make a stand against the lords of the earth! The men of Heart's Desire, confident that the new foreman understood his business, asked few questions as they gathered about the wagon and gazed at the silent captive.

He was a singular-looking man, tall, lean, sinewy, with a high, thin nose and a square chin which seemed not in keeping with his calling. His left nostril was indented by a scar which ran across his cheek, and one ear was notched well-nigh as deeply as that of a calf at a spring branding.

"This feller," said Uncle Jim Brothers, "looks like he come from Arkansaw."

"Maybe *so*," answered Curly. "Anyhow, he shot up two of the boys and killed a horse for us before we got at him. We was out of ammunition—I told you we didn't have enough. After we killed the woollies, and run off them two herders, we rid up the canon. There was him, a-settin' in the door of his ole Kentucky home, with a Winchester that'd go off—which it stands to reason couldn't have happened if he was a real sheepherder. I can't figure that out." Curly scratched his head dubiously, and looked again at his prisoner.

"He ain't saying a vort alretty," said Whiteman.

"He's happy enough without. He was livin' like a lord there, in his shack—four hundred paper-back novels, a keg of whiskey and a tin cup, and some kind of 'hop' that we brung along, and which was the only thing he hollered over."

The prisoner sat up in the wagon. "If you'd be so good as to give me the packet you've in your pocket," said he to Curly, "I'd be awfully obliged to you, old fellow, I would indeed." Curly drew a paper package from his pocket and passed it to the speaker, who opened it with eager fingers.

"Thanks, my good man," he remarked, "thank you awfully." They led him into the deserted Lone Star for further deliberations.

"That's the snuff he's been takin'," Curly explained aside. "I know. It's 'hop.' Sheep, 'hop,' and whiskey! With that for a life and them for a steady diet, I don't believe our friend here'd last more'n about thirty years more." He turned to the captive, who by this time was leaning back against the wall in his chair, the central figure of present affairs, but apparently quite unconcerned.

"How you feelin' now?" Curly asked.

"Much better," replied the prisoner. "Thank you awfully. I was beginning to feel deucedly seedy, you know."

"I'd like to know," inquired Curly, bluntly, "what in merry-hell you're doing down in here, anyhow. Where'd you come from? Where've you been?"

A half-humorous smile came to the face of the captive. "You seem not to know a Sandhurst man, gentlemen, when you see one," said he.

"I said he was from Arkansaw," remarked Uncle Jim.

"No foolin' now, young feller," said Curly, frowning. "You may have more trouble than you're lookin' for. What's your name?"

"I really forget my first name," replied the prisoner, blandly, but not discourteously. "Of late I have been customarily addressed as the King of Gee-Whiz."

"Well, King," suggested the acting foreman, grimly, "you'd better turn loose and tell us your story, about as soon as you know how."

"Very gladly," responded the other, "very gladly. You seem a good sort, and you fought fair. I'll tell you the absolute truth.

"I came from England originally, and not from Arkansaw, as my friend supposes, although I don't know where Arkansaw is, I'm sure. I was long in the British Army, or Navy, I cawn't remember which. I'm quite sure it was one or the other, possibly both."

"I wouldn't kid too much, friend," said Curly, warningly.

"I beg pardon?"

"Drop the foolishness!"

"You misunderstand me, I'm sure," said the King of Gee-Whiz. "At that time it was quite customary, indeed very fashionable, for young gentlemen to belong both to the Army and the Navy. Now, I remember with perfect distinctness that I shipped before the mast on her Majesty's submarine, the *Equator*."

Uncle Jim drew a long breath. "A submarine ain't *got* no mast," said he. "It crawls, on the bottom of the ocean."

"Don't mind him, friend," interrupted Curly. "He come from the short-grass country of Kansas, and he don't know a submarine from a muley cow. Go on, King."

"As I was saying," continued the latter, somewhat annoyed, "I shipped before the mast on her Majesty's sub-marine, the *Equator*, Captain Harry Oglethorpe comman-ding,—a great friend of mine, and a very brave and clever fellow. I knew him well before I got so deucedly down on my luck. But what was I saying?"

"About submarines—"

"Ah, yes, I remember; we left Portsmouth Harbor the 12th of August, 1357. It seemed a gruelling hard thing to us to sail just on the opening of the shooting season, but the wuzzies were troubling a bit.

"One day, as Sir Harry and I were sitting on deck before the mast, having a cigarette—"

"At the bottom of the sea—on deck!" gasped Uncle Jim Brothers.

"Pray don't interrupt me, or I'll never get on," chided the King of Gee-Whiz, politely. "We were smoking, as I said, awfter dinner. I was remarking to Sir Harry that we were having a very good voyage over, when, as he turned to reply, an orderly rode up to us and saluted."

"Rode—rode—rode up!" murmured Curly. "How could he?"

"Let him alone," said Uncle Jim. "Didn't he say he couldn't remember whether he was in the Army or the Navy? The horse goes."

"The orderly saluted," resumed the King of Gee-Whiz, "and said he, 'I beg pardon, but the officer of the day presents his compliments, and begs to report that the ship's a-fire, and upon the point of exploding.'"

"Sir Harry looked at his watch. 'Thanks,' said he. 'Present my compliments to the officer of the day, and ask how long it will be before the explosion occurs.'"

"'I beg pardon,' replied the orderly, 'but the officer of the day presents his compliments, and begs to say that the explosion will occur in about three minutes.'"

Emerson Hough

"'Very well,' said Sir Harry, 'you may go.'—'That will give us time to finish our cigarettes,' said he to me. The orderly saluted and rode away. We never saw him again.

"The officer of the day was a very accurate man, very accurate indeed. In three minutes to the dot the explosion did occur. We never knew what caused it. No doubt the Admiralty Board determined that, but we were not present at the session.

"The explosion was most violent, and no doubt the submarine was quite destroyed by it. Sir Harry and I were blown to an extraordinary distance from the spot. I remember saying to him, as we reached the surface and started upward, that it seemed quite too bad that we'd not had time to get together our personal kit for the journey.

"It's no use my mentioning how long we travelled thus, for I'm not in the least clear about it myself. All I can say is that in course of time we descended, and that we found ourselves on solid ground, on the island of Gee-Whiz. That, you will understand, was an uncharted and hitherto undiscovered land, lying near the 400th parallel west of London and somewhere below Sumatra—several weeks' march from Calcutta, I should say. We'd never seen the place nor heard of it, but were jolly well pleased to alight upon it, under the circumstances. Of the rest of the ship's company we never heard.

"It was a baddish fix, I must say, for to be marooned on a desert island is serious; and it's still more serious to lose one's ship in the British Army. Presently, however, we composed ourselves. 'I say,' said Sir Harry, 'this is a great go, isn't it? Here I am with no luggage whatever except one bar of soap!'

"Presently I saw approaching a band of natives, headed by

a large person, who was apparently their leader or king."

"Then that was the real King of Gee-Whiz?" asked Doc Tomlinson.

"At that time, but not permanently, as I shall presently show you."

"I explained the situation to the King, who turned out to be a very good sort. 'God bless my soul!' said he. 'My dear sir, there's not the slightest occasion for uneasiness, there really isn't, indeed.'"

"You may fawncy the situation! As it was, Sir Harry and I were obliged to make the best of it. We concluded to remain and to take possession of the region in the name of her Britennic Majesty."

"That's the most natural part of your story!" affirmed Uncle Jim, with conviction.

"Thank you. But I must tell you of the complications which now arose. You will see that all these people were sun-worshippers, or something of the sort, and they'd a beastly unpleasant habit, you know, of offering up a sacrifice now and again to appease the spirits, or the like. We learned they'd a valley of gold hidden away somewhere back in the island, and from this the King got all his gold, though even under these circumstances not so much as he wanted at all times. He'd the trouble of most royal families.

"The ruler of this golden valley was some sort of a princess, and she was downright niggardly with her money, as some of these heiresses are, you know. She'd promise the King to bring him an apronful of gold if he'd give her a sacrifice to offer up, but he had no way of providing an offering. No one had come for years in the line of a sacrifice, excepting ourselves. You can imagine the awkwardness this created. The King wanted to sacrifice us, one or both, directly. The princess, who by the by was a regular ripper in her way, was quite gone on Sir Harry, and he on her as well. At this point my own personal fortunes were much involved, as you may understand.

"Sir Harry explained that while he wished to be quite the gentleman about it, and accord me every courtesy, he'd be obliged if I'd be the sacrifice, and leave him to represent her Majesty in the new territory. We talked it over a bit, but came to no conclusion about the matter. It was at this time that one of the most remarkable portions of our experience occurred.

"One morning Sir Harry and I were standing in front of our residence, in our part of the island, talking over matters. Sir Harry was taking a bawth in a wash-hand basin—"

"What's that?" asked Uncle Jim.

"I reckon he means a wash-pan," explained Billy Hudgens.

"At least, Sir Harry was making a deuce of a row with the soap, and he'd the wash-hand basin quite full of bubbles. Just then the King of Gee-Whiz came by, and chawnced to notice the bubbles. You should have seen his expression!

"You must remember he'd never seen a bit of soap in all his life; and no one who has been without it—like the King and myself—can tell what that means. He was deucedly infatuated with the bubbles. In short, he valued them at once far more than all the gold in the valley; and he wound up by telling us flat, that so long as we could make bubbles for him, there would be no sacrifice. He commanded us to appear before him every day and make these bubbles—Sir Harry showed him how to do it with his pipe—every morning and awfternoon.

"Awfter he'd gone, Sir Harry and I looked at each other. 'It's death or bubbles,' said he to me. I pointed out to him that it was either death or no bawth. He was much shocked. Evidently the thing could not go on, for our soap was already very near exhausted. Sir Harry was a sad dog. Said he to me, 'While there is soap there is life,' meaning to say, you see, that while there was life there was hope. Ha, ha!"

"Leave that out," admonished Curly. "Go on."

"About now there went ashore on the island the private yacht of a gentleman whom we found to be Sir Isaac Morgenstern. He was a retired soap-maker, of wealth and station, and was on a voyage to Samoa with his daughter, his household servants, and the like. He'd with him, as chaplain, a missionary, William Cook, a person of very fat habit of body.

"When the boat went ashore, Sir Isaac, his daughter, Lady Sophie, her maid, a Miss Eckerstrom, Mr. Cook, and one or two others were saved, together with certain of their effects—an auto car or so, a piano, a harp, some books, pictures, and a number of other items which made our life much pleasanter. We all settled down together in a bit of colony, and we got on well enough.

"The King by this time was becoming most unpleasant again about his sacrifice. Sir Harry was a sad dog. 'Sacrifice Morgenstern,' suggested he, 'he's used to sacrifice.' You see, in the retail business—"

"Never mind dot," said Whiteman. "Tell vot happenet!"

"A great many things happened. For one thing, the death of Sir Isaac."

"How come that?" asked Billy Hudgens.

"One day Sir Harry met Sir Isaac in the woods, and they'd a bit of talk. Without thinking much about it, Sir Harry explained that he was called on to blow soap bubbles for the King, and that he was in great need of soap, which at that time was worth far more than gold."

"Unt Morgenstern a retiret soap-mager" exclaimed Whiteman, involuntarily.

"Now that was shore hard luck for *him*," added Uncle Jim.

"You may quite believe so," said the teller of the story, gently. "And the saddest part of it, he'd nearly solved our problem before he left us. At once Sir Harry began talking of soap, Sir Isaac began wondering how he could make soap. Ere long he thought of Mr. Cook, the missionary. 'Soap making is simple,' said he, 'if one has fat and a bit of alkali.' The water there was most alkaline, I may add. 'Now there is Mr. Cook?'

"'You cawn't have the missionary,' interrupted Sir Harry, 'until after he has married me and the princess. Then I don't mind.'"

"I've every reason to believe that Mr. Cook was made over into soap. But for once Sir Isaac was wrong. He oversold the market, and that was his mistake. As soon as the King of Gee-Whiz found that there was abundance of soap he lost his fawncy for bubbles. The shock of this lost opportunity prostrated Sir Isaac, and he presently passed away. We mourned him for a time, but presently other events occurred which deadened the loss.

"You will understand that the King of Gee-Whiz was a deucedly good sort. He'd take a nip now and again, of course. The only thing he had to drink was palm wine, which he got by chopping a notch in a tree and catching the juice in a cup."

"That sounds like wood alcohol," said Billy Hudgens, in a professional tone of voice. "It ain't safe."

"Quite right. It wasn't safe. The palm wine itself caused the King to cut a pretty caper now and then; but awfter his mistake, he was far worse—far, far worse. He never got over that, never."

"What happened to him?"

"A most extraordinary thing. I never knew of anything like it in all the world.

"You see, there were two trees which grew close together near the royal palace. One of these was his Majesty's private drinking tree. The other, as it chawnced, was a rubber tree."

Curly deliberately removed his hat and placed it on his knee, wiping, as he did so, a brow dotted thick with moisture. No one broke the silence.

"You will easily understand," resumed the speaker, "that when the King of Gee-Whiz had chopped into the rubber tree with his little gold axe, drinking awfterwards a cupful of pure caoutchouc, it did not take him long to repent of his inadvertence. The results were what I may call most extraordinary. I should judge the rubber juice to have been of very high proof indeed.

"To be brief, I give you my word of honor, the King was turned into an absolutely elastic person on the spot! When he stamped his foot he bounded into the air. 'He's a regular bounder, anyway,' said Sir Harry, who would always have his joke. 'And,' said he to me, as I remember distinctly, 'if his conscience becomes elastic, we're gone, the same as Cook and Morgenstern.' Sir Harry was a great wit.

"Now, the more furious the King became, the more helpless he became as well. He simply bounced up and down and around and about. Reigning monarch, too— lack of dignity—all that sort of thing—must have been most annoying to him. We could do nothing to calm him. In all my travels, I have never seen such a state of affairs; I haven't, really."

"Nor me neither," said Billy Hudgens, sighing, "and I've kept bar from Butte to El Paso."

"Then what happened?" demanded Curly.

"Everything that could happen," said the other, bitterly. "Lady Sophie and her maid, Sir Harry and the princess— the entire household suite of the King of Gee-Whiz— were mad enough to taste also of the juice of this rubber tree. It had the same effect upon them! I say to you, positively and truthfully, that then and there the island of Gee-Whiz was inhabited by the maddest population ever known in any possession of her Britannic Majesty."

"Reckon they was a pretty lively bunch to hold," suggested Curly; "but what happened next?"

"I am not quite clear as to all that transpired awfter that. I know that I was the only sane man left on the island."

"Then," remarked Curly, with conviction, taking a huge chew off his plug, "then that must shore have been one hell of a island!"

But the narrator went on unmoved: "I reproved the others, and they resented it. There was a great battle with the natives one day, of which I remember but little. I seem to have been left insensible on the field. When I recovered, I saw dawncing off across the sea the figures of all these different persons except Sir Harry—who, of course, was with me in the battle. Sir Harry was still with me, quite sober at lawst, and quite dead, I do not know from what cause. I was left alone.

"It was thus, gentlemen, that I acquired, by right, as I think, my title which I assumed—awfter acting for a time as Viceroy for her Britannic Majesty—as the King of Gee-Whiz. For a while I lived there alone. Awfterwards, in some way, which I do not quite call to mind at present, I appear to have been discovered. It was shortly awfter that I received my decoration—I beg your pardon." He flushed a dull red. "It was nothing, of course," said he. "As to saving Sir Harry, it was only what any other fellow would have done in the Army or the Navy—I don't remember which.

"So, gentlemen, I've told you my story as a gentleman should. I've been deucedly down on my luck ever since then, and I cawn't tell you, really I cawn't, how I happened to be here and in this business as you found me. There's many a younger son, in the Army or the Navy, who knocks about and gets a bit to the bad. I hope you'll not lay it up against me, I do indeed!" His head dropped forward on his chest. "I was stone broke," he whispered, "and I'd not a friend on earth."

"And so you drifted here," said Curly. "Well, it's about the right place. Heart's Desire's wide open."

"It wasn't so bad," resumed the stranger, wearily, passing his hand across his forehead; "it wasn't so bad down here for a time. I didn't mind it, being alone, that sort of thing, for you see I was alone on the island for so long. But the trouble was that I was followed all the time—have been for more than a year now—by that cursed King—that damned fiend that I thought I'd left long ago! I'd go out into the sunshine, and there he'd be, walking, and bounding, and jumping along, anyway I'd look! He'd follow me like a—look! look! there he is now. See!"

He raised a trembling finger and pointed to a spot in front of the open door. A black shadow was cast upon the floor by the strong sunlight which shone upon the figure of a leaning spectator.

"Look!" cried the King of Gee-Whiz. "He's there! He's there!" He slipped and sank to the floor, rolling over into an utter insensibility. Curly put on his hat and stood looking down at him.

"Sand, sunshine, and sheep herdin'," said he, "will do up any man in time. I'd 'a' made a good cow puncher out of this fellow, too, if I'd got him in time. By Golly! I'll do it anyhow. I'll have Mac get him a horse and saddle and put him to work. Any feller that kin shoot and lie as good as him has got the makin' of a good cow puncher in him."

They turned over the King of Gee-Whiz gently, that he might rest more easily, where he lay. His coat and waistcoat fell open. Underneath them, upon the left side of his chest, appeared a small, dull-colored cross of metal.

"For Valor"; Curly read the inscription with difficulty. "I knowed it; I knowed he'd been a cow puncher sometime, and just went wrong."

"Great Scott!" exclaimed Uncle Jim Brothers, "that's the Victoria Cross! This here's a V. C. man!"

"I don't know that brand. It ain't registered for this range," said Curly.

"Well," said Billy Hudgens, philosophically gazing at the sleeper, "I reckon 'D. T.' would be easier to understand, all things considered."

"If he ever comes to," said Curly, as he cast away through the open door the contents of the pockets of the King of Gee-Whiz, "we'll try to get him through the D. T. stage as well as the V. C., whatever that is, and I reckon he's good for a job on the Carrizoso range. This country can't afford to be too damned particular about a feller's past."

CHAPTER XXIII

PHILOSOPHY AT HEART'S DESIRE

Showing further the Uncertainty of Human Events, and the Exceeding Resourcefulness of Mr. Thomas Osby

Tom Osby's freight wagon made not so bad a conveyance after all. The first fifty miles of the journey were passed in comparative silence, Constance and her father for the most part keeping to the shelter of the wagon tilt. Tom Osby grew restless under solitude ere long, and made friendly advances.

"You come up here and set by me on the seat," said he to Constance, "and let the sun shine on you. The old man can stay back there on the blankets with my kerosene can of whiskey if he still thinks his health ain't good. Like enough he'll learn to get the potato off'n the snoot of the can before long.

"You see," he went on, "I don't make no extry charge for whiskey or conversation to my patients. Far's I know, I'm the only railroad that don't. I got a box of aigs back there in the wagon, too. Ever see ary railroad back in the States that throwed in ham and aigs? I reckon not."

"Twenty dollars extra!" remarked Ellsworth, "You've

made the girl laugh."

"Man, hush!" said Tom Osby. "Go on to sleep, and don't offer me money, or I'll make you get out and walk." This with a twinkle which robbed his threat of terror, though Ellsworth took the advice presently and lay down under the wagon cover.

"Don't mind him, Miss Constance," apologized Tom Osby. "He's only your father, anyhow, if it comes to the worst. But now tell me, what ails *you*? Say, now, you ain't sick, are you?" He caught the plaintive droop of the girl's mouth; but, receiving no answer, he himself evaded the question, and began to point out antelope and wolves, difficult for the uneducated eye to distinguish upon the gray plains that now swept about them. It was an hour before he returned to the subject really upon his mind.

"I was hearin' a little about Ben Stillson, the sherf, goin' out with a feller or so of ours after a boy that's broke jail down below," he began tentatively. "You folks hustled me out of town so soon, I didn't have more'n half time enough to git the news." From the corner of his eye he watched the face of his passenger.

"A great way to do, wasn't it!" exclaimed Constance, in sudden indignation. "I asked them why they didn't hire men to do such work."

"Ma'am," said Tom Osby; "I used to think you had some sense. You ain't."

"Why?"

"You can't think of no way but States ways, can you? I s'pose you think the *po*lice ought to catch a bad man, don't you?"

"Well, it's officer's work, going after a dangerous man. Wasn't this man dangerous?"

He noted her eagerness, and hastened to qualify. "Him? The Kid? No, I don't mean him. *He's* plumb gentle. I mean a *real* bad man—if there was any out here, you know. Now, not havin' any *po*lice, out here, the fellers that believes in law and order, why, onct in a while, they kind of help go after the fellers that don't. It works out all right. Now I don't seem to just remember which ones it was of our fellers that Stillson took with him the other day, along of your hurrying me out of town so soon after I got in."

"It was Mr. Tomlinson, and Mr. McKinney from the ranch, you know; and Curly wanted to go, but they wouldn't let him."

"Why wouldn't they?"

"Because he was a married man, they said. And yet you say this criminal is not dangerous?"

"He'd ought to been glad to go, him a married man. I've been married a good deal myself. But was them two the only ones that went?"

"They two—and Mr. Anderson."

Tom smoked on quietly. "Well, I don't see why they'd take a tenderfoot like him," he remarked at length, "while there was men like Curly standin' around."

"I thought you were his friend!" blazed the girl, her cheeks reddening.

Tom Osby grinned at the success of his subterfuge.

"If he wasn't a good man, Ben Stillson wouldn't 'a' took him along," admitted he.

"Then it *is* dangerous?"

"Ma'am," said Tom Osby, tapping his pipe against the side of the wagon seat, "they're about even, a half dozen good ones against about that many bad ones. They're game on both sides, and got to be. And we all know well enough that Dan Anderson's game as the next one. The boys figured that out the other night. Why, he'll come back all right in a few days; don't worry none about *that*." He looked straight ahead of him, pretending not to notice the little gloved hand that stole toward his sleeve. In her own way, Constance had discovered that she might depend upon this rough man of the plains.

"Ma'am," he went on after a while, "not apropy of nothing, as they say in the novels, I wish you and your dad would hurry and get your old railroad through here. Us folks may some of us want to go back to the States sometime, and it's a long way to ride from Heart's Desire to any railroad the way it is, unless you've got mighty good company, like I have, this trip. I get awful lonesome sometimes, drivin' between here and Vegas. I had a parrot onct, and a phonygraph, as you may remember, but the fellers took 'em both away from me, you know. I'm thinkin' of makin' up to that oldest girl from Kansas and settlin' down. She makes fine pies. I've knew one of her pies to last two hundred miles—all the way up to Vegas— they're that permernent. She reminds me a heap of my third wife. Now, allowin' I did take one more chanct, and make up to that oldest girl, we'd look fine, wouldn't we, takin' a weddin' trip in this here wagon, and not on no railroad!"

Constance was smiling now. "I've got her gentled and

comin' along right easy now," thought Tom Osby to himself.

"I knowed a feller up in Vegas onct," he went on, "got married and went plumb to New York, towering around. He got lost on a ferry-boat down there somewhere, and rode back and forrard all day; and says he to me, 'Blamed if every man in that town didn't get his boots blacked every day.' That's foolish."

The girl laughed outright, rolling the veil back from her face now, and taking a full look up at the sky, with more enjoyment in life than she had felt for days. Further conversation, however, was interrupted by a deep snore from the rear of the wagon.

"That," said Tom Osby, "sounds like the old man had got the potato loose."

"I'm ashamed of him," declared Constance.

"Natural," said Tom; "but why special?"

"He oughtn't to touch that whiskey. I hate it."

"So do I, when it ain't good. That in the can is good. It's only fair your dad should break even for some of the whiskey he give the Lone Star. They didn't have a drop when I got in. Now, that's another reason why we ought to have a railroad at Heart's Desire. It might prevent a awful stringency, sometime. There's Dick McGinnis, why, he nearly—"

"But it's not coming. It will not be built. They wouldn't let us in. We couldn't get the right of way."

"Now listen at you! You mean your daddy couldn't, nor

his lawyer couldn't. Of course not. But you haven't tried it your own self yet."

"How could I?"

"Well, you'd a heap more sense than to size up things the way your pa did. The boys told me all about what happened. A man out here don't holler if you beat him fair, but if you stack the cards on him, that's different. Dan Anderson done just right."

"He broke up all our plans," Constance retorted hotly; and at once flushed at her own speech.

"What was he to do? Sell out? Turn the whole town over to you folks? Soon as he knows what's up, he throws back the money and tells the road to go to hell. He kept his promise to me, and to all the other fellers that had spoke to him about lookin' after their places. He done right."

Constance looked for a moment at the far shimmering horizon. At length she faced about and bravely met Tom Osby's eyes. "Yes, he was right," she said. "He did what was right." But she drew a long breath as she spoke.

"Ma'am," said Tom Osby, regarding her keenly, "not referrin' to the fact that you're squarer than your men folks, I want to say that, speakin' of game folks, you're just as game as any man I ever saw. Lots of women is. Seems like they have to be game by just not lettin' on, sometimes."

She felt his eyes upon her, and this time turned away her own. For a time they were silent, as the well-worn wagon rolled along behind the long-stepping grays; but Tom Osby was patient.

"A while ago," he resumed after a time, "you said 'we,' and 'our railroad.' That's mighty near right. You two folks right here in this wagon, yourself particular, can save that there railroad, and save Heart's Desire, both at the same time. And that's something, even if them was all that was saved."

"I don't quite see what you mean," answered Constance.

"Oh, now, look here," said Tom, filling another pipe, "I ain't so foolish. I ain't goin' to say that the old days'll last forever. We all know better'n that when it comes right down to straight reasonin'. A country'll sleep about so long, same as a man; and then it'll wake up. I've seen the States come West for forty years. They're comin' swifter'n ever now."

"When we first came here," said Constance, "I thought this was the very end of all the world."

"It has been. And the finest place in all the world, ma'am, is right at the end of the world. That's where a man can feel right independent. A woman can't understand that, no way on earth. A man's a right funny thing, ma'am. He's all the time hankerin' to git into some country out at the end of the world, where there ain't a woman within a thousand miles; and then as quick as he gets there, he begins to holler for some woman to come out and save his life!"

She turned upon him again, smiling in spite of herself.

"The boys have been mighty slow to let go of the old days," he went on. "In some ways there won't never be no better days. We never had a thief in our valley, until your pa come in here last summer. There ain't been a lock on a door in four hundred miles of this country in the last twenty years. When the railroad comes the first thing it'll bring will be locks and bolts. At the same time, it's got to come—I know that. We've about had our sleep and our dream out, ma'am."

"It was beautiful," Constance murmured vaguely; and he caught her meaning.

"Yes, plumb beautiful. Folks that hasn't tried it don't know. A man that's lived the old life here, with a real gun on him as regular as pants, why, in about three years he gets what we call galvanized. He'll never be the same after that. He'll never go back to the States no more. That's hard for you to understand, ain't it? And yet that sort of feelin' catches almost any man out here, sooner or later, if he's any good. It's the country, ma'am."

A strange spell seemed now to fall upon Constance herself, as she sat gazing out in the sunlight. She felt the fatalism, the unconcern of a child, of a young creature. She understood perfectly all that she had heard, and was ready to listen further.

"Of course," continued Tom, "this, bein' South, and bein' West, it ain't really a part of the United States; so I can't save the whole country. But, such as this part of the country is, I reckon I'll have to save it. You'll see my name wrote on tablets in marble halls some day; because I've got a hard job. I've got to reconcile these folks to your dad! And yet I'm going to make 'em say, 'Now is the winter of our discontent made glorious summer by this son-of-a-gun from New York.' You didn't know I read Shakespeare? Why, I read him constant, even if I do have to wear specs now for fine print."

Constance, in spite of herself, laughed outright with so merry a peal that she wakened her father from his slumber. "What's that? What's that?" broke in Mr.

Ellsworth, suddenly sitting up on his blankets.

"Never mind, friend," said Tom Osby, "you go back to sleep again; me and Miss Constance is savin' things. I was just talkin' to her about her railroad."

Ellsworth rubbed his eyes. "By Jove!" he exclaimed suddenly, "that's a good idea. It shall be hers if she says so. I'll give her every share I own if that road ever runs into the valley."

"Now you are beginnin' to *talk*," said Tom Osby, calmly. "Not that you'd be givin' her much; for you and your lawyer wouldn't be able to get the railroad in there in a thousand years. The girl can play a heap stronger game than both of you."

"Well, if she can," responded Ellsworth, "she's going to have a good chance to do it. We're going to build the railroad on north, and we don't feel like hauling coal down that canon by wagon."

Tom Osby seemed to have pursued his game as far as he cared to do at this time. "S'pose we stop along somewhere in here," he suggested, "and eat a little lunch? My horses gets hungry, and thirsty, the same as you, Mr. Ellsworth. Whoa, boys!"

Descending from his high seat, he now unhitched his team and strapped on their heads the nose-bags with the precious oats, after a pail of not less precious water from the cask at the wagon's side. Methodically he kicked together a little pile of greasewood roots.

"We're to have some tea, you know," he remarked. "I don't charge nothin' extry for tea, whiskey, or advice on this railroad of mine. Get down now, ma'am," he added, reaching up his arms to assist Constance from her place. "Come along, set right down here on the ground in the sun. It's good for you. Ain't it nice?

"There's the back of old Carrizy just beginnin' to show," he explained; "and there's the Bonitos comin' up below. That's Blanco Peak beyond, the tallest in the Territory; and them mountings close in is the Nogales. There ain't a soul within many and many a mile of here. And now, with them old mountings a-lookin' down at us on the strict *cuidado*, not botherin' us if we don't bother them, why, ain't it comfortable? This country'll take hold of you after a while, ma'am. It's the oldest in the world; but somehow it seems to me onct in a while as if it was about the youngest, too."

Constance took the counsel offered her, and seated herself in full glare of the Southwestern sun. She looked about her and felt an unwonted sense of peace, as though she were rocked in some great cradle and under some watchful eye. "Dad," said she, quietly, "I'm not going home. I'm going to spend a month at Sky Top."

"Has it caught *you*, ma'am?" asked Tom Osby, simply.

"She talks as though there were no business interests anywhere to be taken care of," grumbled her father.

"Oh, now, interests ain't exclusive for the States," said Tom Osby. "You come all the way out here to steal a town, and you couldn't do it. Give the girl a month, an' she'll just about have the town—or her and me together will. You settin' there talkin' about goin' home! Go on home if you feel like it. Me and Miss Constance will stay out here, and take care of the business interests ourselves."

Emerson Hough

"We're personally conducted, dad," laughed Constance.

"Listen," said their personal conductor, balancing a cup of tea upon his knee. "Now, you folks has got money behind you that's painful. You don't *have* to steal, Mr. Ellsworth. It's only a *habit* with you. Now s'pose Miss Constance comes along, allowin' that God can plat a town as well as a surveyor, and allowin' that the first fellers that finds it has as good a right to it as the last ones—which she *does* allow, and *know*. Now, here's what she says. Says she, 'We'll go in with this outfit, and we won't try to steal the landscape. We'll pay for every foot of ground that's claimed by anybody that seen it first. We won't try to move no ancient landmarks, like log houses that dates back to Jack Wilson. We'll put in the yard at the lower end of the town, provided that Mr. Thomas Osby, Esquire, gives his permission—always admittin' there may be just as good places for Mr. Thomas Osby, Esquire, a little farther back in the foot-hills, if he feels like goin' there. Now I reckon Miss Constance makes Mr. Thomas Osby, Esquire, yardmaster at the new deepot."

"Of course," assented Constance; and her father nodded.

"That'd be fair, and it'd be easy," went on Tom. "We'll fix it up that-a-way, me and Miss Constance—not you. And as soon as we get to a telegraft office, we fire the general counsel, Mr. Barkley; don't we, Miss Constance?" The girl nodded grimly.

"He's fired," said Tom. "You can take care of that the first thing you do, Mr. Ellsworth. Then you can make out my papers as yardmaster and general boss of the deepot. You can be clerk.

"Now here we go, the railroad cars a choo-chooin' up our canon, same as down here at Sky Top. In the front car is the president, which is Miss Constance, with me clost along, the new yardmaster. Your pa is somewhere back on the train, Miss Constance, with the money to pay off the hands. He's useful, but not inderspensible."

"Go on!" applauded Constance. "Who besides us and poor old dad?"

Tom Osby turned and looked at her gravely.

"And there comes down to meet us at the station," he concluded, "the only man we needed to help us put this thing through." Tom Osby finished his tea in silence. Constance herself made no comment. Her gaze was on the far-off mountains.

"That there man," he resumed, shaking out the grounds from his tea-cup, "is the new division counsel for the road, the first mayor of Heart's Desire,—after Miss Constance,—and mighty likely the next Congressional delergate from this Territory. Now can you both guess who that man is?"

"I'll admit he's a bigger man than Barkley," said Ellsworth, slowly. "That boy would make a grand trial lawyer. They couldn't beat him."

"No," said Tom Osby, "they'd think he was square, and that means a lot. They *do* think he's square; and the boys are goin' to do something for him if they can. Now if he gets back—"

Constance turned upon him with a glance of swift appeal.

"As I was sayin', *when* he gets back," resumed Tom, "some of us fellers may perhaps take it up with him, and tell him what Miss Constance wants to have done."

This was too much. The girl sprang to her feet. "You'll tell him nothing!" she cried.

Ellsworth turned to Tom Osby with a sober face. "Young Anderson rode away from us the other morning," said he, "and he hardly troubled himself to say good-by. We used to know him back East; and he needn't have taken that affair of the railroad meeting so much to heart."

"Come!" called Constance, "get ready and let's be going. I'm sick of this country!" She walked rapidly away from the others.

"A woman can change some sudden, can't she, Mr. Ellsworth?" remarked Tom Osby, slowly.

"Look here, Miss Constance," said he, presently, when he came nearer to her, standing apart from the wagon, "there's been mistakes and busted plans enough in here already. Now don't get on no high horse and break up my scheme."

"Don't talk to me!" She stamped her foot.

"Ma'am! ain't you ashamed to say them words?" She did not answer, and Tom Osby took the step for which he had been preparing throughout the entire morning.

"Ma'am," said he, "one word from you would bring that feller to you on the keen lope. He'd fix the railroad all right mighty soon. Then besides—"

She turned away. "The question of the railroad is a business one, and nothing else; talk to my father about it."

Tom went silently about his preparations for resuming the journey. When he came to put the horses to the wagon tongue, he found Constance sitting there, staring with misty eyes at the distant hills beyond which lay Heart's Desire. Tom Osby paused at the shelter of the wagon cover and backed away.

"Something has got to be did," he muttered to himself, "and did mighty blame quick. If we don't get some kind of hobbles on that girl, *she's* goin' to jump the fence and go back home."

Emerson Hough

CHAPTER XXIV

THE CONSPIRACY AT HEART'S DESIRE

This being the Story of a Sheepherder, Two Warm Personal Friends, and their Love-letter to a Beautiful Queen

When Tom Osby came back to Heart's Desire, he drew Curly to one side, and the two walked over to a shady spot at the side of Whiteman's corral, seating themselves for what was evidently to be an executive session.

Tom Osby continued to stuff tobacco into his pipe with a stubby forefinger, and Curly's hat was pushed back from a forehead wrinkled in deep thought.

"It's a good deal like you say, Tom," he assented; "I know that. Unless we can get Dan Anderson and that girl to some sort of an understandin', the jig's up, and there ain't a-goin' to be no railroad at Heart's Desire. But how're you a-goin' to *do* that?"

"Well, I done told you what I thought," said Tom Osby. "I'm a married man, been married seven times, or maybe six. There's just two things I understand, and them is horses and women, which I ought to, from associatin' with them constant. Now, I tell you, if I'm any judge of women, that girl thinks a heap of Dan Anderson, no matter what she lets on. It's her that's got the railroad up her sleeve. The old man just thinks she's a tin angel with fresh paint. Why, he's done *give* her the whole railroad. He don't want it. He's got money now that's sinful. Now, I say, she's got the railroad. Dan Andersen's chances, they go with the railroad. If she could just get *him* to go with the business *chances*, that'd about fix things; and I more'n half believe she'd drop into line right free and gentle."

"Well, why don't she *say* so, then," grumbled Curly, "and stop this foolishness?"

"Now there you go!" replied Tom. "Can't you see that any woman on earth, even a married woman, is four-thirds foolishness and the rest human? With girls it's still worse'n that. If I'm any judge, she's wishin' a certain feller'd come along and shake the tree. But she ain't goin' to fall off until the tree's done shook. Consequently, there she is, still up the tree, and our railroad with her."

"Looks like *he* ought to make the first break," observed Curly, sagely.

"Of course he ought. But *will* he, that's the question."

"No, he won't," admitted Curly, pushing his hat still farther back on his head. "He's took his stand, and done what he allowed was right. After that, he ain't built to crawfish. He's passed up the girl, and the railroad, too, and I reckon that settles it."

"And yet he thinks a heap of the girl."

"Natural? Of course he does. How can he help it? That's where the trouble is. I tell you, Tom, these here things is sort of *personal*. If these two folks is havin' trouble of their own, why, it's *their* trouble, and it ain't for us to square it, railroad or no railroad."

"When two people is damn fools," commented Tom Osby, gravely, "it's all right for foreign powers to mediate a-plenty."

"But what you goin' to do? She won't bat a eye at him, and he ain't goin' to send for her."

"Oh, yes he *is*," corrected Tom Osby; and the forefinger, crowding tobacco into his pipe, worked vigorously. "He's *got* to send for her."

"Looks to me like we can't do nothin'," replied his friend, pessimistically. "I like that girl, too. Say, I'll braid her a nice hair rope and take it down to her. Maybe that'll kind o' square things with her for losin' out with Dan."

"Yes," scoffed Tom Osby, "that's all the brains a fool cow puncher has got. Do you reckon a hair lariat, or a new pair of spurs, is any decent remedy for a girl's wownded affections? No, sir, not none. No, you go on down and take your old hair rope with you, and give it to the girl. That's all right; but you're goin' to take something else along with you at the same time."

"What's that?" "Why, you're goin' to take a letter to her,— a letter from Dan Andersen's death-bed."

"Who—me? Death-bed? Why, he ain't *on* no death-bed. He's eatin' three squares a day and settin' up readin' novels. Death-bed nothin'!"

"Oh, no," said Tom Osby, "that's where you're mistaken. Dan Anderson *is* on his death-bed; and he writes his dyin' confession, his message in such cases made and pervided.

He sends his last words to his own true love. Says he, 'All is forgiven.' Then she flies to receive his dyin' words. You ain't got no brains, Curly. You ain't got no imagi*nation*. Why, if I left all this to you, she'd get here too late for the funeral. You're a specialist, Curly. You can rope and throw a two-thousand-pound steer, but you can't handle a woman that don't weigh over a hundred and twenty-five. Now, you watch your Pa."

Curly sat and looked at him in silence for a few minutes, but at last a light seemed to dawn upon him. "Oh, I *see*," said he, smiling broadly. "You mean for us to get up a letter for him—write it out and send it, like he done it hisself."

Tom Osby nodded. "Of course—that's the only way. There wouldn't either of them write to the other one. That's the trouble with these here States girls, and them men from the States, too. You have to take care of 'em. You and me has got to be gardeens for these two folks. If we don't, they're goin' to make all kinds of trouble for theirselves and each other."

"Kin you disguise your handwritin' any, Tom?" asked Curly. "I can't. Mine's kind of sot."

"Curly," answered Tom, with scorn, "what you call your brains is only a oroide imitation of a dollar watch. Why, of course we can't write a letter and sign his name to it deliberate. That's forgery, and we'd get into the penitentiary for it. That ain't the way to do.

"Now look here. Dan Anderson may be lookin' right well for a dyin' man, but he's on his death-bed just the same. That's needful for the purposes of dramatic construction. He's a-layin' there, pale and wore out. His right arm is busted permernent, and it's only a question of time when he cashes in—though he *might* live a few days if he was plumb shore his own true love was a-hastenin' to his bedside."

"But it was his *left* arm that got shot," argued Curly; "and it didn't amount to a whole lot at that."

"There's you go," jeered Tom, in answer, "with them imitation brain works of yours. It's his *right* arm that's busted. Now, him a-layin' there plumb helpless, his thoughts turns to his bride that might 'a' been, but wasn't. With his last dyin' words he greets her. If she would only hasten to his deathbed, he could die in peace. That's what he writes to her. 'Dear Madam,' says he, 'Havin' loved you all my life, I fain would gaze on you onct more. In that case,' says he, 'the clouds certainly would roll away!'"

"That shorely would *fetch* her," said Curly, admiringly, "but how you goin' to fix it?"

"Why, how? There ain't but one way. The dyin' man has his dear friend Curly, or Tom Osby, or some one, write his last words for him. That ain't counterfeitin'. That's only actin' as his literary amanyensis, and that's plumb legal."

"Things may be legal, and not *safe*," objected Curly. "Supposin' he finds out?"

"Why, then, we'll be far, far away. This letter has got to be wrote. I can't write it myself, and you can't; but maybe several of us could."

"I ain't in on writin' the letter," Curly decided; "I'll carry it, but my writin' is too sot, and so's my thinker."

"Well, I ain't used my own thinker in this particular way

for about twenty years," said Tom Osby, "although I did co'te two of my wives by perlite correspondence, something like this; and I couldn't see but what them wives lasted as good as any."

"It's too bad Dan Anderson ain't in on this play hisself," Curly resumed. "Now if it was us that was layin' dead, and him writin' the letter, he'd have us both alive, and have the girl here by two o'clock to-morrer, and everything 'd be lovely. But us! We don't know any more about this than a pair of candy frogs."

"The fewer there is in on a woman deal the better," said Tom Osby, "and yet it looks like we needed help right now!"

The two sat gazing gloomily down the long street of Heart's Desire, and so intent were they that they did not see the shambling figure of Willie the sheepherder coming up the street. Then Tom Osby's gaze focussed him.

"Now there's that damned sheepherder that broke us up in business," said he. "It was him that got us into this fix. If he hadn't lied like a infernal pirate, and got Dan Anderson to thinkin' that the girl and this lawyer feller Barkley was engaged to each other on the side, why Dan wouldn't have flared up and busted the railroad deal, and let the girl get away, and gone and got hisself shot."

"S'posin' I shoot Willie up just for luck," suggested Curly. "He's got it comin' to him, from the way that Gee-Whiz friend of his throwed lead into our fellers, time we was arguin' with them over them sheep. This country ain't got no use for sheep, nor sheepherders either, specially the kind that makes trouble with railroads, and girls."

"No, hold on a minute," interrupted Tom Osby. "You wait—I've got a idea."

"Well, what is it?"

"Wait a minute. How saith the psalmist? All men is liars; and sheepherders special, natural, eighteen-karat, hand-curled liars—which is just the sort we need right now in our business."

Curly slapped his thigh in sudden understanding. The two sat, still watching Willie as he came rambling aimlessly up the street, staring from side to side in his vacant fashion.

"A sheepherder, as you know, Curly," went on Tom, "has three stages in his game. For a while he's human. In a few years, settin' round on the hills in the sun, a-watchin' them damned woolly baa-baa's of his, he gets right nutty. He sees things. Him a-gettin' so lonesome, and a-readin' high-class New York literature all the time, he gets to thinkin' of the Lady Eyemogene. You might think he's seein' cactus and sheep, but what is really floatin' before him is proud knights, and haughty barons, and royal monarchs, and Lady Eyemogenes.

"It ain't sinful for Willie to lie, like it is for us, because life is one continuous lie to him. He's seen a swimmin' picture of hand-painted palaces, and noble jukes, and stately dames out on the Nogal flats every day for eight years. That ain't lyin'—that's imagination.

"Now this feller's imagination is just about ripe. Usual, at the end of about seven years, a sheepherder goes plumb dotty, and we either have to shoot him, or send him to Leavenworth. Your Gee-Whiz man can maybe take to cow punchin' and prosper, but not Willie. His long suit is imaginin' things, from now on.

"Now, that feller is naturally pinin' to write this here particular letter we've got on our minds. You watch Willie compose."

"Here you, Willie, come over here!" Curly called out.

The herder started in fright. Timid at best, he was all the more so since the raid of the Carrizoso stock men. His legs trembled under him, but he slowly approached in obedience.

"Willie," said Tom Osby, sternly, "I'm some hardened as a sinner my own self, but the kind of way you do pains me. What made you tell that lie about seein' the lady and that lawyer feller makin' love to each other, on the back seat of the buckboard, behind the old man's back?"

"I *thought* I seen 'em," pleaded Willie. "I—I *thought* I heard 'em talkin'."

"Oh, sufferin' saints! Listen to that! You *thought*! Of course you did. You and that Gee-Whiz friend of yours ought to turn yourselves into a symposium and write for the papers. Now look here. Have you got a copy of the 'Proud Earl's Revenge,' in your pocket?"

Willie tremulously felt in his clothing, and did produce a dog-eared volume to somewhat that effect. Tom Osby turned over a few of the pages thoughtfully, and then sat up with a happy smile. "There ain't no trouble about that letter *now*!" said he.

"What—what—what do you want?" asked Willie. Then they told him. Willie radiated happiness. He sat down beside them, his hands trembling with joy and eagerness—conspirator number three for the peace and dignity of Heart's Desire.

"Go get some paper, Curly," said Tom Osby, and Curly departed. Willie remained wrapped in thought, his mind confused at this sudden opportunity.

"It's all about Lancelot," said he.

"What brand did Lancelot ride under? Now, no foolin', Willie."

"Why—why—why," said Willie, "Lancelot, he's at a tournyment. Now, he loves a beautiful queen."

"Shore he does! That goes. What's the queen's name?"

"Her name—her name—her name's Guinevere," replied Willie. "And the proud king, he brooks it ill. The proud king's name is Arthur."

"Oh, no, it *ain't*!" said Tom Osby. "There ain't no man who's name is *Arthur* that has no scrap to him. It ain't *Arthur* that goes on no war-path."

"Yes, he did," insisted Willie. "Lancelot gets herded out. He gets shot up some at the tournyment, so he leaves the beautiful queen, and he rides off for the range all alone by himself. He's like a sheepherder."

"Come on with the paper, Curly," called Tom Osby. "This feller's thinker is workin' fine. Go on, Willie."

"Now, Lancelot, he's layin' at the point of death, and he's thinkin' all the time of Guinevere. I reckon he writes her a letter, and he says, says he, 'Dear Lady, I send thee my undyin' love,' says he. 'I kiss the picture which is a-layin' on my breast,' says he; 'and with my last breath,' says he, 'I shorely yearn for thee!'"

"Meanin' Guinevere?"

"Shore! Says Lancelot, 'Fair queen, thou didst me a injury onct; but couldst thou but come and stand at my bedside, I hadst new zeal in life,' says he."

"Meanin' he'd get well?" asked Curly. "That's the same as Dan Anderson! *This* feller's a peach!"

"Shut up!" admonished Tom Osby. "Go on, Willie."

"It's always that-a-way," said Willie. Tears stood in his eyes. He looked vaguely out over the blue hills which hedged in the enchanted valley of Heart's Desire. "It's always that-a-way," he repeated. "Somehow, somewhere, there's always a beautiful queen, for every fellow, just over the mountains. It's always that-a-way."

Tom Osby reached out a hand and gently shook him.

"Set up, Willie," said he. "Come down now, till we get this business fixed. Now, what happens after that?"

Willie winked his eyes and smiled amiably. "The sick knight, he writes a missive to the beautiful queen," he went on. "He sets his signet ring on to the missive, and he hands it to his trusted henchman, and his trusted henchman flies to do his bidding."

"That's you, Curly," nodded Tom Osby. "You're the trusted henchman."

"I'm damned if I am!" replied Curly. "I'm nothin' but a plain cow hand from the Brazos; but I don't take

Emerson Hough

'henchman' from nobody!"

"Hush!" said his friend. "This feller's a genius. If he don't get side-tracked on Dead Shot Dick, or something of that kind, this letter is just as good as wrote, right now."

"The good knight presses his signet ring on to the missive," resumed Willie, "and his trusted cow hand wraps the missive in the folds of his cloak, and climbs on to his trusted steed, and flies far, far away, to the side of the beautiful queen."

"That's good!"

"And the beautiful queen reads the missive, and clasps her hands, and says she, 'My Gawd!'"

"Oh, *now* we're gettin' at it!" said Tom Osby. "Say, this is pretty *poor*, ain't it, Curly?"

"And then," went on Willie, frowning at the interruption, "the beautiful queen sends for her milk-white palfrey, and she flies to the distant bedside of the sufferin' knight."

"She'll take a milk-white buckboard, more likely," said Tom Osby. "You got any palfreys on your ranch, Curly? But we'll let it go at that. She's got to fly to the distant bedside somehow."

"Oh, that'll be all right," agreed Willie, sweetly. "She'll fly. She'll come. It's always the same. It's always the same."

"Write it down, Willie," ordered Tom Osby, thrusting the paper before him. Willie hesitated, and glanced up at Tom.

The latter balked in turn. "What! Have I got to start it for you? Well, then, begin it, 'Dear Madam!'"

Curly shook his head. "You couldn't never marry a woman writin' to her that-a-way." And Tom, rubbing a finger over his chin, had to admit the justice of the assertion.

"Leave it to Willie," suggested Curly. "He'll get it started after a while. Go ahead, Willie. How did he say it to her, now, when he sent for the beautiful queen?"

Tom Osby's pencil followed rapidly as it might.

"He writes," said Willie, "like they always do. He says: 'Light of my heart, I have loved you for these years, and they have seemed so long. I could love no other woman after seeing you, and this you should know with no proof but my word. If I have drawn apart from you, 'twas through no fault of mine, and this I pray you to believe. If I have not acted to my own heart the full part of a man, 'tis for that reason I have hidden away; but believe me, my faith and my love have been the same. If I have missed the dear sight of your face, 'twas because I could not call it mine with honor, nor dare that vision with any plea on my lips, or any feeling in my heart, but that of honor. Heart's Heart, and life of my life, could you not see? I could not doom you to a life unfit, and still ask you to love me as a man.'"

He passed his hand across his face, as though it were not himself he heard speaking; but he went on.

"'Now I lie here hurt to death,' says the good knight Lancelot. 'This is the end. Now, at the time when truth must come from the soul, I say to you, my queen'—she's always queen to him—'I say to you, I have loved you more than I have loved myself. But if you could come, if you could stand at my bedside before it is too late, before it is too late—too late—'" Willie's voice broke into a wail. The ray of light was almost fading from his clouded brain.

"Go on," whispered Tom Osby.

"'My queen, my darling—' says Lancelot."

Willie's hands, trembling, fell into his lap. "It's always that-a-way," he whimpered vaguely, coming now to himself.

"Willie," said Tom Osby, gently, "I ain't right sure I've got it all down straight, but I think I have. You read her over, and touch her up here and there where she needs it. Curly, look here. I don't believe Dan Anderson would hesertate one minute to sign this if he saw it."

"They sign it with their hearts," said Willie, vaguely. "They always do."

"He signs it with his heart," said Tom Osby, "and it goes!" He folded the paper and handed it to Curly.

"Saddle up that Pinto horse, Curly, if you can," said he, "and make the run to Sky Top as fast as God'll let you. This letter's all right, and it goes!"

So presently there rode down the long sunlit street of Heart's Desire, mounted upon the mad horse Pinto, this courier to the queen, bearing a message from a mad brain and two simple hearts,—a courier bound upon a strange and kindly errand.

The blue mountains, beyond whose rim lived the sovereign, looked gently down, and the stern walls of the canon seemed to widen and make room for the messenger as he swept on, carrying the greetings of an absent knight to his distant queen.

"It's like he said," mused Curly to himself, feeling in his pocket for tobacco as he rode. "It's that-a-way, and I reckon it always has been. I've felt like that myself sometimes. *Ola, Pinto*! *Vamos*!"

CHAPTER XXV

ROMANCE AT HEART'S DESIRE

The Pleasing Recountal of an Absent Knight, a Gentle Lady, and an Ananias with Spurs

Long and weary miles lay before Curly, messenger to the queen, but the bigness of his errand lightened the way, and his own courage and hopefulness communicated themselves to his steed. The mad horse, Pinto, indomitable, unapproachable, loped along with head down and ears back, surly at touch of rein or spur, yet steady in his gait as an antelope. The two swept down the long canon from Heart's Desire, traversed for twenty-five miles the alkali plain below, and climbed then the Nogales and the Bonitos, over paths known only to cattle thieves and those who pursued them. At last they swung down into the beautiful valley of the Bonito, and thence in the night far to the southward, until at length they reached the defiles of the Sacramentos. They pulled up after more than a day and a night of travel, weary but not hopelessly the worse for wear, at the end of the steep trail up the mountains to the Sky Top hotel.

Curly, a trifle gaunt, gave his first attention to his horse, which he unsaddled with a slap of approval, and turned loose to feed as best it might on the coarse herbage of the upper heights. His next thought was for himself, and he realized that he was hungry. Immediately there dawned upon his mind another great conviction. He was scared!

He looked about at the long galleries of the ornate modern log house, wherein civilization sought to ape the wilderness; but it was not the arrogant pretentiousness of the building itself which caused him to shift his glance and stand dubiously upon one foot. It was the thought of what the edifice might contain. There, as he began too late to reflect, was the queen! He, the trusted henchman, was bearing to her a missive regarding whose nature he now experienced sudden misgivings. Suppose Willie, the sheepherder, had not, after all, been able to meet the requirements of a situation so delicate and so important! Curly had known the plains and the mountains all his life. He had ridden in the press of the buffalo herd in the Panhandle, had headed cattle stampedes in the breaks of the Pecos, had met the long-toed cinnamon bear all over these mountains that lay about him—had even heard the whisper of hostile lead as part of his own day's work,—but never before had his heart failed him.

Nevertheless, his face puckered into a frown of determination, he stumbled, a trifle pigeon-toed in his high-heeled boots, across the floor of one gallery after another, and knocked at one door after another, until finally, by aid of lingering Mexican servants, he found himself in the presence of the beautiful queen whom he had sought.

He ratified her title when she came toward him where he stood, twirling his hat in his hands; so tall was she, so grave and dignified, yet so very sweet and simple. Curly was a man, and he felt the spell of smooth brown hair and wide brows, and straight, sincere eyes; not to speak of a queen's figure clad in such raiment as had not often been given Curly to look upon. He gazed in a frank admiration which lessened his fear.

Constance Ellsworth held out her hand, with questions for his own household at Heart's Desire. Was everything right with them? Was Arabella quite well of her accident? Was his wife well? And so on. But all the time she questioned him deeper with eyes large, wistful, eager. She had had no news since leaving Heart's Desire, and now she dreaded any. This, then, she said with tightening heart, was news, but fatal news, long withheld. Had Dan Anderson come back unhurt from his sheriff's errand, there would have been no message at all, and silence would have been sweeter than this certainty of evil. This messenger, reticent, awkward, embarrassed, brought her news of Dan Anderson—of the boy whom she had loved, of the man she loved, debonair, mocking, apparently careless, but, as she herself knew, in his heart indomitably resolved. Now he was gone forever from her life. He was dead! She could never see him again. Ah! why had they not used the days of this life, so brief, so soon ended? It was of his death that the messenger must speak.

Curly, already sufficiently perturbed, witnessed all this written on her face, stumbled, stammered, but was unable to find coherent speech; although he saw plainly enough the subterfuge with which even now the girl sought to hedge herself against prying eyes that would have read her secret. She began again, to ask him of his family, the same questions. "Is anything wrong?" she demanded. In some way they were seated before he could go on.

"It ain't the twins, ma'am," he began. "I got—I got a letter for you. It's from him—from us—that is, I got a letter from Mr. Anderson—Dan Anderson, you know."

He fumbled in his pocket. The girl, thoroughbred, looked him straight in the face, pale, meeting what she felt to be the great moment of her life.

"Then he's alive! He must be!"

Curly shook his head; meaning that he was feeling in the wrong pocket.

"He is dead! And I did not see him. He—went away—" Her chin quivered. "Tell me," she whispered, "tell me!"

Curly, busy in his search for the letter, lost the tragedy of this.

"Tell me, *tell* me, how did it happen?"

"Well, ma'am, he ain't hurt so awful," remarked Curly, calmly. "He just got a finger or so touched up a little, so's he couldn't write none to speak of, you see."

Her heart gave a great bound. She feared to hope, lest the truth might be too cruel; but at length she dared the issue. "Curly," said she, firmly, "you are not telling me the truth."

"I know it, ma'am," replied Curly, amiably; he suddenly realized that he was not making his own case quite strong enough. "The fact is, he got hurt a *leetle* bit worse'n that. His hand, his *left*—no, I mean his *right* hand got busted up plenty. Why, he couldn't cut his own victuals. The fact is, it's maybe even a little worse'n that."

"Tell me the truth!" the girl demanded steadily. "Is his arm gone?"

"Sure it is," replied Curly, cheerfully, glad of assistance. "Do you reckon Dan Anderson would be gettin' *anybody* to write to *you* for him if he had even a piece of a arm left in the shop? I reckon not! He ain't that sort of a *man*."

Curly's sudden improvement gave him courage. "The fact is, ma'am," said he, "I got to break this thing to you kind of gentle. You know how that is yourself."

"I know all about it now," she said calmly. "I knew he would not come back—I saw it in his face. It was all because of that miserable railroad trouble that he went away—that he didn't ever come. It was all my own fault—my fault,—but I didn't mean it—I didn't—"

Curly, for the first time in his life, found himself engaged in an important emotional situation. He rose and gazed down at her with solemn pity written upon his countenance.

"Ma'am," he said, "I don't like to see you take on. I wish't you wouldn't. Why, I've seen men shot like Dan Anderson is, bullets clean through the middle of their body, and them out and frisky in less'n six weeks."

"He *will* live?"

"Oh, *well*," and Curly rubbed his chin in deliberation, "I can't say about *that*. He *might* live. You see, there ain't no doctor at Heart's Desire. The boys just took care of him the best they could. They brung him home from quite a ways off. They—they cut his arm off easy as they could, them not bein' reg'lar doctors. They—they sewed him up fine. He was shot some in the fight with the Kid's gang, out to the Pinos Altos ranch. The sherf tole me hisself Dan was as game a man as ever throwed a leg over a saddle. When he got back from takin' the Kid up to Vegas, the sherf—that's Ben Stillson—he starts down to Cruces. Convention there this week, ma'am. Ben, he allowed he'd get Dan Anderson nomernated for

Congress—that is, if he hadn't 'a' got killed."

"I knew he was a brave man," said the girl, quietly. "I've known that a long time."

"You didn't know any more'n us fellers knowed all along," said Curly. "There never was a squarer, nor a whiter, nor a gamer man stood on leather than him. He come out here to stay, and he's the sort that we all wouldn't let go of. Some of 'em goes back home. He didn't. What there was here he could have. For one while we thought he was throwin' us down in this railroad deal, but now we know he wasn't. We done elected him mayor, and right soon we're goin' to elect him something better'n that—if they ain't started it already over to Cruces—that is, I mean, if he ever gets well, which ain't likely—him bein' dead. Now I hate to talk this-a-way to you, ma'am; I ought to give you this letter. But I leave it to you if I ain't broke it as gentle as any feller could."

Curly saw the bowed head, and soared to still greater heights. "Ma'am," said he, "I don't see why you take on the way you do. We all know that you don't care a damn for Dan Anderson, or for Heart's Desire. Dan Anderson knowed that hisself, and has knowed it all along. *You* got no right to cry. You got no right to let on what you don't really feel. I won't stand for that a minute, ma'am. Now I'm—I'm plumb sincere and *truthful*. No frills goes." There was the solemnity of conscious virtue in his voice as he went on.

"I'm this much of a mind-reader, ma'am," said he, "that I know you don't care a snap of your finger for Dan Anderson. That's everdent. I ain't in on that side of the play. I'm just here to say that, so far as he's concerned *hisself*, he'd 'a' laid down and died cheerful any minute of his life for *you*."

She flung upward a tearful face to look at him once more.

"He just worships the place where your shadow used to fall at, that's all," said Curly, firmly. "He don't talk of nothing else but you, ma'am."

"How dare he talk of me!" she flashed.

"Oh, that is—well, that is, he don't talk so blamed much, after *all*," stammered Curly. "Leastwise, not none now. He's out of his head most of the time, now."

"Then you've not told me everything, even yet," exclaimed she, piteously.

"Not quite," said Curly, with a long breath; "but I'm a-comin' along."

"He's dying!" she cried with conviction. Curly, now taking an impersonal interest in the dramatic aspect of the affair, solemnly turned away his head.

"Ma'am," said he, at length, "he thought a heap of you when he was alive. We—we all did, but *he* did special and private like. Why, ma'am, if you'd come and stand by his grave, he'd wake up *now* and welcome you! You see, I am a married man my own self, and Tom Osby, he's been married copious; and Tom and me, we both allowed just like I said. We knew the diseased would have done that cheerful—if he had any sort of chanct."

The girl sprang up. "He's not dead!" she cried, and her eyes blazed, her natural courage refusing to yield. "I'll not believe it!"

"I didn't ast you to, ma'am," said Curly. "He ain't plumb dead; he's just threatened. Oh, say, you've kind of got me rattled, you see. I've got a message—I mean a missive—anyways a letter, from him. I had it in my pants pocket all the time, and thought it was in my coat. Them was the last words he wrote."

She tore the letter from his hand, and her eyes caught every word of it at the first glance.

"This is not his letter!" she exclaimed. "He never wrote it! It's not in his hand!"

"Ma'am," said Curly, virtuously grieved, "how could you! I didn't *say* he wrote it. He had to have a amanyensis, of course,—him a-layin' there all shot up. Nobody *said* it was his handwriting It *ain't* his handwritin'. It's his *heart*writin'. They sign it with their *hearts*, ma'am! Now I tell you that for the truth, and you can gamble on *that*, anyways.

"I think I had better go away. I'm hungry, anyhow," he added, turning away.

"Soon!" she said, stretching out her hand. "Wait!" her other hand trembled as she devoured the pages of the message to the queen. Her cheeks flushed.

"Oh, *read* it, ma'am!" said Curly, querulously. "Read it and get sorry. If you can read that there letter from Dan Anderson—signed with his heart—and not hit the trail for his bedside, then I've had a almighty long ride for nothing."

CHAPTER XXVI

THE GIRL AT HEART'S DESIRE

The Story of a Surprise, a Success, and Something Else Very Much Better

As Curly stumped away, his spurs clinking on the gallery floor, he encountered Mr. Ellsworth, who held out his hand in recognition.

"I just heard some one was down from the town," he began. "How are you, and what's the news?"

"Mighty bad," said Curly, "mighty bad." Then to himself: "O Lord! I'm in for it again, and worse. I'd a heap rather lie to a woman than a man—it seems more natural."

"Bring any word down with you from up there?" asked Ellsworth. Curly nodded. "I brung a letter," said he.

"That so? What's it about?"

"Well, sir, it bein' a letter to a lady—"

"You mean my daughter? Now, what—"

"Yes, it's for her," admitted Curly; "but it's personal."

"Well, I didn't know but it might be news from that young man, Anderson. You know he went with the posse. Do you happen to know?"

"You ask her. It is, though."

"Did he send you down here?"

"I'm almighty hungry; I ain't had no breakfast, nor nothing." Whereupon Curly bolted.

Ellsworth, disturbed, went in search of Constance. He found her, a crumpled and pathetic figure. The news then had, indeed, been bad!

"Now, now, child," he began, "what's up here? You've a letter, the man tells me."

She covered it with her hand as it lay in her lap. "Is it from him, young Anderson?" he asked. She nodded.

"It's written by a friend of his," she answered presently. "He himself couldn't write. He was too—ill."

"Sent for you?" His voice was grave.

"Yes," she whispered, "when it was too late."

"We'll go," he said with decision. "Get ready. Maybe there is some mistake."

"Don't," she begged, "there is no mistake. I knew it would happen; I felt it."

"By Jove, I hope it's not true; I was beginning to think a good deal of that boy myself."

Constance was passing through the door on her way to her room. She turned and blazed at him. "Then why didn't you talk that way before?"

She disappeared, and left him staring after her, through the open door.

An hour later a buckboard, driven by a silent Mexican, rolled down the Sky Top canon, bound for the northern trail.

Curly finished his breakfast, and then went out in search of his horse, which presently he found standing dejectedly, close where it had been left, apparently anchored by the reins thrown down over its head and dragging on the ground. Curly seated himself on the ground near by and addressed his misanthropic steed in tones of easy familiarity.

"Pinto," said he, "you remind me of a heap of folks I know. You think them reins holds you, but they don't. They ain't tied to nothing. You're just like them, hitched tight to a fool notion, that's all. If I don't take your bridle off, you'll stand there and starve to death, like a good many fool folks I've heard of. You've got to eat, Pinto."

Curly arose and with a meditative finger traced the outlines of the continental maps displayed on Pinto's parti-colored flanks. That cynical beast, with small warning, kicked at him viciously.

"Oh, there you go!" remonstrated Curly; "can't you get tired enough to be decent? Git on away—*vamos*!"

He stripped off the bridle from Pinto's head, and again gave him a friendly slap, as he drove him off to graze, without any precaution to prevent his running away. As for himself, Curly lay down upon the ground, his face on his arm, and was soon fast asleep in the glaring sun. Pinto, misanthropic as he was, did not abuse the confidence reposed in him. He walked off to a trickle of water which came down from a mountain spring, and grazed steadily upon the coarse mountain grass, but every now and then, under the strange bond which sometimes exists between horse and man, wandered around to look inquiringly at his sleeping master, whom he would gladly have brained upon occasion, but upon whom, none the less, he relied blindly.

There were long shadows slanting toward the eastward when Curly arose and again saddled up his misfit mount. He knew that the buckboard was well in advance of him in time, but it must take the longer wagon trail to the westward of Sky Top, while for himself there were shorter paths across the mountains. He rode on until night fell, and the moon arose, flooding all the mountain range with wondrous silvery light, which grew the plainer as he left the whispering pines and came into the dwindled pinons of the lower levels. Then up and down, over and over, he crossed the edges of other spurs, coming down from the great backbone of the range. It was past midnight when he reached the flat-topped mesa near the Nogales divide, where there were no trees at all, and where ancient pottery, relics of a forgotten Heart's Desire of another race and time, crumbled beneath his horse's hoofs. Here Curly loosened the saddle cinches, flung down the bridle-rein over Pinto's head again, and himself lay down to sleep, uncovered, but hardy as any mountain bear that roamed the hills.

When he awoke the red sun hung poised on the shoulder of Blanco, far away, as though to receive the ghostly worship of those who once lived and loved, and prayed here, in the long ago. So now he ate as he might, and drank at the Rio Bonito, a dozen miles farther on, and went his way comforted.

Dropping down rapidly on the farther side of the Nogales, Pinto shambling along discontentedly but steadily, Curly at length came to the wagon trail which led along the edge of the plain on the western side of these ranges which he had threaded. He leaned forward and examined the trail for wheel marks.

"By Jinks! Pinto," he muttered, "the old man and the girl is shore hittin' the trail hard for that there death-bed. I'll bet that pore girl's tired, for they must have made a short camp last night. *Vamos, caballo*!" and so he spurred on to the northward along the hot low flats.

By noon he sighted a dust cloud on ahead, which told him that he had the other party well in hand if he liked, in spite of the speed they were making.

"They travelled all night, that's what they did! If that Mexican don't kill his team, it's a lucky thing." He did not seek to close the gap between them, but on the other hand pulled up and rode more slowly.

"Now, Pinto," he pondered, "whatever in the world am I goin' to do when we all pull into town? Deathbed—and him like enough settin' up and playin' solitaire, or out pitchin' horse shoes. Shucks! If I could git around behind Dan Anderson's house, I believe I'd shoot him a few for luck, so's to make some sort of death-bed scene like is announced in the small bills. We've been playin' it low down on them two folks, and for one, I wish't I was out of it. Pinto, this here particular trusted henchman has shore got cold feet right here."

He trailed behind the buckboard hour after hour, dropping

back into a gully for concealment now and then, and putting off the unpleasant hour of meeting as long as possible. He kept in the rear until the vehicle turned in at the mouth of the canon which led up to the valley of Heart's Desire. Then Curly hastened, and so finally clattered up alongside the buckboard. Ellsworth was gray with fatigue, and Constance worn and pale; seeing which Curly cursed himself, Tom Osby, and all animate and inanimate things. "It's a shame, that's what it is!" he muttered to himself reproachfully, and averted his face when Constance smiled at him bravely and disclaimed fatigue.

The sun was beginning to sink beyond Baxter peak as they came in view of the little straggling town, clinging hard to the earth as it had through so many years of oblivion. It was an enchanted valley upon which they gazed. The majestic robes of the purple shadows, tremendous, wide-spreading, yet soft as the texture of thrice-piled velvet, were falling upon the shoulders of the hills. An unspeakable, stately calm came with the hour of evening. It was a world apart, beautiful, unreal, sweet and full of peace. Far, far from here were all the tinselled trappings of an artificial world, distant the clamorings of a disturbing civilization with its tears and terrors. Battle and striving, anxiety and doubt, apprehension and repinings— the envy and the jealousies and little fears of life—none of these lay in the lap of old and calm Carrizo. Peace, rest, and pause,—these things were here.

The ravens of the Lord had cared for those who had come hither, pausing, dreaming, for a pulse-beat in a frenzied century of rapacity and greed. Would the ravens care for a now pale-faced, trembling girl?

"It's perty, ain't it, ma'am?" said Curly. She looked at him and understood many things.

But Curly left them traitorously, almost as soon as they entered the lower end of the street, intent upon plans of his own. Those in the slower buckboard, whose tired team could ill afford any gait beyond a walk, saw him set spurs to his horse and dash ahead. There came more and more plainly to their ears the sound of a vast confused shouting, mingled with rapid punctuation of revolver fire. As they came into full view of the middle portion of the street, they saw it occupied by the entire population of Heart's Desire, all apparently gone mad with some incomprehensible emotion.

"What's the matter? What's the matter?" Mr. Ellsworth called out to one man after another as they passed; but none of them answered him. Coherent speech seemed to have deserted all. "Here, you, Curly!" he shouted. "What's all this about?"

Curly, after a swift dash up the street, was now spurring back madly, his hat swinging in the air, himself crazed as the others.

"He's in!" he yelled. "We done it!"

"Who's in? What've you done?"

"Dan Anderson—nomernated him for Congress—day 'fore yestidday, over to Cruces. Whole convention went solid—Cruces and Dona Ana, Blanco—whole kit and b'ilin' of 'em. Ben Stillson done it—boys just heard—heard the news!" After which Curly relapsed into a series of yells which closed the incident.

Constance listened, open-eyed and silent. So then, he had succeeded! The joy in his success, the pride in his victory, brought a flush to her cheek; but in the same moment the light faded from her eye. She caught her father by the shoulder almost fiercely. "Look at them!" she exclaimed. "They're proud of their victory, but they do not think of *him*. See! He is not here."

Her father, sniffing politics, was forgetting all else; but sobered at this speech, he now motioned the driver to move on. McKinney was there, Doc Tomlinson, Uncle Jim Brothers—the man from Leavenworth—many whom they knew, but not Dan Anderson.

As they turned from the street to cross the *arroyo*, they saw following at a respectful distance both Curly and Tom Osby, the latter walking at Curly's saddle-skirt, for reasons not visible at a distance. Tom Osby was still continuing his protestations. "You go on over, Curly," said he. "You've done mighty well; now go on and finish up. I ain't in on the messenger part."

"Maybe not," replied Curly, "but both halfs of this here amanyensis is goin' over there together. I told that girl that Dan Anderson was shot to a finish and just about to cash in. Now here's all this hoorah about his bein' put up for Congress! I dunno *what* she'll find when she gets into that house, but whichever way it goes, she's due to think I'm a damned liar. You come along, or I'll take *you* over on a rope."

The two conspirators crossed the *arroyo* and paused at the path which led up to Dan Anderson's little cabin. They saw Mr. Ellsworth and Constance leave the buckboard and stop uncertainly at the door. They saw him knock and step half within, then withdraw and gently push his daughter ahead of him. Then he stood outside, his hat in hand, violently mopping his brow. As he caught sight of the two laggards he beckoned them peremptorily.

"O Lord!" moaned Tom Osby; "now here's what   that

sheepherder done to us, with his missive and his signet ring."

Constance Ellsworth had grown deadly pale as she approached the dwelling. The open door let in upon a darkened interior. There was no light, no ray of hope to comfort her. There, as it seemed to her, in that tomblike abode, lay the end of all her happiness. In her heart was only the prayer that she might find him able, still to recognize her.

At her father's gesture she stepped to the door—and stopped. The blood went first to her heart, and then flamed back into her face. Her cheeks tingled. Her hand fell lax from the door jamb, and she half staggered against it for support, limp and helpless.

There before her, and busily engaged in writing—so busy that he had merely called out a careless invitation to enter when he heard the knock of what he presumed to be a chance caller—there, perhaps a trifle pale, but certainly well, and very much himself, sat Dan Anderson!

"He's alive!" whispered Constance to her heart.

"He's going to live!"

The future delegate from the Territory had slunk away from the noisy street to pen some line of acknowledgment to his friend the sheriff of Blanco. He had succeeded, so he reasoned with himself insistently; and yet a strange apathy, a sadness rather than exultation, enveloped him. The world lay dull and gray around him. The price of his success had been the sight of a face worth more to him than all else in the world. He had won something, but had lost everything. His hand stopped, his pencil fell upon the paper. He looked up—to see *her* standing at his door!

Dumb, unbelieving, he gazed and gazed. She turned from red to pale, before his eyes, and still he could not speak. He knew that in an instant the vision would fade away.

"Oh, why, hello!" said he at last, weakly.

"How—that is, how do you do?" Constance said, flushing adorably again.

"I didn't expect—I didn't know you were coming," stammered Dan Anderson.

She chilled at this, but went on wonderingly. "I got your letter—" she began.

"Letter? My letter—*what* letter?"

Constance looked at him fairly now, agitation sufficiently gone to enable her to notice details. She saw that Dan Anderson's left arm was supported upon the table, but apparently not seriously injured. And he had been writing—with his *right* hand—at this very moment! She almost sank to the ground. There had been some cruel misunderstanding! Was she always to be repudiated, shamed? She stood faltering, and would have turned away.

But by this time Dan Anderson's own numbed faculties came back to him with a rush. With a bound he was at her side, his right arm about her, holding her close, strong.

"Constance!" he cried. "Constance! You! You!" He babbled many things, his cheek pressed against hers. She could not speak.

"You see—you see—" exclaimed Dan Anderson, at length, half freeing her to look the more directly into her eyes, and to assure himself once more that it all was true—"I didn't understand at first. Of *course*, I sent the letter. I wrote it. I couldn't wait—I couldn't endure it any longer. Darling, I couldn't *live* without you—and so I wrote, I wrote! And you've come!"

"But your handwriting—" she murmured.

"Of course! of course!" said Dan Anderson. He was lying beautifully now. "But of course you know I'm left-handed, and my left arm got hurt a while ago, so I couldn't use that hand. I don't suppose my handwriting did look quite natural to you."

Her eyes were solemn but contented as she looked into his face, and saw that in spite of his words he was as much mystified as herself. Slowly she presented to him the letter which he had never seen. His face grew grave and tender as he read it line for line.

"It is mine!" he said. "I wrote it. I sent it. I've sent it a thousand times to you before now, across the mountains."

"Is it signed with your heart, Dan?" she whispered.

"With my heart—yes, yes!"

"It is beautiful," said she, simply. And so they dropped between them the letter to the queen. Hand in hand they stepped to the door, the room too small now to contain their happiness.

Two stumbling figures fleeing, pigeon-toed and sharp-heeled, on the further side of the *arroyo* meant much to Dan Anderson. A laugh choked in his throat as he caught her once more in his arms.

"It looks like Willie had made good!" said Tom Osby to Curly, as he took a swift glance back over his shoulder.

But Constance and her lover had forgotten all the world, as they stepped out now into the glory of the twilight of Heart's Desire.

"You remember," said he—"up there—the other time?" He nodded toward the head of the *arroyo*, where lay the garden of the Littlest Girl.

"You broke my heart," she murmured. "I loved you, Dan. What could I do?"

"Don't!" he begged as he tightened his arm about her. "I loved *you*, Constance—what could *I* do? We've been through the fire together. It has all come right. It's all so beautiful."

They stood together at the little garden spot. Two brave red roses now blossomed there, and he plucked them both, pinning them at her throat with hands that trembled. They turned and looked out over the little valley, and to them it seemed a golden cup overrunning with joy.

"Heart's Desire," he murmured, and once more his cheek rested against hers.

"Yes," she whispered vaguely, "all, all—your Heart's Desire, I hope—and mine—*mine*."

"It's the world," he murmured. "It is the Beginning. We are the very first. Oh, Eve! Eve!"

Emerson Hough

ABOUT THE AUTHOR

Emerson Hough (1857-1923) was an American author, best known for writing western stories.

Hough was born in Newton, Iowa, and graduated from the University of Iowa with a law degree. He moved to White Oaks, New Mexico, and practiced law there but eventually turned to literary work by taking camping trips and writing about them for publication.

He is best known as a novelist, writing The Mississippi Bubble as well as The Covered Wagon, about Oregon Trail pioneers, which later became successful as a movie, running 59 weeks at the Criterion Theater in New York City, passing the record set by Birth of a Nation. Other notable works included Story of the Cowboy, Way of the West, Singing Mouse Stories, and Passing of the Frontier, and writing the "Out-of-Doors" column for the Saturday Evening Post.

Hough was also a conservationist, and was the catalyst behind a law passed by the U.S. Congress to protect the buffalo in Yellowstone National Park. He married Charlotte Chesebro of Chicago in 1897 and made that city his home.

Choose from Thousands of 1stWorldLibrary Classics By

A. M. Barnard
Ada Leverson
Adolphus William Ward
Aesop
Agatha Christie
Alexander Aaronsohn
Alexander Kielland
Alexandre Dumas
Alfred Gatty
Alfred Ollivant
Alice Duer Miller
Alice Turner Curtis
Alice Dunbar
Allen Chapman
Alleyne Ireland
Ambrose Bierce
Amelia E. Barr
Amory H. Bradford
Andrew Lang
Andrew McFarland Davis
Andy Adams
Angela Brazil
Anna Alice Chapin
Anna Sewell
Annie Besant
Annie Hamilton Donnell
Annie Payson Call
Annie Roe Carr
Annonaymous
Anton Chekhov
Archibald Lee Fletcher
Arnold Bennett
Arthur C. Benson
Arthur Conan Doyle
Arthur M. Winfield
Arthur Ransome
Arthur Schnitzler
Arthur Train
Atticus
B.H. Baden-Powell
B. M. Bower
B. C. Chatterjee
Baroness Emmuska Orczy
Baroness Orczy
Basil King
Bayard Taylor
Ben Macomber
Bertha Muzzy Bower
Bjornstjerne Bjornson

Booth Tarkington
Boyd Cable
Bram Stoker
C. Collodi
C. E. Orr
C. M. Ingleby
Carolyn Wells
Catherine Parr Traill
Charles A. Eastman
Charles Amory Beach
Charles Dickens
Charles Dudley Warner
Charles Farrar Browne
Charles Ives
Charles Kingsley
Charles Klein
Charles Hanson Towne
Charles Lathrop Pack
Charles Romyn Dake
Charles Whibley
Charles Willing Beale
Charlotte M. Braeme
Charlotte M. Yonge
Charlotte Perkins Stetson
Clair W. Hayes
Clarence Day Jr.
Clarence E. Mulford
Clemence Housman
Confucius
Coningsby Dawson
Cornelis DeWitt Wilcox
Cyril Burleigh
D. H. Lawrence
Daniel Defoe
David Garnett
Dinah Craik
Don Carlos Janes
Donald Keyhoe
Dorothy Kilner
Dougan Clark
Douglas Fairbanks
E. Nesbit
E. P. Roe
E. Phillips Oppenheim
E. S. Brooks
Earl Barnes
Edgar Rice Burroughs
Edith Van Dyne
Edith Wharton

Edward Everett Hale
Edward J. O'Biren
Edward S. Ellis
Edwin L. Arnold
Eleanor Atkins
Eleanor Hallowell Abbott
Eliot Gregory
Elizabeth Gaskell
Elizabeth McCracken
Elizabeth Von Arnim
Ellem Key
Emerson Hough
Emilie F. Carlen
Emily Bronte
Emily Dickinson
Enid Bagnold
Enilor Macartney Lane
Erasmus W. Jones
Ernie Howard Pie
Ethel May Dell
Ethel Turner
Ethel Watts Mumford
Eugene Sue
Eugenie Foa
Eugene Wood
Eustace Hale Ball
Evelyn Everett-green
Everard Cotes
F. H. Cheley
F. J. Cross
F. Marion Crawford
Fannie E. Newberry
Federick Austin Ogg
Ferdinand Ossendowski
Fergus Hume
Florence A. Kilpatrick
Fremont B. Deering
Francis Bacon
Francis Darwin
Frances Hodgson Burnett
Frances Parkinson Keyes
Frank Gee Patchin
Frank Harris
Frank Jewett Mather
Frank L. Packard
Frank V. Webster
Frederic Stewart Isham
Frederick Trevor Hill
Frederick Winslow Taylor

Friedrich Kerst
Friedrich Nietzsche
Fyodor Dostoyevsky
G.A. Henty
G.K. Chesterton
Gabrielle E. Jackson
Garrett P. Serviss
Gaston Leroux
George A. Warren
George Ade
Geroge Bernard Shaw
George Cary Eggleston
George Durston
George Ebers
George Eliot
George Gissing
George MacDonald
George Meredith
George Orwell
George Sylvester Viereck
George Tucker
George W. Cable
George Wharton James
Gertrude Atherton
Gordon Casserly
Grace E. King
Grace Gallatin
Grace Greenwood
Grant Allen
Guillermo A. Sherwell
Gulielma Zollinger
Gustav Flaubert
H. A. Cody
H. B. Irving
H.C. Bailey
H. G. Wells
H. H. Munro
H. Irving Hancock
H. R. Naylor
H. Rider Haggard
H. W. C. Davis
Haldeman Julius
Hall Caine
Hamilton Wright Mabie
Hans Christian Andersen
Harold Avery
Harold McGrath
Harriet Beecher Stowe
Harry Castlemon
Harry Coghill
Harry Houidini

Hayden Carruth
Helent Hunt Jackson
Helen Nicolay
Hendrik Conscience
Hendy David Thoreau
Henri Barbusse
Henrik Ibsen
Henry Adams
Henry Ford
Henry Frost
Henry James
Henry Jones Ford
Henry Seton Merriman
Henry W Longfellow
Herbert A. Giles
Herbert Carter
Herbert N. Casson
Herman Hesse
Hildegard G. Frey
Homer
Honore De Balzac
Horace B. Day
Horace Walpole
Horatio Alger Jr.
Howard Pyle
Howard R. Garis
Hugh Lofting
Hugh Walpole
Humphry Ward
Ian Maclaren
Inez Haynes Gillmore
Irving Bacheller
Isabel Cecilia Williams
Isabel Hornibrook
Israel Abrahams
Ivan Turgenev
J.G.Austin
J. Henri Fabre
J. M. Barrie
J. M. Walsh
J. Macdonald Oxley
J. R. Miller
J. S. Fletcher
J. S. Knowles
J. Storer Clouston
J. W. Duffield
Jack London
Jacob Abbott
James Allen
James Andrews
James Baldwin

James Branch Cabell
James DeMille
James Joyce
James Lane Allen
James Lane Allen
James Oliver Curwood
James Oppenheim
James Otis
James R. Driscoll
Jane Abbott
Jane Austen
Jane L. Stewart
Janet Aldridge
Jens Peter Jacobsen
Jerome K. Jerome
Jessie Graham Flower
John Buchan
John Burroughs
John Cournos
John F. Kennedy
John Gay
John Glasworthy
John Habberton
John Joy Bell
John Kendrick Bangs
John Milton
John Philip Sousa
John Taintor Foote
Jonas Lauritz Idemil Lie
Jonathan Swift
Joseph A. Altsheler
Joseph Carey
Joseph Conrad
Joseph E. Badger Jr
Joseph Hergesheimer
Joseph Jacobs
Jules Vernes
Julian Hawthrone
Julie A Lippmann
Justin Huntly McCarthy
Kakuzo Okakura
Karle Wilson Baker
Kate Chopin
Kenneth Grahame
Kenneth McGaffey
Kate Langley Bosher
Kate Langley Bosher
Katherine Cecil Thurston
Katherine Stokes
L. A. Abbot
L. T. Meade

L. Frank Baum	Owen Johnson	Stephen Crane
Latta Griswold	P.G. Wodehouse	Stewart Edward White
Laura Dent Crane	Paul and Mabel Thorne	Stijn Streuvels
Laura Lee Hope	Paul G. Tomlinson	Swami Abhedananda
Laurence Housman	Paul Severing	Swami Parmananda
Lawrence Beasley	Percy Brebner	T. S. Ackland
Leo Tolstoy	Percy Keese Fitzhugh	T. S. Arthur
Leonid Andreyev	Peter B. Kyne	The Princess Der Ling
Lewis Carroll	Plato	Thomas A. Janvier
Lewis Sperry Chafer	Quincy Allen	Thomas A Kempis
Lilian Bell	R. Derby Holmes	Thomas Anderton
Lloyd Osbourne	R. L. Stevenson	Thomas Bailey Aldrich
Louis Hughes	R. S. Ball	Thomas Bulfinch
Louis Joseph Vance	Rabindranath Tagore	Thomas De Quincey
Louis Tracy	Rahul Alvares	Thomas Dixon
Louisa May Alcott	Ralph Bonehill	Thomas H. Huxley
Lucy Fitch Perkins	Ralph Henry Barbour	Thomas Hardy
Lucy Maud Montgomery	Ralph Victor	Thomas More
Luther Benson	Ralph Waldo Emmerson	Thornton W. Burgess
Lydia Miller Middleton	Rene Descartes	U. S. Grant
Lyndon Orr	Ray Cummings	Upton Sinclair
M. Corvus	Rex Beach	Valentine Williams
M. H. Adams	Rex E. Beach	Various Authors
Margaret E. Sangster	Richard Harding Davis	Vaughan Kester
Margret Howth	Richard Jefferies	Victor Appleton
Margaret Vandercook	Richard Le Gallienne	Victor G. Durham
Margaret W. Hungerford	Robert Barr	Victoria Cross
Margret Penrose	Robert Frost	Virginia Woolf
Maria Edgeworth	Robert Gordon Anderson	Wadsworth Camp
Maria Thompson Daviess	Robert L. Drake	Walter Camp
Mariano Azuela	Robert Lansing	Walter Scott
Marion Polk Angellotti	Robert Lynd	Washington Irving
Mark Overton	Robert Michael Ballantyne	Wilbur Lawton
Mark Twain	Robert W. Chambers	Wilkie Collins
Mary Austin	Rosa Nouchette Carey	Willa Cather
Mary Catherine Crowley	Rudyard Kipling	Willard F. Baker
Mary Cole	Saint Augustine	William Dean Howells
Mary Hastings Bradley	Samuel B. Allison	William le Queux
Mary Roberts Rinehart	Samuel Hopkins Adams	W. Makepeace Thackeray
Mary Rowlandson	Sarah Bernhardt	William W. Walter
M. Wollstonecraft Shelley	Sarah C. Hallowell	William Shakespeare
Maud Lindsay	Selma Lagerlof	Winston Churchill
Max Beerbohm	Sherwood Anderson	Yei Theodora Ozaki
Myra Kelly	Sigmund Freud	Yogi Ramacharaka
Nathaniel Hawthrone	Standish O'Grady	Young E. Allison
Nicolo Machiavelli	Stanley Weyman	Zane Grey
O. F. Walton	Stella Benson	
Oscar Wilde	Stella M. Francis